OF TAINTED HEART

✣

OLIVIA WILDENSTEIN
KATIE HAYOZ

OF TAINTED HEART
BOOK 2 OF THE QUATREFOIL CHRONICLES

Copyright © 2021 by Olivia Wildenstein & Katie Hayoz

Cover design by *Ampersand Book Covers*
Editing by *Anna Joy Missa*
Proofreading by *Laetitia Treseng*

To making the real world
a little more magical.

GLOSSARIES

(OUR) BRETON

azoù-kaer – beaux arts

bajaneg – idiot

dihuner – clock

diwaller – guardian

erenez e v'am – bind to me

groac'h – shapeshifting water sprite

Istor Breou – History of Magic

kamarad – friend

kaoc'h – shit

kelc'h – circle

Kelouenn – the Scroll

mestr – master

sorser – wizard

tadoù – father

toull-bac'h – jail tomb

FRENCH

au secours – help!

ça va? – how's it going?

chéri(e) – darling

chouchen – mead (Brittany specialty)

chouchou – sweetie

connard – asshole

c'était genial – so much fun

démarrer – start

escargot – snail

enculé – fucker

fraisier – strawberry cake

frangin – brother (slang)

galette – a savory crêpe

guivre – wyvern

ma petite chérie – my little darling

magie noire – dark magic

maison – home

merci – thank you

merde – shit

pain au chocolat – chocolate croissant

pas du tout – not at all

pieuvre – octopus

profiterole – cream puff

putain – fuck

putain de merde – fucking hell

putain de bordel de merde – fucking hell (x 10)

quelle merde – what a shitshow

salidou – salted caramel (Brittany specialty)

pas question – no way

puits fleuri – flowered well

gargote – cheap restaurant

très drôle – very funny

une autre bouteille, s'il-te-plaît – another bottle of wine, please

vin chaud – mulled wine

THE DIHUNER
THE ASTRONOMICAL CLOCK

Adrien Mercier
1997-

Geoffrey Keene
1970-

Camille Mercier
1972-2017

Juda
1946-

Nolwenn
1952-

Matthias
1979-2020

Romain
2005-

Samson &
Arthur
2020-

Pierre Bisset
1963-2004

Audrey Abede
1961-1998

Gaëlle Bisset
1986-

Amandine de
Morel
1976-2004

Viviene de
Morel
543-598

Cadence de
Morel
2003-

Rainier de
Morel
1974-

ne
ers

Rémy Roland
aka Slate Ardoin
2001-

Oscar Roland
1974-2004

Merlin
540-584

Eugenia
Hernandez
1978-2004

1

CADENCE

Magic is real, and yet we failed to bring it back to the world.

I failed to bring it back. Even though I defeated my curse, even though I won my golden leaf, I missed my window to fit it into the astronomical clock. All our hard work and perilous battles were for nothing.

I suppose that's not completely true.

The Bloodstone ring came off Slate's finger. Thanks to our sweat and tears, he lives.

This is the only thing that should matter. That this tortured, beautiful soul, who finds humor in even the shadiest moments, didn't succumb to my mother's fate.

He lives. And he chose to stay in Brume.

With me.

For me.

"Oh, look at that." Slate bumps my knee in the middle of our astronomy lecture and nods toward the auditorium's glass wall that overlooks the *Lac de Nimueh*, hardly visible through the dense fog. "It's snowing. How . . . *delightful*."

I smile, because I know he hates it. He's itching to return to sunny Marseille. Not that I'm a fan of the bitter cold, but I do find snowstorms pretty.

I lean toward him, "If your chimney's swept, we could build a fire. Drink a little *vin chaud*. Roast some marshmallows."

Slate grunts, but there's a spark in his eyes.

"Talk," I add.

His head jerks. "*Talk?*"

"Well, yeah. I mean, I'm assuming Bastian and Alma will be invited to our mulled wine by the fire party."

He shifts in his chair, plucks my hand, with which I was taking notes, and links our fingers. "I was picturing animal pelts and you" —he leans forward and drops his deep voice to a raspy whisper— "sprawled naked on top."

I smile. "Alma and Bastian may find that awkward."

"Alma and Bastian aren't invited to that part of the evening."

"Mademoiselle de Morel," Mademoiselle Claire calls out from where she stands by the whiteboard on which she's been scribbling mathematical equations about interplanetary distances. "Please stop distracting our newest student."

I blink.

Ever since buxom, blonde Claire Robinson learned Slate was Oscar Roland's son, she's been starstruck, which I'd found ironic at first. I mean, she *is* an astronomy teacher. Now I just find it annoying. And disturbing. Claire Robinson is thirty-five. Fifteen years older than Slate. Sure, Slate looks and acts more mature than his age, but that doesn't make her admiration of him any more okay.

Plus, he's *my* boyfriend.

Slate leans back in his chair, keeping my hand clutched in his. "I was actually distracting her, Professor. Carry on."

I don't even try to steal my hand back. I let all my peers gawk, let Claire Robinson absorb my connection with Slate. We may seem like a strange pair to most—me, the shy, almost eighteen-year-old dean's daughter best known for pushing around book trolleys, and he, the shameless twenty-year-old Roland heir who mysteriously vanished at age three and then even more mysteriously reappeared.

They do say opposites attract. And we're definitely opposites and attracted. Sometimes, I think our bond's magical somehow. Yes, magic doesn't exist—because of me—but it's unnatural and unsettling how deeply and swiftly I fell for Slate.

I glance at him, at his black eyes that absorb everything around him, that light up and bow when he's happy, that squeeze and narrow when he's agitated, that glitter when he's plotting how to smite my innocence.

Paradoxically, he's the one putting on the brakes, claiming he doesn't want to hurt me. I've been out of the hospital for almost ten days, and although my body's still marbled in bruises, the swelling's gone and most of the superficial cuts have zippered up. I've never felt better, more alive, happier.

I whisper in Slate's ear, "I'll get Alma to take Bastian on a tour of the ramparts followed by a cleansing snowshoe expedition through the forest. That should give us enough time to *talk*."

Mademoiselle Claire glowers at me, but I don't even feel a twinge of guilt. What I do feel is Slate's fingers closing around mine.

His breathing hitches as his inky gaze turns toward my face, toward my mouth more specifically. I think he has a thing for my lips because he's *always* staring at them. I lick them, and he sits up a little, readjusts his posture, then swings his gaze back to the whiteboard, a nerve feathering his jaw.

The bell rings a few minutes later, freeing us from the cougar's lair. I don't think Claire Robinson would actually try anything on Slate, but she was obsessed with his father. According to Gaëlle, who was in Claire's graduating class, the blonde all but stalked Oscar and was inconsolable at his funeral.

Her green eyes track Slate as we walk out of her class, cementing my desire to chat with Papa about her questionable morals.

Bastian and Alma are both loitering outside the auditorium. Although Bastian isn't enrolled in U of B—technically, he's still attending college in Marseille—Slate's decision to stay in Brume has made Bastian reluctant to leave.

A thought knocks into me as we walk toward Adrien's history class. "Hey, Bastian, why don't you transfer here?"

He stops in his tracks, his rubber-soled boots squelching against the tiled floor of the Bisset Esplanade. Bastian isn't the quiet type, almost as chatty as Alma, and yet he doesn't say a word. Just gapes at me as though I've morphed into Slate's prized cactus.

Here I imagined Bastian would nod so enthusiastically his black-framed glasses would skid off his nose.

Something terrible dawns on me. Did I speak in tongues? Sylvie, the town doctor, informed me that although my brain seemed healed on the CT scans, concussions that provoked comas often caused residual trauma.

"What say you, little bro?" Slate's fighting off a smile.

Oh, thank God. I must've spoken in French.

"I didn't think—I didn't think it was . . . a possibility." Bastian's tone is as thick as Slate's charcoal sweater. "Wouldn't I need to apply?"

"Consider yourself accepted." Slate slings his arm around my shoulders. "Right, Cadence?"

"Of course." I reach up and thread my fingers through Slate's. "There's a place with your name on it. Say the word, and I'll call up Papa."

Slate's fingers twitch at the mention of my father, and it saddens me, because Papa and Slate are the two most important men in my life, and they don't get along. They can barely stand to be in the same room, even though, Brume being tiny, and me being the object of both their affection, forces them to be in each other's company almost daily.

Bastian's lashes flutter as though batting away tears. "I don't want special treatment. I mean, what if I don't qualify to be here?"

Slate snorts. "You're at the top of your class in Marseille. Top of the whole damn school. So shut the hell up about not qualifying. I'm not qualified to wipe your ass, and *I'm* here."

I roll my eyes at my boyfriend's coarse manner of speech. "You've got the grades to get in, Bastian. It's simply a matter of transferring your records and enrolling you. And Papa can do that in his sleep. So, yes or—"

"*Oui!*" Bastian's exclamation makes more than one student stop and stare. He wrenches back his neck and spins. "Yes." He says it quietly this time, reverentially.

The happiness that suffuses Slate's sweet foster brother is almost as potent as the one filling me. My entire life is finally falling into place, all the pieces coming together. A lot like the Quatrefoil.

The analogy makes my heart pinch. Why, oh why, did my mind have to go to the clock and the leaf I failed to lock into its cradle?

I stare out the floor-to-ceiling glass panes, past the thready fog, at the round temple enthroned at the top of our hilly town. And then I stare beyond it at the carcass of the Beaux-Arts building which juts out of the snow like some Grecian ruin.

The arena where I won my battle but lost my piece.

"Cadence." Slate's voice in my ear jolts me. "You're safe."

I paste on a smile. "I know." And I really do know it, the same way I know magic is evil. Yet a quiet longing to try again lingers.

Maybe someday . . .

The curses flash behind my lids—Slate's blood-soaked jaw when he climbed out of the well, Gaëlle's bone-white face when her husband came back from the dead, Adrien's charred scalp when he fought off the *guivre*, Emilie's tiny figure slipping under the water.

I stare at the emerald quatrefoil charm dangling from my bracelet and think: *never again*.

2

SLATE

It's over. The ridiculous race to assemble the Quatrefoil is over. *Putain de bordel de merde.* I didn't think I'd survive it. That Cadence would. I thought for sure we'd end up like little Emilie. Little Emilie whose death I'll forever need to atone for.

I'm relieved as all hell that Cadence didn't lock her piece into the clock. I can't imagine what would've happened if we'd actually brought magic back to the world. My guess is, nothing good.

A few days after her discharge from the campus clinic, Cadence insisted on slogging up to Fifth Kelc'h to view the wreckage of the Beaux-Arts building. She claimed it was to get closure, and perhaps it did offer her *some* closure, but it also opened a can of worms I wanted to keep shut.

She murmured something about having failed us all and that maybe she should try again.

I sandwiched her hands between mine, attempting to tamp down the panic gripping my lungs. "Promise me you won't try. Promise!" I roared like a wild animal.

Color drained from her cheeks, and she nodded. No way was I going to risk losing her again.

Now, standing on the train platform, I hug Cadence to me. I swore I'd never leave her side, but here I am, breaking that promise.

In order to stay in Brume, I have to take care of things back in Marseille and get Spike. The prickly boy's been neglected these past few weeks, and I worry about the state he's in. No way am I letting this damn Quatrefoil crap kill him too.

Cadence's ice-blue eyes are red-rimmed, and a lone tear slides down her cheek.

I wipe it away with the pad of my thumb. "Bastian and I will be back in no time. A few days, tops."

"Promise? I know how much you wanted to get out of Brume—"

I place my index finger on her gorgeous crimson lips. "Promise." The back of my throat goes raw, and I swallow.

Two months ago, I was a criminal with bulging pockets and a hollow heart. Now, the organ pounding behind my ribs is at capacity. How ironic would it be if Slate Ardoin—thief, con man, bully, orphan—went into cardiac arrest for over-caring?

I massage my chest, trying to convince myself the pain is from gorging on croissants at the tavern this morning. I swear, Bastian and I ate as though we were packing on the calories for a trek across the North Pole instead of a cozy, eight-hour train ride south.

The copper-haired tornado, otherwise known as Alma, wraps an arm around Cadence's waist. In her sky-high heels, she's the same height as her bestie. "The faster they leave, honey, the faster they'll be back." She winks at Bastian, whose light-brown skin turns a ruddy shade of brick.

Cadence nods, teeth denting her bottom lip. Jesus. That alone makes me want to stay.

The dull tone announcing that the train's ready to depart has Bastian calling out my name. Although every molecule in my body is screeching at me to stay, I turn and lunge toward the door Bastian's blocking with his body.

Last time I tried to take a train out of Brume, the Bloodstone's magic created an impenetrable wall.

I squeeze my eyes shut, bracing for impact. Instead, my body sails right through the air, and my boots thunder onto the beige vinyl flooring. Bastian moves, and the door suctions shut behind us. We head into first class—what I lack in manners I make up for in posh taste—and throw ourselves into opposite aisle seats.

In a matter of minutes, sunlight rips through the gauze of fog, and the magical town shaped like Merlin's hat becomes nothing more than a wispy cloud floating atop a silver lake.

The past few weeks feel like a dream. Like none of it was real.

I inhale and before I even get the words out, Bastian tilts his head and says, "Yep. It happened. You didn't hallucinate the whole thing. And you're not coming down from some bad trip. You really fought a *groac'h*." He grins. "And won."

I wouldn't go as far as to say *won*, but I appreciate the sentiment.

Bastian flips down the table between our seats and sets a thick manila folder on top of it. The financial records of the Roland estate —*my* estate. All forty-two million euros of it.

Well, forty-two minus the hundred thousand Rainier de Morel gave to the deceased Marianne Shafir. It's not a lot comparatively, and my worrying may seem trivial, but something about that transaction rankles. I've already asked my lawyer, Philippe, to look into it.

Just out of curiosity.

I thumb through the documents. "Hard to believe Rainier signed this over to me." I stare back out at the scrolling countryside, white snow blurring into faded yellows and browns, and think of de Morel revving up his snowmobile, of the cruel glint in his eyes as the ring fell off my finger. "Then again, he was holding out hope the ring would do me in."

"Rainier's scum." Bastian pats his cropped, dark locks. "To be fair, though, if my daughter were in danger because some dude put a ring on his finger, I wouldn't exactly be welcoming him into the family with open arms."

"Yeah, but would you be advising him to jump off a roof?" I can still hear Rainier urging me to end it before the pain of the ring became insufferable. At the time, it made sense. But now, I wonder.

A dark shadow crosses Bastian's face. "If you'd listened to him—"

"Since when do I ever listen to anyone?"

"I never thought I'd be glad you didn't." He lifts his dark eyes to mine, and I see the kid I grew up with. The boy who looked up to me for no other reason than because I gave a shit. The boy whose goodness kept me from becoming a callous monster.

Oof. I rub my chest. Acid reflux is a bitch.

Speaking of which . . .

I unzip my bag and pull out two warm aluminum foil packages.

"Nolwenn gave me these for the road. I'm her *chouchou* now." Our mutual distrust of Rainier cemented our relationship faster than my leaf bolted to the clock.

To think she's the one who sent me away from Brume seventeen years ago. I haven't told anyone because it's a dangerous secret. One that would expose Rainier for the shady, manipulative man he is. Not to mention, Nolwenn's eyes have been shadowed with dark circles for days now, and I don't want to add to her stress.

Bastian swipes one of the foil packages and opens it. The odor of bacon wafts through the carriage as he bites into the savory crêpe, moaning like a lovesick puppy. Where he puts it all, I have no clue. There's not an ounce of fat on his gangly frame.

I'm about to open my foil packet—heartburn be damned—when the train enters a tunnel. The lights flicker, creating patchy darkness around us. My ears pop, and my muscles seize up.

I'm back in the well again, struggling to breathe, feeling the razored edges of the water fairy's teeth sinking into my neck. Sweat beads along my forehead, and I let out an involuntary snarl. Sunlight shocks me back to reality. My *galette* is on the floor, egg and cheese smeared under my boot.

Bastian blinks. "Slate? You okay?"

Fucking mermaid PTSD. I take a deep breath and nod.

THREE DAYS LATER, Bastian and I are packed up and ready to get on the road. For the time being, I've decided to leave the apartment without a tenant. It's not like I need rent money. I take one last look at the sun sparkling over the Mediterranean, the sky behind it an unearthly cerulean, before flicking on the switch that lowers the blinds.

Even with the windows shut, the brine and sunshine penetrate. No hint of steely gray fog anywhere. I'd almost forgotten what it was like to live in a town where I wasn't always part-popsicle. I bet the ache I felt in my chest leaving Brume wasn't love. It wasn't even heartburn. It was my goddamn nipples finally thawing.

To think I'm counting down the seconds until I get back to that icy hell: forty thousand, if Bastian and I drive without stopping. Forty thousand seconds until Cadence is back in my arms.

I punch in the code for the alarm, then lock my armored door. As I wait for the elevator, my phone rings. *Philippe.*

"Calling to see how Spike's doing? Because the answer's not good." I'd asked my idiot lawyer to check up on him two weeks ago, and what did he do? He moved Spike closer to the window and into direct sunlight. Enter a freak winter heatwave, and poor Spike got a nasty sunburn. A wicked scar now bleaches two of his branches.

"Spike?"

"My pet cactus?"

A beat of silence. He's probably rolling his bulbous eyes. "I'm callin' about that old lady you asked me to dig into . . . Marianne Shafir."

The elevator doors ding. I don't step in, don't want to risk losing the network connection.

"She was indeed on the faculty of the college for four decades, but there's no medical file on any cancer. Which doesn't mean she didn't have one, but I'll have to do more diggin' if she was in private care. Which will require more time. Which will require more—"

"Money. Yeah. Fine. Anything else?"

"That's all for now, boss."

I shut down the call and jam my finger into the elevator button. The doors slide open, and this time I step in and ride down to the garage, my stomach folding upon itself. I bet Marianne didn't have cancer. Until I have proof, though, I'm keeping my trap shut.

I don't even tell Bastian, who's tightening the bungee cord holding a cargo carrier to the roof.

It's an atrocity. A horror. An abomination. My Aston Martin, usually a sleek, silver bullet, currently resembles a bloated *escargot* knocked up with triplets.

I slip on my dark aviators. "You better read all those books I saw you pack," I grumble. "Don't know why I bothered buying you a Kindle."

"I brought it, too. And I've already read most of these . . ." Bastian's voice trails off at my pointed glare.

"Then why the hell did you take them?"

"Because books aren't simply to read. They're also to *own*. Where I live, they live."

At least, he'd smoothed a protective blanket under the industrial plastic cargo case. It better preserve my Skyfall Silver paint job.

"High maintenance. That's what you are."

Bastian snorts. "Right. Says the man traveling with a meter-high Eve's Needle named Spike and his harem of juicy succulents."

He may have a point. His crap is strapped to the roof because, between the Mexican Snowball, the Burro's Tail, the Roseum, the Panda Plant, the Jade, the Aloe Vera, and the others, there's no room in the trunk. But I'm a gentleman. I take care of the ladies. Even Spike's.

My Eve's Needle isn't just any cactus; he's a rescue that started life with no advantages and no luck. I found him on a street corner, his pot broken, half of his needles ripped off. He was small and pale and pretty damn pathetic. That was two years ago. Now he's a tough-ass dude that's taller than a toddler and living proof that even the doomed can rise from their ashes.

Bastian puts his hands on his hips and stares at the big lug. "So, how are we gonna do this? We strap Spike to the roof, too? He's too long to fit in the trunk."

"He's already gotten one sunburn. I won't tolerate a second." I eye his pale scar. "He's going on your lap."

"You're kidding?"

"It's a two-seater. Where else would he go?"

With a heavy sigh, Bastian slides into the passenger seat. "Okay. Hand him over."

I wrap my arms around the painted terracotta pot and heave it onto his thighs. We angle Spike just right, lower the window, and then shut the door. His top half hangs out the window.

I get in and rev up the engine. "The air whipping through his needles will cool his burn."

Clicking on his seatbelt, Bastian sighs. "If anything will cool his burn, it's Brume."

I tap the town's name into the GPS, my finger hovering over the *démarrer* button on the touchscreen. "Can't believe we're going back."

Cadence's blue eyes and red lips flash behind my lids. Scratch that. I *can* believe I'm going back.

I press the screen, and the map lights up, announcing it will take around eleven hours to reach Brume.

I swerve out of the parking lot as a tinny, female voice announces, "*Destination: maison.*"

Yeah . . . I'm going home.

3

CADENCE

Slate's coming home tonight.

I feel like he's been gone an entire month, but it's only been three days. Time hasn't ticked by this slowly since the Quatrefoil hunt when we had to wait for the pieces to appear. I nibble on my bottom lip as the memory of my battle flits before my eyes, so vivid in spite of my concussion. I wonder if that chapter in my life will ever dull. All at once, I hope it does and I hope never to forget. For all its horror, it was also exhilarating.

Our housekeeper, Solange, is slicing up a roasted goose which she's just removed from the oven—the skin is crispy, the meat browned, and the juice that sluices out clear and pungent. A pot filled with a mixture of sautéed chanterelles, roasted chestnuts, and Brussel sprouts already graces the table. The vegetables glisten beneath the sculptural chandelier Maman fashioned from a medley of bronze maple leaves and glass ones. I'm glad she chose maple and not clover-shaped ones. I couldn't have stomached looking upon the palm-sized, rounded Quatrefoil leaves every day of my life.

Papa even more so, since it was a leaf that cursed him into his wheelchair.

Just as I think of him, he drives into the open-plan kitchen-dining room. "It smells divine, Solange."

"Hope it tastes divine, Monsieur de Morel."

"Always does." I sit, tucking my sleek, wool pencil skirt beneath me.

To take my mind off Slate, Alma and Gaëlle took me on a surprise shopping trip in Rennes yesterday. I don't particularly enjoy clothes shopping, but it was nice to get out of Brume and away from the frozen campus with its compact fog and icy cobbles.

Plus, I got to buy a housewarming present for Slate, a neon cactus light. It's super kitsch, and he'll probably hate it—the man loves fine things—but it made me think of him. Unfortunately, I only remembered those sheepskin pelts we'd joked about once we were already on our way back.

"You look so chic today, *ma Cadence*."

"*Merci*, Papa." I touch my hair, which I've smoothed with my flat iron. Instead of dull brown, it shines a rich chestnut. Unlike Alma, I'd never have the patience to do my hair all the time, but doing it occasionally is quite fun and surprisingly relaxing.

Through the glass tabletop, I spy my father massaging his thighs. "Jacqueline was hard on you this morning?"

Jacqueline is his physio coach, a nervy and severe middle-aged woman. I don't know how Papa stands her. I guess she's good at what she does, but she's not pleasant to be around.

"No more than usual."

"Then why are you massaging your legs?"

"The cold makes them sore."

I meet his eyes, a darker shade of blue than mine. If I'd succeeded, he'd be walking again. He'd be rid of the pain. Not once has he made me feel guilty, yet guilt chokes me.

I know I said never again, but it's only *one* leaf. I won it once; I could win it again. Especially if Adrien, Gaëlle, and Slate fight alongside me. They wouldn't be able to touch whatever dark monster the leaf conjures up, or they'd get cursed, but just having them there would steady my hands and nerves.

Slate will say no, of course, but what about the others?

As Papa shakes open his napkin and drapes it over his emaciated lap, he asks, "What's got your forehead so puckered?"

I slide the tip of my index finger along my curved fork tines. When Solange leaves the room, I say, "I want to try again. For Emilie. For you."

Papa doesn't speak for a long, *long* time. Then, "If walking were as important to me as this town, as the memories that keep me here, we'd have moved to a place where I wouldn't be cursed into a chair."

"But—"

"I almost lost you once. I will not chance losing you again. Not for anything." My father's such a selfless man, not to mention violently protective of me, that he'll never be on board with me trying again.

"But, Papa, I *was* successful."

"A building crashed on your head. You were in a coma for *four* days!"

All of Brume heard about the dean's daughter getting stuck in the art center after a freak earthquake jostled the town. So many excuses we had to come up with to cover up the Quatrefoil's evil magic.

The well that overflowed: a canal obstruction.

Adrien's house that caught fire: a gas leak.

Cursed Emilie who died: a runaway child.

My heartbeat quickens as I daydream of how wondrous it would be to reunite Emilie with her mother, reverse the damage the town withheld, and free my father of his wheelchair. One battle could bring about so much joy.

I clutch my water glass and take a sip, electing to drop the subject and segue to the topic of Claire Robinson and her depravity.

"Claire was a great fan of Oscar's."

"I know, but—"

"She wouldn't jeopardize her position at our school for an affair." Papa saws into a Brussel sprout. "But if she did, and Slate responds to her advances, there's not much anyone could do. After all, he's an adult. A consenting one. If I were you—"

"You're not me." He's convinced Slate's a gigolo and will dump me as soon as I've served my purpose.

Except I've served my purpose—which was saving his life—and he's still interested.

Papa sighs. "Claire Robinson might be a moot point if he doesn't come back."

"He's coming back."

"I didn't say he wasn't."

I spear a mushroom and shove it into my mouth. "You were insinuating it."

Papa glares at the goose as though it's wronged him. "After losing your Maman, you became my only reason for existing, so forgive me for caring about your heart."

Remorse for snapping at him bites me in the behind. "Papa, can you please give him the benefit of the doubt and accept that I'm not an awful judge of character?"

Lines bracket his mouth, but when he finally looks at me, they soften. "I'll try, but if I hear the merest rumor about him—"

"You'll verify its accuracy before sharing it with me or confronting him. That's what you were going to say, right?"

It takes him a second to answer. "Right."

The tension relaxes after that, and I get my nonjudgmental father back. The one who spins the best tales and shares the most interesting pieces of news. By the time lunch is cleared and dessert served, I'm feeling content again.

Solange places an espresso in front of my father before bustling down the stairs to the laundry room.

The dark liquid reminds me of the stain on the scroll. "Did you manage to contact that art restorer for the scroll?"

"I did. Didn't you notice it was gone from my office?"

"No." We usually meet around the table or in the living room. Rarely in his home office. "When did the restorer say they'd get it back to you?"

"They warned it could take weeks. And they also warned me that removing the ink smudge might strip the text underneath."

I lick the tiramisu that clings to my spoon, then dip it back inside my little bowl. "How do you think it got there?"

"I'd rather not share my presumptions."

"Why not?"

"Because it might tarnish the image of someone you cared about."

The spoon slips from my fingers and clatters into the bowl. Someone I *cared* about? Past tense? That means that person's no longer here . . .

"Maman?" I whisper.

"*Non.*" Papa sips his coffee. "Think about it, Cadence, the translations vanish. Then—"

"Camille?" My mouth parts around a gasp. "You think Adrien's mother wrecked it?"

"Well, someone took those translations and the laptop on which she'd backed them up. I hate to even think this, but what if she caught something in that part of the scroll, something she didn't want anyone else to read?"

My palm climbs to my mouth, my emerald quatrefoil charm shivering against the goosebumps pebbling my skin. Could Camille be to blame? And if she did do it, what on Earth did she read on there? Is that what led her to commit suicide?

Oh, *mon Dieu*.

My father places his tiny porcelain cup back on its gilded saucer. "I might be completely off the mark, though, so please don't mention my speculations to anyone, Cadence. Not to Slate, not to Gaëlle, not to Alma, and certainly *not* to Adrien."

"I won't."

Papa's theory makes terrible sense. We're no longer hunting the Quatrefoil, and may never endeavor to put it back together, but dread—combined with my desire to understand what was written on the scroll—makes my skin go as clammy as the night I faced off against Ares.

4

SLATE

Brittany feels like it's a whole world away from the South of France. Marseille can get cold, but it's nowhere near the arthritis-inducing chill that envelops the North.

Once we hit the area, Bastian's teeth start chattering. I swaddle him in the spiffy new blanket from my winter survival kit and Spike in a cashmere throw, then turn off the two-laned highway onto a dirt and gravel road, headlights barely cutting through the mist.

Like everywhere else in France, a simple rectangular sign of white rimmed in red announces the town. Evenly spaced black letters spell out B-R-U-M-E. Like this place is a normal, plain-old town. There's no billboard warning: *You are entering the ice crack of Hell.* No historical marker stating: *Merlin got murdered here.* Not even a welcoming banner of: *Bienvenue, sucka!* Nope. Just a fork in the road with iron lampposts, cobbles to the left, and slushy-dirt and darkness to the right.

The cobbles lead to the train station, the public parking, the lakefront, and the ramparts of the town; the dirt road leads to the edge of the forest. I put the car in gear and cut into the deep, foggy freeze of Brume, following the lane enclosed by a canopy of firs and pines.

"They better have finished at the house." I hired Brume's Broom —Brume's finest (and only) professional cleaning service to make the Roland home livable. I'd already gotten the electricity and water taken care of last week. That just left moving stuff around and getting rid of seventeen years' worth of dust, cobwebs, and rodent droppings.

Tonight will be the first time I sleep in my home instead of my elfish hidey-hole of a dorm room. Absently, I bring my hand to my forehead. It might be permanently misshapen due to all the beat-downs I got from the ceiling beam in that place.

"You know, I can go stay at the dorms if you—" Bastian starts.

"You're staying at the house."

"But maybe you want the place to yourself."

"Bastian?"

He turns to me, his slightly crooked teeth still chattering. "Yeah?"

"Shut the hell up."

He shakes his head but grins.

My place is his place. Although I will ask for a bit of privacy when Cadence comes to visit. I can see it now: her; me; a crackling fire; warm, bare skin. That gets me gunning the Aston and hoping the animal pelts I asked Bastian to order have arrived.

When we pull into the drive, my headlights illuminate the red shutters and tapestry of ivy choking the stone walls. Fresh tire treads lead away from the house and toward town. Brume's Broom must've finished not too long ago. They left the porchlight burning, just as I asked.

The GPS croons, *You have arrived at your destination.*

I step on the brakes, and my Aston Martin skids to the right before stopping. Yeah. I thought about the survival kit but forgot about the winter tires. Hopefully, there will be some chains in the garden shed.

"Can't. Feel. My. Legs." Bastian tilts his head to Spike.

I round the car, ease the door open, and gently lift the cashmere throw protecting Spike. He's still scarred from the sunburn—will be for life, most likely—but his needles are a healthy yellow. I think the ride did him good.

"Come on, boy." I pluck the cactus off Bastian's lap.

The three of us make our way to the front stoop and the candy-apple-red door.

Bastian tries the handle. "Locked. Please tell me the cleaning service didn't leave with the keys."

I shift Spike so that I'm supporting him with my left thigh. With his pot and dirt, he's a lot heavier than he looks. I tap my right foot on the front mat. "Under there."

Bastian crouches and lifts the bristly rectangle. *Bienvenue* is printed in curly script across the thing. I need to change that. Get something that reads *Enter At Your Own Risk* instead of *Welcome* to better fit the town spirit.

Gold flashes under the porch light, but before Bastian fits the key into the lock, he looks at me. An odd, dreamy expression crosses his face, and he smiles. "I never thought I'd see the day that Slate Ardoin lived in a place where you could keep the key under the front mat."

I roll my eyes. "Stop giving me shit."

"I'm not." His voice gets as thick as the fog. "I just—I'm just so happy you decided to give up thieving and get yourself a legit life. Instead of worrying about losing you, I can concentrate on school and our future."

Putain. Again with the chest pain. "Open the door or I'll freeze to death before I can even start my legit life."

Last time I was here, the place was an icebox and reeked of mildew. Now, heat hugs us, and the odor of wood polish and bleach permeates the air. Bastian flips on the light, and the house that once belonged to my parents comes to life.

The decor is awful. The sky-blue walls of the living room and dandelion-yellow of the kitchen are way too cheery. The white-washed furniture and pale oak floors too cozy. The square nine-paned windows with lace curtains too fairy-talesque. Even the granite fireplace somehow manages to give off happy vibes.

"This house cleans up nicely." Bastian's gaze surfs over everything.

I grunt, because I'm a fan of rich brown and charcoal, dark wood and oriental rugs, open spaces with bay windows.

As I set Spike on an end table by the couch where he'll get diffused light but no nasty drafts, Bastian points to the chimney. "You took the family pictures down."

I don't want pictures of people I can't remember. I don't say it, because Bastian might not understand. I also had the Brume's Broom team put all of the nursery items in the attic. My old crib, mobile, everything. For extra cash, they agreed to assemble the queen-sized bed I ordered and paint over the galaxy wallpaper. That room should now be a wool-gray oasis that Bastian can set up however he wants.

At the moment, he's eying the open bookshelf separating the living and dining areas. There's twenty squares of shelf space, all half-filled with tomes on astronomy. I kept those because I don't hate astronomy. The math doesn't scare me like I thought it might, and the whole idea of the unexplored universe awakens that same part of me that got excited when it heard magic was real.

The magic bit's snuffed out, but the astronomy part lives on.

I'd assumed studying killed people's ability to form opinions and assert views. In my few days at U of B, I've come to realize instead that it's a lot like thieving and conning: it takes planning and skill, comes from the gut, and if done right, gives back a hell of a lot more than one puts in.

"There just might be enough room for my books here, if we stack'em in tight." Bastian empties a shelf, moving a book on black holes and another on physics. "And Spike's harem can go here, too. A succulent in each square."

I grimace. "You make it sound cheap. Like the ladies are on display, purely for his pleasure."

That gets a snort.

"Fine. Let's get those ladies inside. Along with your books."

"Aren't we supposed to meet Cadence and Alma at the tavern?" He checks his watch, a Breitling I bought him right after the Bloodstone came off.

"I shot Cadence a message we'd be a little late." I thumb the patch of skin at the base of my finger. Sometimes, I swear I can still feel the gold band gripping it. "I wanted to get our shit organized first." I've got plans for later on, and none of them include unpacking.

We unhook the carriage trunk and lug it inside. As Bastian begins arranging his prized possessions on the shelves, I brave the cold for the succulents.

Once I set them at Bastian's feet, I wiggle my eyebrows. "So? You and Alma? Anything happening there?"

His cheeks flush. "We're just friends." In an almost whisper, he admits, "She's a little scary."

A month ago, I would've agreed. I thought Alma was all tooth-and-nail and would rip Bastian to pieces. But then I met a certain *groac'h* who really was all tooth-and-nail and really did rip men to pieces. Alma's a kitty cat in a tiger fur coat.

Bastian tucks a book in, jostling it so hard it drops on the other side. "I mean, she's a lot more confident and . . . um . . . experienced than anyone else I've been interested in. Besides, I'm probably not her type."

I collect his fallen book—*Symposium* by Plato. Just the cover is yawn-inducing. I slide it through the open shelf. "'Fuck you talking about *not her type*? You're everyone's type. You're the brainy hero."

"That's an oxymoron."

"An oxy-whatta?"

"A figure of speech made up of contradictory terms." At my smirk, he adds, "You were just pulling my leg. You knew what it was."

I don't confess that I did. I've got a rep to uphold after all. "If you like her, make a move."

He blushes all the way down to his roots. "Hand me the Mexican Snowball," he mumbles.

I return to his side of the shelf and snatch the rose-shaped succulent. As I hand her over, she slides out of my fingers. Bastian performs a sort of backbend. With an impressive and painful-looking twist of his arm, he catches her before her little pot goes splat.

"Does Alma know you're so flexible?"

He shoots me a glower that bombs its purpose considering the scarlet hue of his skin.

After we've placed the ladies on the bookshelf, I step back to admire our handiwork. Bastian's right—the girls *do* look good here.

"I'm just worried she's not interested in me like that."

"You're such a moron. Anyone can see how Alma looks at you. She's not making a move because, well, we've all been preoccupied with . . . *oh* . . . surviving. But if there's one good thing that came out of almost dying, it's the realization that life's really short. Screw uncertainty and indecision. You've gotta go for it. There's nothing worse than regret."

I study the Burro's Tail that Bastian put in front of his box set of fantasy hardcovers. The witchy covers make me think of the first night I met Cadence in her cosplay regalia.

Same night I put on that damned ring.

I decide the good outweighs the bad when it comes to the Bloodstone-chapter of my life. I got the girl. The house. The trust fund.

Face screwed in concentration, Bastian pivots the Aloe Vera, once, twice, then steps back. "Home sweet home."

"When I was in juvie, and I contemplated my future, this was not at all where I pictured myself."

"In a house, or in Brume?"

"Both. I like big cities. I like modern and sharp. Sunshine. Heat. Noise." I gesture to the coziness surrounding me. "Not *this*."

"So you're worried life will get boring now that you're no longer relieving people of their possessions or fighting dark magic?"

I raise a smile because, for all my complaining, I'm ready for boring. "Bring on the boring."

I don't know if I could stay here forever, but for now, I'll take a calm, little life in this hilly cobbled town with its pounds of snow and fog.

I grab my duffel bags from the carriage case in the foyer and bring them upstairs. I left most of my wardrobe back in Marseille. Only my heaviest winter clothes are suited for Brume's deep freeze.

The master bedroom spans the area above the living and dining rooms, a big-ass space for such a teeny house. It smells like cedar air-freshener and laundered bedding.

My parents were a little more reasonable in their decorating choices up here. The walls are ivory, the curtains simple sheaths of blue cotton twill. At the foot of the bed sits a worn, wooden trunk. My mother's maiden initials are on it—E.H. Eugenia Hernandez. I don't know why I didn't have it put up into the attic with the rest of my parents' personal crap. Maybe because it'll make for a good bench when I put on my socks.

A navy duvet blankets crisp white linens on the king-sized bed.

Above the carved headboard hangs a framed black-and-white photograph of the university temple, looking formidable with its massive oak doors and domed cupola. The stained-glass cupola is no more, thanks to the earthquake caused by Cadence's leaf, and the doors are now bandaged with timber.

Setting my duffel bags on the trunk, I go about arranging my stuff in the antique set of drawers. I hesitate before hanging my pants in the wardrobe. Cedar panels line the inside, nothing fancy. But the cherry-wood doors match the headboard, decorated with swirls, curlicues, and a quatrefoil shape carved around the brass keyhole. Knowing my luck—and Brume—this could turn into some Narnia-loophole. I could find myself in eternal winter after I hang up my pants.

Hmm. Maybe Brume *is* Narnia. Maybe if I step through the wardrobe, I'll find myself on a sunny beach sipping Mai Tais in the Bahamas.

After I hang everything up, I feel up the panels. No magical portal.

Probably best, because if I get sucked anywhere, then I won't get to see my girl.

Which reminds me . . . *the animal pelts.*

Bastian's standing on the threshold of his bedroom. "I liked the galaxy wallpaper. Gave the space a certain *je ne sais quoi.*"

I couldn't stomach it. "Paper your walls with pages from one of your favorite novels."

He goes white as though I just suggested murder.

Chuckling, I head back downstairs and into the kitchen where I told the cleaners to put my mail. Sure enough, a cardboard box sits on the round wooden table. I grab it and return upstairs.

Bastian nods to the box. "The pelts?"

The night we got back to Marseille, he caught me surfing the web for some decorative fur rugs. My finger had hovered over *add to basket* when he'd *huh*ed. When I asked him what *huh* meant, he refocused on his eight-hundred-page fantasy novel about fae folk.

"Harboring some caveman fantasies?" He flipped a page.

"Just thought it would make the house . . . comfy." *For Cadence's naked ass . . .*

Smirking, he returned to his book while I scrolled through a page of bear pelts, complete with claws and head. Bastian glanced at my screen and grimaced.

Jesus. "What now?"

"Better go vegan."

"Vegan?"

"Murdered animals are unethical and definitely *not* a turn-on."

I balked at him for a full minute, before huffing and typing: *vegan animal pelts.* I clicked on the first link.

Bastian cleared his throat. "Not that company. It's got a bad rep for paying its workers unreasonably low wages."

How the hell did he know this? *Whatever.* I shoved my phone and credit card into his chest. "You're so fucking knowledgeable. *You* order them. I want two. One for my bedroom. One for the living room."

Now, Bastian leans against the doorframe of my bedroom as I rip the tape off the box, already envisioning everything Cadence and I will do on those pelts. As I pull out the first rug, he lets out a howl of laughter. There are two giant "pelts" in the box—a fluffy white one with four floppy legs and a headband of yellow daisies, and a purple faux-fur unicorn thing, complete with rainbow sparkles.

"You ordered a poodle and a fucking unicorn?" I spear him with a look nastier than any I shot the *groac'h.*

Between gasps of mirth, he squeaks, "Sheep. Not poodle." His giggling fit goes on.

I dump both back in the box and rub my hands, worried some of the sparkles might've transferred to my palms. And then I smile. "Retribution will be sweet."

"Worth it." Pushing his glasses up, Bastian wipes away his tears. "Want me to help you set them up by the fireplace?"

I shove him out of my room. "Go take a shower, you ass. We leave in fifteen."

I shut the door on his grinning face, pluck off my T-shirt, then drop the rest of my clothes and step into the bedroom's connecting bath. The tub doubles as a shower. I yank the new charcoal curtain closed. I had the worn wood walls repainted gray to complement my parents' Moorish-style black-and-white tiles.

As the warm spray hits me, and I scrub up, I think how I could get used to this. A life full of pranks, and soap that doesn't come on a stick.

5

CADENCE

I stare out the window of *La Taverne de Quartefeuille* at the bouquet of flowers in the bucket above the well. Nolwenn replaces the plastic poinsettias, presently dusted in snow, with real flowers when spring descends upon Brume. Considering today is February 1ˢᵗ, we have, oh . . . another five months ahead of us.

"Cadence?"

I blink away from the well and up into Adrien's face. It's still bare of eyebrows and lashes, but at least the burn marks are gone. His dark blond hair has started to grow back evenly, though it's still buzzed within a centimeter of his scalp. He looks so different, but I guess I do, too.

Our crazy leaf hunt left its marks on all of us.

He pulls out the chair next to mine and sits. "Are you okay? Did Slate—"

"The reason I asked you to meet me has nothing to do with Slate." I shift on my seat, then dip my palms between my lap as far as my pencil skirt will allow. "Actually, I don't want Slate knowing about this at all."

Adrien sits up a little straighter. "*This*?"

"That we're meeting."

Adrien glances around us, then leans toward me. "If you didn't want him to know, perhaps we should've met somewhere more *private*."

It's Wednesday night. Where the tavern is packed on weekends, weekdays are much quieter. Out of the ten tables on this floor, only three other tables are occupied. One by some U of B faculty, one by a group of juniors, and the last one by a couple who doesn't seem to be enjoying their date. If I'm not mistaken, the guy's one of our town's firefighters. I'm guessing the girl across from him is his girl-friend, soon to be ex.

"You're right. I probably should've picked somewhere else, but Gaëlle said she was coming here with the kids for an early dinner."

The lines on his face rearrange in wariness. "Gaëlle's coming?"

I nibble the inside of my cheek just as she trundles through the door, arms wrapped around one of her twins while her stepson holds the other eight-month-old. I raise my hand to catch her atten-tion, which is ridiculous considering how small the tavern is. It's not like she could miss me.

Gaëlle nods, then says something to Romain I don't hear but imagine it's to go upstairs, because he climbs up with his ward while she comes over with hers.

After she takes a seat across from me, I release the lining of my poor cheek. "I'm going to cut right to the chase. I want to get your opinion on something."

My fellow *diwallers* eye each other warily. They must sense it's about the Quatrefoil. I mean, what else do a student, a history professor, and a young mother have in common?

"I was talking with Papa today and was reminded that if . . . if I hadn't dropped the ball—or rather, the leaf—" Neither smiles. So much for easing the mood. "He'd be free of his wheelchair."

Adrien touches my forearm. "You didn't drop anything."

I shoot him a sad smile, because the fact is that I did. Otherwise, we'd be meeting to discuss how to use our powers instead of how we don't have any. "Anyway, I asked him what he thought about me trying again."

Gaëlle hisses.

"He better have told you it was a bad idea," Adrien growls.

"He did. He told me not to even consider it."

"Good." Adrien crosses his arms.

"And Slate?" Gaëlle pulls off her son's yellow wool hat, which reminds me of the scarf she stuffed in the mouth of her husband's ghost.

"Slate made it clear that it was out of the question and that he'd return to Marseille if I did something that stupid." I try to smile but end up grimacing.

"Such a shame that would be."

"Oh, come on, Adrien. You don't hate him anymore." I knock my knee into his, jostling the foot propped on his gray suit trousers. He's wearing them with an uncoordinated herringbone jacket that somehow matches, maybe because it's the same shade of steel as his pants.

He sighs. "Just because I'm glad he didn't die, doesn't mean my opinion of him has improved."

"Let's put your opinion aside for a second." I prop one elbow on the table, keeping the other tucked under it. "*If*—"

"No way." Gaëlle shakes her head, making her long brown curls rush over the beige wool coat she's unbuttoned but hasn't removed.

"*If* I put the ring back on, would you guys help me?"

"You can't be serious." Adrien reaches over and this time latches on to my hand. "We almost lost you."

"I know, Adrien, but I had it." Heat stings my eyes. "I can get it again. I know I can."

"We're aware you can, Cadence"—Adrien's tone isn't harsh but by no means is it gentle either—"but we don't want you to put yourself in that sort of danger ever again."

"But you'll help me?"

Adrien's fingers tighten around mine. "Tell us you didn't . . ."

A tear trickles down my cheek as I pull the hand still burrowed in my lap out of hiding and lay it flat on the table. The Bloodstone swirls as though real blood sloshes inside the oval dome. Probably not an illusion.

"No, no, no . . ." Gaëlle's brown skin turns as ashen as Adrien's house after our fight against the *guivre*.

"I'm sorry. I understand if you don't want to help me. I managed just fine on my own the first time around, so—"

"Shut up." Adrien's grip turns vise-like. "Of course, we're going to help you."

"Of course." Color progressively returns into Gaëlle's cheeks.

Not that she seems happy about the situation, but at least, her horror has receded.

"I can't believe you did this." Adrien's hazel eyes flash with dread, or is it disappointment?

"I can't believe I did it either." I bite down on my lip. "The worst that can happen is that I'm unsuccessful, right? I mean, your pieces are locked into the clock forever, and Slate didn't die, so . . ." I try to pull my hand out of his, because he's squeezing so tight he's cutting off my blood flow. "Adrien, I can't feel my fingers."

He doesn't let go, but his eyes seem a little glazed, as though he's somewhere else. Maybe back at his birthday party.

"If you don't fucking unhand her, Prof, I'll go borrow one of Juda's knives. I hear he keeps them nice and sharp."

I jump at Slate's voice. He stands beside my chair, Bastian right behind him. "You're home," I say all breathily, jamming my hand, the one with the Bloodstone, back under the table.

"Hello, Bastian. And welcome back, Rémy." Adrien finally releases my fingers. Instead of apologizing, his eyes turn slitted as he focuses them on Slate.

"Don't call me Rémy."

"Shh." I spear my fingers through Slate's. "You guys, everyone's looking."

Slate's black eyes slam into me. I know it's not me he's mad at. At least, not yet. He's going to be extremely mad in a second, though.

"I'm going upstairs." Gaëlle gets up, hiking the baby further onto her hip. "Glad you're back, Slate. You, too, Bastian. We're going to need all the help we can get." She squeezes my shoulder. "And, Cadence, I'm here for you always, but I really wish you'd have come to us before you made the decision."

I swallow back my guilt. In many ways, this doesn't actually affect them. Just me. The ring's on *my* finger and it's *my* piece.

I shouldn't have told them anything.

"Before you made *what* decision?" Slate's tone is so sharp it slices right through my thoughts.

I stare up into his face, at his stubble-covered jaw that's ticking. *Actually* ticking. This wasn't how I'd pictured our reunion, but after lunch . . . after Papa retired to his bedroom to read a book, I snuck into his office and input the code on the safe.

If there was even one chance I could bring back Emilie, Maman, and everyone else who'd perished because of the Quatrefoil, I was taking it. After all, we were talking about *one* battle. *Mine.*

Of course, a small voice in my head had hissed: *What if it makes everything worse?*

I'd almost slammed the door shut, but as I'd stared at the oval crimson cabochon, I remembered the smooth weight of my leaf and decided ignorance wasn't bliss. I snatched the cursed ring, read the inscription, *Erenez e v'am,* then slipped it on.

Licking my lips, I steel my spine and slide my hand out from underneath the table. I think Slate's stopped breathing because his chest doesn't rise and fall and his nostrils don't flare. He's preternaturally still. Only his eyes move. From the Bloodstone to my face.

"I leave for three days and you can't fucking take care of things around here, Prof?" Slate's low voice snaps Adrien's attention toward him.

I pull my hand out from Slate's. "Adrien's got nothing to do with this. You want to be mad at someone, be mad at me! It was *my* decision." As I stand, my eyes collide with Bastian's, which have gone as square as his lenses. "And you know what? All of you . . . I've changed my mind. I don't want any of you involved."

No one else should suffer my reckless, guilt-fueled decision.

I try to shove past Slate, but he steps into my path and slinks one arm around my waist, all at once pinning me against him and hiding me from the busybody diners.

I really should've picked a quieter place.

"The hell we're staying out of it," he says all low and growly.

Adrien gets up. "You're not alone in this, Cadence. We're a team. And this time, we'll be there for you." He doesn't stroke me with more than his eyes, but it buffets the chaotic pulses of my heart.

"Thank you," I whisper.

He nods, glares at Slate, says good evening to Bastian, and then leaves.

"Will you go back to Marseille?"

"Why would I go back to Marseille?"

"Because you're mad at me."

"I'm not mad; I'm fucking furious. But I'm also fucking staying."

I snake my arms under Slate's coat and hug him. "I was afraid you'd leave."

He snorts. "That would make *some* people only too happy." After a beat, he asks, "Why did you put it on?"

I take in a breath. "Because I had to."

He's quiet for a second, then says, "I'm still pissed off. Colossally pissed off. But I get it. I get you wanting to finish it."

I tighten my grip. "Tell me you don't hate me."

He presses his lips to the top of my head. "I could never hate you."

I start crying now, because what I did finally catches up to me, and I'm scared.

Slate winds his hand through my hair, paring my face from the collar of his black button-down. "I won't let anything bad happen to you, but in order to do that, I'm going to be sticking to you like white on rice. Everywhere you go, I go. And I do mean, *everywhere*."

"Okay."

"Now that our sleeping arrangements are in order, let's eat. I need sustenance before our reunion with my favorite clover."

I loosen my grip. "Sleeping arrangements?"

"I said *everywhere*, to which you said, *okay*. Bastian"—Slate looks over my shoulder—"who's standing a little too close, heard you, too."

Bastian *is* standing close, so close I can smell his cologne. "I'm trying to hide the Bloodstone from view." He tips his head to a table behind him.

"Oh." Slate shoots the nosy college students a withering glare. "Good thinking." He drops his hand to mine to cloak the Bloodstone and guides me back to the table before dropping into Adrien's vacated chair.

Nolwenn bustles over. "Welcome home, Marseille." Did she hear any of our conversation? The worry lines bracketing her pursed lips tells me she definitely senses something's up. "What can I get you?"

After Slate says, "The usual," and she leaves, I whisper, "I didn't think you meant at night too."

"Not excited to sleep with me?"

Heat prickles my cheeks, and my pulse thunders, but for a whole other reason than the ring.

"If you didn't want to share my bed, Mademoiselle de Morel, you should've contemplated your choice of accessories a little longer."

I square my shoulders. Might as well make the most of this situation. After all, I do want to sleep with Slate. "If that's the case, I should've put it on sooner."

His mouth parts. Have I shocked Slate Ardoin? That'd really be something. I mean, he's seen it all. Done it all. I didn't even think anything *could* shock him. But he's definitely shocked.

He shakes his head and tows the hand he's still holding into his lap, making my body contort since it's not the arm closest to him.

I continue, "Fire. Pelts. You. Me. Tonight."

"Don't forget, Bloodstone," he mutters. "And it's a negative on those pelts." He slants Bastian a look that makes his brother smirk.

"I sense a story." I scoot my chair nearer to Slate and lay my head on his shoulder. "I could really use a story right now."

Grin turning into a chuckle, Bastian recounts how Slate now owns two cute, fuzzy rugs.

A moment later, Alma torpedoes into the tavern, her amber locks twisted into a top bun and her whiskey-colored eyes accented by liquid liner. "What'd I miss?"

As she drops into the chair beside Bastian, he starts from the beginning again.

I tip my head up toward Slate's. "I'm glad you're home."

"I'm glad I'm home, too, princess."

I love that Brume has become his home.

6

SLATE

While Cadence, Bastian, and Alma demolish their *salidou* crêpes, I get up to supposedly use the bathroom, but instead, head straight through the kitchen and out the back door. Juda's white caterpillar eyebrows crawl under his puffy chef hat as I pass by.

As he separates a chicken into parts with a few deft whacks of a meat cleaver, he doesn't ask where I'm going or why I'm using the backdoor. Even though he may still consider me strange, I'm no longer a stranger. I'm a Brumian through and through.

I emerge onto a steep, pocket-sized patch of snow overlooking the cobbled road linking First and Second Kelc'h and breathe in the frigid air, reveling as its icy fingers grip my lungs. The pain reminds me that I'm alive. That the damn ring came off, despite Rainier's warning it wouldn't. And Cadence, too, will survive, no matter what monster comes at her this time.

I bang my fists against the gray wall of the tavern and choke back a roar. I want to rip this town stone by stone. I want to nab Cadence and whisk her away, back to Marseille, or anywhere really. But now that she's put on the ring, there's no escape.

Putain de bordel de merde.

I want to shake her, ask her what the hell she was thinking, even though deep down I know. A girl who succeeds at everything can't stomach failure. I should've seen it coming. I should've kept the fucking ring myself. Why the hell did we entrust the devil with it?

The kitchen door opens, and Nolwenn steps out. "*Ça va, Marseille?*"

Just need a minute to process the news, I think but don't spit out. For all her involvement in my childhood, it's best she doesn't involve herself in my present.

She takes a gold case from the pocket of her apron and slides out one of those thin cigarettes advertised as 'feminine.'

She holds it out to me, but I shake my head. "Didn't know you smoked, Nolwenn."

A chagrined smile pleats her skin. "Only when I'm stressed." She lights it, sucks on it. When she pulls it from her mouth, the white paper's ringed in hot-pink lipstick.

As she blows out the smoke, I notice how much older she's been looking. How tired. Even the layer of makeup she wears can't hide the fact that her skin is sallow. I'm about to ask her how she's feeling when she says, "The ring is on Cadence's finger."

My stomach twists some more. So much for keeping the news under wraps.

She sighs. "Rainier will finally get what he wants: the Quatrefoil put back together."

I stare down the hill in the direction of the manor. The fog's wispier tonight, and yet the house isn't visible from this pocket of darkness. I can feel the old stones breathe though, like the dragon in Adrien's flue before it soared out.

How I loathe Cadence's father. Even his genuine affection for his daughter can't redeem him in my eyes. "Cadence says he doesn't know she put it on."

"*Ah.*" Doubt echoes through the pale rings of smoke Nolwenn puffs out.

"You think he's behind it?"

"I think that if he didn't want his daughter to wear it, he would've found a way to get rid of it. He's good at getting rid of things."

"*Things* or people?"

Her dark eyes flick to me, her only response.

I scrape a hand through my stiff curls, tearing through the gel that's supposed to tame them. "I need to go back inside. I can't let Cadence out of my sight until—"

"The *magie noire* reveals itself," Nolwenn finishes for me. "She'll win her battle, the same way she won her last one."

"At what cost?" I growl.

She lifts the cigarette. "Marseille, you must worry about what happens *after*."

"After?"

"Do you really think a cursed artefact will bring light, beauty, and happiness into the world?"

I leave her to finish her cigarette in the dark, dread spreading like a cancer in my stomach. When I get back to the table, I'm more agitated than when I left.

After dinner, we walk Alma back to Third. She's now aware of the ring on Cadence's finger and insists on coming back with us, but Cadence tells her it's unnecessary, that she'll see her on campus.

Reluctantly, Alma inputs the door code of her dorm cottage. As we walk home, leaving the lit cobbles of town, my pulse trumpets. I peer into every shadow for danger. At some point, I think I feel a rumbling and check with the others, but they didn't feel a thing.

At home, I get no pleasure watching Cadence *ooh* and *ahh* over how we cleaned up the place. I smile at the neon cactus light she gives me but don't go looking for a nail to hang it with. I just stand in the foyer with my arms crossed like a stone gargoyle, letting Bastian guide her around the bottom floor. When he's done, I pluck her hand and lead her up to my bedroom, leaving Bastian to lock up.

This is the moment I've been waiting weeks for and yet it's completely wrong. In every scenario my mind's cooked up of this night, Cadence isn't wearing the ring, all of her bruises have healed, and we're both slightly giddy.

I try to pretend, though. That the ring isn't on her finger. That the scar and the faint purple bruise beside her brow are gone. That my heart's knocking around my chest in anticipation instead of trepidation. I try to sink into the moment and concentrate on the pale moonlight licking her soft curves as she sheds her sweater, revealing a silk camisole.

I cage Cadence's face between my clammy palms and kiss her perfect mouth, but then my thumb grazes the scar on her eyebrow. She jerks, and my house of cards topples.

I lower my hands and take a step back. "Neither of us are in the right headspace."

Her lips purse as though she wants to object, but a full minute ticks by, and she doesn't. "I'm sorry, Slate. I'm so sorry."

I nod. I sense she wants words, but I can't give her any. None that will reassure her anyway.

After I kick my shoes off, I sit on the bed with my back against the headboard and pat the spot beside me. Cadence removes sexy thigh-high boots and arranges them neatly beside my mother's wooden chest, then unzips her skirt. My dick springs to life, but the Bloodstone glints and deflates my erection before it can firm up. She keeps her opaque tights on and climbs into bed beside me, nestling her body into the crook of mine. I'm so angry that I attack her mouth but keep myself zipped up. I don't want her first time to be rough and stained by irritation.

When her hand ventures across my thigh, I rip my mouth from hers. "I can't."

"I think you can."

I cinch her wrist and gently hold it back. "I want this to be special for you. I'm not in the right place to give you special."

With a sigh, she curls up around me, laying one palm on my leg, at a safe distance from my pulsating groin, and we talk about life, about the one I've just left behind and the one I'm starting anew.

At some point, her breathing eases, and she drifts off. I hold her hand, tracing the Bloodstone with my thumb as though if I run my nail enough times around the setting, I could carve out the jewel. Heat pulses from it the entire night, but the red never flares.

Until my girl gets her piece, I ain't looking away from that stone.

7

CADENCE

After Adrien's history class the following day, I head over to the temple library with Bastian and Slate. We have two hours before Mademoiselle Claire's astronomy class, and the Quatrefoil only knows how much time before my piece shows up.

I keep glancing toward the Bloodstone, keep expecting it to light up like it did each time a leaf came into play, keep expecting my muscles to cramp and my veins to fill with fire. Which is why I suggested getting the clock cleared.

Once I have my leaf, I don't want to have to wade through shards of glass to find my element; I want to fling the piece of the Quatrefoil into its cradle and yank off the ring. Be done with the whole thing.

The sun pierces the fog for several seconds, revealing the Nimueh Lake in all its glory.

Slate jerks to a stop.

"What?" My heart takes off at a gallop. "What did you see?"

His voice is scratchy as wool. "Emilie's body still hasn't surfaced."

Papa and Geoffrey insisted we weigh her body down to keep her death a secret. Slate couldn't do it.

I swallow the thick buildup of grief. "It's not spring yet."

Slate drops his smudged gaze to my mittened hand and sighs. "Let's do this."

He didn't sleep last night whereas I surprisingly did. Or maybe, it's not surprising. When I'm with Slate, I have this feeling that nothing bad can touch me.

When we reach the boarded-up door kept shut with a chain and padlock, Slate pulls out his keychain.

I smile. "I don't think your house keys will work."

Bastian bounces on his boots to drive warmth into his legs. The air's particularly brisk today.

"Watch and learn, Mademoiselle de Morel." Slate smirks. "Watch and learn."

I frown as he pushes the keys to the side and grips what looks like a tiny flashlight.

He rolls the bottom, and a silvery wand rises from its hollow depth. "This is called a lock pick. I've had this retractable one specially made."

"Do I want to know why you have a retractable lock pick?"

Slate starts to work on the padlock, ignoring my question. "Why didn't you just phone up the fire department to open it up again?"

"Because my father doesn't know I put on the ring. If he thinks I'm trying to access the clock, he'll figure it out."

Bastian blows air into his palms. "You don't think he knows? Didn't the ground rumble when you put it on? Slate said it rumbled when he put it on."

That's true. "I have to admit, I was shaking so much I didn't pay attention."

"Wouldn't you have felt it, though?"

"You know what? I don't think the ground shook this time. I mean, Adrien and Gaëlle didn't mention anything."

"I have a theory," Slate says just as the padlock clicks. He slides it out of the heavy chain, then shoves open the wooden door bandaged with planks of timber.

Bastian grabs ahold of the door and drags it farther out. "What's your theory?"

Slate points a gloved hand to his ear.

Tick ... tick ... tick ...

"The ground rumbled when the clock started up. Since it hasn't stopped ticking, no need for magical earthquakes."

"Huh." Bastian bobbles his head. "Solid theory."

"Thank you, little bro." Slate taps the flashlight on his phone and goes in first.

Although they tied tarps over the missing cupola to keep the inclement weather out, the air is frosty and humid inside the cavernous hull. At least, there's no snow.

I turn on my cell phone and swing the beam around, my heart tightening as I take in the devastation. Novels litter the tiled floor like dead birds. Two curved bookcases are still standing. All the others have tumbled like dominoes and lay in heaps of splintered wood that remind me of witch pyres.

A frisson of desolation races up my spine.

Slate finds my hand in the darkness and tucks it into his. "You okay, princess?"

I nod. Books are replaceable. Well, the ones on this level. The ones in the archival room aren't. My gaze goes to the hatch door on the opposite end of the temple, but I can barely make it out. The muddy sunlight seeping through the coated green tarpaulin and the three neon rays radiating from the elements carved into the recessed clock's golden case are hardly enough to illuminate the entire space.

Glass crunches underfoot as we wind through the wreckage, careful not to trample the fallen tomes. To think that, soon, my element's green light will shine alongside the red, white, and blue beams. A jolt of excitement temporarily overtakes my trepidation.

Bastian comes to a stop in front of Slate's Water element. Bright blue flecks the air around his face. "Wouldn't happen to have a broom on the premises? Or on you?"

I smile at his wicked humor. "Not a real witch yet, remember?"

Slate impassively scrutinizes the steel-gray enamel within the swooping golden Quatrefoil outline, the blue-ombré lunar dial, and the constellation-flecked star one, before releasing my hand to grab a thick wooden board that used to be a shelf.

As he sweeps the chunks of colored glass off the clockface, I gasp. "Careful! It's an antique."

He cranes his neck to look at me from his crouch. "Glass rained down over the clock, the ground shook, and you're worried I might put a scratch in the enamel?"

He has a point, but still, I watch him like a hawk. Once he's cleared the entire face, and I've surmised that neither the golden band carved with our four elements nor the gunmetal-gray enamel bear a single dent, I relax.

Why I'm surprised the clock's unscathed is beyond me. After all, magic protects just as fiercely as it destroys.

The ring suddenly feels heavy as an anvil.

I shudder, which makes Slate jump out of his crouch and stride toward me. "What is it, Cadence?"

I shake my head. "Nothing. It's nothing." I can't believe I put the ring on. What if another innocent dies? Maybe I should tell Monsieur Keene to put the town under lockdown again.

My teeth chatter from the cold and dread spooling and unspooling through me like tentacles. Slate sighs and drags me into his body, holding me in a hug that slowly but surely soothes my foreboding.

"The clock's right on time." Bastian's looking at the moon dial. The hand is at the far edge of the whitest part, heading toward navy. "We're twelve days from the new moon."

I nod, my head still resting against Slate's shoulder. "At least, this time around, we know the ring will come off."

Slate's body goes taut. "You'll still have to fight to get the piece."

"And I will."

Slate puts a finger under my chin and lifts it so I'm looking him in the eye. "Yes, you will." His thumb grazes my bottom lip, making my blood fizz.

"So what do you both think? Why isn't this hand working, too?" Bastian juts his head toward the golden hand tipped with a star that lays motionless over the smaller dial, the one with diamond-like gems embedded like constellations into the enamel.

"I would think it'll work once I put my piece in, and magic is restored."

The three of us stare at the clock, trying to imagine exactly what the world will be like then. I think of Papa, walking. I think of us swimming in the lake during the summer. Snowshoeing through the forest in the winter. Slate will be with us, no more hatred between the two of them. I feel an itch in my fingertips and wonder if I'll be able to make plants grow or flowers bloom. When my thoughts start to slide toward darker images, ones like in *Istor Breou* of parched earth and desiccated forests, I shake my head.

Slate, too, must be thinking dim thoughts, because a shiver goes through him.

I look up. "Are you okay?"

A crooked smile blooms on his lips. "I was just thinking how I can't wait to show you some magic."

Heat pools in my belly. But then Bastian walks over and flicks Slate's temple. "I'm hoping that magic will give you some better lines. Cadence won't admit it, because she doesn't want to hurt your feelings, but that was pathetic, bro. You're off your game."

I laugh.

Slate shakes his head. "I'm not off my game. I have no game. No need for it." He hugs me tighter. "I got everything I want right here."

Soon, I'll have everything I want, too.

8

SLATE

The noise that jerks me awake sounds like a choking rattlesnake. I bang the back of my head on the wall and nearly fall off the stiff, wooden chair I lugged up from the dining room to my bedroom two nights ago when I felt myself dozing off.

All in all, I've been successful at staying awake at night when everyone else sleeps, only allowing myself to drift off during classes, and even then, in increments never exceeding fifteen minutes.

The strangled buzzing sounds again. Cadence stirs, and I swear under my breath, hurrying out of the bedroom. I'm fully dressed and ready for anything the Quatrefoil throws at me. I'm hoping it's a cup of coffee.

The noise is my doorbell. Guess I need to get that fixed. Or possibly removed. I twist the lock and yank open the door to find Adrien on the stoop. He agitates a paper bag with *Merlin's Baguette* stamped across it. The movement sends the buttery scent of croissants and *pains au chocolat* my way.

"Didn't know you doubled as a food delivery guy, Prof. Let me get my wallet."

"Funny." He comes inside, even though I didn't invite him.

I flick on all the lights, because the sky's a foreboding lambswool gray. It'll probably snow. Fucking Brume.

Adrien pulls the hat from his head. Between his lack of

eyebrows and the blond fuzz, he could double as a newly hatched chick. Or an ostrich egg. I mention it for old time's sake. He smiles; I smile. We're good. For now.

I lead him to the kitchen-nook-slash-game-room when suddenly, I stop and turn around, a huge grin tugging at my mouth.

The skin between his nonexistent eyebrows folds. "What?"

"Your nickname. It's perfect now."

"What nickname?"

Have I never called him Professor Prickhead out loud? "Forget it. Why are you here at"—I check my Daytona—"eight o'clock on a Saturday morning?"

He shrugs out of his wool coat and settles in a wicker chair, the rungs creaking under his weight. He's not as bulky as I am, but he's not thin either. Beneath the tweed, there are muscles. Lifting heavy historical tomes is good for more than the mind. Unfortunately. I'd much rather he were scrawny. Cadence may be into intelligence, but a brain on a bony man would've surely been less attractive. At least, he doesn't have facial hair.

I pull plates and cups from the cupboard, then fill the coffee machine with water. Like everything else in this house, the dishes are cheery—white porcelain with bright buttercups painted along the edge. The ceiling groans above me. Sounds like Bastian's up.

My phone vibrates in my back pocket. I pull it out.

A message from Philippe: *All clinics, hospitals, private docs coming up empty. If this Marianne Shafir had cancer, I'll eat my own balls. I've got an in on her bank account. I just need more money to persuade some people to look the other way.*

I rub a hand over my chin. It feels like I've got a hedgehog growing there.

Fine, I tap in response.

The amount of money I'm wasting on this might be crazy, but I've got a gut feeling. And my gut is rarely wrong.

Slapping his leather gloves against the scratched wooden table-top, Adrien pulls my attention from the phone. "My first stop was the manor, but Rainier informed me Cadence hasn't been home since Wednesday."

The muscles of my abdomen lock up. "Do you often bring Cadence croissants in the morning?"

He crosses his arms over his chest. "I wanted to see how she was doing. Haven't run into her since my class on Thursday."

"She's safe and sound. Tucked in my bed as we speak."

Adrien goes very still. "She'd be safer in town."

I gesture to my frozen backyard, the repository of Gaëlle's husband's bones, visible through the nine-paned window above the steel sink. "We're still *in town*."

"You know what I mean."

Yeah. He means she'd be safer *away* from me. I don't remind him that the ring's on *her* finger, not mine.

I slide the dainty coffee cup under the chrome spout and punch the brew button, even though what I really want to punch is Prick-head's face. After everything we went through, he still doesn't trust me. I may think he's an overrated, overdressed, overpampered rich boy, but I trust him.

Well, mostly. I trust him to be a team player and I trust him with my life, but I don't trust him not to sway Cadence away from me.

The gurgling stops as creamy foam settles on top of the espresso. "I know everyone likes to think I'm the *love 'em and leave 'em* type, but I only left to come back. I'm here, so don't give me shit about her not being safe with me."

Adrien runs a hand over his scalp. "This is really not the time for her to be playing house. She doesn't need to be distracted. She needs to be protected. She needs to be with someone who's thinking with his brain not his dick."

I take a step toward him, fists balled. "You fu—"

"Slate, stop!"

I freeze and turn.

Cadence stands in the entryway, wearing one of my shirts over her tank top and sleep shorts. Her hair's mussed like I've been running my fingers through it all night.

If only . . .

Bastian pops up behind her, whistling a tune, his stride full of bounce until the tension in the room smacks him like the icy fog curling outside the window. "Uh . . . good morning?"

We all ignore him.

Cadence stalks past where I stand between the kitchen and the nook, her bare feet slapping the honeyed hardwood. She rips the cup from underneath the coffee maker, and some of the foam sloshes out, dribbling over her skin. I reach for her but she holds up her palm.

She glares at Adrien, blue eyes luminous with displeasure. I'm glad I'm not on the receiving end of that look. "I don't need to be protected. I survived last time without your help."

Adrien's mouth pinches. "You might've survived but you almost—"

"I. Survived." Half the coffee is out of the cup now, drips of mud-colored liquid splashing on her glossy red toenails. "And I'll survive again. Both of you need to stop patronizing me. I'm neither a child nor am I made of glass."

"*Patronizing* you?" Adrien sputters. "We're all just worried."

"What he said." I rub the zippered-up scar on the back of my neck and stifle a yawn.

She gulps down the dregs of her coffee like it's *chouchen*, then shoves the cup under the spout again. "Sorry. I didn't mean to yell, but I'm tired of hearing the two of you fight over me. Adrien, I know you consider me like your sister . . ."

The hell he does.

"And I appreciate your affection, but Slate isn't a vagrant or a deviant."

When color stains his cheeks, my lips begin to tug into a grin.

"As for you, Slate."

My glee dies a slow death.

"Fists are *never* the answer."

I want to disagree. Sometimes they're the only answer, but I doubt Cadence wants to debate the merits of knuckle sandwiches. Besides, disagreeing would only feed into Adrien's 'hotheaded, unreliable protector' impression of me.

I drop into the chair across from him and make peace by jutting my chin toward the brown paper bag. "Prof brought us breakfast."

Cadence's eyes lose their frosty edge. "Thank you, Adrien."

This time when I reach for her, she lets me wind my arm around her waist and pull her onto my lap. Adrien turns his face toward the window, eyes narrowed on the shed, which is a miniature version of the house, complete with stone walls and a poppy-red door.

Bastian sets four glasses and a bottle of Danao on the table, then tips the pastry bag onto a plate. He grabs a chocolate croissant and shoves it into his mouth, before washing it down with the milky-fruit drink which he's guzzled by the carton since he got a taste for it at age twelve.

"Wow." He chews down another morsel of flaky dough. "Merlin sure can bake."

I steal a sip of coffee from Cadence's cup before she slips off my lap to take the last seat at the table.

As she reaches for a croissant, Adrien finally returns his hazel eyes to her. "I stopped by your house before I came here."

Her hand freezes in midair.

"You didn't tell your dad about the ring." It's not a question.

"I didn't want him to worry." Both her gaze and fingers lower to the croissant.

Adrien leans forward, reaches toward Cadence's arm, but a glance in my direction halts his progress. He flattens his palm on the tabletop. "Perhaps you should go see him. Sleep under his roof. It'll reassure him."

When hell freezes over . . .

She rips off the curlicued end of her croissant, grimacing. "He doesn't know about the ring, Adrien. And it's not exactly like I can walk around my house in gloves." She dusts her fingers and buttery flakes fall like raindrops.

"He's convinced you've been sleeping in the dorms with Alma."

That's the story Alma fed him when she picked up some clothes for Cadence the other day.

"If he knows I'm here, he'll—" The strangled sound of the bell cuts off Cadence. "Please tell me that's not him?"

I lean back in my chair to peek through the lace curtains, find Alma standing on the stoop, hugging her arms to her middle, looking disheveled and miserable in a pair of flannel pajama pants and a short fur coat. And behind her, atop the souped-up snowmobile that almost ran me over the night of the new moon, is none other than the man I loathe even more than winter in Brume *and* the Quatrefoil: Rainier de Morel.

9

CADENCE

"Daddy dearest is here, along with Alma." Slate's chair legs, which airlifted when he leaned back to look out the window, bang into the floor. "Bastian, the door?"

As Bastian goes to let them in, I palm my snarled hair. What is Papa going to think? I attempt to finger-comb it, but a strand snags on the ring. I slowly tow my hands down. *Yeah . . . it's not my hair* he'll be looking at.

Adrien sighs. "I didn't tell him you were here. In case you were wondering." He glowers at Slate as he says this.

Slate mirrors his look. How much more crap must we endure before these two get along?

Sliding my lip between my teeth, I stand up. The cold air smacks into my bare legs and pebbles my skin, reminding me I'm wearing Slate's shirt over my pajamas.

"Cadence de Morel, come out here right this second!"

Blood drains from my face. "I need pants," I whisper to Slate.

"Whatever for?"

"Slate, he's going to slap a chastity belt on me if he sees me dressed like this in your home."

"Good thing I have a nifty lock pick." He smiles. Actually smiles, like this situation is comical.

"Please get them for me." I flick my gaze to the landing. "Please."

Smile in place, Slate climbs the stairs two at a time.

"Cadence!" my father thunders again. "I know you're in there!"

"Coming, Papa!"

"Fine." As Slate comes into view of my father, he gives him a two-finger salute. "Morning, Rainier. Apologies that the parking spot I reserve for snowmobiles hasn't been cleared."

I hear Papa mutter something but don't catch what.

Alma walks over to me, shivering hard even though she has on more clothes than usual. "I'm s-s-sorry. He w-w-woke me and—"

I give her a one-armed hug. "It's okay. It's okay."

"Want to help me build a fire?" Bastian nods to the living room.

Adrien's fresh cologne—springtime grass and vetiver—sinks into me as he approaches. "If he forces you to go home," he says quietly, "I can sleep over in the guest bedroom to keep you company."

I manage a small smile. "Thank you, Adrien. That's really considerate of you."

"Like you said, you're like my sister, and family is everything."

My throat tightens. What a family we both have. Both of us down one parent. At least, we *have* a parent. I glance over at Slate, who's trundling back down the stairs. Even though he's sporting dark circles beneath his eyes, his gait is surprisingly lithe and spritely. Probably pumped up on adrenaline and caffeine.

He hands over my jeans. Since his shirt covers my ass, I wiggle out of my sleep shorts and slide my feet into the skinny denim. The second I zip them up, I stuff my hands into the back pockets and amble toward the open door.

"*Bonjour*, Papa." I slap on a hopefully cheery smile.

"You said you were sleeping in Alma's dorm room. Imagine my surprise when I didn't find you there." His words snap out of his mouth like the wisps of silvering blond hair around his face.

The wind's definitely picked up since yesterday.

I shift from one bare foot to the other, wishing I'd asked Slate for some socks. "Sorry, Papa. I should've told you the truth. I just didn't want to worry you."

His cheeks are ruddy, and I can't tell if it's from the glacial air or his rising fury, because he. Is. Furious.

I glance over to where Slate stands shoulder to shoulder with Adrien as though they were brothers-in-arms instead of nemeses.

Adrien's expression is inscrutable, but Slate's isn't. It's very readable. He's grinning—eyes, mouth, and all. Getting under my father's skin always procures him such joy.

I shoot daggers his way, and one must've hit its mark, because his smile withers like most plants in Brume.

I turn back toward my father, deciding to rip off the Band-Aid. At this point, I'd rather he focus on the ring than my nonexistent sex life. I whip my hands out my back pockets and hold the one with the ring out.

Papa blinks.

And blinks.

Milky air puffs from his gaping mouth. "Tell me that's not what I think it is."

"I want to try again."

"Cadence," he whispers my name, his expression completely horror-stricken. "Slate made you do it, didn't he?"

Slate bounds toward me, nostrils flaring, fingers jamming into fists. "Now wait a minute, de Morel. I—"

I slap one of my palms against Slate's chest, and a little *oompf* drops from his lips, replacing whatever tirade he was about to unleash on my father. He looks down at my splayed hand . . . my jeweled hand.

Alarm replaces my anger when I notice how crimson the ring seems. My gaze slams into Slate's just as the ground gives a single hard shudder.

My Earth piece has arrived, and with it, a bolt of gut-shredding pain.

10

SLATE

Everything happens at once. The ring ignites, and Cadence folds over, releasing a shrill whimper that ices my marrow. The ground bucks under Rainier's snowmobile, and he tilts back, gripping the handlebars like the reins of a bronco. The icy crust atop the snow cracks and widens, snowflakes bursting out in puffs as though subterranean woodland creatures are waging a Nordic pillow fight. From the newfangled dugout in the road, a massive root rises and bends like a cartoonish worm.

The second it aligns with Cadence, it slams back into the ground and heads for her, splitting my two stone steps before splintering the hardwood floor. I crush Cadence to me and back her up. The timbered tentacle trails our retreat, springing nails from the floorboards.

The whole house shakes. Alma shrieks, or maybe it's Bastian. Adrien knocks into me, his cologne so strong I smell it over the odor of wet earth and wood. He reaches for the stair post to steady himself, but the ground shudders again, and he ends up grabbing me.

I snarl, "Paws off!" but it's drowned out by Cadence screaming, "Papa!" She tears away from me and runs toward Rainier, whose snowmobile is now teetering on the edge of a wide crevasse.

Fall in, fall in, fall in, is the refrain in my head as I watch the old man's blue eyes widen in fear, his aristocratic pallor paling even further. How satisfying would it be to see him swallowed up by the frozen ground? Despite the obvious surprise on his face when Cadence showed him the ring, I still believe that somehow, someway, he's responsible for her putting it on.

The root curls in on itself and trails Cadence out, making the ground buck. The snowmobile lists to the side. Rainier slips . . . and slips.

I scream her name, and she freezes, barefoot in the snow, a hairsbreadth from her father. The tuber stops, lifts like a periscope, stretching almost the full length of Cadence's body, and levels on her face. My breath jams inside my lungs.

No one moves, not even the creepy-ass crawler.

A mound of snow slides off my slate-shingled roof and lands with a splat on the ground. And then there's a deep groaning sound, and the snowmobile noses downward, but by some miracle doesn't plunge into the trench.

"Slate!" Cadence cries. "Papa!"

She called my name first.

"Slate!"

Oh . . . she called on me to *help* her Papa.

Adrien jumps into action, and I lunge after him, muttering a litany of *putain de bordel de merde*s. We both grab onto the handle sticking out of the snowmobile's back, above the snow flap, and heave. The vehicle staggers forward instead, making both Adrien and I skid.

"Pull, Slate!" Adrien shouts. "Pull!"

"What do you think I'm doing? *Pushing*?" The thought does give me pause, but then Cadence whimpers, and I toss all temptation aside, drop into a squat, and lean my weight back, thigh muscles on fire.

The root's still watching her, but it hasn't moved.

Adrien groans while I growl obscenities at the Quatrefoil. The snowmobile finally gives and then slides backward. We drag it a full meter away from the trench that's carved up the road as far as the eye can see in this fog.

Adrien pants and wheezes. "Rainier's safe, Cadence. Rainier's safe."

Her eyes are glazed with tears. "Th-thank you." She wipes her cheek. "I d-don't . . . I'm afraid t-to move. I'm a-afraid."

"We're all right here, princess." I step toward her, but she holds out her hand, the one with the ring. The stone swirls and swirls like a rotating beacon.

"D-don't, Slate. D-don't. The th-thing . . ."

The hell I'm not going to her. When I reach her side, I wrap an arm around her quivering body.

She gasps my name, tipping her head up.

"Shh. It's all right."

Her scarlet lips spasm just as hard as the rest of her. "If it touches you . . ."

I'm cursed. I sigh, and then grind my jaw as I remember little Emilie. "Curses aren't instant, though. You'll have vanquished this" —I shift my attention to the tapered brown thing—"turd before it would take effect."

Adrien sniffs the air. "Doesn't smell like an excrement."

"Just a figure of speech, Prof." I would have snickered had Cadence not been rattling in my arms. "We need to get you socks and shoes. And your coat."

"It follows me," she whispers, the shirt she borrowed from me flapping around her flimsy tank top. "I c-can't move."

"Okay." I'm about to release her and dash back into the house, when I spot Alma and Bastian in the doorway. His eyes are as round and wide as an owl's, or rather as Alma's mouth. "Guys, get her stuff! In our bedroom."

"*Our?*" Rainier scoffs.

"Not the time, Papa." Cadence doesn't move her eyes off the root while I scrutinize my destroyed foyer.

To think I just had the floorboards oiled . . . Quatrefoil *de merde.*

Bastian and Alma rush back out carrying Cadence's furry boots and new puffer coat that's the exact same shade as her lips, and as her toes, and I'm not talking about the polished bits.

"Hold on to me, princess."

Cadence's hand settles on my shoulder as I lean over and lift her leg. I press her sole onto my denim-clad thigh to get rid of excess snow, then rub her icy foot between my hands to drive heat back inside before pulling on her sock and then her boot. I repeat the process, then zip her into her coat.

Her teeth chatter, and her skin's a patchwork of alabaster and scarlet. "How am I su-supposed to k-kill it?"

"There are gardening tools in the shed," Adrien suggests.

I swing my gaze toward him. "You think a weed whacker will work on this magical tuber?"

"Tuber? What tuber?" Alma whispers.

"Must be all magical if you guys can't see it." My voice plumes out of my mouth. Unlike the statue of Ares, which existed before the Quatrefoil shot it up with magic.

Adrien spears his arms into his coat, which he's just retrieved from inside the house. "Here." He hands me mine, probably trying to earn brownie points with Cadence, but I thank him nonetheless.

"What should I do, Papa?"

My ego prickles that she's turning to Rainier for advice.

The old man runs his gloved palms over his shrunken thighs. "Get her an axe."

Bastian shuffles over to us, squinting as if that will help him see through the magic.

A low slither makes my attention dart back to the thick root that expands and contracts like a massive vein feeding an invisible heart.

"What's wrong with you, Bastian?" I bark. "Get the fuck back."

"Is it moving?" Alma hugs herself as though her fake-fur jacket is some favorite pet. "Do tubers move?"

"Not move, per se, but they do grow laterally," muses Bastian, the human encyclopedia.

"Get back!"

"It can't touch him. Only *he* can touch *it*, remember?" Rainier mutters.

"I still don't want him anywhere near it." I jam my fingers into a fist, regretting I didn't let Rainier's ride slip into the crevasse. Especially since Adrien was holding on. Two birds, one snowmobile.

The warmth of my coat reminds me that Adrien's not a complete asshole. Just Rainier de Morel.

Prof crosses his arms over his chest. "If this is the root, then what size is the plant?"

"Giant," I mutter, looking toward the town for a monstrous growth. Problem is, the town's choked in mist, which makes it impossible to spot *giant trees*, or anything else for that matter.

Adrien fishes out his phone and presses it to his ear. "I'm calling Gaëlle. Maybe she sees something from her window."

Rainier throttles the engine. "I'll go check."

"Papa, no!"

I've never heard Cadence raise her voice at Rainier. Warms my balls right up.

"The piece is no longer on its way, *chérie*; it's here."

"What if the trench widens, and you fall inside? Just stay next to us, okay?"

Rainier purses his lips but cuts the engine. "What's Gaëlle saying, Adrien?"

Prof nods and utters a bunch of *yes*es before removing the finger he used to plug his ear and lowering his cell. "She's getting dressed and coming to us, but from what she can see, the damage doesn't extend to Second."

"That's a relief." Rainier rests a hand on his trouser leg, squeezes the muscle underneath. "Call your father. Tell him to put a blockade at the entrance of the town, so no one leaves and stumbles into the trench. Now let's go see where it stops."

Cadence shivers. I take her hand, which is radiating heat even though her teeth are clacking. "Th-the axe."

"I'll get it." I dig my keys from my pocket and release her. "Don't move."

"I won't. I swear."

I stride through the snow toward my shed, unlock it, and squint until I catch the gleam of a serrated blade. A saw, not an axe, but I don't see anything else, so it'll have to do. I pluck it from its peg, then haul ass back out. My molars slam together when I notice Adrien's hand on Cadence's shoulder. I tighten my grip on the saw's handle.

I must be giving off feral vibes, because Adrien's palm springs off her body, ruffling the black fur lining of Cadence's hood.

I trudge back over and am about to swing the weapon at the root when she grabs my bicep. "Stop! You can't touch it."

"I've decided that I don't care. It's the last piece."

"But I care. *I* care." She wrangles the saw from my fingers. "Now, get back."

As the weight of the weapon settles inside her palm, she whispers, "Oh my God. I'm going to be sick."

I cup her cheeks to make her look at me. "You've got this." I swallow down a rawness building in my throat. "You've got this."

"Okay." Her throat bobs.

I step back, and she lifts the saw, then drags it over the root. The serrated edge bites into the membrane. Something viscous and red oozes around the cut, then drips into the snow.

"Is that . . . blood?" Adrien's voice rents the quiet, that's ringing louder than my furious pulse.

Suddenly, the root squirms and retracts, ripping the saw from Cadence's hand and diving back into the trench. She flails from the momentum, falling onto all fours. I spring toward her and grip her waist, then help her back up.

"Did I—Did it . . . Did it work? Is the thing dead?"

Adrien follows the bloodied smear to the ditch and peers inside.

"Is her leaf there?" Rainier sounds out of breath even though he's sitting pretty on his snowmobile.

"*Non*, Rainier."

"The saw is, though," Bastian says, coming up next to Adrien. "Should I retrieve it?"

"No!" I yell at the same time as Alma asks, "How deep is the trench?"

"Not too deep. Three meters, maybe. I'd need some rope."

"No," I repeat, walking over to him in case he decides not to listen and jump in.

"Where did it go?" Alma asks, standing arm in arm with Cadence next to me on the snow-crusted embankment.

I reach over and clasp Cadence's hand, so she doesn't slip, and because I'm possessed by a need to hold on to her.

Adrien shines the light of his phone, and the beam catches on a thick, shiny trail that leads straight toward the town.

"I guess we need to follow the bloody-red road," I say.

"Let's go." Bastian takes a step forward.

"Oh, hell no." I turn to him. "You and Alma get your asses back inside the house. Make sure Spike doesn't freeze to death."

"One step ahead of you there, bro. Spike's wrapped up in the unicorn faux pelt."

I grind my teeth. I really don't want Bastian anywhere near this thing.

"What other tools do you have in the shed?" Adrien asks.

"Let's go find out." As I back up, I growl, "Just me and Adrien. No one else moves, got it?"

As we make our way toward the gaping red door, I quip, "We need all the weapons we can get. Maybe ask Gaëlle to grab her rolling pin."

Our crewmate's method to widowhood obliterates Adrien's stern countenance, and he snorts. "You're a real prick, you know that?" His tone is good-natured, so I don't take offence.

Besides, I *am* a prick, through and through. It's what's allowed me to survive.

Working together, we gather an impressive amount of crap that we dump onto an old sled and fasten to the back of Rainier's snowmobile with a garden hose. We're now equipped to poison, chop, beat, dig, and choke whatever monster awaits Cadence at the end of the slithering trail of bloodied sap.

11

CADENCE

Like those rattling cans newlyweds tie to the back bumper of their cars, we set off behind Papa's snowmobile.

I'm quiet. Quietly contemplating the trail of blood we're following.

You destroyed a goliath. You can do this. I try to find strength in my past, even though my past led me to this moment . . . Oh, the cruel irony.

My finger burns, but the heat unfortunately doesn't extend to the rest of me. My teeth chatter in spite of Slate holding me tight to him and Adrien walking alongside me, close enough that our arms keep bumping.

Bastian and Alma pull up the rear, whispering theories of what the tuber might lead to. Nothing good, that's for sure.

Papa's cricket ringtone chirrups over his growling engine. He digs his phone out of his coat pocket, then barks Geoffrey Keene's name followed by the word *crypt*.

After yelling at Adrien's father to *set up the blockade already*, he stuffs his phone back into his pocket. "The trench ends at our mausoleum."

That can't be a coincidence since it's my piece.

The naked linden trees poking around the cemetery like emaciated scarecrows come into view and then the rows of tombstones and the four founding families' crypts. In the distance, I hear Geoffrey Keene bellowing orders. The fire brigade's utility vehicles appear through the mist, their dark outlines sharpening as we get nearer, and then the mayor's imposing frame materializes like the prow of a ship cutting through a tempest.

Like his son, Geoffrey's tall with broad shoulders and a proud gait. He walks up to the other side of the meter-wide trench, the mist curling around his dark pea coat and silver hair. A slighter body comes into focus beside him, hourglass-shaped, feminine—Gaëlle.

"Mon Dieu," she whispers loudly.

"What the hell's happening, Rainier?" Geoffrey glares at Papa. "I thought this was over!"

Papa sighs and looks over at me, which eggs Geoffrey's attention my way. I pluck my hand from my pocket, then from my glove, and hold up my index finger to display the ruby-bright oval stone.

He blinks at the ring, then at me. "How—Why—"

Slate's arm falls from my waist. "Looks like you'll get your precious seat on the Council after all, Monsieur Mayor."

Bellowed orders behind him make Geoffrey glance over his shoulder, but quickly his attention returns to me. I don't usually like the way he stares, as though he sees Maman, the woman he was apparently attracted to in spite of both my mother and himself being happily married, but I like it even less right now because his hazel eyes shine with panic.

I *can* do this.

I *will* do this.

Papa shuts off the engine of the snowmobile. "Make sure all the firefighters stay back. We don't want any of them . . . *seeing* anything they shouldn't."

They wouldn't see much, but I'd rather they stay back. Less chances of collateral damage.

Gaëlle walks toward the mausoleum, then vanishes from sight. A moment later, she reappears on our side of the trench, brown locks whipping around her cheeks. She takes me into her arms for a quick hug. "We're all here, Cadence. You'll be fine."

I whisper a hollow *merci*, finding comfort in the familiar waxy scent of the hair product she uses on her curls. After she lets go, I slip my glove back on.

"What happened to Viviene's statue?" Bastian's standing by the gated portico, gazing up at my ancestor's effigy, or rather, at where the statue *should* be. Instead, shards of paper-thin granite rest on the ground like the hollow shell of a Kinder egg missing its prized plastic toy.

Geoffrey rubs his graying scruff. "We had reports of a vandal two days ago."

I turn to Papa. "Did you know?"

He nods. "Geoffrey informed me."

That explains his lack of outrage. "Why didn't you tell me?"

"I thought you were with Alma and didn't want to bother you." His jaw tightens, snaring Slate with a barbed look. "Seems I *should* have bothered you."

There's a commotion at the cemetery gates as the fire brigade drops one of the long, wooden barriers. Geoffrey jogs off toward them.

Something gleams among the rubble near the foot of the stone burial mound; something outfitted with a broad, shiny blade.

I frown. "Is that a . . . an axe?"

Bookended by Slate and Adrien, I walk over to the portico and grip the icy bars.

Slate squints. "I'd say it looks more like a meat cleaver."

"What's there?" Papa calls.

I look over my shoulder at him, perched on his snowmobile, pale as the air. "A really big knife."

"Maybe it's to help you defeat your curse." Adrien's head is tipped down, the rim of autumnal green cinching the golden-brown center of his irises alight with stress.

"Since when does the Quatrefoil provide tools?" Gaëlle's reasoning makes my heart trip over a beat.

"What if Viviene's the piece?" Alma says from her spot near Papa.

"Her statue's ruined, Alma," I say, even though doubt creeps in. *Could my piece breathe life into yet another statue?*

"What purpose would that root have had then?" Papa asks.

"It led us here." Adrien gestures to the line of blood.

"The trench would've led us here." Slate's logic matches my own.

"The root is my piece, not her." My inflection is deadened even though every nerve inside my body is jangling.

Slate brushes back a strand of my hair, his fingers winding behind my neck, locking there. "It bled. *You* didn't."

Not yet. I don't voice this. He's worried enough as it is.

Alma's pajama bottoms twist around her legs. "So . . . the knife?"

Papa rubs his arms as though to drive warmth into them. I want to tell him to go home, but I know he'll refuse. "Take it, *ma chérie.*"

"No." Slate's eyebrows hang low over his eyes.

"Yes," Papa bellows.

"Like Gaëlle said, why would the Quatrefoil hand over a tool to destroy it?" Slate snaps. "I bet it's a trap."

I look at Adrien who's scrutinizing the broken granite husk. "What do you think, Adrien?"

"Why do you care what he thinks?" Slate's nostrils pulse out a breath.

I lay my hand on his chest, right over his battering heart. "Because he's calm, and you aren't."

"What does that have to do with anything?" Slate's eyes exude such darkness, but I can't tell how much of that is annoyance and how much is fatigue.

"I think if it's there, you should use it," Adrien says.

"And I think it's a trap." Slate's voice is rough with irritation.

I whirl around. "Maybe Viviene's helping me!"

Bastian inches closer. "I can see the knife, so it's not magic. Alma? Can you see it?"

She nods. "Yeah. I can."

I look up at Slate. "So it's not a trap."

Slate side-eyes the damaged statue. "Fine," he grumbles. "Let's go get it. Is the only way in through the crypt?"

Papa shifts on his seat. "There's a gate. The keyhole's hidden in the scrollwork of the last bar."

Slate edges along the cage protecting Viviene's tomb until he reaches the mausoleum wall. He runs his thumb over the metal. "Well, I'll be damned."

I rub my hands together, the Bloodstone's band singeing my flesh.

"De Morel, you don't happen to have the keys on you?"

"They're at the house."

"I can go get them," Adrien volunteers.

Slate tugs the gate and metal screeches. "No need, Prof. Looks like our vandal left it open."

It's snowed since then, though, and the door is stuck in inches of white powder.

Slate tramples the area in front of the door. "Bastian, when's eventide?"

"It's the last piece, Slate," Adrien interjects. "It can surely be locked into its cradle at any time."

I'm slightly envious of how serene he sounds. Then again, this isn't his battle; it's mine.

"Seven twelve to seven forty-nine," Bastian says.

"And what time is it now?" Slate asks.

Bastian checks the digital clock on his phone. "Nine forty a.m."

Slate grips the door, drawing it wide enough for us to step through.

I swallow. Ten hours. I won't need ten hours.

Hopefully.

I stare at the frostbitten land and dark trench before focusing on the cleaver.

Like my heart, the Bloodstone pulses, making my fingers prickle in both anticipation and trepidation. I curl them into my palms, steel my spine, and step inside the cage, praying I wasn't wrong...

That Viviene won't suddenly come to life.

SLATE

L ike mist on Brume, I'm on Cadence's heels as she strides across the snow-swept portico to the ruins of the statue. I'm so close I smack into her when she stops.

She cuts me a look. "Slate, for the last time—"

"For the last time, I don't give a fuck about being cursed. I'm not leaving your side."

She shakes her head and lets out a long, resigned sigh. Like she's finally realized she can't talk me out of this.

Yeah. I won't back down. Every muscle, every nerve in my body is on high alert, ready to spark into action. Anxiety slithers like a coiling snake over the surface of my skin. I can't lose Cadence.

I won't.

Outside the cage, the bloody trail tapers like an ominous arrow toward the three tiers of waist-high stone upon which once stood the enchantress.

I lower my eyes to the ground where the statue lies in pieces. The face is entirely intact, an abandoned mask staring up at the steel-wool of the sky. Her lips are slightly parted, as if the artist had captured her midbreath. A jolt of surprise makes me suck in a lungful of arctic air at her resemblance to Cadence—same intent gaze, same full lips, same pointy chin. She glimmers, merely the effect of the filtered sunlight glancing off the stone but eerie none-theless.

Cadence shivers as her eyes trail over the face of her ancestor she must've gazed upon thousands of times. "I've never seen it from this close. It's so . . ."

"Delicate," I supply while Cadence says, "Real-looking."

That, it is. And marginally creepy.

"People say Maman looked just like Viviene."

"I was thinking she looked a lot like you."

"According to Monsieur Keene, I'm my mother's spitting image, so . . ." She shrugs. "Guess none of the women in my family are all that original." A smile tugs at her lips even though it's laced with melancholy.

Rainier calls out from his snowmobile, "What about the knife, *ma chérie*?"

The cleaver handle is encrusted in frost and looks to be half frozen to a slick of snow and ice. The flat side of the blade shines so brutally I can see our reflections in it.

Cadence takes a deep breath. "Slate, I beg you . . . back up."

I cup her face between my palms and press a kiss to her forehead. "Not happening. Now, do you want to grab that knife or should I?"

Cadence squats, her breath fogging the blade as she wraps her gloved fingers around the handle. She's not expecting the ice to let go easily, so when the handle just slips from winter's grasp into hers, she pitches backward. I lurch and grab her elbow.

She gasps. "Slate, you're touching me! Don't touch me." She tries to wrench her arm free from my grip.

"Your piece is the root," I remind her.

"But if this is part of my battle—"

The sound of scraping stone cleaves the air. Cadence holds her breath. So do I.

Nothing happens.

The sarcophagus doesn't move.

The ground doesn't shake.

Even the snowflakes seem to have stopped swirling.

Rainier squints. "What's going on?"

Cadence opens her mouth to respond when metal and stone screech. The trench plows through the portico and fissures all three slabs of stone. Before either of us can jump aside, the granite cracks, opening up like the maw of some prehistoric beast, and swallows us whole.

My stomach pinwheels as air whooshes past my ears and my body ping-pongs through a tangle of branches, flowers, and leaves. Something stabs me between the shoulder blades and then in the neck, right where the *groac'h* bit me.

Jesus, it's like being back in juvie, except this time instead of being prodded with toothbrush shivs, I'm attacked by a shrub. Warm blood trickles down my cheek and spine, because the branches have better aim than my cellmates ever did.

With an unceremonious *oomph*, I hit the sodden ground and peel my lids up to take in a spectacle that will forever stay seared into my retinas: a massive tree full of glowing white blossoms, with roots that skitter around like snakes.

Creepy-ass town with its creepy-ass flora.

Cadence bursts through the canopy of leaves and lands on the ground right beside me. The impact knocks the knife from her hand. It cartwheels over the jumble of roots before planting itself blade down in the muck.

I heave myself onto all fours and crawl over to scan her for injuries, find a long scratch along her cheek and several rips in her puffer jacket. "You okay, princess?"

"Just a little banged up, but otherwise I'm—" Her eyes widen. "You're bleeding!"

I snort. "That's what I *do* in Brume, remember? I bleed." I don't mention my wounds feel like they're sizzling over Juda's gas stove.

I inhale, then regret it. What is that smell? Like a rat dung-wrestled a skunk to its death. I look around for an army of cadavers or a sewage leak, but there's nothing. Nothing to explain the eye-watering stench.

We both get to our feet and look up at the crevasse through which we fell, two stories up. Cliffs of darkness rise on either side, and for a second, the memory of the well and its toothy inhabitant floods me. I close my eyes, pitching the water fairy away. When I open them again, my pulse is almost back to normal.

I tally up all the positive points: we're together and not in total darkness (no thanks to the anemic Brumian sun). What lights up the cave are the milky blooms peppering the tree.

"Cadence!" Alma screeches from above.

One by one, each member of our crew pokes their head over the edge of the trench—Alma, with her big eyes and copper curls; Bastian, who luckily shoves his glasses up the bridge of his nose before they tumble off; Adrien, whose expression is problematic to gauge since his eyebrows have gone the way of the dodo; and Gaëlle, who gnaws on her lip.

I think I catch wisps of Rainier's silvery-blond hair, but it must be my imagination because Cadence's father, for all his nosiness, wouldn't risk his life.

Gaëlle motions to the canopy of branches that stretches four meters up and six meters wide. "Since when can trees grow underground?"

"Tree?" Both Alma and Bastian echo. *Ah. They can't see it.*

"Not a real tree, Gaëlle." Prickhead shoves his hat back to briefly scratch his foreskin, I mean, forehead.

"Felt pretty real, Prof," I yell.

"What sort of tree is it?" Gaëlle asks.

I point to the phosphorescent flowers. "I'd say a magical one, but I could be wrong. Could be that the run-off from an underground nuclear test site winds up here, in this lovely subterranean orchard."

Someone snorts, and it echoes against the rocky dirt walls.

Adrien squints down at the leaves and flowers. "Hawthorn."

"That's why it smells like Black Death!" Cadence's eyes shine like the tree. "Hawthorn blooms are reputed to smell like the plague, because they produce the same chemical as a decaying corpse." Her fear's momentarily replaced by awe, history buff that she is.

"Hawthorns have a long history in magical lore. They're said to be bad luck," Prof adds.

"Fabulous," I mutter.

"They're not all bad." Gaëlle fingers the collar of her coat now that she no longer has a scarf to fiddle with. "I sell teas at the store made from hawthorn leaves. They're great for blood pressure." She shoves a brown curl off her face. "And the heartwood can be carved into pretty beads."

"Wonderful." I peer back at the glow-in-the-dark blooms. "Once we kill it, we can string up the spoils to wear at the Nice Carnival."

Cadence's lips quirk. "Although I'm really pissed at you right now, I'm also really glad you're here."

"White on rice, princess."

Bastian points. "What about the cleaver?"

Cadence traipses carefully over the thick tangle of roots that extend from the base of the trunk like wheel spokes. Before her fingers can make contact with the handle, a root bursts out of the ground and lassoes around her wrist, pinning her hand in place.

I leap toward her, ducking beneath another flailing root, and seize the knife just as one cuffs my ankle. I go down but not weaponless.

"Oh, hell, no." I hack into the root that's shackled me, making it bleed and shrivel down to the size of an earthworm.

It releases me and scampers off, twisting toward the mothership. I whack through the boa-like thing holding Cadence's wrist in a vise. Viscous red liquid splatters both of us as it frees her.

A quiet whoosh followed by a burning pain in my shoulder makes me jerk. "What the . . .?" I crook my arm and pat my shoulder. My finger trips over a thin piece of wood that's penetrated my coat. Swearing, I yank it out and hold it up. "The tree has thorns?"

"It touched you!" Terror and incredulity shake Cadence's voice. "It's not supposed to touch you!"

"I'm guessing I'm fair game since I touched it first."

Her face pales beneath the bloody sap dotting it.

"What's happening down there?" Bastian yells.

"What's happening is, we're getting attacked by a fucking tree! How the hell do we kill a magical hawthorn?" I wrench my neck as far back as I can, my shoulder throbbing like a mother. "What did we bring from the shed? Dump it all in!"

Bastian vanishes from the opening.

"We have this knife, Slate. I probably don't need anything else." Cadence eases it from my fingers and eyes the roots that have grown alarmingly still.

"A tree dies without roots," Prof yells down.

A frown turns down Cadence's crimson lips. "So I have to chop all the roots?"

"Or fell the trunk," I add. "Don't take my word for it, what with me not being a lumberjack, but I'm pretty certain a tree can't live without a trunk."

"Watch out!" Bastian pitches our gardening cargo through the crevasse. Most of it gets stuck in the branches. He looks down. "Why's it hovering?"

"'Cause you dumped it onto the tree, bro."

"Sorry."

"S'okay." I roll my stabbed shoulder. It feels like barbed wire is working its way under my skin.

A rattling, creaking sound echoes through the cavern as the roots begin to shift anew.

Cadence drives the cleaver into one that runs over her boot. It turns into a bloated slug. "Slate, behind you!"

I whirl around and crouch, eyeing the closest weapon—a bag of clothespins—but then see a pointy garden spade just beyond it. I reach it just in time to impale my barky assailant. The root bleeds and withers. This time, I don't wait to be attacked. Like Cadence, who's swinging her cleaver like a warrior queen, I pounce on the writhing roots and gouge each and every one of them. My shoulder joint screams, and putrid blood sprays me, but I don't stop. Not even to scrub my face on the sleeves of my pea coat. To think I just got the damn thing. I growl at the tree.

"I will end you!" My battle cry booms through the grotto in time with Cadence's grunts.

"Cadence!" Prof shouts.

I spin around just as something grazes Cadence's cheek and lodges itself in her hood. The tree's using us for dart practice. I leap over roots to reach her, my upper back so stiff I almost lose my balance.

"Slate, watch out!" She smacks her knife so close to my groin that my dick shrivels up like the root that flops at my feet before reeling back toward the tree. "Sorry."

"Try not to injure it before we use it."

Another thorn whizzes at us, slicing right through the air between our bodies.

"What's it shooting at you?" Gaëlle asks.

"Thorns!" I step in front of Cadence to shield her from the next airborne missile. I grit my teeth when it hits my waist.

Cadence starts batting at them.

"Concentrate on the roots," I grunt, fire racing across my body. "I'll protect you."

We dance—or rather, she dances, I scuttle—around the trunk until she's butchered each root.

By the time we've completed our first walk-around, I resemble Spike from all the thorns I've received, and Cadence is covered in enough blood to have just walked off the set of a slasher flick. I fucking hate horror movies.

And trees.

And mermaids.

And Rainier.

And the Quatrefoil.

And wells.

And snow.

The list is *long*.

"We did it," Cadence whispers.

I swivel my neck that's as stiff as a steel rod to cop a look. No more giant roots. "Can you see your leaf?"

"No." She looks up at the crew, and the light from the hawthorn blossoms catch on a patch of skin on her cheek that looks odd. Crackled and brown. Probably dried blood. "Can you guys see anything shine?"

I try to lift a hand to her cheek, but a cold burn sweeps across my muscles and bones, immobilizing them. "Cade—" Her name gets lost as my tongue creaks, then petrifies.

My skin tightens and itches, and then the embedded thorns in my body pop out like champagne corks and white flowers bloom in their wake. The sight ices my heart, and the smell . . . it turns my insides.

"Oh my God, Slate." Cadence raises her palm to her mouth.

I roll my eyeballs—which thankfully, still move—and discover I look like a modern table centerpiece with my bark skin and floral galls.

Tears stream down Cadence's face, raking through the scarlet sap. A single white flower blooms from her cheek. When her fingers hit its petals, she yanks at it. It grows right back.

"Why is Slate frozen? What's happening to him?" Bastian's voice is a wet holler.

I move my eyes upward to see him, but two flowers have grown from the top of my head and hinder my vision. He better not be contemplating jumping in.

"Cadence!" Prof shouts. "The roots!"

What's happening with the roots?

Cadence's mouth parts around a soundless scream as a root we must've missed—unless they're all growing back?—seizes her around the waist and carries her away from me.

13

CADENCE

My lungs are pinned to my spine as the root swings me through the air. I curl into myself, protecting my face with my forearms just before I hit the lowest branches of the hawthorn. The flower that's sprouted from my cheek tickles my eyelashes. I want to rip it out but I'm clutching the giant knife for dear life.

The knife!

Remembering I'm armed, I swing the blade into the vine-like root laced around me. It freezes, then with a whoosh of air, loosens and falls like a rope, before shirking away. I plummet fast and hard to the ground, and the momentum rips the cleaver from my gloved fingers.

Caked in muck, I heave myself onto all fours and scan my surroundings for my weapon, find it resting beside Viviene's crumbled tomb. Sprinting over, I rip my gloves off with my teeth and seize the handle just as a new root lashes at me.

The things are growing back!

There are still nicks in the bark from my previous assault, but they've stopped weeping blood.

I pirouette, knife brandished, pounding the blade into three elongated roots. I've never reviled nature before, but right now, I'm hating on all things leafy and flowery. After this, I'm putting in a request for a new element.

I snatch the new bloom from my cheek and toss it to the ground where it withers instantly. "How do I defeat this thing!" I yell at my crew, because I could use some ideas.

My gaze goes to Slate, and a whimper crosses the thin divide of my lips. I'm so angry at him. So, *so* angry that he followed me down this wicked rabbit hole. But I can't let my feelings distract me. I have to vanquish the damn tree, send it back to the pits of hell from which it grew. Once I fit my piece into the clock, it'll break his curse. He'll be free of the bark and glowing blooms.

Focus, Cadence. Focus.

I slam my knife into four more roots before I hear Bastian squawk around great sobs, "Since it's a tree—maybe you need to reach—the heartwood."

He's a mess. I'm a mess too, but I'm so pumped on adrenaline that my worry for Slate has taken a backseat. Besides, I'm confident that I'm going to win this.

If I don't . . .

No, no, no. No going there.

"What Bastian said! Go for the heartwood!" Adrien yells.

"And where exactly is the heartwood?"

"In the middle of the trunk," Bastian answers, voice thick.

"Anywhere in the middle?" I ask, panting like an out-of-shape triathlete.

"Yes." Adrien's calm tone is wrought with nerves. "It runs from the base to the crown."

So chopping down a tree it is.

I send a little silent thank you to whoever left me the hatchet-like knife before tearing out my new facial accessory *again* and prowling toward the trunk. A root winds around my ankle and yanks me back. I fall flat on my face, the newest sprouting bud cushioning the impact.

Never thought I'd be grateful to have a plant growing out of me.

My hood flops over my head as I get to my knees, towing the cleaver across the mud toward me. It feels like it weighs a freaking ton and it wasn't light to begin with. I suck in a breath as needle-sharp thorns whizz around me, most embedding themselves in the mud with a squelch. A few hit my back, but I don't think they penetrate my puffer coat, because I don't experience the fiery pain presently radiating across half my face.

Another volley of wooden darts rains down. Four puncture my jeans, lodging themselves inside my calves. My muscles seize.

I scramble to my feet before my legs turn to bark, because if I'm immobilized like Slate, I won't be able to get close to my mark. Fire lances up my shins and pools into my knees, making me feel as though I was made of clay.

Oh, the irony . . .

The top of my fur hood grazes the lowest branches of the magical tree as I drag my arm back and take a swing at the trunk. A wood chip flies. I yank the cleaver back and whack the bark again. And again. A root tickles my ankle as it laces around both my weighty legs. When it begins to tighten, I almost lose my balance, but even it can't dislodge the two trunks upon which I'm standing.

Sweat beads beneath my hood, drips down my spine. When I faced down Ares, I was terrified yet I still destroyed him. I use the fear presently chewing through my insides to fuel my resolve to end the Quatrefoil.

Alma shouts, "Come on, Cadence. You can do it, hun!"

Gaëlle, too, is chanting encouragements.

And from farther away, I hear, "You can do it, *ma Cadence!*" I can't see Papa but knowing he's there, supporting me, injects courage into my heart.

Focusing on their voices, I roar and smash my blade over and over into the trunk. My progress is slow but substantial. The rough, dark bark chips off, revealing a layer of honeyed brown.

"How will I know when I reach the heartwood?" I holler, hoping they can hear me over the ruckus of metal striking wood.

The root tangled all the way up my legs has now looped around my waist and is inching its way higher, trying to stay my arms. I redirect the blade and dig it into the wooden cord. It immediately softens and loosens its grasp on me. Not that it does me much good since I'm paralyzed from the waist down.

I think of Papa. Of the curse he's endured for almost two decades. "Soon you will be free, Papa. Soon, you will walk."

"Bastian says it'll be darker than the sapwood!" Adrien bellows, before barking something about the garden hose and snowmobile.

"No!" Gaëlle yells. "Look what happened to Slate. You can't go in there. She'll be fine."

My heart, that's been walloping my rib cage since the ground split open, stills. I pause with my knife bobbing in the air and shout, "Don't you dare come down here, Adrien! Listen to Gaëlle. I've got it. I swear, I've got it."

I redouble my efforts, groaning as I land blow after blow, revealing more and more of the trunk's entrails. How freaking deep is this heartwood?

Just as I have that thought, the tree groans louder than I do. I blink, but between the bloom and the sweat and the blood caked over my face, I can't see a thing.

I claw at the bloom and lob it off, finally catching sight of the hawthorn's dark core. Is that the heartwood? I grip the cleaver and give it another satisfying thwack. The branches swing, and then the tree is listing, listing . . .

Something falls from a branch above me and smacks the crown of my head.

It takes me a second to see it's the chain we brought over from Slate's house. *Great.* I'm getting battered by my own tools.

Blood pools from the heart of the tree, runs over the bark. My heart holds still, my lungs too, but not my arms. No, they resume their battle to mince the wretched tree. My fingers cramp so suddenly I almost release the cleaver. Two thorns protrude from the knuckles of my right hand. My left hand, for what I can see of it past the bouncy white petals, is thorn-free.

I hack faster. A minute later, the knife slides through my wooden fingers. I squeeze my other hand around the hilt as though it were Papa's hand and he were being swept out to sea. My backhand is fierce.

A deep crack rends the air and then the trunk tips like a drunkard.

"It's falling, Cadence. Get away from it!" Gaëlle cries.

I can't move my legs. Thankfully, though, the hawthorn is falling away from me.

If Slate weren't presently stuck in his bark shell, he'd probably yell, "Timber!" and scoop me up and out of harm's way, but he can neither crack jokes nor carry me to safety.

Tears and sweat run down my cheeks, blurring the sight of the collapsing tree. I blink to clear my vision and immortalize the moment. Long minutes after the tree settles, I jerk my head back to throw off my hood and lock eyes with the others.

The whole cavern glimmers. Probably a special effect caused by my tears of euphoria and exertion. With my still supple hand, I scrub my face and pluck out the flower. I expect it to grow back, but it doesn't.

It doesn't.

"You did it!" Gaëlle's full-on sobbing. "You did it, sweetie. You did it."

"I'm so proud of you, hun!" Alma cheers.

Adrien smiles down at me, relief smoothing out his creased face. He swipes his hand across his cheek, and I realize he's crying. Bastian, too, is crying. More like wailing. But I don't think it's because I almost gave up the ghost.

"Your piece." Adrien jabs his thumb toward the trunk.

Atop the ebony heartwood lies the fan-shaped gold leaf. I drop my weapon and reach out, but my body's still stiff and my blood feels as syrupy as *salidou*. My legs are finally bark-free; my hand, too. My fingers inch closer and closer.

"If you're any slower, it'll be the new moon before you grab that piece."

I spin around at the sound of that voice, and then on a sob, I lurch toward Slate and strangle his neck, my biceps trembling like tambourines. His strong, solid arms wind around my waist and pull my body flush against his.

"Oh, Slate." I soak his neck with my tears.

"*Shh.*" His warm breath blows against a clump of hair sticking to my neck.

"You're alive."

"I told you, Mademoiselle de Morel, nothing's going to take me away from you. Not an endless winter. Not your papa. Not the Quatrefoil and its wicked flora. I'm yours for as long as you want me." He leans back and pushes a rope of hair plastered to my cheek, tucks it behind my ear. "Scratch that. Even if you don't want me—"

"I'll always want you."

He bumps my nose with his. "Can I get that in writing?"

"Don't you trust me?"

"You, I trust."

"Then trust that I'm yours."

His lips slant over mine as a loud wolf whistle, followed by joyous hooting, rains down around us. Rising to the balls of my feet, I kiss Slate hard, putting all my anguish and all my heartbeats into the man who followed me into the bowels of the earth, because my life mattered more to him than his own.

14

SLATE

C adence wrenches her lips off mine and whispers, "We're going to have magic," then tips her head back and squeals it for our four—scratch that—three-person audience.

Adrien's not there. Guess he didn't enjoy our show.

"Yes we are, princess. Yes we are." Although I don't share in her excitement, still undecided about this whole magic thingamajig, I'm relieved we're well and truly done. "Can one of you Peeping Toms get us out of this dump?"

"On it, bro!" Bastian bobbles his head like a dashboard dog.

The cloud cover breaks, and insipid light filters down. I take a deep breath, immediately feeling worse for it. Cadence wasn't downplaying the plague-reek of those blooms.

She tucks the cleaver under her armpit and picks up the golden leaf she worked so hard to earn. Her hands shake, and I'm not sure if it's from fear or awe.

I put my hands on her hips, and she startles and tries to back up.

"I've already been cursed, Cadence. Touching you while you're holding the leaf won't make a difference."

The worry in her eyes darkens the blue to navy. "What if turning into a tree was your curse, and now that it's over, you're cursing yourself all over again?"

"You were turning to bark, too. So it wasn't unique to me. And remember that Emilie"—I clear my throat of the sudden Bloodstone-sized lump jamming it—"didn't come into her curse until the next day."

"Which means you'll be cursed tomorrow . . ."

"Except we'll have magic by tonight. Any curse will be gone. Because of you. Because of how fiercely you fought." I tug her closer and press my forehead to hers. Mud and sap are caked along her hairline. "What will you do once you have power? Have shoots of grass sprout with every step you take? Create volcanic eruptions?" I drop my mouth to the soft shell of her ear and whisper, "Or bind me with ivy and have your wicked way with me?"

She wrinkles her nose. "Not until you've taken a shower."

I smile away the stress of the past few days. "How fortunate that water's my element, then."

There's a commotion from above. Voices and a motor.

Bastian's face pops back over the trench lip. "Heads up! I'm throwing down the box for the piece!"

With no branches to block his way, Bastian's aim is close enough. The thing lands with a heavy thud near the crumbled remains of Viviene's tomb. Cadence crouches, opens the latch on the lead-lined birch box, and puts the piece inside.

Alma lowers the hose we took from my place. "We've tied it to the snowmobile. Rainier can help pull while you climb up."

The green rubber unspools like a snake, hovering centimeters off the ground.

I take the cleaver from Cadence. "Ladies first."

We tie the hose around her waist.

She grips it, tucking the box under her arm. "Now!"

Rainier revs up his engine. The limp hose gradually tightens and airlifts Cadence. Clumps of dirt fall as she inches upward. Finally, she reaches the top, and Bastian and Adrien grip her arms, propelling her over the edge.

When the hose tumbles back down, I breathe a sigh of relief and secure myself, gripping the green rubber like I held on to the twenty-euro bill I found on the street when I was nine. My memories of that glorious day are still clear. I gorged on madeleines, the extra buttery ones from the bakery.

By the time my head pops out of the fetid grave, I actually appreciate the frozen tundra that is Brume.

"Slate!" Before I'm even fully standing, Bastian wraps his arms around me, nearly knocking me back into the crevasse. He sobs into my shoulder, then punches me right in the snotty wet mark he left. "That's for scaring me."

If this scared him, it's a damn good thing he wasn't present the day I went into the well.

I rub the ache. "Hey, promise me that when I die, you won't bury me. Cremate me and use me for fertilizer. Didn't you see what a good-looking tree I'd make?"

Actually, *did* he see?

"You looked like you died just standing there. It was terrifying." He punches me again.

"Oww! *Putain!*"

He sniffs. "And you'd make horrible fertilizer, so you'd better just stay alive."

I hand Cadence the cleaver, then wrap Bastian in a headlock and muss his hair with my knuckles before letting him go. "No worries, little bro. Not planning on leaving this life anytime soon."

The others circle around Cadence. Even Adrien's human slug of a father is there, hazel eyes dark with ambition.

He sidles up to me and, in a voice sticky like syrup, says, "Monsieur Ardoin, I hope your promise to hand over your Council seat hasn't slipped your mind."

Could I pretend to have forgotten? Maybe I could play it off as an early onset of my curse.

I tuck my hands under my armpits, picking rectitude, because I'm not in the mood for another fight. "Hasn't slipped my mind."

"What time shall we meet at the temple?" Geoffrey's sleazy gaze roves over Cadence as if he's scrubbing the tree sap off her with his eyes.

I step right into his face, near enough to sear his corneas with my vicious scowl. I feel sorry for Prickhead, which is saying a lot considering the creeps I had as father figures.

"At eventide." Cadence's candid joy slips into me, chipping my desire to rearrange the mayor's face.

After making sure to convey what I think of his leering, I drape my arm around Cadence's shoulder and murmur into her ear, "What do you say we go home and shower the tree innards off?"

"Um." She pushes a lock of hair back, her cheeks flushing under the gunk. "Well . . ."

Rainier's eyes flash our way. He couldn't have heard what I said, but he's the one who answers. "Cadence needs to bring the piece safely home, and then she and I must discuss certain *things*. Like her choices these past few days."

Cadence sighs.

Rainier's stare is so abrasive, I feel the burn of it when he peels it off my face. "We'll see the lot of you on Fifth at seven fifteen. Don't be late."

"Or what? Your fancy snowmobile turns into a pumpkin, de Morel?"

Bastian grabs my wrist and tugs me back. "Don't mind Slate. Emotions are running high right now. It's all the adrenaline."

Nope. Not adrenaline. Festering antipathy.

I shake Bastian off and crouch, scooping handfuls of snow to clean some of the gunk off my face.

"You still have a little . . . over here." Gaëlle taps her cheek.

While Alma asks Cadence what I'm covered in, I rub. I must miss the spot, because Gaëlle sticks her thumb inside her mouth and swipes it across my cheekbone. Suddenly, her eyes go wide, and her finger pops off my skin.

"Oh *mon Dieu*, I'm sorry, Slate. I'm so used to cleaning up my children. That was . . ." She wrinkles her nose.

"I'm covered in way nastier stuff than your spit." Besides, it was sort of heartwarming. I never had a mother fuss over me before. My heart gives a hollow bleep at that, and my attention swings in the direction of my parents' mausoleum.

I ease the meat cleaver from Cadence's fist—not the most ideal tool for my task but it'll do—then take her hand and help her onto the snowmobile.

The cleaver comes satisfyingly close to Rainier's hair. Might even have lopped a few strands. Definitely transferred some tree sap over.

He leans away and hisses, "Be careful with that knife."

"Beheadings aren't my jam, de Morel." I regret he can't see the tree sap, because smiling while covered in blood would surely have given Rainier a few nightmares, though I imagine he's got plenty of his own.

He revs up the snowmobile's engine, and I leap away before he can knock me down and squash me like the bug he thinks I am. It reminds me of the night the ring came off, right before his daughter dashed through the snow and flung herself into my arms.

How adamantly he'd pushed me to take my own life.

How disappointed he'd been when he failed to take it from me.

He invited me to Brume, and now that I've served my purpose, he wants me out.

Because of his daughter, or because I got a whiff of something foul . . . something he's trying to hide?

15

CADENCE

I look over my shoulder at Slate and make the phone call gesture. He gives the faintest nod as Papa and I glide toward the wrought-iron gates of the cemetery. When I swivel back around, I catch Adrien's eye. There's something guarded about his expression, some emotion that's turned the hazel of his irises to a deep mahogany. He refocuses on the Head of the fire department and whatever lie Geoffrey's feeding him.

Once we've passed them, Papa zips over the deep snow blanketing the side of the road. The Bloodstone feels heavy and hot around my finger. To think that tonight, I'll be rid of it. Unlike Maman, who never managed to pry it off her finger. A shudder runs through me, and I tighten my arms around my father's middle, flexing my tired muscles and gummy arms to keep him close.

How lucky we were to figure out how to lock the leaves into the clock. If only Papa and the others had known back then . . .

Once we reach the manor, I help Papa into the wheelchair he's left under the raised garage door, then step into the glacial concrete space and remove my boots before heading straight to my bedroom.

As I run myself a bath, I catch sight of myself in the mirror. I'm disgusting. How could Slate even kiss me back there? I mean, sure he was also covered in mud and blood, but I'm candied in the stuff.

I shed my clothes and wrap them in a towel which I'll toss in the laundry before Solange can grab them from my hamper. I really hope my coat will be salvageable considering the number of rips. To think it's brand new.

I step into the shower as the bath fills and scrub the muck off my skin and charm bracelet, then have a go at my hair. My arms tremble from the effort it takes to massage my scalp and untangle my mid-length locks. Once the water runs clear and my hair no longer feels like dreads, I turn off the shower, step carefully over the heated stone floor, and lower myself into the steaming bath.

A sigh flees my lips as I let my head loll against the curved porcelain rim and shut my eyes.

A KNOCK on my bathroom door jolts me awake. I splash water that has dipped below tepid onto the marble floor.

"Mademoiselle Cadence, it's almost four. Your father asked me to come and check if you wanted anything to eat."

"Thank you, Solange. I'll be down in a minute." I hoist myself out of the bathtub, muscles screaming. Even though I'm now clean, my skin is covered in red gashes and sprinkled in bruises. I apply antibiotic ointment and plasters to the worst offenders, then don a bulky turtleneck and fleece-lined leggings.

After grabbing my ball of soiled clothes, I take the elevator down to the basement, stick everything in the washing machine, dump detergent inside, and select a long spin cycle. Only after the door clicks and the machine fills with water do I realize I left the faux-fur trim on my coat. Oh well, it can't look much worse than it does already.

When I arrive in the kitchen, I'm surprised to find Papa isn't alone.

Adrien's sipping tea at the table. "Hey. How are you feeling?"

"I fell asleep in the bathtub."

Papa refills his cup. "I should've sent Solange to check on you earlier."

"I'm happy she didn't. I needed the rest." I dig into the meal our housekeeper's placed on the table. "Is she still here?"

"She just left." Papa takes out a Churchill and cuts the tip. "Did you need anything?"

"No. I wanted to talk about what's to come and didn't want to do it in front of her." I scan the open-plan space expecting to find the birch box, but it's not here. Papa probably put it in the safe.

Adrien leans back in his chair, the light from the leaf chandelier glazing the short bristles of dark blond hair growing atop his head. "What is it you want to know?"

"How will it work? Will we each get the magic of our element? Will the whole world get magic? And what sort of magic will we get?" I take a mouthful of my spaghetti, biting into a roasted cherry tomato. A sweet and slightly smoky flavor dances across my tongue. God, Solange is a good cook.

"All four of you will get the magic of your elements, which means you'll be able to control that element and *only* that element. Everyone else will need to touch the symbols on the *dihuner*, but from what your mother grasped from the text, Adrien, you four will somehow need to act as a conduit between the Quatrefoil and the person desiring magic. She wasn't sure if that meant you'd need to touch the symbol at the same time, hold the person's hand, or simply decide to give them access. I guess we'll find out soon."

"How I wish those translations hadn't been stolen." Adrien's mouth is pinched, but I can't tell if it's resurging grief for his mother or irritation at the theft.

Theft or sabotage.

I return my attention to my father who's puffing on his cigar. "Any news on when we'll get the scroll back from the restorer?"

My father releases a cloud of lavender smoke that buffs the sharp edges of his features. Like all of us, he's in dire need of some R&R. "Hopefully, next week."

Adrien leans his forearms onto the glass tabletop. "I spent the past week going over the pictures Slate took of the *Kelouenn* but the only reference to the transmission of magic was a line indicating those who wield it should be pure of heart. Also, to prevent one person from having too much power, every human has an affinity for a single element. No one has controlled all four since Merlin, Viviene, King Arthur, and Morgane le Fay, the co-creators of the Quatrefoil. Even after those precautions, we know from *Istor Breou* that it didn't stop evil from running the show."

"So people won't be able to choose their own element?" I ask.

"From what I gathered, the Quatrefoil will choose for them."

I wrap more pasta around my fork tines. "Your father wants Slate's seat on the Council—"

"I've tried talking him out of it." There's a defensive edge to Adrien's tone.

"That's not why I'm bringing it up. The reason is, what if his affinity isn't Water? Will he still be able to take Slate's place?"

Adrien and Papa exchange a glance that speaks of past conversations on the subject.

Finally, Adrien looks back at me, hazel eyes swirling with . . . remorse? "Yes."

Papa bats away the veil of smoke screening him. "Once the Quatrefoil is whole, you'll pour a drop of your blood on your symbol to bind yourself to your element. Geoffrey will need to put his blood on the Water symbol in order to become its keeper."

"Was that in the translation?"

"Yes and no. The *Kelouenn* alludes to something of the sort, but I dug deeper, compared notes with what was written in *Istor Breou* and other medieval stories about magic." Papa tucks his cigar between his lips, takes a long drag, then lets the smoke curl out one corner of his lips. "And although Geoffrey claimed I kept what I knew from Amandine, I shared all of my findings with your mother. She and I had no secrets from each other. The only reason we didn't rush to tell the others is that we *presumed* that was how it worked. We hadn't even made the connection with the *dihuner* at the time. Until the Quatrefoil was assembled, and our theory was tested, it remained exactly that . . . a theory." He lifts the cigar back to his mouth. "Perhaps, it won't work. Perhaps Council seats cannot be transferred. Perhaps the blood must come from a *diwaller* descendant. We won't know until we try."

Tonight will be a night of great discoveries.

Adrien spins his teacup between his long fingers. "Since Slate is staying, I imagine he no longer wants to give up his seat."

"I imagine he'd rather keep it," I say. "And quite honestly, I'd rather he didn't give it to your father. Your family already has a seat on the Council. Taking another is greedy and unbecoming of a guardian."

Adrien stops whirling his cup, and his eyes flick to mine as though I've personally insulted him. His mouth thins. "Dad can have my seat then."

"I'd rather have you on the Council, than him. I trust *you*." The implication of my words go unsaid but not unheard.

"Would you rather have me or Slate on the Council?"

"Don't put me in that position, Adrien."

"My father won't back down, so it's a choice you'll have to make. You *and* Gaëlle."

I concentrate on my plate of pasta. "I said I'm not choosing, and I'm not."

"Cadence, you know Adrien. Slate's still—"

"Still what?" I snap at Papa.

"A stranger."

"Perhaps to you, but no longer to me."

The skin around Papa's eyes tightens at my chilliness.

Even though I haven't put a dent in my bowl of pasta, and my stomach is growling, I pat my lips with my napkin and stand. "If you gave him half a chance, he'd no longer be a stranger to you either."

"*Ma Cadence . . .*"

I hold up my palms. "Don't. Don't make excuses for yourself." I back up under both men's watchful gazes. "I'm going to go back upstairs until it's time to leave. I'll meet you in the foyer at seven."

I toss my napkin on the table, pick up my bowl, and put it in the sink, then leave them to their whisperings.

The second I'm in my room, I text Slate the mechanics of Council-seat transference but don't mention Adrien's offer. If he's serious about it, he'll reiterate it tonight.

16

SLATE

E veryone but Alma and Bastian take off.

Bastian stands by the trench, looking down into the pit of darkness. I go and tug him away from the edge.

"I wasn't going to jump." His boots are planted firmly in the packed snow.

I shrug. "Brume has the unique quality of making you think you'd be better off six feet under. Better safe than sorry."

"What are you looking at?" Now Alma peeks into the void.

Fog curtains off the sun, so Bastian turns on his phone's flashlight. Its beam barely makes a dent in the dimness but highlights the twisted branches of the felled tree and the crumbled mass of Viviene's coffin.

"The statue." He points to the shell of Viviene's statue that lies split open, a delicate outline of the enchantress. "I read somewhere that this kind of statue—impossibly thin granite—was called a *toull-bac'h.*"

"Tool bench?" I ask.

Bastian scoffs. "No. *Toull-bac'h.*" He drags out the *-atch* sound at the end. "They were reputed to be jail tombs. Since they were crafted from dark magic, and seriously complicated to make, people only created *toull-bac'hs* for the worst of the worst. Murderers, degenerates, you know . . . dangers to society."

My eyebrows rise. "How the hell do you know all that?"

"Because I *open books*. I *research* stuff." He stands a little straighter. "I'm currently teaching myself some Brumian Breton, you *bajaneg*. And in case you were wondering, that means idiot."

It's been a shitty morning, but Bastian can always make me smile. "*Bajaneg*." I roll the word around on my tongue. "I like it."

Alma clears her throat. "Okaaaay. So, you think Viviene's statue was a jail tomb?"

"Why not?" Bastian shrugs.

"Because that would mean Viviene was an awful person."

I study the granite carcass below. "She did trap her lover inside a cave."

"Supposedly," Alma says. "And no one can get the story right. Cave. Tree. She probably just got a bad rap because she was a strong woman. Not too popular at the time."

I twirl my cleaver. "Maybe one of Merlin's many lovers decided to avenge him."

"Or maybe she was too good a soul. Those are usually the ones who pay the worst price."

At the thought of good souls paying a price, cold fear slithers up my spine. Don't I know it. My rotten soul is the only reason I've survived this long. But then you have good, shiny people like Bastian or Cadence. Staring down at the statue, I'm struck again by how Viviene looks so much like Cadence. Too much like Cadence. I don't like seeing Cadence's likeness frozen in stone and broken into pieces. I don't like any reminder that Cadence could suffer. Or die.

Bastian sticks his phone back into the pocket of his coat. I'm glad Viviene is once again cloaked in darkness.

I shake off my dread and lift the butcher knife. "You two up for a little outing?"

Alma hugs herself tighter. "We're not going to murder anyone, are we? Because you're giving off some serious serial killer vibes at the moment."

I squint through the fog. "Actually, the opposite. I want to bring someone back to life."

Alma shifts closer to Bastian. "Um. What?"

I let my arm fall and cross through the expanse of white dotted with granite headstones. Bare linden trees populate the wider spaces, mist and ice crystals garlanding their branches. When I reach my destination, Alma sucks in a breath.

The Roland mausoleum sits at the foot of an ancient and gnarled oak. The little domed building is a third of the size of the de Morel mausoleum, small and round. There's no portico, no fancy statue, just a curved granite façade split by an arched wooden door that's been carved to resemble a Carnac stone. ROLAND is engraved above the door. And down the right side is a list of names and dates of death starting with the most recent to hundreds of years into the past. But I don't read them all because my gaze sticks to the very top where RÉMY is etched right beneath EUGENIA and OSCAR.

My grip on the butcher knife tightens.

"Guess your fam wasn't the type to waste coin on the dead," Bastian points out.

I snort. "Lucky for me. I'd rather have it burning a hole in my pocket than filling one in the graveyard."

Alma sticks a finger into a part of the door that's rotted through. "And there are holes aplenty."

"So what's the plan?" Bastian asks.

The weary sunlight glances against the blade as I give a hard thwack to the stone. "Rémy Roland's not dead." I swing again. "So I'm scratching out his name."

"Scratching, huh?" Bastian backs up.

Once I've obliterated the four letters, I attack the dates.

"Technically, this isn't bringing anyone back to life," Alma says. "You're merely erasing Rémy's existence."

"Good riddance." A small chunk of stone crumbles onto the snow by my feet. "That kid with the charmed life never existed."

Alma sighs. "That kid's standing right here with a big ol' knife."

She may be right, but it feels so damn good to erase this false truth, because it also erases the *could-have-beens* and *should-have-beens* running on a loop through my head and leaves what *is*.

A broken hull.

Me.

The messed-up, defaced bit of the Roland bloodline.

The damaged goods.

I have the Quatrefoil and Rainier de Morel to thank for that.

Once I've removed all legible bits, I wipe my brow and lift my face to the breeze battering the cemetery, then tap my boot's toe against the door of the mausoleum. The door doesn't even rattle. Instead, it splinters and crumbles like it's made of dust, leaving a foot-sized gap just above the threshold.

Quality craftsmanship.

I try the knob.

Lo and behold, it opens.

I flick on my phone's flashlight to peer into what seems like an empty little cave until I notice the slabs of marble, granite, and slate lining the thinly plastered walls and floor. Each have a name and date etched into them. There's got to be a hundred souls stuffed inside this broom closet of a crypt.

"Creeeeepy." Alma's eyes bug out as she takes in the musty space.

Bastian wipes dust and dirt off one of the older slabs on the floor. "Wow. This dates back more than a thousand years."

I point the light around until I detect the shine of new marble. Three slabs, all on the wall directly across from the door.

The middle one reads *RÉMY ROLAND, PARTI DE CE MONDE TROP TÔT*. No shit, he left this world too soon. Like a psycho-killer, I plunge my knife into the marble and swear at the pain that reverberates up my arm. The cleaver clatters to the floor.

Bastian picks it up and hands it to me. "Is this a good time to remind you that the last time you defaced something in a crypt, you awakened the Quatrefoil?"

Guilt still slugs my gut that Cadence saw her mother's ravaged corpse. "This is different. There's no other family member alive to give a shit about the state of this place. And this stupid-ass plaque deserves to come down. It's a lie. I'm not gone."

With renewed vigor, I swing my tool. It's a hell of a lot harder to make a dent in the marble. After several unsuccessful attempts at pulverizing it, I slide the flat edge of my blade underneath the white funerary tablet to pry it off the wall. Unbelievably, it works. Before long, the marble monstrosity falls, missing my feet by a hairsbreadth, and cracks.

Waving away the cloud of dirt and dust it created, I nod. "Mission accomplished."

"Whoa! What's that?" Alma steps over the broken memorial, stopping only when her nose practically hits the wall.

A section of plaster came off with the slab, leaving behind a window onto the original stone wall. A drawing in faded reds and blues and yellows fills the space. A quatrefoil frames an oak tree which frames a weird little cave-like mound erected at its roots, a Carnac stone rolled in front of it. It takes me a second, but then I realize it's this spot—the oak, the crypt, though long before they added the Roland name and the actual door to the building. A word is printed in a Bible-like font inside each leaf of the quatrefoil.

Bastian leans in, pushing his glasses farther up his nose. "*Tadoù. Sorser. Mestr. Kamarad.*"

"What does it mean?" Alma asks almost reverently.

After pulling his phone from his pocket and tapping the screen a few times, Bastian finally answers, "*Father. Wizard. Master. Friend.* It's an epitaph. And a really, really old one, considering the plaster that covered it was already ancient. I'm guessing this inscription was for one of the very first people to be put in this crypt."

The tree, the cave, the Carnac stone, the inscription . . . "Merlin," I breathe.

"Oh my God! You're right!" Alma sounds way too excited about this particular information.

Only half-joking, I say, "I could turn this into a cash cow. Charge visitors ten euros a pop just to have a peek at the old wizard's tomb. Twenty if they want a picture."

Bastian reaches out toward the drawing but stops just before he touches it. "That's probably why they plastered over it in the first place: too much exploitation."

"Guys, you do realize what this means, right? Slate is Merlin's descendant!" Alma grabs the lapels of my coat and hops in place, before remembering I'm covered in icky sap. Nose crinkled, she snatches her fingers back and lifts them in front of her face. "Do I have tree blood all over me?"

"Nothing a little snow won't get rid of." As she retrieves some outside, I frown hard at the blunted drawing. "I thought Merlin was Cadence's ancestor."

Alma returns, rubbing a handful of snow between her palms. "He and Viviene were lovers, so some people assumed as much, but according to the old texts, they never had kids together. Apparently, Amandine's grandmother traced her family's lineage back to Viviene and some minor druid." The snow melts and slops off her fingers, effectively stripping them of blood. "But Viviene's great and only true love remained philandering Merlin."

"She had a funny way of expressing it." I gesture to the inscription, before thrusting a hand through my hair, which feels stiff where the sap dried. "Kind of hard to make a relationship work when you imprison your partner in a cave or tree or whatever."

Alma ignores my jab. "This is a divine decree! Merlin and Viviene were star-crossed lovers, even though they turned their backs on that destiny. You and Cadence are their descendants. You two are fated to be together. Karma's turn to get things right."

I snort and roll my eyes, stifling a smile. "Ridiculous."

"I think Alma's onto something. Maybe not about the fated part but about the descendant bit." Bastian points to my jaw. "I mean, with that thing living on your chin, you're starting to look like a grizzled old sorcerer."

I put a hand to my stubble. "Cadence likes my facial hair." I think, then mop down my forehead again. "I need a bath. And a drink."

"Yes. Let's celebrate." Alma puts an arm around Bastian's waist. He stiffens before draping his arm over her shoulders as though she were made of glass instead of snark and the energy supply of a nuclear power plant.

We head out of the cemetery, passing the barriers the fire brigade set up at the gates, and take the steep stairs to Second even though my Moorish-tiled bathroom is yelling out to me. One drink, and then one bath.

It's noon on a Saturday, the temperature a degree below *numb your nipples* and almost down to *freeze your privates off*, yet there are actual people out in the square, munching on crêpes, drinking coffee, and smoking cigarettes beside the wishing-well-slash-siren-den.

Between Alma in her hot-pink plaid flannel pajama bottoms, wedge-heeled boots, and furred jacket, and me in my tattered wool coat, gashed forehead, and crazy hair, I brace myself for an onslaught of curious once-overs. We get zero. I mean, sure we get looks, but none that linger and not a single raised eyebrow. Brume takes jaded to a whole new level.

"Monsieur Roland?" a feminine voice calls out. Claire Robinson stands outside *Merlin's Baguette*, a smile stretched across her face. Her green eyes rake over us, and like everyone else in this weird-ass town, she doesn't flinch at our appearance. "How fortuitous I've run into you." She grazes my upper arm, and her tan suede gloves come away stained with magical tree sap. Not that she can see it.

"Hiya, *Professeur*."

She shakes her head, her bouncy, bleached-blonde tresses frolicking around her cream wool coat, which she wears like a cape over a lime-green top. Professionally whitened teeth pin down the pink frosted line of her lower lip. "Please. We're not in class. Call me Claire."

Yeah . . . don't think so. "Is something wrong?"

"Oh, no. *Pas du tout*. It's just that I heard you kept your father's astronomy books. And seeing as he had *such* an amazing collection, I was wondering if I could stop by your place to have a look at them. Borrow a few." Her hand goes to the golden brooch pinned to the lime-green material straining to hold in her breasts. "I'll return them, of course."

Alma quips, "You can't get them in the library?"

"Not those in question." Mademoiselle Robinson—the suitability of her name only strikes me now—flaps her sooty lashes. "I'm free today."

"No can do today."

Disappointment dims her green eyes. "Tomorrow perhaps? Not much to do on Sundays in Brume."

Tomorrow, I might be busy learning how to create a tidal wave, but I want to get this over with. "Sure. Fine. See you tomorrow."

Her smile widens, and she squeezes my arm. "*Fantastique!*" She whirls around and takes off across the square.

Alma wrinkles her nose. "What a cougar."

I heft up an eyebrow. "If Claire Robinson is a cougar, what does that make Adrien?"

"That's different. He grew up here. He was friends with families here long before he ever became a teacher. And Mademoiselle Claire is *old* old. Adrien's only twenty-four."

"Flawed logic if you ask me."

She elbows me and winks. "Not that you need to worry since you and Cadence are destined to be together."

I snort as I shoulder the door to the tavern and hook the velvet curtain to draw it open. We step into the steamy warmth just as Nolwenn bustles through with a platter of dirty dishes, practically skidding to a stop at the sight of us.

Ah. That's reassuring. At least *one* person in town picks up on our unkemptness.

"Marseille!" Her gaze glides over my wild hair and scratched-up face before traveling over the two others. "Where's Cadence? Is she —did she—I felt the ground shake this morning."

"She's fine."

"Thank the Qua—God." Color climbs back into her cheeks. "There's a free table upstairs."

As the other two head up, Nolwenn calls me back. I know what she wants to discuss: Cadence's quest. I lower my voice, though between the hum of the dining room and the French folk song spilling from the speakers, I doubt we'd be overheard anyway. "It's done. Cadence succeeded at getting the last leaf."

The lines around her eyes pucker with worry. "She's not hurt, is she?"

"No. She's okay."

I spot the shadow of a bruise on her chin, hidden beneath a thick layer of makeup. My vertebrae stiffen, and a familiar burn rages in my gut. "Did Juda hurt you?"

Confusion deepens the folds of her wrinkles. "What?"

I step closer. "Juda. Did. He. Hurt. You?"

Surprise widens Nolwenn's eyes, and then she laughs. "Oh, dear. No, no, no." One last chuckle bursts out, then she shakes her head, solemn again. "No. I swear to you, Marseille, he's never, ever raised his hand or voice to me."

Relief pools in my stomach. "How did you get that bruise then?"

She sighs. "By thinking I could change the world with a well-aimed swing."

A sliver of the kitchen is in my line of sight, and I imagine Juda there, chopping onions. That's when the knife left in the snow flashes through my brain. Not just any knife. A meat cleaver. Something from a chef's kitchen.

Nolwenn abhors magic.

Suddenly, it's all clear. "*You* ruined Viviene's statue?"

Her face is just as impassive, just as much of a mask as Viviene's.

"Why? Why would you do that?"

The glasses rattle on her platter, which she shakily slides onto the bar. "When I was a kid, we told stories about the statue. One of them was that magic existed because Viviene was alive in that granite hull. Some believed breaking it would kill Viviene and magic." She shakes her head. "There was no sorceress inside. It was a simple statue. My ruining it did nothing to hurt magic. I only hurt myself."

At least, the mystery of where the weapon came from is solved.

"Can't blame me for trying, *n'est-ce pas?*"

"If it's any consolation, that knife came in very handy."

She grips my fingers in her overworked, overwashed ones. They feel thinner and bonier than before. In fact, all of her looks thinner and bonier. "Please, Slate. Don't bring magic back." I think it's the first time she's used my name. "I've seen what it can do. Experienced it firsthand. Lost a son to it. Nothing good will come of giving it back to the world."

Nolwenn has reason to be scared. It's an unstable and enigmatic force, which in the hands of our greedy species, will undoubtedly cause a massive amount of destruction. But Cadence still wears the ring. And even though Rainier said it slid off mine without consequence because we locked the pieces into the clock, it's never felt like the truth.

Hell. Even if it is, this is the Quatrefoil. I doubt we'll get lucky twice.

Luck or not, I want that ring off Cadence's finger. Plus, if there's even the slightest chance Emilie's curse can be reversed and the little girl revived, I'm taking it.

Gently, I extricate my hands from Nolwenn's grip. "We don't have a choice. We need to get the Bloodstone off Cadence's finger, and to do that, we need to place the piece with the others."

Nolwenn sighs, a deeper wariness overcoming her demeanor.

"If nothing else, keep an eye on Rainier. The Quatrefoil has been an obsession of his for decades."

"You're preaching to the choir. You may have lost track of me in the system, but he found me and let me rot there. As far as I'm concerned, his soul's darker than my own."

"Good. Now go upstairs, and I'll bring you some *chouchen*."

I don't get a chance to drink the home-brewed mead, though, because Cadence sends me a text about Geoffrey and blood-binding. I leave Bastian and Alma in the tavern and trek up to the temple.

17

CADENCE

As eventide approaches, I head downstairs in slim gray jeans and a tight black turtleneck I found at the bottom of my teetering pile of sweaters. I haven't worn it in years, because I favor boxier fits, but tonight, I want to look badass, and chunky sweaters don't exactly scream witchy-fierce.

Adrien and Papa exit the living room just as I reach the bottom of our split staircase. I don't smile at them, just head to the coat closet and grab an old coat and Papa's cashmere jacket. Wordlessly, I help him thread his arms through, while Adrien pulls a wool hat low over his ears and brow, concealing his absent eyebrows.

"You have the box, Papa?" I ask, as I spear one arm through my own coat.

Adrien moves to my side and grabs my other sleeve, holding it up, forever the gentleman.

"Right here." Papa pats the leather pocket of the wheelchair. "I also brought a needle to prick your fingers."

"You think of everything." Those are the last words I say until we reach Fifth. Not because I'm mad at him but because I'm deep in my head, turning over what's about to happen.

What if magic gets out of hand? Can we banish it back into the Quatrefoil? How do we banish it? Do Adrien or Papa know? I'm tempted to ask but don't want to sound defeatist.

Papa and Adrien don't say much either, probably having

exhausted subjects of conversation and my father's stock of cigars considering the smell wafting from them both.

As Adrien goes to unlock the padlock on the library doors, I lower my voice and whisper into my father's ear, "At the end of the day, hating Slate will only make *you* miserable."

He tips his head up, his features and blond hair silvered by the waning moon. "You're gravely mistaken if you think that boy can make *you* happy."

"*That boy* is kind and selfless and—"

"Entirely wrong for you."

I gasp. "He jumped into a pit with me!"

"He *fell* in."

I set my teeth. "He fought the cursed tree alongside me."

"Well, he *was* down there and enjoys brawling."

I ball my fingers into fists. "You're not being fair." I back away from him but then remember the box. I snatch it from the leather pocket of his wheelchair, then go stand beside Adrien.

He holds up the heavy lock. "It was open. You wouldn't know anything about how that happened?"

"I came here with Bastian and Slate after your class on Thursday. We wanted to clear the space so that we had an easier access to the clock once . . . once I was done."

I still can't believe I'm done. Soon I may be able to grow crops in barren soil and silence shifting fault lines. Unless I merely get an enhanced green thumb . . .

Loud, happy chanting echoes through the quad, over the old stones and crisp snow.

Si je meurs, je veux qu'on m'enterre
Dans une cave où il y a du bon vin;
Dans une cave, oui, oui, oui . . .
Les deux pieds contre la muraille
Et la tête sous le robinet;
Et la tête, oui, oui, oui . . .

Two bodies sway our way to the rhythm of the old French drinking song—a broad one and an average-sized one sporting a thick furry coat.

Adrien crosses his arms. "I'm guessing Slate rested at the tavern."

I tighten my hold on the birch box as two more bodies cut through the mist, arm in arm. Gaëlle and Bastian. Considering they're both walking straight, I'm guessing they stayed away from Nolwenn's *chouchen.*

Slate skids and goes down, the momentum knocking Alma off her feet. Laughter explodes out of my friend. I feel Papa's eyes on me, and yes, I would've preferred Slate hadn't arrived inebriated, but I won't give my father the pleasure of seeing me annoyed, so I paste on a bright, albeit tight, smile.

"We're good." Slate bounces onto the balls of his feet quite nimbly. "Right, Thumbelina?"

Alma just snickers while I'm thinking he's got a nickname for her. Not to mention, his arm around her.

"Where's dear old dad, Adrien?" Slate asks.

Adrien's arms tauten, creasing the fine gray wool of his coat. "On his way."

"Huh." Slate sidles in next to me and drops an arm around my shoulders. He smells like a cork dipped in blood. "Would've expected him to be the first man on site."

I duck from underneath Slate's arm. "I take it you didn't go home?"

"Wanted to, but Alma said we have reason to celebrate, because—"

"Not yet we don't." My voice holds the same bitter chill as the dark air.

Slate's merriment goes the way of blue skies in Brume. "I'm not drunk, Cadence."

Then why do his eyes shine like shards of black glass?

"I really hope you aren't, because we're about to bring something uncontrollable back into this world."

His tone dampens further. "I'm aware."

"You'll never guess what we found out, Cadence," Alma chirps. "Merlin is Slate's ancestor! He's buried, or at least commemorated, in the Roland mausoleum."

Disappointment surges within me that Alma learned this before I did.

My father snorts. "That's positively ludicrous. And surely fake. Merlin's bloodline was always shrouded in secrecy. Not to mention that mausoleum is much too plain a burial spot for the greatest wizard that ever lived."

"Maybe it's plain because *he* wasn't a pretentious asshole," Slate says under his breath.

"Hope you haven't started without me?" Geoffrey trots up to us, tailored wool coat snapping from his hurried pace. He eyes the lot of us, lingering on me, which makes me wonder, not for the first time, how obsessed he was with my mother. His nose lifts, and he sniffs the air. "Already celebrating, I see."

"Some of us," I mutter, spinning on my boots and shoving the thick oak door.

The hinges creak, and the wood groans, mirroring the sound of my bones and muscles. The soles of my boots crunch over the occasional piece of glass that escaped our cleaning as I head toward the recessed clock with its three vertical beams of neon light.

Alma catches up with me. "Are you angry?"

"Nope."

"You look angry."

"Do I?" When I position myself in front of my symbol, the slashed, upside-down triangle, I tell her, "Back up, will you? I'd hate for you to *accidentally* topple into me while I'm holding my leaf."

Alma expels a deep breath. "I'm sorry we started partying without you. It was totally unpremeditated. And Slate wanted to tell you in person about the whole Merlin thing."

"I told you, I don't care. What I do care about is not hexing you, so . . . back. Up." I unclasp the box and stare down at my leaf, my breaths coming hard and fast, partly from annoyance and partly from nerves.

Everyone gets situated around the clock. Papa parks beside Gaëlle, in front of the Air symbol. Adrien stands in his element's red light. Geoffrey's alone by the Water symbol because Slate's insisting on being my shadow. Bastian and Alma stay back, beyond where the protective plexiglass used to be.

I pluck my leaf and set the box aside. The smooth, warm metal makes the Bloodstone pulse out heat and red light. "Is it time?"

"Seven nineteen," Bastian announces.

"I'm ready." Geoffrey's holding out a small knife, which I suppose he intends to use to slice his skin and smear his blood on the Water element. I'm tempted to steal a glance at Slate, but don't because he said he took care of things, and I trust that he did.

"Dad," Adrien starts, eyes refracting the red beam. "About the Council seat . . . take mine."

The air seems to change consistency behind me, as though Slate has stiffened, and his posture has somehow affected it. "No need for grand gestures, Adrien. I promised your father my seat, and I'm a man of my word."

Adrien's eyes go to Slate. "Are you certain?"

"Yes."

"You won't regret this once you're sober?"

"I'm already sober." Slate's voice has gone deep and low, almost growly.

Geoffrey taps the blade of his knife against his open palm. "May we commence before the sun rises?"

"We don't want to miss our slot," Papa adds, for once in agreement with his nemesis.

Blood blazing, from the ring and my heightened emotions, I crouch and press my palm against my symbol. A beam as green as summer grass shoots up, followed by a grinding noise that drowns out the clock's ticking as my cradle lowers in the middle of the clock's leaf, dragging the gunmetal enamel down in the shape and size of my piece.

I lick my lips nervously. "Do I just slide it in?"

"That's what we d-did." Gaëlle's teeth chatter as though she were cold.

"There'll be a gravitational pull. Don't resist it," Adrien adds, obsessively fingering a button on his coat, popping it in and out of the hole.

I take in a breath, then a second one, and a third. I may not be heading underwater, but I *am* about to dive into something. I'm not even sure what, which is more terrifying than leaping off the bow of our boat into the deepest and darkest part of the Nimueh Lake.

For the trillionth time, I consider the repercussions that placing the leaf in the clock will have on the world. I can hardly wrap my mind around the enormity of it. Maybe putting it in is a mistake. Maybe—

Papa's stick-thin legs impel me to stay the course.

Just as Adrien warned, the cradle jerks my hand nearer the teardrop-shaped depression and tears the gold leaf from my grip. It clinks against the enamel as it settles into its designated place.

A gust of cool air snakes through the temple, whipping up my hair and icing the nape of my neck. I look around to make sure a skein of ghosts hasn't descended upon us. When I see no smoky outlines, I puff out a relieved breath.

The ticking pauses, the gears grind, and then both hands on the clockface spin and spin.

Like the *dihuner's* hands, my gaze cycles over the others' faces. "Is that normal?"

"It did it last time." Adrien doesn't lift his eyes off the clockface.

Suddenly, the frenetic rotations halt, and the slow *tick, tick, tick* resumes. The crescent-tipped hand has returned to its rightful slice of moon. The star-tipped one has shifted . . . I think.

Shoot. Has it? I should've paid better attention.

Forever-observant Bastian confirms it's swung ninety-degrees.

"Is it me"—Alma's squinting at the constellation dial—"or have the stone-stars moved?"

Adrien leans forward a little. "They haven't moved, but some have . . . *turned on.* They're definitely brighter."

A wall of heat licks up my spine. "The ring, princess. Take it off." Slate's quiet voice propels a shiver through my body.

Right. The ring.

I pull on it, expecting the band to have loosened, but no matter how hard I tug, the metal remains fused to my skin. "It's stuck."

Slate's hand lands on my waist, and he spins me to face him. "What do you mean, it's stuck?"

I demonstrate.

He thrusts my fingers aside and gives it a try. "Why isn't it coming off?" he yells.

"I don't know." I bite the inside of my cheek. "Maybe because it isn't the new moon?"

Slate's chest is vibrating with barely-checked anger. "But we're done!"

The ground chooses that moment to groan.

"Everyone, get down!" Slate yells, hugging my body and driving us to the floor.

I shut my eyes as the ochre honeycomb tiles rattle beneath me. Glass plinks. The tarp overhead snaps. Wood creaks. Stones chafe. A whirlwind of air tornadoes through the temple.

I don't want my last words to Slate to have been the caustic ones I delivered in front of the library. "I'm sorry I snapped at you. You're the best thing that's ever happened to me," I croak, keeping my lids sealed and my limbs compact under his unyielding ones.

Slate's hot breath pulses up the side of my throat. "Yeah?" For all his confidence, he sounds uncertain about my declaration.

I turn my head slightly, finding his mouth in the cacophonous darkness. "Yes."

If I die tonight, then I can't imagine a better way to go than connected through skin and heart with Slate Ardoin.

18

SLATE

I'm still kissing Cadence when the air in the temple finally grows quiet. Have we died? Is this the afterlife?

Every molecule in my body suddenly compresses, squeezing smaller and smaller until I think I may expire from the pain. "*Putain de bordel de merde.*"

Guess that was a negative on the dying part.

The pain vanishes just as abruptly as it set in.

Underneath me, Cadence is shaking and expelling breaths at warp speed, her eyes screwed shut.

I half-sit, pulling her up with me. "You did it. We're alive. We're okay."

Her eyelids flutter open, and she glances around, probably to ascertain that no one got speared with a shard of glass or impaled with a wooden shelf or suffocated by the tarp.

I don't know what I'm expecting but certainly not what I behold.

There's no broken glass. No splintered wood. Not even a tarp tatter in sight.

The massive curved bookcases stand tall again, novels and textbooks and travel guides lined up on the varnished oak shelves. Above us, the cupola is intact, the stained glass salted with snow. Instead of the howl of the wind, the tick of the clock and hum of heaters fill the air.

I didn't drink *that* much. Sure, my head's a little fuzzy, but I know reality from . . . well . . . not reality. And this is most definitely real.

Cadence slow-blinks, her lashes sweeping up and up and up as she takes in the restored library. She bolts to her feet, and I stand too.

"Try getting the ring off now."

She yanks at it.

Nothing.

I yank at it.

Nothing.

Fuck.

A moan grabs her attention. Her ponytail slaps me in the face as she swivels her head. "Papa!"

She releases my hand and rockets across the clock toward where Rainier lays sprawled on his stomach, body spanning the breadth of a *dihuner* petal, wheelchair tipped next to Gaëlle, who's simultaneously peeling her body off the tiles and massaging her temple.

A few caveman grunts make me pivot. I find Bastian spread-eagled behind me, glasses askew. I stride over and lift him to his feet before he's even gotten his lids up, then shove the black frames in their rightful place.

My brother's brown eyes lock on mine, relief scored across his pupils. I scan him over quickly for bleeding scratches or worrisome bruises. Find none. Once I'm sure he's stable, I crouch by Alma.

"For all that is holy, I swear I'm never drinking again." Alma's words are muffled seeing as she's face down on the tiles. She presses her palms into the floor, heaving herself up. "That was *not* pleasant." She wrinkles her nose, which jostles her little bump.

"Agreed. But look around." I gesture to the space. "Worth it, no?"

"Um . . . yeah?" She rubs her head. "I guess as far as libraries go, this one's original and cool, but—"

"Original and cool? What it is, is fixed!" I announce.

"You mean the clock?" Bastian asks. "It wasn't technically broken."

"I'm not talking about the clock. I'm talking about the library." At their blank stares, I frown. "It was in shambles."

Alma lowers her hand from her forehead. "It was?"

"Wait a minute. Do you guys not remember?"

Alma and Bastian exchange a look.

I spin around, lock eyes with Geoffrey who stands beside his son, both dusting their pressed trousers in perfect synchronicity. "Do you remember the destruction, Geoff?"

His hands freeze on his pant legs, and his hazel eyes shoot over to me. "My name's Geoffrey, Monsieur Ardoin."

I flick my hand, because now's really not the time to discuss preferred monikers. "So? Do you?"

The mayor stares around him, eyebrows tapered over squinty eyes. "Something was destroyed?"

Cadence's gaze locks on mine before returning to her father, whom she's knelt beside. "What about you, Papa?"

"I don't remember the library looking any different." Displeasure edges de Morel's tone at being left out by magic.

I walk around the clock and right his overturned wheelchair. Despite myself, a needle of sympathy pierces my chest. I may detest Rainier, but I'm used to seeing him radiate power and disdain. It almost pains me to see him looking so helpless.

Almost.

Cadence's eyes rove over Rainier's motionless lower half. "Your legs. Can you move them?"

Rainier cranes his neck and peers at his suede boots. When they don't even twitch, his head lolls back to the floor, and his mouth thins. "*Non.*" He steals his hand out of his daughter's and presses it into the gray enamel of the *dihuner*, managing to heave his upper body to sitting.

Cadence gasps, raising her palm and swiveling it. Ruby-red blood stains her pale skin. "Papa! You're bleeding!"

With the help of Adrien, we grip Rainier under the armpits and hoist him back into his chair. He doesn't look at either of us, but once he's back in his cushy leather seat, his gaze collides with mine. The hatred there tells me that if Cadence hadn't been here, he would've picked staying on the ground over benefiting from my help.

Cadence looks him over for other injuries, but the only one he sports is the long slash across his left palm.

"Must have cut it on some glass when I fell. With how hard the ground shook, I thought the whole library was going to come crashing down."

Cadence runs off toward the front doors of the library, panting something about a first-aid kit. That's when realization hits. I look down at the clock, and the dregs of my compassion for Rainier de Morel disappear.

Oh, Rainier. You conniving bastard.

A streak of scarlet crosses the gold ringing the clock. And, oh so conveniently, cuts right across Gaëlle's glowing white symbol.

I cross my arms. "Wow. Must've been some cut, de Morel. You bled all over the *dihuner.*"

His pupils dilate as Cadence returns, toting a hard plastic case. She sets it in her father's lap, clicks it open, then selects an individually packed disinfectant wipe which she pats over Rainier's palm. He hisses in a breath.

I unbutton my coat and pull a square cloth of black microfiber from the inside pocket. Like my lockpick, this goes with me everywhere. Comes in handy should I need to wipe fingerprints from my phone's screen, off Bastian's glasses, or, well . . . other surfaces. One can't always wear gloves.

"Guess I'll clean it up. Make it spiffy. Wouldn't want to usher in magic with a gory mess."

Rainier stares daggers at me as I kneel down and spit, then wipe off every smudge of red from the slashed triangle, all the while whistling. Once I'm done, I stand. Cadence's body is rigid, the corners of her mouth downturned.

Yeah, princess. Daddy's a wily magic thief. He was surely hoping his blood would bond him to the Air element if he plastered it on there before Gaëlle.

I ball my hand into a fist and feel a bandage rub against the cashmere lining of my gloves. I know that's what Rainier did, because I did the same. I came in here earlier and dribbled my blood on the Water symbol. Only I was more discreet. Geoffrey would have to put his nose right to the clock to make out anything.

I feel that sense of satisfaction that comes with a job well done. I haven't lost my touch—or appetite—for trickery.

Cadence comes back to life slowly. She removes the soiled wipe from Rainier's hand to apply a Band-Aid. "It was an accident, right? You weren't trying to"—she licks her lips—"to take Gaëlle's magic."

Rainier's eyebrows pinch. "I understand why you ask but can't help being disappointed that my own daughter would suspect me of something so vile. That this *boy*"—he ticks his head in my direction—"thinks poorly of me, I can live with. That you think me capable of such a thing . . ." He closes his fingers over the armrests of his wheelchair, strangling the black leather. "I would never rob someone of their birthright."

Her trust trickles in and chases her somber expression. "I believe you."

Love really does make people blind as bats.

"Adrien, your eyebrows!" Gaëlle gasps.

Adrien pushes the wool hat up, feeling up his face for the two brown caterpillars that went MIA after his battle with the wyvern. "They're back!" He rips the hat from his head. His hair's still buzzed short, though. Probably because the Quatrefoil didn't give him the haircut; Cadence did.

My girl grins. "Incredible."

I shove the cloth back into my coat and cross my arms again, disliking how gleeful she sounds about Prof's facial hair. I preferred Prickhead moon-faced.

"Slate, your coat's clean." Gaëlle points to the dark wool.

She's right. There's not a speck on it. You'd never guess I mud wrestled murderous tree roots.

"How long were we out?" Geoffrey asks.

"Four minutes." Bastian's hair is sticking out in all directions. He keeps thrusting his fingers through it as he inspects every corner of the clock.

Gaëlle squeezes the bridge of her nose and shuts her eyes. "Four whole minutes. That's the most rest I've gotten since the twins were born."

Adrien chuckles, and Cadence smiles at him.

I wish his eyebrows away. They stay stubbornly planted atop his hazel eyes.

Geoffrey retrieves the knife he brought to our clock*ish* gathering. "Well, I didn't come here to chat. I came to secure my place on the Council." He slashes his skin. Blood beads along the small cut in the meaty part of his index finger.

"Dad—" Adrien begins.

"Adrien." Geoffrey's voice is low and threatening. "Don't you dare."

Prof shuts his mouth, but just for a minute. Then he looks at me. "No regrets?"

I shrug. "It's just a title."

Rainier juts his chin to Cadence's hand. "The ring hasn't come off, Geoffrey. I fear we'll have to wait until the new moon for the blood-binding."

"Unless the ring and blood-binding are unrelated." Geoffrey tips his head to the side and regards the Bloodstone as though it were a big, red bug.

I exchange a look with Cadence. The pitch of her eyebrows tells me she's worried. I dip my chin, communicating that all's well, and her eyebrows level out.

"Then I guess the rest of you will be needing the needle I packed." Rainier fumbles with the leather bag strapped to his chair, his eyes spasmodically flicking to the Air symbol. He's probably hoping I didn't do too good a job of cleaning up after him.

"No need for a needle. They can use my knife, Rainier." Geoffrey hands it to Adrien.

I wonder what his blood mixed with mine will do. Hopefully, we're in a first-come, first-served situation.

"That's barbaric." Rainier turns his nose up at Geoffrey. "*Chérie,* take the needle."

Cadence indulges him and pricks her finger, then grabs a disinfectant wipe from the box still sitting on Rainier's lap, and hands both to Gaëlle.

Bastian sidles in next to me, expression stern. He's not happy I'm standing back, just letting it happen. Maybe I should've told him and Alma what I went off to do earlier, but they both wear their hearts on their faces . . . or sleeves . . . or whatever.

"Does anyone else feel like we're part of a creepy cult?" Alma asks, as Geoffrey, Adrien, Gaëlle and Cadence get into place.

A corner of my lips kicks up.

"On the count of three," Adrien says.

"Wait!" I grip Rainier's chair and yank him as far back as the newfangled plexiglass barrier will allow. "Safety first. Bastian, Alma. Back up."

"I was fine where I was," Rainier grumbles barely holding it in check, his skin a sickly shade of lavender.

Adrien shovels in a deep breath. "One . . . two . . . three."

At the exact same time, they touch their bloody fingertips to the glowing symbols. We all wait for something to happen . . . anything really.

A little rumble.

Increased neon beams.

Frantic ticking.

A zombie marching band.

Geoffrey grumbles, "*Kaoc'h*."

"What does that mean?" I ask Bastian, whose phone's glued to his palm.

He jerks at my distraction but indulges my curiosity by tapping the word into his Breton translation app. Shaking his head, he murmurs back, "You're going to love it. It means *shit*."

I feel a smile coming on as I refocus on the clock.

Adrien straightens. "Rainier, do you have your lighter?"

Cadence's old man snaps to life beside me and forages through his wheelchair's pocket. When he finds the shiny, solid silver canister, he hands it to Adrien, who fires it up, then squints at the flame and utters a few words under his breath.

The flame stays shallow and pointed.

I can't help it, I cackle. Starts off as a giggle before gathering force until I'm shaking.

Cadence throws me one hell of a glare.

I clear my throat, trying to stifle the laughter, but then I think of Adrien going cross-eyed, and it starts up again. "Sorry," I wheeze. "Don't mind me."

Adrien snaps the lighter closed.

"Why didn't it work?" Alma chews her lip.

Rainier sighs. "I'm afraid it might not be the end."

That finally sobers me up. "The Quatrefoil's got more shit up its leaves?"

Bastian's eyes are trained on the gradient blue of the lunar dial. "Maybe it all ends on the new moon. You just have to wait."

"For years, you've been saying we had to get the leaves together and that was it, Rainier!" Geoffrey's voice echoes off the stacks.

"It's what I assumed. What we *all* assumed, Geoffrey." Rainier pauses, and his Adam's apple bobs. "I guess we were wrong."

"But we put the leaves together! We did it!"

"*We?*" I skewer Adrien's old man with a look, because all *he* did was feed the town excuses for the chaos.

"What about the stones?" Alma gestures to the star dial. "Some of them are brighter. Must've happened for a reason."

We all squint at the celestial dial, trying to find rhyme and reason for the shininess. I go through the zodiac in my head, trying to remember different constellations and their formations of stars when it hits me. "It's a constellation."

Cadence frowns. "Which one?"

"Not one of the major ones. One from Brumian myth." Learning the ancient constellations was an extra-credit assignment suggested by Mademoiselle Claire which—unbelievably—I did, on my own, for pleasure. Next, I'll start wearing argyle sweaters and shiny black dress shoes.

Bastian grins at me. "It's called *Wrongful Death.*" Apparently, he perused the same book I did. "It's named that way because it supposedly resembles a murder victim."

As I step onto the clock, Cadence studies the body shaped by the luminescent stones.

"It's a clock, Roland, not a carpet," Rainier growls.

I don't react, just plod right on, toward the topaz-encrusted dial and crouch to touch the stones. The instant my skin skims the chilled surface of a lit one, I find myself nose to nose with yarn. Beneath a neat pile of colored wool and cashmere sits a skeleton, threadbare cloth and blackened skin adhering to its bones. It reaches toward me, empty eye-sockets full of sadness, and although it doesn't open its mouth, I swear I hear it whine. "Home. Bring me home."

I snatch my hand back and fall flat on my ass. *Nice.*

The vision fades, and I'm back in the temple, the others gawping with round eyes.

Cadence treads toward me. "What happened?"

I explain my fucked-up vision. All except Rainier drop into crouches and touch one of the glowing stones. My fellow *diwallers* get a vision.

Adrien scratches his chin. "I didn't see a skeleton. I saw your mother's bonsai statue, Cadence. Under something fluffy and white. What about you?"

"I saw the *Kelouenn*. It was mixed up with some navy towels, I think. Really weird." Cadence sniffs the air. "Does anyone else smell laundry detergent?"

"I saw a plank with the initials C + A carved into it." Gaëlle winds her long hair into a thick rope. "You think we need to find and gather these objects?"

"And do what with them? Bring them back here?" Cadence seems a little flushed.

I nod to the stone I touched. "The skeleton specifically asked to go home."

Cadence touches my stone. She must get the same vision because the blood leaches from her cheeks.

Gaëlle sticks her hands inside her coat and nods to the clock. "What do the rest of the stones show?"

Adrien grazes them. "Skeleton, plank, bonsai, skeleton again, *Kelouenn*, bonsai." Suddenly, he goes as pasty as Cadence and whirls on his father. "You kept it?"

"Kept what?" Cadence asks.

Geoffrey's throat dips. "I did. I've kept everything of Camille's."

"But the cup she used to commit suicide?" Adrien hisses. "That's —that's—*Why*?"

"Do I question what you do, son?"

Father and son gaze at each other for a long moment.

Adrien stands. "Maybe there's something in the *Kelouenn* about why we need all these *things*."

"Except the real *Kelouenn* is at the restorer's. Right, Papa?"

Rainier has gone as still as a statue. "Right."

Lie. Lie. Lie. I want to chant this out loud but somehow keep my mouth zipped.

"I should go over the pictures Slate took of the scroll. They might tell us why we're seeing such random objects." Adrien retrieves his hat from his coat pocket and pulls it on. "I'll just go home and—" His gaze jerks to the massive oak door.

My adrenaline levels spike. "What?"

"Home. I'm wondering if I have my house back." He vaults over the low plexiglass wall and strides out of the library before I can ask him for help with Rainier.

However tempted I am to keep Cadence's father in the clock paddock, I nod to Bastian. Together—Geoffrey doesn't even offer a hand—we get Rainier and his chair over the guardrail. And then I help the girls up and over.

"What if we don't do anything? What if we just wait until the new moon?" Gaëlle's voice is thin in the vast space.

"The ring's still on Cadence's finger." My teeth barely separate as I say it. "We don't stop until it's off."

"I thought—because it came off your finger—I thought—" My incendiary look makes Gaëlle stutter.

"It probably will come off at the new moon, but we're not taking any chances."

Gaëlle sighs. "Can we at least wait until morning?"

Even though my body and brain ache like a mother, I don't want to waste a single second and am about to protest when Cadence touches my arm.

"Gaëlle's right. We all need some rest. Especially you, Slate."

Adrien bursts back inside the library as though he's being chased by my fanged *groac'h* and his pet *guivre*. "You guys will never believe—what's happened—to Brume."

19

CADENCE

My blood zings as I walk toward Adrien, who's shouldering the library's heavy door. I glance up into his face, familiar again. It's funny how something so trivial as eyebrows can make such a difference. His eyelashes have grown back and bat excitedly. Although, is it excitement?

Nothing the Quatrefoil has thrown at us up until now has been exhilarating. Pulse-pounding, sure, but not thrilling in the positive sense of the word.

Right before emerging onto the snowy lawn, I peer over my shoulder and meet Slate's wary gaze. Like me, unease is eating at him, crimping the edges of his eyes and mouth. He looks like he's aged a decade since I slipped on the ring.

The ring, which is still attached to my body.

To my blood.

I ball my fingers into a fist, reviling the damned jewel. I won my leaf, but of course, that isn't enough for the devious Quatrefoil. I'm starting to wonder if this isn't some never-ending sick game that'll cost us our sanity and eventually our lives. After all, everyone from the last *diwaller* generation died. Even Camille ultimately lost her mind and desire to go on.

My boots sink through a patch of brittle snow as I scan the abounding darkness for what caused Adrien's stupor. Through wisps of mist silvered by moonlight, I make out the *Arzoù-Kaer*—the

Beaux-Arts building. Its limestone walls stand straight and tall again. Its long strips of windows sparkle like thin ice. Gone is the disemboweled cadaver of stone and plaster. I take a step forward and another until all of it comes into view, including Maman's giant terracotta warlord who thrones like the God he is in the attached veranda.

"Holy *kaoc'h*." Slate stands next to me, the shape of his dark eyes uncharacteristically round and their shine rivaling the frosted flagstone walkways of Fifth.

"Incredible," Gaëlle whispers from where she stands on my father's other side. "Simply incredible."

"Um . . ." Alma's arms are crossed over her faux-fur jacket. "You're talking about the fact that the Beaux-Arts edifice is presently thataway?"

"No, we're talking about the fact that it's not demolished." I sigh. "You don't remember, do you?"

"It was destroyed, too?"

"The Quatrefoil's apparently reversed all the destruction it inflicted on Brume," Adrien says.

"And stirred up something new." Slate gestures toward the art center. "Any theories why it's overlooking the lake?"

I suck in a breath, because he's right! It used to give onto the forest, not the lake. I pirouette. The four buildings are still in the correct order—beside the *Arzoù-Kaer* sits the Bisset Esplanade with its glassed-in promenade, then the square castle that houses the Mercier Humanities Center, and finally, the circular stone and glass amphitheater named after Slate's family.

"The *kelc'hs* have spun." Adrien blows warm air into his gloved hands. "At least, Fourth and Third did. I didn't venture all the way down the hill."

"Why?" I find myself asking.

"Yo, de Morel. Why'd Brume pop its cork?" Slate asks. "Or rather, twirl its *kelc'hs*?"

Papa scoffs. "How should I know? We never got this far."

"Anything in the *Kelouenn* manual?" Alma asks Adrien.

"I . . . I didn't make it to the house. I'll go now, though." Adrien starts toward the stairs but then stops and backtracks. "Almost forgot. The stairs are broken up because the town didn't spin on a single axis." He takes off toward the curlicue road but pauses. "If any of you have time to spare to go over the scroll with me, meet me back at my place in fifteen."

"I'll be there." Once he's gone, I turn toward Bastian. "You said the star-tipped hand moved. Do you have any idea what it's measuring?"

Bastian rubs the back of his head, adding more volume to his already messy brown hair. Soon he's going to be giving Nolwenn's poufy do a run for its money. "I didn't study it long enough, but I'll go back there and see if I can figure it out."

Alma stifles a yawn. "Wait up."

"Alma, you don't need to—"

"Sidekicks stick together." She threads her arm through his, and they plod back toward the library.

"Put your ringer on," Slate calls out, forever the worrywart older brother.

Bastian nods before drawing the door open for Alma.

"And you call us if . . . if you find anything." Slate presses his lips together.

I sense that wasn't what he meant to say. I assume, *if something goes wrong* was his first thought, because it was mine.

"If you want to stay with them, I can go help Adrien—"

"They can handle it."

"Well, I'm going home and staying home until you all figure out what's wrong with the cantankerous Quatrefoil." Before taking off, Geoffrey lifts his coat collar like I imagine all villains do.

"Entitled *bajaneg*," Slate mutters under his breath.

"For once, I couldn't agree with you more," Papa intones.

Gaëlle doesn't say anything. She rarely says anything bad about anyone so it isn't surprising. I think the one and only time I heard her talk badly was about Matthias.

"Can you take Papa home?" I ask her.

"Or Gaëlle can go with Slate to help Adrien—"

"She has young children, Papa."

He grumbles something that gets snatched by the whirring of his wheelchair as he takes off too fast toward the road.

"Slow down! Your wheels might skid."

He doesn't heed my entreaty.

"I've got him, Cadence. Don't worry." Gaëlle runs off after him, sliding twice before managing to latch on to the back of his chair.

I stare until the mist envelops their bodies.

Knuckles bump into my chilled hand, and then a single warm finger hooks around mine. "Thanks for staying with me."

I lean into Slate. "Like Alma said, sidekicks stick together."

He turns toward me, eyebrows drawn over his inky irises. "You're more than my sidekick. Hope you know that."

I smile. "I do."

He looks back toward the hazy lake. "You really think the Quatrefoil reversed all the damage it did?"

"Papa's still cursed, so I assume it's just the damage it did to our generation."

"Do you think Emilie's still . . . dead?"

"I don't know."

Pulling up his coat sleeve so he can peer down at his watch, Slate releases a frustrated sigh. "Kind of late to go ringing a six-year-old's doorbell."

"Tomorrow. We'll pay her a visit tomorrow. Or call . . ." I realize I don't want to know yet about Emilie, because if her curse isn't reversed, if she's still dead— I'm not ready to lose hope. "Maybe we need to wait until the new moon for curses to reverse."

Slate sighs as he spears his fingers through mine again. "It's so damn cold out here, I'm going to end up losing a significant part of my anatomy if we don't get a move on."

"Ah, romance isn't dead." I peck his lips and squeeze our palms together. As we make our unhurried way hand in hand to Third, marveling at how everything looks different and yet the same, I say, "When I was a kid, I loved jigsaw puzzles. Papa and I used to work on them together. A new one each week. One of them was so huge it covered our entire dining room table." I smile nostalgically. "However difficult they were, we never gave up and we *never* failed."

"I bet you didn't."

I rest my cheek against his shoulder. "But I'm beginning to think this Quatrefoil puzzle is going to be the first we fail at. I mean we have *all* the pieces. We even put them together. Yet we're not done? How are we supposed to succeed when new pieces, that don't have any discernible sockets or tabs, enter the game?"

"We just need to figure out how they line up. Which we will." Slate kisses the top of my head. "If the Quatrefoil didn't want to be solved, it'd stop tossing pieces at us. It's egging us on."

I reach up to touch the scar on my eyebrow. Encounter no raised skin. "Slate, my scar's gone."

I stop walking and so does he. The bronze sign of Third clanks over our heads as it swings on its chains.

He frowns as he inspects my face. "Huh." He releases my hand and touches the nape of his own neck. "What about mine? Can't feel anything through these gloves."

I push up on tiptoe and tow his jacket and shirt collars down to inspect his skin. "Gone." Then I run my fingers against the edge of his jaw, encountering only thick stubble. "Both gone."

"Hope you still find me irresistible without my battle scars."

"It isn't your scars that drew me to you, Monsieur Ardoin."

"You seemed pretty transfixed by the ones on my chest the first time you saw me naked. You had drool"—he taps the corner of my mouth—"right. There."

I roll my eyes even though I might've had a little drool. I decide to focus on that first part of what he said. "I actually still haven't seen you naked."

"Not for lack of trying on my behalf."

Fingers still resting on his jaw, I press my smile to his. It isn't a long kiss, but it's a sweet one.

"How about we go back to my place to work on the puzzle. I find I focus better when naked anyway."

A laugh bursts from my mouth as we start up again. "You're terrible."

"Unarguably so. I'd even go so far as to call myself wicked."

My laughter wanes at that word. I don't like it because that's what the Quatrefoil is. Wicked.

Voices drift from the open second-floor window of a faculty house, followed by a cork popping. The sound of how I imagined our evening ending.

I release a sigh that puffs out like a cloud. "Do you think the townspeople will notice Brume has spun?"

Slate peers around the deserted street. "The non-*diwallers* noticed, so I'm guessing, yes."

We reach Adrien's place at the same time as he does. He's panting and shaking like the folder he retrieved at his father's place. "I remembered something!"

He reaches for his doorknob and barrels inside, lobbing his hat and coat onto the coatrack, and then drops down into his brown suede couch while I stare around the living room at the twin swords crisscrossed by the door, the bulky, varnished Tudor furniture, Camille's oil portrait.

My heart fires up a melancholic beat at the sight of the gentle oval face framed by dark blonde tendrils of hair. I wish the Quatrefoil hadn't just warped our town's streets but its timeline. What I wouldn't give to feel Camille's hand on my brow . . . my mother's . . . meet Slate's parents.

We sit opposite Adrien, Slate tugging on me until I'm almost on his lap.

"So, what is it you recalled, Prof?"

"Remember how the Quatrefoil graces the center of the scroll, and all around it, there are texts and drawings?"

"Yeah?"

"Well, I think we have to focus on everything that's written around the Quatrefoil."

"The missing pieces of the puzzle," I whisper.

"Exactly." Adrien looks up from the pages he's taken out of the folder and lined up to recreate the scroll. At the sight of my proximity to Slate, his mouth warps, and he drops his gaze back to the acres of marked-up paper.

To lessen Adrien's discomfort, I release Slate's fingers and lean into the armrest. Slate's eyes scrape across the side of my face, clearly annoyed I've pulled back, probably because he imagines my reasons for doing so are linked to my former crush. I want to explain I'm just trying to be respectful when he rolls his shoulders forward and drops his elbows onto his spread knees.

"I just thought of something." Slate twines his fingers together and bounces his wrists. "Since the Quatrefoil reversed all the damage it caused, maybe it wiped your ex's mind clean. You two could finally get back together."

He levels a smile on Adrien that the latter does *not* reciprocate.

"I'd rather focus on getting the Bloodstone off Cadence's finger than winning back my ex."

Their little staring match lasts for so long that I clear my throat and pick up a paper. "We better get started, because I'd love nothing more than to get the bloody heirloom off."

Actually, I would love something more. I'd love for Slate to make peace with Adrien and Papa, because, whether he likes it or not, they each own pieces of my heart. Very different pieces but pieces that nonetheless interconnect.

Just like the Quatrefoil and its leaves.

20

SLATE

Something rare and unprecedented wakes me.
Sunlight.
In Brume.
Bright enough to make my eyes water.

I push the granny Afghan off my torso, sit up, and work out a crick in my neck. I expect to see Cadence on the other end of Adrien's suede couch. But the place is empty, the dregs of our dinner cleaned up and put away.

Only minutes after Cadence and I got to Prof's house last night, Bastian and Alma arrived, none the wiser about what the star hand of the clock was measuring. Herbal tea led to Adrien roping them into the shamrock wordsearch. For the rest of the evening, the four of them pored over printed photos and paged through Adrien's books, while I did my part and played delivery boy—again—grabbing food both late and early to feed their buzzing brain cells. Any chance of me and Cadence sharing an intimate evening flopped the moment Adrien brought up the damn *Kelouenn*, 'cause little revs up my girl like history.

I intend to change that and introduce her to *my kelouenn*.

Huh. Quite catchy.

The odor of freshly ground coffee beans lingers in the air. I vaguely remember Cadence kissing me earlier, the taste of *pain au chocolat* on her lips, telling me to sleep, that she'd wake me when it was time to meet up with Gaëlle and discuss the next steps.

I'm guessing it isn't time.

They're probably touring the twisted streets of Brume. Unless they're all working on their suntans. I close my eyes as I stand in front of Adrien's kitchen window and absorb some much-needed Vitamin D while I chomp on leftover pastries. I can't stomach wasting half-eaten food, a remnant of my time in foster care.

Too lazy to figure out where Adrien keeps his fancy Nespresso capsules, I shoot down someone's unwanted glacial coffee. The snow sparkles like Alma's glittery eyeshadow, marred only by boot prints. If I weren't so jaded, I'd say this morning feels like a brand-new beginning, happy and bright, the sunny-side of an egg. But I've seen what this town can do, how it can maim and obliterate. Whatever I'm feeling is an illusion. Or a spell. Might as well call it a spell considering . . .

I yawn and check my Rolex. What the—It's almost noon! Did I sleep through Cadence's call? After a little game of hide-and-seek, I locate my phone between the couch cushions. No missed calls.

I swipe to send Cadence a text, but her name doesn't pop up.

I type it in with no results. Did she change it on me? Maybe she put something cute in there. I scroll through my short contact list, which consists of select Brumians, a few establishments, my lawyer-slash-banker Philippe, and Bastian. Oh, and Spike. His number's made-up, but Bastian input it, along with a great stalk-shot, and since it made my brother giggle like a schoolgirl, I kept it.

No new, cute nicknames pop up. No new, *not so cute* ones either. Most of my contacts are gone. Either a goddamn update ate my info, or I rolled over my phone and somehow deleted my address book.

Quelle merde. Good thing I'm old-school and have a great memory for number sequences thanks to memorizing my Milieu contacts—storing them would've been problematic for business.

I tap her ten-digit phone number. The call rings and rings. When her prerecorded message comes on, panic sets in. I call Bastian, but his number also goes to voicemail. What the hell? Bastian *always* answers when I call.

I whip on my shoes and coat before bursting out into the surreal

Brumian sunlight. I jog across the road and down a set of steps, only to find that they abut someone's house. I mentally flog myself for forgetting about the circles turning and head back up toward the road.

A shrill, "Ahh!" freezes my legs.

I put a hand out and catch myself on the rough wall.

Hope forces my lungs to expand and my breath to stall. The cry comes again. My heart thrashes wildly, the sound of it so loud in my ears that it almost drowns out the childish voice which is as familiar as my own. I hear it every night, over and over, as I wait for sleep to pull me under.

The child's scream comes again.

Where before there was a hen house above and a patch of scraggly trees below, now the shifting circles have lined up two snowy backyards. They angle steeply down, then even out to a flat ridge right before Second Kelc'h.

A little girl with yellow snow boots and long golden curls is hurtling down the newfangled slope. I sprint like a racer at the shot of the pistol, dashing toward her, part-running, part-skidding, part-rolling in the snow.

When she reaches the bottom of the hill, she tumbles into the white powder. A red disk pops out from underneath her, skidding lower, stopping against a snowbank.

I reach her then. Her body's shaking as if she's crying uncontrollably. "Emilie," I murmur.

I kneel down next to her, ready to cradle her in my arms, when she flops onto her back, wiping off her cheeks, a gurgling sound coming from between her lips.

Laughter. It's laughter. She's laughing so hard that she can barely keep it together.

The world around me expands, sparks ignite at the edge of my vision.

Emilie.

I'm dizzy with happiness, my head spinning, my soul floating. I let out a laugh of my own. "Emilie! Emilie!"

Then she turns her face to me and I see her eyes are green, not brown. Her nose is straight and long where Emilie's was short.

I swallow back disappointment sharp enough to slice right through my throat.

"*C'était génial!* The best! So scary but so fun!" The girl sits up. "Are you Stéphane's dad?"

I drop onto my elbows, dipping my forehead to the frozen crust of snow. I manage to choke out a, "*Non.*"

"Well, my dad says the *kelc'hs* moved, that's why our yard is now on top of the Dumonts'. The Dumonts are too old to enjoy sledding. But in the summer they have a vegetable garden. I know because they gave me a cucumber once . . ."

Wetness leaches through the wool of my coat and numbs my skin. Why can't it numb my soul?

The girl's still rambling. "And Maman says not to be scared about it, that the town was built like a clock. The *kelc'hs* are like the dials, but instead of measuring hours and minutes and seconds they measure other stuff, we just don't know what. But whatever they measure just changed, and it feels like an earthquake but it's not, it's—"

Thankfully, one . . . two . . . three more kids come whizzing down the hill on saucers, shutting off the tap on this girl's torrent of words.

"About time! Let's do it again!" She scrambles toward her plastic sled, digs it out, then treks up the snowy hill.

I close my eyes but see Emilie's body sinking into the water, so I snap them back open. Emilie is still dead. The magic didn't reverse the curses. All this sun, all the repaired buildings, all the scars that healed . . . good-for-nothing magic.

I don't know how long I lie there, listening to the whooshing of the kids' snow saucers, their screams of delight, the warbling of a stupid-ass bird who forgot to fly south for the winter. I'm too empty to feel the cold. My eyes close once again, and I nearly drift off, but then remember why I left the comfort of Adrien's surprisingly cozy couch.

I heave myself up, shedding some of the despair that's weighing me down, and stride across the ridge to the broken, winding road, heading toward Second, assuming some of my crew will be at the tavern, lunching away. The nearer I get to the square, the more the buildings start encroaching on each other, resembling rowdy drunks holding each other up. In the narrow space between the rough stone walls snake crooked alleyways and pocket-sized courtyards.

The square hasn't changed—the dreaded mermaid den still stands among the frosted cobblestones. Smells of garlic and butter waft about. Through the steamy window panes of the tavern, I catch sight of Cadence, Alma, Bastian, Gaëlle, and Geoffrey Keene. Once I get over the old man's dubious sense of fashion—he sports a preppy vest atop a Vichy-print shirt that matches the cloth napkin on his lap—the question of why he's there with my crew, sucking down a salt-meadow gigot, careens into my mind. They better not be going over the game plan without me. I don't care if the bags under my eyes are hefty enough to require an extra fee at the airport, starting *sans moi* isn't cool.

I open the door and step through the curtain keeping out the cold. Immediately, a blanket of warmth, the clanking of silverware, and the smell of sizzling lard surrounds me. Nolwenn's working her way across the dining room, tray in hand. I catch her eye and nod my greeting. She nods stiffly back, wearing an uneasy smile.

Guess she's having a bad day.

Winding around two other tables, I reach my crew. Through mouthfuls of food, they're discussing the lit topazes in low tones. Cadence has her back to me, chestnut hair draped over her left shoulder, revealing the curve of her right ear. I step quietly behind her. They're all so deep in discussion that no one but Bastian even notices me.

I put a finger to my lips, then bend over, take the plump bit of Cadence's earlobe between my teeth and whisper, "Hello, beautiful."

Pain explodes on the side of my head as something warm and slimy oozes from my hair down my neck.

"*Bordel de merde!*" I straighten, rubbing my throbbing temple.

Cadence scoots her chair back and stands, brandishing her ceramic plate like a weapon while her scalloped potatoes skid down my chest. Her cheeks are bright pink, her eyes gone navy with rage.

"Good morning to you, too, princess. Any chance I can get a

kiss?" I reach out for her, but the skilled lumberjack that she's become raises her weapon higher and swings, nearly hacking off my head.

As I duck, she yells, "I don't know who you are, but you're out of your mind if you think I'd kiss some random guy."

21

CADENCE

"Some random guy?" The curly-haired stranger lowers the hand rubbing his temple and narrows his already rather thin eyes at me. "Did I sleep right through to April first?" Under his breath, he adds, "Would explain the weather."

Adrien, who was in the bathroom when I got accosted, strides through the tavern as soon as he notices my raised, bobbing plate. He puts a hand on my hip and eases me away from the stranger wearing my lunch. "What happened?"

"The boy tried to kiss her," Gaëlle says.

"The *boy*?" The stranger's attention whizzes toward her. "I'm still dreaming. That's it, huh?"

"Dreaming?" Alma smirks. "Nope, but if you want me to pinch you, I'll be glad to do it. I'm a really great pincher."

Bastian shifts on his seat, vexed that Alma has sort of propositioned the stranger. I'm too perplexed by how the stranger in question nibbled my ear to chide my best friend. Although I'll definitely have another talk with her about leading men on. Poor Bastian.

The sweet transfer student's been infatuated with her since he landed in Brume a month ago, and although they haven't hooked up, he clearly wants something to happen. He's been wanting something to happen ever since he spotted Alma in the library and ended up running into the clock's guardrail—a rough meet-cute, which left an impression on Alma, and then on the rest of us when he helped us battle the Quatrefoil.

"Little bro, can you tell the weirdos to drop the act? It's no longer *très drôle*." The stranger's staring straight at Bastian, who glances over his shoulder at the diners behind him.

"You know this kid, Bastian?" Adrien asks.

"*Kid*?" The stranger pops the word out as though it's an insult.

He does look more like a man than a kid, but to Adrien, anyone below the age of twenty-one is a kid. Unfortunately. Although recently, I feel like he's seeing me as less of a kid and more of an equal, especially since he broke up with Charlotte.

When Bastian suggested Adrien call her to check if maybe she'd forgotten about the whole fire-demon-hexing debacle, he avoided answering, lifting instead his eyes to mine as though seeking something in their depths. An answer to a question.

I'd shivered because there'd definitely been heat there. The same way there's heat in the palm he's fastened to my hip. The stranger's eyes taper on that point of contact. His already dark irises dim to throat-clenching black. Why does he look like he wants to hack off Adrien's wrist?

Adrien tightens his grip, pulling me so close that our sides touch, eliciting yet another frisson from me. "Can I see your student ID?"

The boy snaps his gaze back up to Adrien's face. "Are you fucking kidding me, Prof?"

"No. I'm not *fucking* kidding you. I'm very serious right now. Either show me your ID, or I'll have to call campus security."

The stranger pats his jacket pocket, retrieves a wallet, and pulls out a driver's license, muttering curse word after curse word. One of them sounds Breton. Maybe he actually is from around these parts. "Will this do, Mercier?" he spits out each word as though they taste sour.

The name *Slate Ardoin* sits next to a picture that looks more mugshot than photobooth-posed, what with the scowl and chaotic black corkscrews falling helter-skelter around his head.

"You wouldn't happen to have your student ID on you as well, Slate?"

"He knows your last name, Adrien," Gaëlle putters in, "so he probably is a student."

"Okay. Now you're all just being rude. Especially you, Adrien. Please take your fucking hand off my girlfriend."

My lips pop open. "Girlfriend?" He thinks we're dating?

"That's enough. I'm calling security." Geoffrey takes out his cell phone.

"What the hell's up with the circus act?" Slate's complexion is reddening, like the lump at the juncture between his forehead and temple where I struck him with my plate.

Everyone's staring now. Even Juda's stepped out of the kitchen, gripping a big knife, the blade of which he taps against his open palm.

Nolwenn, who isn't scared of anything or anyone, pulls open the curtain blocking the entrance. "No brawling inside my tavern." She nods to the door, her white puffy hair so stiff it doesn't even bob. "Out."

Slate raises a dark eyebrow. "Even you're in on this, Nolwenn?"

"Security's on its way." Geoffrey slides his phone back onto the table.

Slate's cheeks puff. "This is complete and utter bullshit."

I spot two men in campus uniforms and downy winter jackets through the frosted glass of the tavern, and then a gust of icy air slithers past the drawn curtain. When my teeth chatter, Adrien's hand moves over my ribcage to drive heat into my chilled skin.

I realize now's really not the time to revel in his touch, yet I melt right into him.

Alma eyes us from over her hammered copper mug filled with piping hot coffee.

"Cadence, can you come outside with me so we can talk?" The gravelly voice makes my attention slam back on the boy.

Either he's a stalker or a student. I mean, he knows *all* our names.

"She's not going anywhere with you." Adrien says this calmly but a slight vibration warps each word.

One of the guards hooks Slate's arms. The boy jolts, but then his shoulders roll forward, and he pulls his arms free, before pivoting and slamming a fist into the guard's nose. Something crunches.

"Don't you fucking touch me."

The other guard reaches for his Taser.

"I'm a Roland, you—" Before Slate can finish his sentence, the guard pulls the trigger of his yellow, gun-shaped weapon.

The stranger's eyes roll back, and he slumps into a table, before flopping onto the tiled floor.

The urge to yell at the guard and drop to my knees to nurse him seizes me out of nowhere. I lunge forward, but Adrien tows me gently back.

"Don't, Cadence. We don't know *what* or *who* he is."

"He's obviously from around here." I wave to the electroshocked boy. "I mean, he knew *all* our names, as well as the Rolands."

"Who are dead." Geoffrey, forever the observant soul, pours himself some more red wine. *"Une autre bouteille, s'il-te-plaît, Nolwenn."*

"Why do you think he brought up Oscar and Eugenia?" Alma asks. "Ooh. You think he's some long-lost nephew of theirs?"

"Neither of them had any relatives, so I doubt it." Geoffrey gurgles down the dregs of the first bottle which he shared with Gaëlle and Adrien.

"He did look an awful lot like Oscar, didn't he?" Nolwenn muses.

"If Oscar had a perm. Don't you remember how straight his hair was? Eugenia was the one with the curls." Geoffrey looks down his nose at the stranger called Slate, who's being carried out of the tavern. "I suppose, if they'd had time to produce a kid before that awful car accident, this boy could've been it."

My heart squeezes as I stare through the window at the boy's lolling head and dragging feet, scrolling through my memories for some glimmer of him.

I suck in a breath and push up on my toes to reach Adrien's ear. "You think he's part of the Quatrefoil?"

Adrien's pupils dilate, covering up the golden browns and vivid greens. He raises a hand and touches his neck and ear, all the while looking down at me a tad strangely. A tad intensely.

"Adrien?" I snap my fingers in front of his face.

He blinks and coughs. "What?"

"Do you think the Quatrefoil sent him?" My pulse races as the guards cart the subdued stranger out of sight.

The wind must've risen because the mist licks at the cobbles and curls off walls. If I'd been a stranger to Brume, I might've seen the weather turning as an omen. But this is Brume. Brume *means* mist.

"Cadence?" Adrien touches my cheek. He must've said my name a few times. Perhaps even said something else considering the others are all looking at me with varying degrees of worry, as though I'd been under some spell.

"Sorry. What?"

He reels his fingers back and makes a fist. "The pieces can't touch us, remember? Yet he touched you *and* the guard."

"I wasn't insinuating he was a leaf. We already *have* all the leaves." I close my eyes and knead my temples, the Bloodstone exceptionally heavy on my finger.

Why won't it come off? I'm so desperate for all of this to make sense.

And to end.

I open my eyes and aim them at Adrien. "Do you think we'll ever be done?"

"Yes." He pulls me into a hug. And somehow, even though he's hugged me dozens of times in the past, this hug feels different, more intimate.

Maybe it's because Adrien's palms press me into the solid length of his body. I reason that he's simply being charitable, trying to make me feel safe, but his heart thuds just as fast as mine beneath his tan cashmere sweater.

22

SLATE

P*utain de bordel de merde.*

This has gone too far.

So I've pulled some pretty petty jokes on Bastian over the years; stupid stuff like filling his pencil case with dead flies or gluing the pages of his books shut. I'll even admit I recently input a shortcut in his phone's autocorrect that changes *Hello* to *Help! I can't retrieve my head from my ass.* But this is taking things to a whole new level.

I was fucking tased.

TASED, dammit.

And now . . . *now*, I wake up slouched on a stiff leather armchair with zip ties around my wrists, in a locked room I'm assuming is an old waiting room turned campus holding cell.

I've resided in my fair share of fenced holding cells. Some were shared spaces that smelled of puke. Others were puny, private boxes with padlocked doors and a scattering of cockroaches. One was a simple cot laid out in a fishbowl of bars, erected right smack in the middle of the police chief's office.

This, however, is a special level of hell—a giant oil painting of Rainier de Morel stares me down, the painted blue eyes just as hateful and glacial as in real life. On either side of him are paintings of other old, white men, wearing the university insignia pin on their lapel.

I squint. Someone before me has scratched off the paint near Rainier's thigh in the shape of a limp penis. *Ha.* My type of hooligan.

Keys jangle on the other side of the door, which swings outward and reveals Rainier, one hand on the arm of his wheelchair, the other holding my driver's license.

"Well, Monsieur"—he glances at the laminated card between his fingers—"Ardoin. Your antics have taken me away from my home on a Sunday. I'm told you created some sort of scene at *la Taverne.* What do you have to say for yourself, young man?"

"I say, as far as jails go, although comfy, this isn't very impressive."

"We have no need for jails. People at my college behave themselves."

"Of course, they do."

He hands me back my driver's license and clips the piece of plastic binding my wrists. "My name is Rainier de Morel, and I'm the dean here. Campus security was called because the mayor thought you were a student. But, like I said, *my* students behave themselves."

"This is getting real old, real fast, de Morel." I roll my wrists as I stand. "We've got work to do. Like figuring out what the damn clock is telling us to hunt for. I don't want to take any chances of that ring not sliding off Cadence's finger."

Color drains from Rainier's cheeks, leaving him white as the starched collar poking above his sky-colored sweater. "How—what —" For once, he doesn't seem twelve feet tall sitting in that chair. For once, he looks small and scared. "Who are you?"

Rainier's a damn good actor. I mean, he's got the whole town fooled, thinking he's a good guy when he's really the devil's spawn, but the expression of confusion and fear on his face is genuine. There's no faking that.

Which means . . . *Putain,* what does that mean?

Something occurs to me. Something awful.

Dread churns in my gut.

I drop onto the chair arm so we're almost face to face. "I'm—I'm Oscar and Eugenia's son."

"Oscar and Eugenia didn't have a son."

"Yeah, they did: *me*. I know everyone thinks I died in the fire like they did, but—"

"They died in a car accident. On their way to Paris."

My lungs suddenly feel packed full. Like I can barely take a breath without popping them. But I press on. "Okay, well, I'm still of the Roland bloodline. One of the founding families. A *diwaller*. Come on, Rainier. You *know* this." In my head I'm begging him, *Please fucking know this.*

He barks out a short laugh, his fear turning into derision. "You almost had me there, young man. Too bad for you, you didn't do your homework. The Rolands were never a founding family. The founding families are the de Morels, Bissets, Merciers, and Keenes. Since 1350. Better go check your sources."

Black and white spots float in front of my eyes. I slither down the arm of the chair and onto the cushion.

No.

No, no, no.

"I'm letting you off with a warning, Monsieur Ardoin, because I was young once. Did stupid things, too. Now, I don't know what kind of alcohol or drugs you took to give you these ideas, but I suggest you stick to sobriety. And get off my campus. Next time we cross paths, I won't be so kind."

He powers his wheelchair out of the room, leaving the door agape. I stare at the empty space he left behind and attempt to even out my breathing.

It's been more than twenty-four hours since I touched Cadence's piece.

Emilie's curse took effect the next day.

This is my curse. To be forgotten.

To be scratched out.

Just like I scratched out Rémy.

The Quatrefoil has a very, very sick and twisted sense of humor.

Breathe, Slate. Breathe. In. Out. In. Out.

All my life I was told I was a nobody.

I'm not a nobody.

I'm not.

I'M NOT.

Breathe. In. Out. In. Out.

I can't be forgotten.

I rush out of the room with a sudden need for fresh air and follow a labyrinth of hallways until I find the front doors. They spit me out onto the snow-covered campus green of Fourth where I spin around to get my bearings. The fog is back, along with a bitter cold that freezes my eyeballs. Heart hammering with each step, I follow the fractured road down, then begin to run and don't stop until I've reached my house.

Thank fuck. It looks like it did pre-Armageddon root. Same gabled roof. Same red trim. Same multi-paned windows overlooking the drive.

I peek through one of those windows and let out a long sigh of relief—Spike's there, surrounded by his harem of succulents.

I pull my keys from my pocket, finding only two: the one for my apartment in Marseille and the one for my storage unit near Nice. Where the hell are the rest of them? Where's the keyless remote to my car? Where *is* my car?

Shoving down the panic pacing up my spine, I turn the knob to the front door. It opens.

A *Maître Gims*' song is blaring. So is laughter. The place is filthy, decorated with beer cans and ashtrays overflowing with cigarette butts, the occasional food wrapper shining like tinsel in the bits of sunlight breaking through the mist. The bookshelves still separate the living room and dining room areas, but instead of a dining table there are two unmade single beds. My earlier relief sours.

Spread out on a ratty couch is a redheaded dude. It takes my pissed-off mind a moment to realize it's the guy who has a thing for Cadence. The one I almost fed soap-on-a-stick. What's his name again? Pierre? Patrice? Peter?

He sets down his phone and peers at me from under bleached lashes. "Yo. Who you here for?"

His name comes at my brain like a punch. "Paul."

He half-sits. "Do we know each other?"

Boots thunder down the stairs and two other guys I've seen around campus nod a *hey* as they plod past me on their way out the door. My family home has become a fucking spillover for the dorms.

Fists clenching, I stare around me. The floorboards are stained and scuffed. I just had those oiled!

Paul squeaks, "Um . . . who are you again?"

The only thing that remains untouched by my curse is Spike and his ladies. He's still in the same pot I brought from Marseille. A hand-painted terracotta beauty with his name emblazoned across the front in white.

I cross the living room in three steps and haul him into my arms.

Paul stands, his pale skin blotched pink. "What're you doing with Steve?"

"Who the hell's Steve?"

He gestures to Spike. "Our dorm mascot."

I shoot Paul the mother of all glares. How dare he rename my Eve's Needle? "His name's Spike. And he's not a fucking mascot. Especially not *yours*."

"His name's Steve. It's on the pot."

I relax my grip and stare in horror at the white letters. The first and last are the same, but all the ones in the middle are wrong.

No. Effing. Way.

This is Spike's pot. *Spike.* Not fucking Steve. I growl out a string of obscenities and continue to the door. That's when I notice a grocery store pack of individually-wrapped madeleines. I grab those, too, mushing the bag into the wide inner pocket of my coat.

Paul stammers, "B-Bastian won't like it if you take Steve. He loves his cactus. Brought it from home. And those are his madeleines. Loves those, too."

I turn around. "*Bastian.* Wait. Bastian Binah?"

"Uh. Yeah."

In my new cursed reality, Bastian lives in my former family home, eats my cheap madeleines, and owns my Eve's Needle? Not only that, he named him *Steve*? Jesus. Why not name him Bob? The kid has no sense of flair.

My gaze flicks to the succulents on the overcrowded bookshelf. I stomp over, swipe the Mexican Snowball, and drop her into Spike's dirt. Bastian believes she's Spike's favorite, so she's coming along.

"Hey!" Paul hops off the couch.

I bare my teeth, which stops him in his tracks. As I stalk back into the foyer, I catch sight of the neon cactus Cadence gifted me. The idiots propped my fragile light directly on top of a hissing radiator! Hand shaking with barely contained rage, I unplug it, then pound out of the house, nearly plowing into Claire Robinson.

"Oh!" Her frosty pink lips part wide.

Hope buoys my mood. If she remembered to come get the astronomy books, then maybe she remembers me. "You here for the books, Professor?"

"Why, yes. Bastian Binah said I could grab them at my convenience."

Of course.

"Are you a new professor at the university?" She takes a step closer, and I get a whiff of her powdery, floral perfume.

"A student." I don't say *your student* because I fear she'd take it as a come-on. "Gotta hit the road. Take good care of those books."

They're better off at her place for the time being than in a frat house.

I head toward town, anger fueling me forward. That is, until I reach the cemetery and realize I have nowhere to go. At least, nowhere in Brume.

My coat pocket vibrates. I heft the pot in the crook of my elbow, lean my cactus light against Spike, and fish out my phone. I'm hoping it's Cadence, but she probably doesn't have my number, since I currently don't exist to her. I read the caller's name before accepting the call.

"Philippe?"

"Bad time, Slate?"

"You remember me?"

"Remember you? Hard to forget someone who mistakes your hand for an ashtray."

My whole body suddenly feels light and floaty. Like I've got helium running through my veins. "Oh, man. You remember me. You remember me!" I squeal, not even caring that I sound like a schoolgirl.

Philippe clears his throat. "Are you high?"

"Nope." I sandwich my phone between my ear and shoulder. "So, what's up?"

"I'm calling about Marianne Shafir. I just got her health records back, and they're squeaky clean. No cancer."

I head up to Second, then Third, Spike's pot digging into my hipbone. "So, what was the money for?"

"Not sure yet. However, I was checking up on her credit card usage, and it led me to this *gargote* in Rennes. I phoned them up, and they knew exactly who I was talking about. She used to go there on the regular. The owner's her cousin's nephew or some crap. Anyway, they remembered the last time she ate there because she didn't come alone. She sat with a younger gentleman."

"Go on . . ."

"A wheelchair-bound gentleman. They didn't know who he was but gave me a description. Mid-forties . . ."

Philippe's voice fades.

The street lined with dorms fades.

Rainier de Morel isn't the only man in a wheelchair. And technically, he and Marianne were work colleagues, so hanging together isn't completely unusual, but why in Rennes? Why not at the tavern? And why the lie about her cancer?

What shady business necessitated a trip out of town?

The world swims back into sharp focus, and I realize I'm standing in front of my old elven haven.

"The waitress told me she remembers Marianne handing a letter over to the man, and the man wheeling himself out of there without ordering anything to eat or drink. Considering this woman's background, I'm guessing the guy was a client who needed a graphologist to create a forgery of some sort. Want me to cross-check the date with anything that might have gone on locally?"

In other words: *fork over some more moolah or I'm done digging.* "You do that, and I'll wire over some more funds."

"You got it, boss."

I hang up and eye the heavy door with the Quatrefoil etched into the stone above it. I still know the code to the dorm building. All I'd need to do is pick my way into the room. At least I'd have a place for Spike to stay.

Or . . .

Or I could leave. Since Philippe remembers me, only those in Brume are part of the curse.

Yeah. I'm not leaving. Bastian and Cadence are here. Curse or no curse, they need me.

The keypad beeps once as the door unlocks. I head up the rickety stairs to cell number three, praying it isn't currently in use. It takes me only four seconds to pick the ancient lock. The room's exactly how I left it—bare mattress, empty dresser, puny nightstand, ugly armoire decked out with a bouncy spiderweb. I bet the squashed cockroach is still by the bed.

I flick on the lights and take a step, smacking my head on the low-hanging beam. Don't know about the cockroach yet, but the beam's still there. As I rub my forehead, I slide Spike onto the floor, pop his little friend onto the dresser, then delicately set my neon light next to the succulent and plug it in. Basking in its lime-green beam, I sink onto the bare mattress and strategize.

The crew needs me whether they realize it or not, and I need to solve the Quatrefoil puzzle in order to break my curse. Trying to convince them I'm not a stranger won't help with the puzzle. If anything it'll waste time, because I might get tased and tossed into Rainier's little shag-carpeted holding cell again.

Which leaves me with only one thing to do: convince the lot of them of my use and sanity.

I'm back at square one. I smile, because it reminds me of the snakes and ladders boardgame I used to play with Bastian, the one I painted on a piece of cardboard I'd fished out of a bin, because I didn't have twenty euros to buy him one of those pretty toy store ones.

No matter how many squares I'd tumble down, I always got up and went forward.

Cadence de Morel, be warned, I'm about to scale every fucking ladder in Brume to make it back to you.

The memory of Adrien's hand on my girl rids me of my smile but does wonders for my determination.

23

CADENCE

Adrien sets down the rolled-up *Kelouenn* on his glowing element. Nothing happens. He unrolls it. Still nothing. He drapes the parchment against the glowing jewel that showed us the vision of where to find it. Still nothing.

Same goes for the backpack full of bones Bastian and Alma collected from a corner of Papa's walk-in closet. Or rather, *Alma* collected. Bastian took one look at the patches of leathered skin swathing the skull and fainted, pulling down a shelf full of Papa's cashmere sweaters along with him. That charmed Alma more than any heroic act would have considering her passion for sensitive souls.

I was worried that Alma or Bastian touching anything related to the Quatrefoil would curse them, but, when we went through the *Kelouenn* again this afternoon, Adrien pointed out that only applied to our leaves and their manifestations. He even read the passage out loud to put my mind at ease.

Unfortunately, when it comes to the Quatrefoil, my mind's never at ease.

"Maybe you have the wrong items," Geoffrey declares.

How fitting he didn't say *we* since he didn't help look for anything, just barked directions while sucking down a glass of Sauvignon. I still can't believe he defeated the water fairy in the well on his own. He's so useless.

"Those are the right items, Geoffrey." Gaëlle moves the copper bonsai we located under Papa's pillow atop where my leaf sank into the clock. "Maybe we need to put them all on the clock at the same time?"

"Then we'll need to get the last items." Maman's sculpture shimmers in the milky light. "Are they still the same, Adrien?"

Since Adrien's crouched over the center dial, he touches the lit stones. "The plank from your dock." His eyes glaze over. "The one in which you and Alma carved your initials."

Alma's lips kick up while I blush because the A, in the A + C surrounded by a heart, doesn't stand for Alma; it stands for Adrien. Relief that he hasn't figured it out doesn't help temper my blush.

"There's pebbles and foam around it, so I'm imagining it's on the shore somewhere." He moves his fingers to the next glowing topaz. "We also have to get the . . ." He swallows.

My heated skin turns clammy, because I know what he's seeing. I almost go over to him and rest my hand on the juncture between his rigid shoulder blades but stop myself, because I shouldn't be touching him. However much I like Adrien, he's six years older than I am *and* a professor while I'm still a student. *His* student.

"Mom's cup." Another swallow.

The delicate porcelain one with the hand-painted flowers and scalloped rim still blemished by his mother's lipstick. The one Geoffrey kept despite the fact that it was the instrument to Camille's death. According to the mayor, he stored the cup on the top shelf of his kitchen, inside a Tupperware pot. Now, it's somewhere dark and small, a cupboard of sorts. Adrien and I turned my house upside down after we located the scroll amidst a tumble of fluffy towels in my dryer, but came up empty-handed.

"Any idea where it could be?" Alma asks.

I shake my head. "Only that it must be on First."

Since all the other things were located somewhere on First, we suspect this one is too. It's the conclusion Bastian came to during lunch, right before the strange guy arrived, the one who licked my ear. I reach up and touch my lobe which tingles, even though I'm neither into ear licking nor handsy strangers.

"Maybe it's inside a casket?" Alma claps her hand around Bastian's arm to prevent him from swooning.

Geoffrey's lips pinch, bracketed by so many fine lines it looks as though his skin's turned liquid and is rippling outward. For all his arrogance and gross fascination with my mother, he truly was in love with Camille.

Heaving a sigh, Adrien rises from his crouch. "Plank and cup. Who wants what?"

Father and son look so bereft I make my way to the plexiglass. "You and Geoffrey take the plank. Bastian and Alma will babysit the clock and all the objects we found. Gaëlle and I will take the cup."

Gaëlle's eyes whip up to mine as I land on the other side of the guardrail.

She palms her neck repeatedly. "Um, okay." Clearly, she's as excited as I am to go looking for the vessel that robbed us of Camille, but leaving the woman's son and husband to find it is too cruel.

"Don't forget your swim trunks!" I chirp, trying to lighten the atmosphere.

Adrien's expression eases. I think he mouths a *merci*, but he could just be stretching his jaw muscles.

"Swim trunks? It's the middle of winter. Why in the world would we wear swim trunks?" I hear Geoffrey ask his son as Gaëlle and I push out the library door.

I roll my eyes.

"Not the most potent potion on the shelf." Gaëlle wrangles her great mass of hair into a bun which she hooks into place with a clip she produces from her coat pocket. "So, where should we start? Town Hall?"

I bite my lip as we meander down the road toward Fourth. Only the gym and cafeteria glow, what with it being so late on a Sunday afternoon. Usually, the library would be in use as well, but Papa has barred it from the public for the time being. Sure, it's not destroyed anymore, but we don't need any lurkers snapping pictures of the clock that not only ticks but beams neon light from all four elements. In case some nosy professor or student stumbles upon the *dihuner*, he's prepped a plausible explanation, but hopefully, we won't need it. My father hates lying just as much as I do.

I text him to tell him about our lack of success, while Gaëlle phones Romain to tell him she'll be a little late, and could he bathe the twins?

PAPA: *You're probably right about needing all the pieces. Good thinking.*

ME: *All Gaëlle.*

PAPA: *Let me know what happens next. I may not be able to run around town, but I can help in other ways.*

Right as we pass under the clanking sign of Third, a heavy door thuds, and there, on the stone stoop of one of the dorm buildings, stands the boy who nipped my earlobe.

"So, he really is a student . . ." Gaëlle murmurs, while I just stare.

I don't realize how fast my heart is beating until I taste metal. Since it's not exertion that's boosted my pulse, I'm guessing it's fear. Except I don't feel very scared. I feel . . . *flummoxed*.

Especially when he strides over, his long legs devouring the icy cobbles. "Fancy running into you again, Mademoiselle de Morel." He peers down at me, hands nestled in his coat pockets. "Must be my lucky day."

I finally look past him, at the dorm. "You live *here*?"

He hooks a look over his shoulder and sighs. "Woefully, I do."

I cross my arms and square my shoulders. "When did you start at U of B?"

"At the beginning of January."

He's been here for a month? I iron out my surprise before it can transpire. "And where are you from?"

"Here and there, but my last residence was Marseille."

I frown because Bastian's from Marseille, and when we were at the tavern, Slate looked over at him and called out his name as though they knew each other, even though Bastian swears they don't.

"What are you studying?" I continue.

"At the present moment, your lovely face."

My cheeks blaze. "I meant, in college." Hopefully, the setting sun camouflages my blush. Of course, the second I think this, the cast-iron lantern overhead flares to life.

"Astronomy."

"Really?" I cock up an eyebrow. "I'm in that class, and I've never seen you there."

"I sit in the back."

"Maybe I do as well."

"No. You like the front row."

The vein in my neck throbs and throbs because it's true. I do like to sit at the front. I tighten my arms in front of my chest, hoping to tame my heartbeats. "What's the name of the professor?"

"Claire Robinson." He says this with zero hesitation.

Gaëlle touches my arm. "Cadence, I suspect this young man truly attends our college."

The lantern glazes Slate's mussed black curls, one of which has tangled into his thick, sooty eyelashes. Everything about this boy is so very dark. "So, what are you two ladies up to?"

"Nothing," I lie.

"May I join you in doing nothing?"

"Why?"

"Because it's dark out, and it wouldn't feel right to let you two wander these streets alone. What if there's another earthquake that makes the kelc'hs spin? I wouldn't want either of you to be tossed into the lake. I hear the water temperature isn't too pleasant at this time of year." Under his breath, he adds, "I suspect, at any time of year."

"That's very considerate of you," Gaëlle says.

I balk. She can't seriously be considering his offer. The guy licked my freaking ear and called me his girlfriend!

"No." I shake my head, hook my arm back through Gaëlle's, and stalk away. "Absolutely not. I'm not bringing a stranger along. Especially one who looks so . . . so . . ." I glance over my shoulder at the black-eyed boy with the dense stubble and unruly hair we've left behind.

"Cute?"

I whip my attention back toward Gaëlle. She's smiling. *Smiling.* "More like, wicked."

"But he is quite cute."

"Kittens are cute. That guy's *not* a kitten."

Her features, which have been strained ever since Geoffrey stole the ring off my mother's cold hand and put it on, soften a little. "Honey, I know it's none of my business, but Adrien—"

"That's not why I'm turning down a stroll with a rando, Gaëlle."

My skin heats up some more, and even though it's probably minus twenty, I unzip my coat. "You and Matthias had a thirteen-year gap."

Her face warps, and I feel awful stirring up painful memories, but I don't want to discuss my crush, or have anyone diabolizing it.

"We did, but we started seeing each other when I was in my late twenties. At that point, a decade doesn't make much of a difference." She pats the forearm I've looped through hers. "At the end of the day, though, I'll support anything you choose, because I know you're so much more mature than most eighteen-year-olds. Almost eighteen. Speaking of, do you want the same *magie noire* birthday cake as I make you *each and every* year?"

My throat bobs with a swallow, because what if I don't reach my next birthday?

Don't go there, Cadence. Magic or no magic, I'll blow out eighteen candles next month. I tighten my resolve until optimism seeps through my pessimism and lightens my footfalls. "Why change a winning team?"

We start at Town Hall, searching every nook and cranny and drawer. We empty the display case in the entryway, the one that holds pieces of Brumian history: a wooden sign that reads *First Kelc'h* dating back to medieval times, before the copper ones were hung; a map of Brittany drawn on a piece of aged parchment, which I believe should be preserved in the archival room; an ancient, cross-shaped paving stone whose four sides are painted a different color: blue, green, red, and white; a lead bucket and rotted rope from the *puits fleuri.*

We look behind it all, under it all. Nothing. We move on to Geoffrey's apartment at the top of the government building, which the night watchman unlocks for us. Gaëlle takes the rose-velvet boudoir that Camille used as a study, because I can't step into that room without seeing her body slouched over her desk. I wasn't the one to find her, and I never actually saw any crime-scene pictures, but my mind's conjured up the moment so many times over the last four years that it almost feels like I was there, standing beside her as she drank her arsenic tea and rested her cheek on her suicide note.

We find no plastic container containing a cup in Geoffrey's home, only dust balls. Just as we step past the tall gates surrounding Town Hall, the tree branches over our heads begin to rattle and a shudder races through the cobbles.

"What now?" Gaëlle moans.

"Grab on to something!" a deep voice bellows.

I assume it's the night watchman but find the black-haired boy sprint-stumbling toward us.

The ground heaves, and I lurch forward, reaching out for the cast-iron fence but merely grazing it.

"Crap," I mutter as the ground bucks again, and I'm thrown backward. I make contact with a human body that smells of sweet spice and charred coffee.

Arms wind around me just as the boy's baritone tickles my ear, "Always falling into my arms, princess."

I blink. Then blink again, because what the hell? "I don't recall *ever* falling into your arms."

I can't be sure, because the wind's howling through the trembling town, and the waves are crashing upon the lake shore, but I think he whispers, "One day soon, you will."

24

SLATE

The shaking stops almost as soon as it started, though I manage to keep Cadence in my arms a few more beats. When she finally pulls away, a shadow of confusion passes over her flushed face, because she's feeling the same way I am . . . that we fit together like—

"Did you follow us?" she hisses.

Apparently, our thoughts aren't aligned. "Only to keep you safe." When her eyes narrow, I add, "This town's eerie."

"Did the *kelc'hs* spin again?" Gaëlle picks up her phone from the snow, wipes it on the hem of her coat, then taps it before lifting it to her ear. "Romain, honey, are you all right? . . . The boys? . . . *Merci, mon Dieu.*"

"Adrien!" Cadence exclaims. "He was on the shore. I hope he's okay." She takes out her phone, quickly tacking on, "And Geoffrey, too."

Fuck me. One memory blip, and Cadence is back to being hot for her teacher.

After a rapid phone conversation with Prickhead, she announces, "They're on their way here," then taps her screen a few more times before exhaling. "And Papa's fine, but our generator went out for a few seconds. It's back on, though."

"Glad Papa's okay." The sarcasm slips out before I can think better of it. I'm trying to get them to like me, not think I'm an arrogant prick.

Gaëlle blinks at me. "How come you're here?"

Cadence's phone vibrates. *Alma* flashes on the screen. In a pitch that leaps out of the receiver, she screeches, "The objects! They're all gone!"

My brows collide. "What does she mean, gone?"

Cadence puts the call on speakerphone.

Alma's voice echoes loudly. "They just dematerialized. Faded. Right before our eyes. But Bastian and I aren't *diwallers* so maybe we just can't see them anymore?"

"Where are they?" I ask Cadence.

"The library," she answers, then frowns. "Why am I telling you?"

"Wait! Who is that? Is that the guy from the tavern?" Alma asks.

"The one and only. The original." When Cadence's brow lifts, I stop talking.

"What's he doing there?" Alma whispers, probably believing she's not on speakerphone.

"I was worried." I pretend to readjust my gloves. "There've been so many earthquakes around these parts. You'd think Brume sits on its very own fault line."

Cadence shoots me a pointed look, which I catch thanks to Gaëlle using her phone's flashlight like a lightsaber. "Can we refocus?"

"I'll call Rainier." Gaëlle slices through the darkness once more before poking her screen. "To check if the bonsai's back under his pillow."

Rainier doesn't pick up.

"I'll just pop over and—" Gaëlle starts to back up but then eyes me. "Actually, let's wait for Adrien and Geoffrey to arrive."

Even though I get this means she doesn't trust me, I still appreciate her intentions.

They keep discussing the Case of the Missing Objects, and it distracts them so much that Cadence and Gaëlle forget I'm here. I take advantage of that and step just outside the trickle of yellow light spilling from the lamppost. I need to figure out how to gain passage into their little posse.

The darkness slips over me and tosses me years backward, to the shadowy closet doors and narrow bed slats I'd stare at unblinkingly, until the scuffing waltz of a drunken foster parent or the quieter gait of the truly sick ones vanished back down the hall.

I swore once I got old enough, I would never hide again.

This is different, but it still leaves a bitter aftertaste.

Professor Prickhead's super slug of a dad arrives, slightly out of breath and empty-handed. Geoffrey makes a sweeping gesture to include the whole town. "The *kelc'hs* haven't moved. But the plank's gone. It was in my hands when the ground shook and then it vanished."

"Same with the objects on the clock!" Alma shouts from the phone.

"Where's Adrien?" Cadence squints into the obscurity behind Geoffrey.

Geoffrey lights a cigarette, the end glowing brighter as he takes a puff. As usual, his eyes graze over Cadence longer than they should. I ball my hands into fists.

"He went back up to the clock to see what the stones say. To check if our task has changed."

Gaëlle frowns. "Why would it?"

Geoffrey lets out a long stream of smoke. "If all the items disappeared, we need to know if we're still supposed to hunt for them, and if so, are they all where they were before."

"He's here!" Alma says, just as a heavy clang echoes over the receiver. "Adrien's here!"

After a minute of quick chit-chat with Alma and Bastian about the vanished items, Adrien's voice crackles over the phone. "The stones are still showing me the same visions."

"The star hand moved, though." I hear Bastian say in the background. "It's returned to where it was when we started last night."

Geoffrey glances at his Apple watch. How very twenty-first century of him. "Twenty-four hours exactly. Guess we had a deadline."

Cadence bites down hard on her bottom lip, worry dancing in her eyes. "And what? There's no consequence? We're just granted a do-over? This doesn't sound at all like the Quatrefoil."

"Look around you, Cadence. Everyone's safe." Gaëlle squeezes her arm, but my girl's brows stay knitted.

Is she thinking of Emilie and how we thought everyone was safe before the kid showed up like a hologram in my dorm room a day after running into Matthias's ghost? Because that's where my mind's gone.

Alma sighs. "Maybe it's taking pity on us, and we're getting a no-strings-attached do-over?"

"Pity?" Cadence sputters.

Right there with you, princess. The Quatrefoil hath no pity.

The ticking *dihuner* drones from Cadence's phone, the perfect soundtrack to this eerie town.

"Whoa. Wait!" Bastian exclaims.

Geoffrey coughs, retches, then spits. Once he's done being classy, the *tick tick tick* comes back into sharp focus.

"It's faster!"

Cadence's eyes dart to Gaëlle, then to Geoffrey.

"You're right." Adrien's voice rends the silence. "Twice as fast."

"So, what?" Gaëlle messes with her curly hair. "We have half the time to find the items this round?"

Geoffrey flicks the ashes of his cigarette, and they almost land on my boot. "Better start now if we only have twelve hours to lug all the stuff to Fifth and put them on the clock."

Wait. *What?* Why would they haul everything to Fifth? Was no one listening when I told them what the skeleton said last night? That it wanted to go *home*?

Guess this is my moment. "You guys have got it wrong," I tell them as I step out into the light. "The items don't go *on* the clock."

The shock on everyone's faces confirms they'd completely forgotten I was there.

Stings.

Geoffrey yanks the cigarette from his mouth, crushing it between his index and thumb. "You're the kid from the tavern."

I telegraph my thoughts on being called a kid with a lingering glare.

"He was worried about Cadence." Gaëlle wears a small smile, as though deciding I'm sweet. Hopefully she'll find me trustworthy next.

One person on team-New Slate. A handful to go.

"Rainier let you off without even a tap on the wrist? If that's the case, the man's going soft—"

"You're talking about my father, Geoffrey, so careful what you say."

Cadence and Geoffrey stare at each other a few heartbeats before he sighs and turns to me.

"Get." He wriggles his fingers toward the road. "None of this concerns you."

"Ah." I lean against the lamppost. Put my boot up. "You're never going to defeat the Quatrefoil and get that ring off Cadence's finger if you do it wrong."

Cadence's mouth parts. "How—"

"How do I know that? Because . . ." I pause while I think up a good lie. "Because I love history, especially Brumian history. It's the reason I came to this college."

"You said you were studying astronomy."

"Right. Double major."

They all blink at me.

"I recently got to read *Istor Breou*." The lie comes out so fast my brain has trouble catching up with my tongue, but then it all clicks, and I forge on. "And other interesting materials about Merlin, Viviene, and the infamous Quatrefoil."

Cadence's brows slope toward her nose. "Who let you into the archives?"

"The librarian on duty that day. I don't remember her name. Unlike you, she didn't leave much of an impression."

Even though Cadence crosses her arms and lifts her chin, a blush streaks her cheekbones.

I hold both my palms up in the air. "I swear I only followed you guys to help."

Anger glosses her eyes and absconds with her blush. "If you're here to *help*, then what the hell were you playing at back at the tavern when you licked my ear and called Bastian your brother?"

"I . . ." I scratch the back of my head, trying to come up with a valid excuse. "You're a tightknit group, and . . . well . . . it made me socially awkward."

"You mean, socially impudent?" Geoffrey butts in.

I stop scratching my head. That's fresh coming from this leering old man. *You need to win them over,* I remind myself, setting aside my antipathy. "Yes."

See me, Cadence. Remember me.

Her eyes don't soften.

"What I said and did was out of line. I'm sorry about that." And I mean it. I don't ever want Cadence to be on the receiving end of something she doesn't want. Even if it's from me.

"And what?" Cadence asks. "You expect us to trust you? We have no idea who you are."

Intellectually, I know she doesn't remember me and I shouldn't take offense, but emotionally, her words scrape out my insides like a grapefruit spoon.

"I'm Slate Ardoin, student and lover of Brume." *What a load of shit.* "Look, I know about you putting the Quatrefoil together. I know about this strange little treasure hunt that the celestial dial of the clock is sending you on. I'm not here to hinder you. I'm here to help. Trust. Me."

"How do you know all that?" Gaëlle's fingers have stilled in her hair. That woman really needs a new scarf or she'll be bald by the end of this hunt. "Have you been eavesdropping on our conversations?"

"Just now. You were talking about it. That's how I know about the hunt. About the rest, I saw the clock and the destruction."

Cadence's brow flattens, and I don't blame her—my story has so many holes it's a sieve—but she needs to set her suspicion aside and listen.

"You *saw*?" Geoffrey guffaws. "Dear boy, that's impossible."

"I know it sounds crazy because everyone else has forgotten, but I swear I saw it all and remember it all."

"Adrien had some pictures on his phone, and even those are all gone," Gaëlle says.

"On my birth certificate, it says I come from here, so maybe I have *diwaller* blood?"

"You *know* about *diwallers*?" Gaëlle's eyes are huge.

Cadence hugs her arms around her jacket. "They're mentioned in *Istor Breou.*"

"Look, I heard you say the skeleton wanted to be brought home. Skeletons' homes are usually graves." Although it looked quite cozy in Rainier's closet. "My guess is that you probably have to put all the stuff you find back where it's supposed to go."

Geoffrey drops his cigarette, not bothering to snuff it out under his shoe. As it hits the snow, it hisses. "You said you were born here. Who are your parents?"

"There were no names on my birth certificate. Just a time and place. I assumed I was Eugenia and Oscar Roland's, but apparently they didn't have a son." Annoyance tightens my jaw. "I'll gladly sit down with you at a later date to unearth whose bastard son I could be, but exploring my genealogical tree isn't going to help Cadence get that damn ring off her finger."

Her eyes expand at my determination to save her beautiful, cursed ass.

"What Slate says makes sense." Gaëlle joggles her head. "About putting objects back in their rightful spot. What do we have to lose by trying it? If it doesn't work, we forfeit an hour. Probably less since everything's on First anyway."

"Fine, let's try it," Geoffrey says, just as Adrien, Bastian, and Alma reach us, all three panting like they've run uphill instead of down.

Adrien digs his fingers into a stitch in his side. "How I miss the *kelc'h* staircases." Suddenly, he straightens, and his breath stops pluming out of his mouth. "What is this guy doing here?"

"He saved Cadence," Gaëlle volunteers with a bright smile.

"He didn't save me," she mumbles.

"He's apparently of *diwaller* descent." Geoffrey pats down his gray hair. "He remembers what Brume looked like before the earthquake."

Adrien slides me a look. "Really?"

He and Cadence are one tough audience.

"He suggested we put the things we find in their original spots." Gaëlle pulls on her coat lapels, nestling her face so far into it that her nose vanishes. "And if he's wrong, we start over. *Again.*"

Cadence's phone buzzes in her palm. She glances at the screen, then answers with warmth in her voice, "Yes, Papa?" As she listens, her hand crawls up to her mouth. "No. Oh, no, no . . . I'll be right there." She hangs up, hands shaking. "Something's happened to Solange."

We should've known that failing comes at a price.

25

CADENCE

We all stumble into the kitchen, shady new guy included, to come upon Papa wielding a broom handle like a cattle prod. A drooling, snarling Solange keeps reaching for him, her hands curled like talons. Her usually dewy skin is now a pasty gray, bits of it rotting. A fly sits on the globe of her right eyeball, and she doesn't even blink it away.

Geoffrey lifts his coat collar to his nose. "She smells as bad as the hawthorn did. Possibly worse. Absolutely revolting."

I resist both the urge to vomit and to cry. Gaëlle leans over the sink and does both.

Papa pushes Solange back with a hard shove of the broom. "Get her out of here!"

"I'll grab her. Lock her up in a room." Adrien takes a step toward her.

Slate catches his arm. "However much I'd appreciate you becoming a zombie, Prof, I don't think direct contact is too swell an idea. Ever seen an apocalypse film?"

"Don't call me Prof and don't touch me." He plucks Slate's fingers off his herringbone jacket, then wipes his sleeve a tad too dramatically.

"He's right, Adrien." God, I hate to admit it. "You shouldn't touch her. What if the zombie stories are true, and a bite or scratch is contagious?"

Slate swipes the broomstick from Papa's hands and pushes Solange back with the end. "Why is she like this, de Morel?" He makes it sound like Papa's personally responsible.

"Because we failed," I say.

"Right. But why *her*"—he gestures to Solange with his chin before turning to Papa—"and not *him*?"

The whir of Papa's wheelchair as he reverses undercuts Solange's snarling. "How should I know? One minute she was suggesting the week's menu and the next she was trying to make me part of it. She transformed in a matter of seconds."

"One person cursed per fail? So if we fail again, you might be drooling along with her?" Slate says to Papa, his tone almost upbeat.

At the same time as Solange lunges for Slate, cutting off further speculation, Bastian proceeds to the industrial-sized fridge and rummages around.

Alma whisper-hisses, "How can you be hungry at a time like this?"

He takes a large bundle wrapped in brown butcher-paper, opens it, letting the paper and drippings fall to the floor, then wiggles a pink cut of veal. "Here, zombie, zombie! Come and get it!"

Solange's nostrils flare and then she's turning in slow motion and inching toward Bastian.

I give him a thumbs-up and gesture for him to follow me as I back out of the kitchen, my rubber soles squeaking against the foyer's marble floor. When I reach the guest toilet under the stairs, I wrench the skeleton key hanging from the inside lock.

"Lead her in here," I say calmly, so as not to spook Solange. Can zombies even be spooked? They probably do all the spooking.

Bastian jiggles the raw steak in the air as he adjusts his route. Solange follows docilely, moving so slowly she looks like a character in a flipbook.

Slate closes the rear, clutching the broomstick in his hands like a raised sword. "Whatever you do, don't let her touch you." His voice is edged with real panic.

Solange claws at the air, blackened nails almost making contact with Bastian's raised hand.

Slate whacks her wrist with the broom. "For fuck's sake, be careful, bro!"

The impact splits her gray skin. Pus oozes from the wound and dribbles down the sleeve of her button-down blue uniform.

I flatten myself against the wall as Bastian reaches me at a full trot now. He lobs the steak into the bathroom. The raw meat hits the striped black-and-silver wallpaper with a wet slap before slithering down onto the china tank.

Solange stops, rheumy eyes locked on us. Slate raises the broom and hovers it in front of my chest. In front of Bastian's too. A slender fence between us and my plagued housekeeper.

The fly drones on her eyeball but doesn't take off. Her upper lip hikes up, revealing rotted teeth and sore-infested gums. Any higher, and we'll get a glimpse of the cartilage in her nose. She cranks up her head and sniffs the air.

In slow motion, her face rotates toward the toilet tank and then the rest of her body.

"Get behind me," Slate whispers.

Bastian and I creep along the wall like spiders and then peel ourselves away. Where Bastian puts a kilometer between him and the creature toddling into the bathroom, I remain right behind Slate, so close that my breath lifts the hair curling at the nape of his neck.

I'm itching to shove her inside, but she's cursed, and won't get uncursed if I morph into a zombie too.

Finally ... *finally*, she crosses the threshold.

Slate lunges and grabs the chrome handle. He rams the door shut with a loud thwack. "The key! Where's the key to—"

"Right here." I sidestep him and fit the metal into the slot just as the doorknob starts rattling. My heart drills my ribs, and my fingers slicken. The key dips, then falls to the floor with a hollow clank that my eardrums barely register over my thundering pulse.

"Take your time, Cadence," Slate murmurs. "I've got the door. She's not coming out."

"Okay." I lick my lips. "Okay." I crouch, scoop up the key, and tighten my grip on the metal. And then I perform the inhuman task of inserting the key in the lock and making it click while thinking how fortunate it is that this is a two-way lock.

There's banging and moaning, but the door stays sealed.

I let out a protracted breath and wipe the sweat beading along my brow as we head back to the kitchen.

Smiling, Slate sets down the broom. "Look how good a team you and I make."

"Let's not forget Bastian."

Slate looks in the direction of our shaking zombie lure who keeps repeating, "I can't believe I did that," his face rivaling Solange in its colorlessness.

"That was really brave of you, B." Alma pushes up on her tiptoes and plants a kiss on his cheek.

He freezes, and his eyes grow wide. Finally, he shrugs off his daze. "It was in the *Kelouenn*."

"What was?" Adrien's leaning against the kitchen doorframe, arms crossed, expression closed off.

"The curse of the undead. The drawings were kind of primitive, but now it makes sense. It wasn't a corpse but an undead."

Adrien blinks. "So the drawings outside the quatrefoil shape represent the new curses . . ." He pulls out his phone and begins scrolling through the images he's saved. "I'm guessing the rest of these indicate more—"

"Any tips in the *Kelouenn* on how to revive the undead?" Alma nervously twirls a lock of hair around her finger.

"The text passages were harder to interpret. I'm not sure—"

"The clock!" Slate gasps. "I think it's tipping us off."

"*Us?*" I ask at the same time as Adrien says, "How?"

Slate's eyes have gone a little hazy, as though he's up in the temple instead of here with us. "The constellation of Wrongful Death."

We all stare at him. *How? How does he know?*

Bastian's the first to recover. "According to Mademoiselle Claire, the constellation represents the hidden secrets of murderers. You guys think there's a correlation between the items we're finding and *actual* murders?" He drops his voice on that last bit, even though there are thankfully no murderers around.

"Cadence, a word?" Papa, who's wheeled himself beside Adrien, snaps his head toward the living room, eyes excavating a hole in Slate's chest.

Sighing, because I know what this is about, I follow him into the dimly-lit room.

"Why is this stranger in our home?"

"Because he has *diwaller* blood."

Papa laughs, but it's not a melodious sound. It's more of a bark-sneer. "Don't tell me you believe him?"

"He remembers the destruction, Papa."

My father is definitely no longer laughing. "He also remembers being Oscar and Eugenia's son, and they didn't have one."

I bit my lip. "He must be of *diwaller* descent, though. No one else remembers."

"Unless a Keene, a Bisset, or a Mercier had an illegitimate child —and as far as I know, none did—then I don't see whom he's descended from. Certainly not from your mother."

I hadn't even considered Slate could be my half-brother but am extremely relieved he isn't. I'm not even sure why, really. I always wanted a sibling even though Alma more than made up for the lack of one.

"I suppose, if he's anyone's kid, it would be Geoffrey's. That man scuttled after anything with a pulse in his younger days." Papa's lips pinch in disgust, probably because he's remembering when Adrien's father had a thing for my mother. "I'll call Sylvie. She can collect a hair sample and map out his—"

"Papa, I don't think now's the time to look into his DNA. We need to focus on the Quatrefoil hunt."

"And, what? You're planning on letting the impostor tag along?"

"I don't think he's an impostor." Although . . .

No, he remembers.

Unless he heard us discussing the destruction?

Papa continues. "What if he's an embodiment of dark magic?"

"I don't think so, but everything is different this time."

Papa forges on, "Perhaps he's part of your trial, and you have to defeat him."

"I've already gotten my leaf. And he wasn't in any of the visions in the stones . . ."

"Sorry to bother you, Rainier"—Alma pops her head into the doorway—"but can Bastian and I go into your closet to collect the bones?"

My father's eyes bulge. "There are *more* bones?"

"No, the same ones." I stare past him at the starlit frozen lake shining behind the mist like a fogged-up mirror. "The clock's reset everything, because apparently, we have a time constraint." My spine prickles with remorse. "Which is why Solange was punished. Because we failed."

"And now we have half the time because the clock's going crazy. So, do we have permission to enter your closet, Rainier?" The blue Ikea bag Alma must've found in the kitchen closet crinkles like the tarp which covered the broken cupola until the Quatrefoil magically repaired it.

It gives me hope that Solange isn't doomed, but then my gaze alights upon the lake again, and I think of Emilie. Emilie, who hasn't returned. I rang her mother's doorbell this morning to check.

My lids shut for a fraction of a second. When I raise them, Alma's no longer in the wide doorway, and the others' voices ring against the marble in the foyer.

"I have to go. We need to finish this hunt before anyone else gets hurt." First stop, my father's bedroom to grab my mother's bonsai. Twisted Quatrefoil that it is put her sculpture underneath his giant goose-down pillow.

"Why did we sign up for this task again, Alma?" Bastian grumbles as he follows Alma up the stairs, complexion ashen and slightly green.

She rolls her eyes. "Because we've already been there. Done that. I know where every phalanx lies."

"I'll go get the plank from your dock," Geoffrey announces on his way out the door.

"By the way, did you guys locate the"—Adrien's throat bobs—"you know . . . before—"

"I'll get the scroll." Gaëlle rushes across the foyer in an evident hurry to be off the teacup search party.

I shake my head. "I'll get back to looking for it. It wasn't in Town Hall, so it has to be here."

"Unless it's in the cemetery?" Slate suggests.

The thought wraps my skin with another layer of ice. "It was in a really small place. Like a cupboard. Not a . . . casket." I swallow. "Adrien, how about you help Gaëlle put the scroll back in the plexiglass case. Actually, get the bonsai. I'll continue looking for the last item."

A raspy voice drones in my ear, "I guess you and I are on cup-duty, princess."

I look up into the boy's chiseled face, at the hard cut of his jaw dusted in thick, black stubble. "There is no *you and I*, and please stop calling me princess."

The stranger presses his lips together.

"Since the kid wants to help, why doesn't he go collect the bones?" Adrien's glowering at Slate. "And you and I can get the bonsai, Cadence."

"For fuck's sake, I'm not a kid. As for the bones, the last time I . . ." He moistens his lips with the tip of his tongue. "The last time I got together with a skeleton, it wasn't pretty. For neither the skeleton nor me."

"Not *pretty*?" Adrien asks the question on everyone's mind.

A beat. Then, "I'm skeletonphobic."

"And you think Alma and I aren't?" Bastian wraps his hands around the wrought-iron rail and stares down at us from the first-floor landing. I guess he stayed out of the closet this time.

"What I think is that Cadence's father doesn't want a total stranger pulling the skeletons out of his closet. Right, de Morel?" I can't tell if Slate's holding back a grin or a grimace.

I peer over my shoulder at where Papa sits, the edges of his body highlighted orange from the glow of the living room.

"Right. I neither want you near my things nor near my daughter."

"Papa," I hiss. "Stop it."

Breathing a little hard, Gaëlle streaks back across the foyer, gripping the folded scroll. "Got it."

"Adrien's going to help you frame it," I say. "And, Adrien, maybe try a flashlight or something, see if it's possible to view the words behind the ink stain?"

Something pings behind us. Papa's chrome lighter lies on the floor. I head over to pick it up for him. His hands are shaking. This perverse treasure hunt must be dredging up such terrible memories for him.

I give him the lighter, then squeeze his hand. "Why don't you go watch some TV? Get your mind off all of this?"

"*Non.* I'll go up to my office to help them with the scroll."

Papa watches Slate like a disgruntled hawk as he drives himself over to the glass elevator.

When the doors slide open, Slate steps in front of me, probably to become the sole focus of my attention. "What closets and cupboards haven't you searched?"

I appreciate his pragmatism. And I also appreciate not being alone on this quest. My heart's already too full of grief. I list all the places we've searched, which turns out, is everywhere but the attic and garage.

"Just follow me." I lead Slate up the stairs.

"To the ends of the earth."

His reply makes me stub my foot on the first step.

Slate catches my flailing arm and steadies me. "Whoa there, prin—Cadence."

I blink into his thickly-lashed eyes, then blink again, because I have this very odd sense of déjà vu, or rather, *déjà entendu*, as though someone uttered this very unoriginal line to me recently.

"Are you okay?" His eyebrows lower, darkening his irises which are actually a deep mahogany and not a moonless-black.

"Sorry, I—um . . ." I rub my temple and ease my arm from his grip. "It's been a long day." Dwelling on my auditory hallucination keeps me distracted and silent during all three flights of stairs. Not that Slate's attempting small talk. Judging by his wandering eye, he's much too intrigued by the manor I live in, and judging by his quiet smile, much too entertained by Bastian's intermittent squealing followed by Alma's raucous laughter.

Once we reach the attic stairs, I pause to down several lungfuls of oxygen.

"What is it?"

"Nothing."

"It's not nothing." Slate raises his hand, as though to cup my cheek, but must think better of touching me, because he balls his fingers into a fist and lowers them.

"My mother's things are in boxes up there." It's not like I haven't been up there recently. I did find my New Year's Eve costume inside a trunk of her clothes.

Concern etches fine lines across his brow. "Wait down here then."

As he reaches for the door handle, I suck my lower lip into my mouth, then release it on a deep exhale. "It's okay."

I'm about to face stacks of boxes, not a decomposing corpse. I almost tell Slate what Geoffrey did on New Year's Eve, desecrating our mausoleum, but think better of sharing too much information, because what if Slate *is* a charlatan?

I glance up at him, and he gives me an encouraging smile.

I find myself kind of liking whatever he is.

I'm just not entirely certain why.

26

SLATE

The attic is a bust.

We spend more than two hours unpacking and repacking boxes and trunks full of junk with nothing to show for it. As Cadence pulls out her mother's old clothing, books, and photos, I need to refrain from wrapping my arms around her and kissing the top of her head. She fingers all the objects with a haunted expression on her face. It occurs to me that neither of us ever really knew our mothers. Yeah, she's heard stories from her dad and has all these items to sift through, but, like me, she doesn't remember the sound of her mother's voice, or the lilt of her laugh, or the warmth of her touch.

I pick up a creased photo. The colors are muted and the focus slightly off, obviously taken before digital cameras were a thing. In it, Rainier and Amandine grin at the camera. Behind them are others. A man with his arms around a woman who bears a striking resemblance to Gaëlle. All of them are on ice skates, holding on to each other for dear life.

They look . . . *joyful*.

It strikes me that, since arriving in Brume, I've never seen Rainier smile. I find it hard to pair the man I know with the one in the picture. And then I think: *Magic blew his life apart, too.*

Magic took his friends from him. Took his wife and his ability to walk.

Never thought I'd have empathy for the guy.

Cadence's eyes mist over when she spots the glossy photograph tucked in my hands. "Those are Gaëlle's parents. *Were*. Pierre and Audrey. She passed away from cancer when Gaëlle was twelve, and he died while trying to collect the leaves—he went after the wrong one." She stares down at the scene, shaking her head. "Look at my dad. He looks so . . ."

"Happy?" I venture.

"Yeah. Happy. Carefree." Her eyes meet mine, and immediately my chest constricts because her expression is so damn desolate.

Magic didn't take Cadence from Rainier, but I almost did. Maybe that's why he's so abrasive with me. Why he encouraged me to jump off a roof. Practically pushed me himself.

If I tell Cadence the truth about the night the ring came off, how desperate he was to end me, maybe she'll see her daddy for who he is.

But I can't do that to her. Not yet.

And certainly not now.

I throw the photo back into the shoebox. "Time to move on to the garage."

Cadence nods, and from the quick way she darts out, I can tell she's relieved to leave this gabled, dusty memory trove.

On the way down, she checks her phone. "Alma and Bastian are having a hard time figuring out which grave the skeleton came from. They're going through the plots one by one." At the sound of animalistic mewling and splintering wood, her gaze snaps off her phone and sets on our makeshift zombie jail cell. "How long do you think Solange'll be contained?"

"How thick is your door?"

"Thick. I think."

"Any idea where we could get some two-by-fours?"

"Um. No. But once we're done, I can help you look for some."

I like having a shared project to look forward to.

Cadence leads me into the kitchen and then through a door I have yet to step past, into a space that stinks of motor oil and bleach. Florescent lights buzz to life in a spasmic burst and reveal the cleanest garage I've ever laid eyes on. The walls are a pristine white. Every item—from empty flower pots to tools to the ladder—

has a delineated space on the wall. Apart from the recycling bins and a riding lawn mower, the only other thing not hanging or on a shelf is a van with wheelchair access.

"Is it the house elf that's this OCD or your father?"

A soft groove indents the smooth skin between Cadence's brows. "House elf?"

Regret rocks my stomach as *I* remember us having this conversation but *she* doesn't. "Forget it," I mutter, poking around.

We're another thirty minutes into the search when I hear Cadence gasp. I turn away from the toolbox I'm prying open to see her standing next to the passenger side door of the van, one hand covering her mouth.

There, in the glovebox, is a clear plastic Tupperware container housing a flowered porcelain teacup stained with brick-red lipstick.

Kaoc'h. I was hoping to be the one to find it so I could spare her.

"Hey." My gaze collides with hers.

She stares at me, her pupils so enlarged they nearly blot out the blue. I squeeze her arm and wait a beat for her to push me away. When she doesn't, I slide my hand to her back and gently tug her toward me until I can feel the warmth of her breaths through my sweater. She hesitates before resting her cheek against my chest.

I drop my chin and inhale the scent of her shampoo, the silk of her hair. It takes everything in me not to kiss her right there and then.

Slowly, she eases out of my arms and clears her throat, skating her palms up and down her arms. I hope it's the biting cold air and not an endeavor to wipe away the residue of our hug.

"Sorry. I . . . Sorry." Suddenly, I feel like twelve-year-old me, the kid with a crackling voice and an inability to talk to girls. I run a hand through my hair and clear my own throat before taking the plastic container from the glovebox. "So this is what we're looking for?"

Cadence nods, keeping her eyes on the clear plastic and the cup beyond it.

I tuck the thing under my arm to get it out of her sight and close the glovebox. "Let's go, then."

But when I move toward the door, Cadence is still rooted in place.

"Cadence?"

"The note's in there."

"What?"

"Her suicide note. It's in the box." Her voice unravels with each word.

I set the box on the passenger seat and pry open the top. A poof of chamomile escapes as I extricate the folded piece of stationery from underneath the teacup. Like the porcelain, it's decorated with stamped pink roses and hand-drawn ribbons. I scan the letter, which reads more like a literary novel than a note someone would write before poisoning themselves.

My dearest Geoffrey, my dearest Adrien,

For years now, I've struggled to rid myself of the demons of my past. Guilt, sorrow, and regret reside so deep in my soul they devour any happiness or peace that comes my way. I cannot live with all these feelings any longer. I ask you to forgive me and to go on with your lives without shedding a tear for me. Allow yourselves to be happy and free. Know that I am in a better place where despair cannot come for me.

Yours truly,
Camille

Cadence whispers, "I still can't believe she did it. I mean, I didn't live with her, but I saw her every single day when I was growing up. She was like a mother to me. I swear she wasn't depressed. Not one bit."

"Sometimes people are really good at pretending." I know from experience that it's possible to wear lies like full-body armor.

"Maybe. Yet I'm not the only one who couldn't believe it." She shakes her head like she's hoping to get rid of old ghosts. "Geoffrey had a graphologist analyze her handwriting to be sure it wasn't staged."

Blood pounds through my eardrums. "Which graphologist?"

"A professor named Marianne Shafir." She eases the suicide note from my clenched fingers and replaces it in the box, which she clicks shut. "She's dead now too."

Ice. My blood becomes ice. And then thaws and turns into lava.

The letter Philippe said Marianne handed Rainier wasn't for some get-rich-quick scheme—it was Camille's note! Camille's note, which Marianne herself wrote and then Marianne herself authenticated. This is what the wire transfers Rainier made from my account were about!

I grab onto the car door to steady my rage. There's no doubt left in my mind that the son-of-a-bitch killed Adrien's mother. But *why*? What did she have on him?

"Slate, are you okay?"

I shake my head. "Sorry," I mutter. "Just a dizzy spell. I skipped lunch."

Cadence hugs the box against her chest. "We'll grab something from the kitchen on our way out."

"Wait." I touch her shoulder. "Text Bastian and Alma to check Camille's grave." Then something else occurs to me. "And Marianne Shafir's too, while they're at it."

Her eyebrows slant. "Okay . . ." She pulls out her phone and one-handedly types out my message. "Done. Now let's go." As we head back into the kitchen, she nods to the chrome and wood bread box.

I open it and extract a slightly crusty baguette. Even though my stomach's a pit of snakes, I chomp on it as I trail Cadence out into the foyer where her undead houseguest is still using the door and walls as a drum set.

Cadence calls out, "Papa, we found the teacup! We're off to Town Hall."

The squeak of wheels on marble stops us, and then de Morel's frosty eyes settle on the container. He doesn't look alarmed. He really should be. "Where was it?"

I'm foaming at the mouth to yell, "Murderer!" Instead, I take a large bite of afternoon-old bread and work the crusty dough until it's mush between my molars.

"In the van." Cadence releases a deep sigh. "The Quatrefoil's so twisted."

I pulverize another chunk of baguette.

Magic didn't strip him of all his friends. Nope. He stripped himself of one. Maybe he stripped himself of the others.

I go through the baguette like a beaver on crack.

If only I'd found out yesterday when I wasn't some total-ass stranger. Rainier wouldn't have been able to dismiss my accusations as those of a boy who showed up out of nowhere and decided to encroach on the Quatrefoil fight.

But it's too risky to say anything to him now. Or to Cadence. Or to anyone, really. I have to prove my worth and get my damned curse reversed before I can take down daddy-dearest.

Cadence draws her front door open, and a bitter wind sidles inside. "You should lock the living room doors. Just in case Solange gets out."

Rainier nods.

I have visions of Solange escaping and eating his brains. I'm so fucking tempted to unlock the door it's not even funny, but that would make me no better than the cockroach king sitting before me.

Outside, the mist is heavier. I follow the splash of red that is Cadence's jacket through the fog toward Town Hall.

"Are you feeling better?"

"Better?"

She nods to my stomach.

"Oh, yeah. Great. Thanks." I fitfully rub my belly while thinking, *Your father is a murderous prick!*

Just before we reach the spiffy black gates hedging Town Hall, Cadence's phone buzzes. "Yeah? . . . Marianne's grave was Slate's idea . . ." She raises her limpid eyes to my murky ones. "I'll tell him." After she disconnects, she slides the phone back into her pocket. "You were right about the bones. They were Marianne's. How did you know?"

"You mentioned she was dead."

Her brows are still ruffled as she leads me past the gates and into another mansion of marble, wainscoted walls, and priceless oil paintings.

"When did Marianne die again?" I ask.

"Just after Camille."

How convenient. Especially since she was de Morel's only tie to Camille.

27

CADENCE

S late and I meet up with the others at the lake after we deposit the Tupperware container in Geoffrey's pantry. Like my leaf with its cradle, the plastic container dragged itself to its rightful spot on the shelf, proof that Slate was correct about putting the objects back where they came from.

"The skeleton recomposed itself after we dumped the bones in. It was so eerie." Alma's voice bounces over the wet slosh of the lake lapping at our pier.

"No eerier than the actual skeleton." Bastian's still not back to his usual coppery complexion.

I glance over at Slate. Ever since he read Camille's note, he's climbed inside his head, as though her goodbye letter is affecting him on a personal level. Maybe someone he cared for committed suicide. I don't dare ask.

"Then how come this plank isn't sliding into its rightful spot?" Geoffrey's eyeing the piece of wood as though it's wronged him.

I'm staring at it as though it's yelling out that I have a crush on his son. Thank God Alma and Adrien share the same first initial.

"You're sure it goes here?" Geoffrey asks.

I purse my lips. "I put it in myself."

"But where was it before?"

"It washed up on the shore. Since a few of the original planks were rotted through, and this one fit, I hammered it in." Well,

Camille and I had. Papa had wanted to hire someone to fix our little pier, but Camille thought it would be good for me to learn a bit of DIY.

I wonder if *she* knew who the 'A' stood for. *Probably.* She didn't miss much.

"Then maybe we have to throw it into the lake instead," suggests Bastian.

"Rainier would know." The beam emanating from Alma's phone catches on a reddened streak on the plank, right beside my carved heart.

I crouch to take a closer look. "Did you cut yourself, Geoffrey?"

He frowns. "No. Why?"

I point to the large blood stain on the wood. They all crouch and stare.

"Whoa. Is that—That's—" Bastian swoons.

Slate jolts to his feet and catches him under the armpits, then rocks him back onto his feet. The stranger possesses some startlingly great reflexes.

Alma giggle-snorts. "B, seriously? You faced off with a zombie, but a little blood fazes you?"

"You should see him around spiders." Slate looks like he's fighting off a grin, which might've made me grin, but what the hell? How does he know Bastian doesn't like spiders? *I* didn't even know that.

Our shocked expressions make the smile freeze on his lips.

He rubs at his mouth, his finger pads producing a scratchy noise when they hit stubble. "I, um, saw him jump when he passed Tracy's tank the other day."

Alma shudders. "Gaëlle's tarantula gives me the heebie-jeebies too. One time, I thought she'd gotten loose, and I . . ."

As she tells the story of Romain's April Fools' joke, I eye the stalker. He doesn't meet my gaze but I bet he feels my scrutiny.

"So, some things *do* faze you too," Bastian ends up saying to Alma.

"Only spiders."

He shifts around on his boots, arms crossed. "You're not scared of snakes?"

"Nope. I love snakes. All types of snakes. The bigger, the better actually." I don't miss her lascivious wink, but considering the incline of his eyebrows, her innuendo completely flies over Bastian's head.

"Not to interrupt this fascinating conversation"—Geoffrey flips the plank over as though hoping repositioning it might help it magically fit—"but can we get back to the job at hand?"

Alma stands. "Rainier might know where this plank came from. Should I call him?"

I nod.

Papa's voice rises from the phone's speaker.

After Alma explains the situation, there's a lengthy pause.

Then, "When the dock was being built, there was a particularly bad windstorm. Some of the wood piled up flew into the lake. Perhaps it's one of those planks."

"Thanks, Rainier," Alma chirrups as she hangs up.

"So who's gonna jump in to get the plank if the water isn't the correct spot?"

"Not me," says Geoffrey.

I think Slate mutters, "Of course, not you," but between the groaning ice, lapping water, and sporadic bursts of wind, I can't be sure.

"I'll do it," I say.

"No. I'll do it." Slate's tone is dark and grumbly. "I live in the dorms where the boilers are outdated, so I'm used to bathing in freezing water."

Geoffrey collects the plank and is about to toss it in when Slate catches his arm. "Wait. Shouldn't we take a sample of the blood?"

"It's probably paint, Slate," Alma says. "If it was real blood, and the wood had been in the lake, it would've washed away."

"Maybe the plank's a magical replica."

"The cup was real, as were all the other objects." I stand and rub my gloved hands together to drive heat into my numb fingertips. "Or I think they were. Adrien's studying the scroll with Gaëlle as we speak, matching it to the pictures he took on his phone, so he'll be able to confirm if it's a replica or the real deal."

"The pictures *he* took?" Slate scoffs.

I frown at him.

"Nothing." Slate flips up the blade on a Swiss Army knife. "Maybe the plank's real, but the blood's a replica. Maybe the Quatrefoil is trying to tell us something. Maybe that's why there's blood here."

"Don't!" I say as he approaches the tip to the wood.

"Why?"

"If you damage it, the Quatrefoil might not accept it."

He stares at me, then at the wood, then sighs and pockets his knife. "You're probably right."

"Shall I toss it in?" Geoffrey asks.

Slate dips his chin into his neck, ogling the hell out of the bloodstain. "If worst comes to worst, we'll have to fish it out."

Geoffrey lifts his head a little higher. "*You* will."

The air seems to grow warmer, as though Slate's mood is impacting the very temperature.

"Here goes." Geoffrey lobs the plank into the slushy depths of the Nimueh.

A chill sets into my bones, because it reminds me of Emilie's body. I shut my lids and press the sight away.

After a few heartbeats, Geoffrey's voice cleaves through the wrought silence. "It's floating. Is that a good sign?"

I crack open my lids and watch the flat vessel bob like a vestige of a shipwreck, vanishing behind the mist before reappearing a second later.

"Wood only sinks when its density exceeds that of water." Moonlight glances off the lenses of Bastian's glasses. "So—"

The pier shivers beneath our boots, followed by a low whine that interrupts Bastian's explanation.

"Everyone, back to shore!" Slate whips out his arms as though to herd us there.

Somehow, my boots meet the sloping, snowy knoll that leads back up to the house, and yet I can't remember moving my legs.

"Is the clock resetting?" I hear Alma whisper.

"We definitely still had time." Bastian keeps pushing his glasses up the bridge of his nose which shines with perspiration. "Unless the hand sped up. I can go—"

"No one move." Slate's voice rumbles over the incessant grinding.

I'm not sure what to think of his take-charge bossiness. On the one hand, I'm glad we have one more brain in the mix; on the other, this extra brain literally came out of nowhere. For the umpteenth time, I ponder the odds that the Quatrefoil sent him. It did provide me with a weapon to chop down the hawthorn . . .

"Is it me, or is the *kelc'h* turning?" Alma asks.

I append my gaze to the church steeple across the lake. It keeps coming in and out of sight behind the mist, but when it does reappear, it's not at the same place. I catch Slate staring above my head and pivot.

I'm expecting to see the other *kelc'hs* spinning as well but they're static. Only First moves.

Suddenly, the unhurried revolution stops.

The grinding stops.

It all just stops.

"Look at that. The *kelc'h* is back to where it should be." Geoffrey's pompous tone thickens as though he single-handedly accomplished this feat.

"How can you tell?" I ask.

"Because the forest is no longer visible."

He's right. All we now see from the shore is lake. Not even a hint of the dense forest that unspools from the cemetery. "Does that mean we succeeded?"

"I think it does." Geoffrey smiles smugly.

"If we're done, then Papa can use his legs," I continue. "And Solange is no longer a zombie."

And Emilie will resurface . . .

"What are you talking about?" Alma's voice is as thick as it was last night, when she stumbled up to Fifth on Geoffrey's arm, loaded on *chouchen*. "Who's a zombie?"

I frown. "Solange. Remember? Bastian lured her into the guest bathroom with raw meat?"

Bastian's eyes nearly pop out of his head. "I did?"

Slate eyes Bastian and Alma. "The Quatrefoil must've erased the non-*diwallers'* memory. Just like with the ruined buildings."

Geoffrey turns to him. "How do *you* remember?"

"The real question is, how do *you*?"

"Because I'm a *diwaller*, kid," Geoffrey snarls.

Slate's eyes taper closer to his nose as he stares down Adrien's father. "Well, I've got *diwaller* blood. Believe me now?"

He's still a stranger I'm not sure I can trust, but I do believe him. "Yes."

"I suggest we go celebrate the end of our bonus trial with some Roederer up at the temple." Rubbing his palms together excitedly, Geoffrey whirls on his heels and starts up the hill, flanked by Alma and Bastian, who pepper him with questions along the way.

Can this really be over? I stare at the lake for any sign of the little girl we buried there, but since we slid her in its deepest part, it may take a while for her to surface.

"Cadence?" Slate touches my cheek with a gloved finger, redirecting my attention toward his troubled face. "How did we meet?"

I jerk out of my morose musings. "What?"

He doesn't say anything, just keeps staring with unnerving intensity into my eyes.

"You sprang up behind me in the tavern and licked my ear." Suddenly, the reason he's asking hits me, and I find myself smirking. "Were you hoping the *kelc'h* sliding back into place would cleanse my mind of all that happened today, too?"

His chest hardens with a sigh that plumes out of his mouth a moment later. "One can always hope for a second chance at making a first impression, right?" There's an edge of sadness to his tone, but then he swallows and shouts to the others. "Listen up! You're not done!"

Alma, Bastian, and Geoffrey freeze midclimb.

"What do you mean, we're not done?" Adrien's father asks.

"I mean the Quatrefoil isn't done messing with us yet." Slate's gaze drifts toward the temple at the top of the hill, at the glass dome that sits on the fog like a glistening dew drop.

"And how would you know that, kid?"

A nerve flexes in Slate's jaw. "Because the four other *kelc'hs* are still oriented wrong, that's how."

I gasp. *Of course.* How did I miss that? "Do you think First sliding back into place fixed Solange, though?"

The first-floor window of Papa's office opens, and Adrien sticks his head out. "A plague! A plague is next," he yells across the steep, twilit expanse.

"Aw, man," Bastian mumbles. "I don't like the sound of that."

"And people say Brume isn't exciting," I mutter, which makes Slate's lips quirk.

His eyes, too. They mirror his mouth but symmetrically, like tiny black bridges. He's quite handsome, in a villainous sort of way.

When he catches me staring, heat billows into my cheeks.

"See something you like, Mademoiselle de Morel?"

"Nope."

As I spin around and stride up the grounds toward the manor, unzipping my coat to cool myself off, a deep chuckle reverberates over the land and lake.

28

SLATE

I follow a trail of sweet, roasted cardamom all the way from the clanking copper sign of Second to the glass door of *Au Bon Sort*. The fragrance is so potent, it seems to have absorbed into every old cobble and timbered slat on the way.

My stomach growls as I elbow my way through the Monday lunch crowd, toward the back of Gaëlle's little shop where Cadence, Bastian, and Alma have pushed together two small round tables. In front of them are pint-sized cauldrons, steam curling off the creamy orange contents.

As I shrug out of my jacket, Cadence's blue eyes lift toward me, and it takes everything in me not to lean over and plant a kiss on her lips.

She gestures to one of the undersized cauldrons. "We got you a bowl of Pumpkin Potion, but if you don't—"

"I'm not picky." I scrape the chair out and sit, then spoon the soup into my mouth. I almost spit it out when it hits my tongue and chars my tastebuds all the way down to their roots. I grab my glass of water and chug it. "Wow . . . these bowls really keep in the heat, huh?"

Cadence's lips curve in amusement. "I was just about to warn you to wait a while."

Alma snorts. "Like, a half-hour minimum."

Sweat beads along my upper lip as I refill my glass with what's left in the carafe sitting beside the napkin holder. My tongue is entirely numb now.

Bastian's cleaning his fogged lenses on the hem of his gray tee with enough force to pop them out of the frames. "The Emmental crackers are edible immediately in case you're hungry." His tone is uncharacteristically abrupt.

We left on good terms last night, so I don't think I'm the reason behind his foul mood. "You okay, man?"

"Yeah. Fine."

He doesn't sound fine. I look around the table to see if one of the girls may have insight, but both simply shrug.

"How was class this morning?" I reach out and snatch a cracker from the purple fabric basket.

Even though Cadence fed me last night after I nailed a bunch of planks over Solange's hidey-hole—the *kelc'h* spinning didn't reverse the housekeeper's magical affliction—I'm ravenous, so I chomp it down without tasting it. Food is fuel, and I'm going to need lots to get through another frigid day of being absolutely no one in absolutely bumblefuck nowhere.

"I didn't go," Alma admits, "but those two went."

"It didn't distract me half as much as I would've liked," Bastian grumbles.

Cadence drags her finger through the condensation on her glass, then dries the tip on a paper napkin. "Hard to focus when you know a plague's coming."

After we got back from de Morel's dock last night, Adrien explained what he found on the *Kelouenn*. The illustrations, which supposedly represent curses, were harder to interpret. So all in all, Adrien's information was useless since he wasn't sure what type of plague it would be or when it would hit or what would happen if we failed.

"Where are Adrien and Geoffrey?"

Cadence breaks off a corner of her cracker and slips it into her mouth. "Geoffrey's monitoring the star hand, and after his morning classes, Adrien went back to the manor to work on the scroll. He seems to think this won't be over for a while. That we'll have a trial on every *kelc'h*."

"Wouldn't put it past the Quatrefoil," I say around a mouthful of dry, cheesy crumbs that feel like wet plaster. "Was he able to see what the inkblot's hiding?"

Cadence takes another bite of her cracker. "No. That ink spill really damaged the scroll. Papa doubts even the restorer will be able to get rid of it. But he said he'd bring it to him—well, *back* to him—tomorrow."

A grunt somehow escapes my cemented molars. "That inkblot didn't get there by accident."

Alma's eyebrows tilt downward. "You really think someone sabotaged the *Kelouenn*?"

Not someone. Cadence's daddy. I don't have proof, but I'd swear it's all connected to Camille's untimely death.

Cadence's screen lights up with a message. I catch the name THE MAYOR.

"Is it the stones?" Bastian scoots forward, getting another faceful of pumpkin steam. "Did they finally light up again?"

"They'd turned off?" I ask.

"Yeah. They all went dark after you solved the . . . treasure hunt."

More like manhunt, Bastian. The clock's clearly trying to nail Rainier.

"They're all still dark." Cadence sighs. "My fellow *diwaller* is just requesting that one of us bring him a sandwich and an espresso."

How any of them deem Geoffrey an actual *diwaller* is beyond me. The man's a joke. "Why is he babysitting the clock again? I mean, the ground *will* rumble, since that's what happens every time the clock resets."

"He's hanging out up there in case the star hand starts ticking without provoking an earthquake." Alma lifts her spoon to her mouth, blows, then takes a birdlike sip. The bump on her nose jostles as she grimaces.

Bastian cleans his glasses *again*, mouth back to being warped.

My little brother's so rarely in a mood that I can't help but dig. "Okay. Spill. What's wrong?"

He huffs. "It's really not important."

"It is to you."

He stops wiping his glasses and blinks as though surprised I care. After another few mouth contortions, he places his glasses back on his nose and sighs. "Some guy waltzed into my dorm and stole Steve."

"No way!" Alma's mouth becomes a perfect circle.

He nods frenziedly. "Yes way. I'm *so* mad. Not just mad. Furious."

The cracker I've just airlifted from the basket ends up in my cauldron of pumpkin lava. I pretend like it was my intent by hammering it into pieces with my spoon and stirring.

"Do we have a description of the plant-napper?" Alma asks.

"Paul said he was big and ugly with really scary eyes."

Ugly? That's fresh coming from Paul who looks like a two-toned paint-by-number canvas. Scowling, I mutter, "So a big, fugly dude stole your cactus?"

Cadence tips her head to the side. "How do you know Steve's a cactus?"

Sharp. So sharp, Mademoiselle de Morel. She could give Arsène Lupin a run for his fame.

"By deduction and observation." I gesture to my amber-haired neighbor, who's drinking her soup sip by tiny sip. "Alma mentioned it was a plant-napper; Bastian's a university student. What plant would a college guy, who doesn't smoke pot, have? Cactus is really the only answer."

"He's not just a cactus; he's an Eve's Needle." Bastian follows my lead and crushes a cracker into his soup, then mixes it in so vigorously orange slop sloshes over the cast-iron rim. "Want to see a picture?"

Before I can even nod, Bastian exhibits a selfie of him with Spike, both of them sitting pretty. He's got one arm around the terracotta pot like it's his girl. I'd say it was pretty damn pathetic, but I have the same one—or *had* the same one—but of me and Spike in my living room in Marseille.

"The thief also took my Mexican Snowball. What kind of twisted person does that?"

One who loves his Eve's Needle enough to give him a companion, dammit.

"Are you sure Paul isn't pranking you? Don't roommates do that sometimes in college?" I finally attempt another spoonful of soup. This time, the soup goes down without broiling my palate and throat.

"You think?"

I shrug. "Crimes are like passing gas; the person responsible always blames someone else."

Alma snorts. "Nice analogy, Slate."

I wink. "By the way, have you guys figured out the significance of the items we had to find on First? Could help us understand the point of this second round of trials." *And get everyone to finally see Rainier's true colors.*

Bastian puts his phone down. "What were they again?"

"Yeah, you guys are going to have to refresh our memories." Alma takes a gutsier spoonful.

"The bonsai, the *Kelouenn*, the skeleton, the plank, and the teacup." Cadence ticks them off her fingers.

"Seems pretty random to me," Alma says.

Except I know that the suicide note stuffed alongside Camille's teacup and Marianne Shafir's bones aren't random at all. Not to mention, the plank with the bloodstain is pretty damn suspicious. The *Kelouenn*'s stain, too, is anything but innocent. Now to figure out how the bonsai figures inside Rainier de Morel's murderous plot.

"You guys said the constellation displayed on the dial was that of Wrongful Death, right?" Bastian's voice is barely above the hissing noise of the chrome coffee machine behind the glass bakery counter.

I nod. "The secrets of murderers."

Cadence's head straightens. "So, the Quatrefoil is trying to tell us someone murdered Camille?"

"*And* Marianne Shafir." I crack my neck that feels stiff. "Why else were her bones in play?"

Cadence's complexion turns as pale as the desiccated white blooms packed in the row of Mason jars behind her. Before I can think better of it, I reach out and wrap my fingers around one of her hands. Perhaps because she's in shock and hasn't realized I've made contact, she lets me hold on for two glorious seconds.

But then she blinks and glides her fingers out from underneath mine. "Nolwenn didn't think it was cancer." Her voice has gone so low, Bastian, who sits the farthest, asks her to repeat herself.

"Seems like the Quatrefoil is testing our investigative worth," he says.

"Or trying to stir up trouble," Cadence mutters. "The items have absolutely no connection to each other."

Wrong.

If the Quatrefoil hadn't erased my existence, I may have decided to become buddy-buddy with it, but cursing me in this manner . . . it's a hard pill to swallow. Then again, I didn't die.

The thought of Emilie crushes my tenuous good humor.

"How's lunch?" Gaëlle bustles over with a bright smile, a sheen of sweat glossing her forehead.

"Fantastic. As always." Cadence nods to the student in the apron manning the register. "Is Romain okay, by the way?"

"Sure." Gaëlle looks over her shoulder, eyebrows knitted as loosely as the yarn on her yellow murder weapon that went up in smoke a couple weeks ago. "Why?"

"Because he usually works weekday lunches."

I've only seen Romain once or twice. The dude ringing up the dwindling line of students and faculty isn't him.

"Oh. He has exams this week, so he grabbed lunch and went upstairs—"

The ring flares just as a shudder races through the ground and rattles the glass jars and wooden shelves.

Cadence's fingers curl into a fist. "It's starting." Her voice is shrill with a cocktail of nerves and fear, and from her crimped expression, pain.

Gaëlle looks around her shop worriedly. "I need to evacuate the premises."

"Cadence?" Another tremor makes my water glass tremble. "Call Geoffrey to see if the star hand started."

Gritting her teeth—*devil ring*—Cadence plucks her phone from the table and dials him. As she hits speaker, Gaëlle narrows her eyes at Bastian. Quicker than I can steal a wallet, she swipes something small and yellow off his sleeve.

"What was that?" Alma has gone extra still.

"Oh, just—um—fluff." Gaëlle sucks in a breath as a spider, no bigger than my pinkie nail, scuttles up one of Alma's long curls.

Since I'm closest, I lean over and flick it off.

"Oh. My. God. Something was in my hair?" Alma scoots back her chair, knocking into the shelves behind her, rattling a row of tea canisters.

Geoffrey's phone goes to voicemail.

Cadence dials again, flinging a reassuring smile Alma's way. "It was nothing, honey. It was just a—" She looks toward me for help.

I open my mouth to complete her sentence when Bastian screeches, "Spider!" in a voice shrill enough to wake the dead.

The little culprit scuttles across the table at top speed.

Bastian and Alma jump out of their chairs and climb atop them. Despite her stilettos, Alma accomplishes this in one go while Bastian stumbles twice before managing to tuck his legs up. I'm tempted to remind them both that higher ground only works with mice, but think better of destroying their false sense of security.

Gaëlle swears under her breath while I smack the spider with the menu tucked between the napkin holder and salt shaker. Bastian heaves a sigh of relief while Alma thanks me like I've just saved her from being disemboweled by a serial killer.

Bastian's sigh reminds me of past creepy-crawler incidents. Spiderwebs never bothered him—he considers them an engineering marvel—but the arachnids themselves have always turned him to jelly. The first time I saw him freak out, he was eleven and came nose to nose with a daddy longlegs in our dingy bathroom. He streaked out, running smack into our foster mother who was rolling curlers into her short hair. Toothpaste foam dripping down his chin, Bastian begged her to kill the bug, but she refused and barred me from rescuing the innocuous insect, insisting Bastian needed to man up, go back in there, and squash the bug himself.

I'd slipped out through the bedroom window, ran around the house, and rang the doorbell, then raced back inside, sidestepped Bastian who was still sniffling, grabbed a square of toilet paper, and squashed the bug. I hadn't really wanted to kill it but knew Foster Mom would require proof of death. I forced the wadded-up paper with the smooshed insect inside Bastian's fist just as she returned from checking the front door, muttering something about neighborhood urchins.

"Geoffrey's still not answering." Cadence's upper lip is slick with sweat, but her voice is steadier. The Bloodstone must've stopped singeing her blood. "I'll try Adrien."

Alma winds her hair into a bun at the top of her head with a shaky hand. "Spiders are the spawn of Satan."

"Spiders are actually a sign of good luck to come. Romain wrote a paper on them for school last year." At everyone's raised eyebrows, Gaëlle nods to the tank in her shop window. "There's a reason I have a tarantula as a store mascot. Arachnids are said to bring great wealth."

Bastian peeks out from behind his knees. "I suppose they *are* vital to the ecosystem. Still don't have much affection for them."

I chuckle quietly just as something drops into my soup, splashing my face. Ringing cell phone clutched between her fingers, Cadence leans over and peers inside my bowl. After I wipe my chin, I go fishing with my spoon. Eight miniscule legs paddle in the pumpkin jacuzzi.

A tiny missile plunks against my raised hand, drops to the table, and squirms.

Alma screams bloody fucking murder when she notices it's another spider.

Like raindrops, they fall from the ceiling.

Drip. A tiny green one.

Drip. A medium-sized brown one.

Drip! A huge, furry-ass black one.

"Oh my God! Oh my God! Oh my GOD!" Alma jumps off her chair and dashes for the door.

Bastian blanches and falls off his perch, crushing a bunch of creepy-crawlies on his way down. Shrieking just as loudly as Alma, he swipes them off his jeans and T-shirt sleeves and races out, bumping into other customers equally frantic to escape Brume's den of horror.

"I guess we figured out the plague." I smash a big furry spider under my boot. "Now the question is, how do we stop it?"

29

CADENCE

Even though the Bloodstone's vein-curdling burn has dwindled, my index finger still feels as though it's sitting on Juda's cast-iron stove and my arm muscles keep spasming. Despite my pain and fear, I'm relieved.

All night, I stayed up thinking about the plague the scroll foretold, wondering how it would manifest and how we'd defeat it. By brewing a potion using ingredients from *Au Bon Sort*? With meat cleavers and wooden planks? With copper wire? What if the plague was a river of blood? What if it was a swarm of vampiric crickets or a battalion of howling ghosts?

I wasn't that far off with the crickets. Just got the arthropod wrong.

And from the chaos around me, I realize again that this isn't like the magic of the Quatrefoil leaves. Everyone can see and be touched by the spiders. Like with the items we found, it's a whole different set of rules.

Something plops on my head, and I hop out of my chair. I don't scream like Alma, but my breathing hitches, and chills sprint up my spine. Slate reaches over and plucks the arachnid off my hair, then flings it onto the floor and smooshes it under his boot.

Spiders of all sizes and breeds scamper over the timbered ceiling before plummeting like soft-bodied missiles. Frozen, I watch a squad climb my sweater sleeve.

Table legs shriek against the hardwood floor as Slate creates an escape route for me. When I still don't move, he bowls the spiders off with a sweep of his palm, then spears his warm fingers through my clammy ones, and twirls me toward him. It's pathetic, I know, but his fearlessness and attentiveness funnel right into my heart and wake my body from its daze.

As he stomps, soles thundering against the floorboards, I come back to life and whack the creatures, my arms blurring from how fast they move. Creepy-crawlies squirm over my hair, my back. My spine tickles as one slides inside the collar of my bulky V-neck sweater. I seize the hem and flap it until the spider shoots out.

Because there's no way we can squash all of them, and because this is a trial, not an actual infestation, I attempt to come up with a strategy.

Gaëlle's trying to calm the sobbing customers who've huddled in small groups, pointing to the window.

I squint and catch a dark wave rolling down the cobbles. I must gasp, because Slate's eyes skip over my face, over my body, then back to my face.

"What is it, Cadence?"

I nod to the window, to the breaker of invertebrates.

"*Putain . . .*" he grumbles. "I bet Bastian and Alma have fainted by now."

My phone rings. How I can hear it over the cacophony is a miracle. I grab it from the table and hit speaker.

"Dad just called," Adrien pants. "The stars lit up. Apparently, the constellation they form is the ancient Brumian one called Web of Lies. He looked it up in the archives—that's why he wasn't answering. Anyway, all the ones he touches—are showing him a spider. I'm guessing that's the—plague."

"No shit, Sherlock," Slate mutters under his breath as a spider sneaks into his ear. He digs it out and swears a blue streak.

"Second is full of them, Adrien." I slap my neck, striking a brown spider with thick legs. I wipe off the dusty smear it leaves behind on my jeans, my stomach clenching with disgust. It's truly a miracle that I'm not losing it. Actually, it's not. I just keep telling myself they aren't real. Just leggy bits of magic. "How do we get rid of them, and how long do we have?"

188 | OLIVIA WILDENSTEIN

Slate turns fully toward me and skates his palms across my back, my neck, my head, my front. I'm fully aware he's battling spiders, and yet my blood beats against my skin each time his hands connect to my body.

Slate tips his head to my phone.

I frown until I hear Adrien bellow, "Cadence, are you still there?"

In a voice thick as syrup, I say, "Yes. Sorry." I lower my eyes to Slate's throat, to his sharp Adam's apple that dips and rises slowly. "What did you say?"

"The stones show Dad the exact same spider. Not several. I'm guessing this is like the first challenge and we need to find that one."

"So what does the furry son-of-a-bitch look like?" Slate's voice rolls from his chest right into mine.

I shiver again.

"Slate's with you?" Adrien asks.

I swallow, hoping to thin out my voice. "He met us for lunch." *Yeah.* I still sound like a spider's spinning its web around my vocal folds.

"What does Spider Zero look like, Prof?"

Adrien breathes harshly into the phone. "I can't believe you invited him to lunch!" His voice hits the ear not propped close to my phone's speaker, and I jump.

Adrien's here, in the shop, face flush with exertion, eyes flush with annoyance. I'm guessing he's annoyed a stranger is still knee-deep in our magical business. I'm about to remind him that Slate has *diwaller* blood, when the door of *Au Bon Sort* shatters, and a mottled carpet of spiders unfurls over the broken glass and wooden floor.

On the bookshelf behind Slate, I spot a huge tome entitled *Spells for Modern Witches*. I reach out and grab it, hand it to Slate, then grab the one titled *Brewing Up the Best Social Media Posts* and fling it toward Adrien. Both begin whacking anything with more than two legs. I heft a crystal ball off a shelf and bowl a whole bunch of critters over, flattening them.

"They turn to dust when they die!" Adrien bellows, smashing his papery weapon on Slate's back.

Slate stumbles before whipping around. "What the hell?" He raises his tome, ready to bat Adrien.

"There was a spider on your sweater, Slate."

Slate's eyes narrow as though he doesn't believe there was. I have to admit I was too busy watching the pests disintegrate to notice.

"Tarantulas!" Someone shouts above the crying and yelping and howling.

"Tracy's a tarantula," I breathe.

The boys blink away from each other, refocusing their anger on the plague we're supposed to defeat.

The dark wave outside has thickened to include all kinds of tarantulas—black, brown, orange, purple, striped, spotted, uniform. They seep into the store.

Adrien barks, "We need fire. Spiders hate fire."

Slate murmurs, "Too bad you banished your pet *guivre* in the tajine dish."

Both Adrien and I freeze. But then I remember Adrien walked out of his house with the silver pot. Slate was probably among the gawking crowd. Although, how he knows Adrien fought a *guivre* is beyond me. Did he hear us discussing the battle? Or did he catch sight of the creature's fibrous wings and tail through the charred-off roof?

Adrien's phone dings. He lifts it slowly to his ear, never once looking away from Slate. "Yes, Dad . . . You're sure? . . . Okay." He nods. "Got it. Bastian and Alma are with you?" His eyes meet mine. I try to find comfort in his stare, but there's so much panic I end up feeling antsier. "How long? Are you guys *sure*? . . . Fuck." Since Adrien never swears, I know it's well and truly awful.

"How long do we have?" My pulse is so wild I taste metal.

"One hour. Less now."

"And what happens if we fail?"

Adrien shoves his phone back into his fitted coat. "My guess is some transformation. Into an insect or arachnid."

I blanch. "People will turn into spiders if we fail?"

Slate squeezes my hand, which I hadn't even realized he was holding.

Adrien glares at Slate's fingers. "At least, the spiders are contained on Second."

I pull my hand away. "The items we had to find last time were only on First. When Solange got cursed, she was on First. Maybe to be cursed, you have to be on the *kelc'h* under siege."

Slate inhales quickly and deeply. "We need to evacuate Second."

Gaëlle, who's tiptoeing her way back to us, freezes. She must've heard us discuss the cursing mechanism, because she suddenly sputters, "The kids!"

As she races up the stairs that connect the shop to her apartment, Slate climbs on a chair and barks, "Hey, everyone, get your asses off Second. There are no spiders on any other *kelc'h*. Run! Tell everyone you see to head to a different *kelc'h*!"

People blink, then wheel around and streak out of the shop, yelling the news to others as they sprint up and down the road like headless chickens, leaving the four of us to deal with half a million spiders.

In the absence of all the screaming, the whoosh of thousands of furry legs resounds against my skull.

Something comes back to me, and I whip my attention toward Adrien. "You said the stones were only showing Geoffrey one spider. Which one?"

He runs a hand over his cropped hair. "A large tarantula with reddish-orange legs."

My lashes reel way up. "That's not just any tarantula. That's Tracy! We need Tracy!"

Gaëlle clambers down the stairs, breathing hard. "The sitter's rushing the twins out and Romain's on his way to school. What were you saying about Tracy?"

"She's the key to stopping this." Adrien stares at the tank as though trying to puzzle out how to use her.

Gaëlle carefully arrows toward the shop window and plunges her arm into the terrarium, digging her fingers into the soil and knocking over the half-log shelter. She spins around, eyes bulging with dread.

"Tracy's gone!" She roots around the tank again, sending leaves and sticks flying. "She's missing!"

Of course she is.

30

SLATE

"No one take a single step! Tracy won't hurt you. Tarantulas are peaceful and harmless." Gaëlle's curls bounce out of her hair tie as she scans for her pet among the sea of arachnids washing over our feet. Her apron is twisted. Instead of reading *Au Bon Sort,* it reads ABORT.

Yeah. If only.

I feel a sting, and then it's like a thousand little fires ignite simultaneously under my skin. I fling a giant, hairy tarantula off my neck. "They're not fucking peaceful and harmless, Gaëlle!"

"Please don't hurt them. It could be Tracy."

Cadence eyes my throat. "How venomous are tarantula bites?"

"They don't usually bite." Gaëlle gets on all fours to look closer at the creatures. It doesn't faze her when the spiders use her as a human highway. "They usually use their barbed hairs as a defense mechanism when they get scared."

"Are the *hairs* venomous?" Cadence's voice goes up.

Gaëlle waves a hand in the air. "There might be some swelling and pain, but it won't kill you."

I slide my hand across Cadence's collarbone, knocking over a midnight-black bugger. It's only a matter of seconds before another one takes its place.

"Good to know," I say as another monster gets me on the

earlobe. "*Putain*! They keep stinging me. Are they going after anyone else?"

"Tarantulas have a thing for snakes." Adrien shoots me a smug look, proud of his little dig.

I take a menacing step toward him. "Look here, Prof—"

"Hey!" Cadence holds me back with a hand on my chest. "The only *looking* we're doing is for Tracy." She gives me a little shove. "Got it?"

I take a step back and grumble, "Got it."

After swatting two spiders off her sleeve, Cadence grazes my earlobe and neck. "Those bites are really swelling up. Are you okay?"

The whole right side of my head feels like rubber. "I'm fine."

Adrien frantically shakes his blazer, a shower of spiders falling from it. "You look like you're growing a second cranium."

Gaëlle stands, gently pulling insects off her apron, then pokes my ear and neck. I don't feel a thing. "I've got a salve for that."

"Against cranium growths?" I slur.

"No." She manages a teeny smile. "Against skin irritation. But first, we need to find Tracy. She's a Mexican Red Knee."

"Because she has red knees?" Cadence asks.

"Yes. Be extra gentle when you grab her. She's delicate."

Another jab sends needles of pain down my right arm. "Delicate, my ass," I grumble.

By now, the whole shop is a wriggling, furry mass. I slide my feet on the floorboards because it's nearly impossible to take an actual step without squashing something. And I don't want to be responsible for flattening Tracy.

Outside, the road and the buildings surrounding it are all covered with arachnids. Spiders don't scare me, but the sight of those spindly legs makes me shiver in disgust. I run my hands down my arms, and a dozen drop to the ground.

"Ow!" Adrien tosses a tarantula, then sucks on the side of his hand.

Ha. About time.

"Don't throw them!" Gaëlle cries. As the tarantula turns to dust, she says, "Oh God, was that Tracy?"

Adrien lowers his hand, lips contorted in pain. "I don't think so."

Among the furry throng, I count several red-legged speci-
mens. "Have you trained Tracy by any chance? Does she come
when you whistle?" I snap my fingers. "Tray-tray! Come here,
girl!"

That earns me an eyeroll and a smile from Cadence. I'm hoping
this means I'm back on track to win her heart, which remains my
paramount trial.

"Put any tarantulas you think could be Tracy in the tank. If she's
in her rightful spot, it should stop the plague." Adrien glances at his
watch. "And do it fast. We don't have much time."

"Got any bags, Gaëlle?"

"Yes. Under the cash register."

I head over and pluck four paper bags, hand one to my fellow
diwallers, then puff up my own. "You and Cadence stick to the store,
Gaëlle. Adrien and I will go search the street."

Among the thousands that scurry past, there are handfuls that
match Tracy's profile. Prof and I scoop them up, then drop them
into our shopping bags, before wading back to the shop and
emptying our loot inside the tank.

As the minutes tick by, my field of vision narrows, inflammation
from the spider hairs and bites making my face puff up like a souf-
flé. By the time my right eye is swollen shut, the ten-gallon
terrarium is full of Tracy-doppelgangers.

Still, the *kelc'h* hasn't moved, and the plague hasn't ended.

The four of us stare down at the tank.

"How long—" Cadence's voice splinters. "How long do we have
left?"

"Five minutes." Adrien nabs a tarantula. Because its legs are
yellow, he chucks it back onto the shelf of love potions.

"We're not going to make it." Gaëlle's dark eyes are wild. "Thank
God the kids got out of here."

But as she's talking, footsteps sound on the stairs. I shuffle my
feet and turn around to see Romain. He's got a backpack slung over
one shoulder, a shoebox in one hand, and is loping down as if he
has no worries in the world. But then he stops, mouth dropping
open, as he takes in the chaos.

"Whoa . . ." he says, clearly awed.

"Romain!" Gaëlle screeches. "You're supposed to be in school!"

"My exam isn't for another twenty minutes. Where did all these spiders come from?"

"You've got to go. Right now! You agreed!"

"I, uh . . . I thought you said I had to clean up my room." He grimaces. "Sorry. I had my airpods in."

"Why would I ask you to clean up your room?" Gaëlle screeches but then lowers her voice at his spooked expression. "Honey, I need you to run. Run to Third or First and stay there!"

"Okay, okay!" He scrambles down the rest of the stairs and creeps over the spider rug. But instead of heading directly for the door, he turns toward Tracy's terrarium.

"Romain! Go!" Gaëlle's wheezing so hard I fear she may hyperventilate herself unconscious.

"Hurry!" Adrien bellows. "There's less than a minute left."

"A minute left for what?" Romain turns his big brown eyes toward his stepmother.

"Just GO!" Gaëlle blubbers. "Please, baby, go!"

"Okay. Okay." Romain shoves the shoebox into Adrien's hands. "Can you put Tracy back for me?" He eyes the tank. "With . . . uh . . . all her new friends."

Adrien blinks. A tiny spider swings from his eyelashes. "Tracy?"

"Yeah." Romain hopscotches over the tarantulas. "She was studying with me. Keeping me company."

"He had her the whole time." Cadence laughs.

"Put her in the fucking tank, Adrien!" I bark.

Holding the shoebox with his left hand, Adrien uses his right hand to ease the fitted screen off the top of the terrarium. It catches on one end, snapping back into place. "Dammit!"

I help him lift the screen. With my eye out of commission, my depth perception is off, so it takes me two attempts. As it finally comes loose, the ground lurches.

Adrien flips over the shoebox and dumps Tracy into the tank.

The whole shop shudders, shaking loose the spiders on the ceiling. A torrent of them collapses on top of us. Cadence and Gaëlle scream. I try to reach Cadence, but the floor tilts, and I tumble down, down, down.

More fires blaze over my exposed skin. I make the mistake of swearing, and a spider darts into my mouth, crunches between my teeth, tasting like rotten crab and then like dust.

The ground stops squirming as all the spiders burst, and a deep grinding noise resounds inside my bones as the *kelc'h* rotates.

We did it.

We fucking did it.

31

CADENCE

I clutch my throat, trying to catch my breath and quiet my stampeding heart as the spiders—all except Tracy—shimmer into oblivion. No magic repairs the store, though, and Gaëlle gives a little whimper as she takes in the mess.

"Whoa . . ." Romain whispers, blinking.

Adrien levels eyes stricken with apprehension on me. What does Romain's non-*diwaller* mind make of the destruction?

"Um." I lick my top lip, then my bottom one, refocusing on Romain. "*Whoa* what?"

"The last time the *kelc'h* turned, it was just a tremor. This time, it was like a real earthquake."

Gaëlle sighs through a smile. "It's going to take a while to clean up."

"I'll help after—" Romain scrunches up his brow. "Weird. I can't remember what I was rushing off to do."

"You were putting Tracy back in her tank before heading out for your test, honey."

Romain slaps his forehead. "Oh, right." He strides toward the door, but stops as he catches sight of Slate, whose exposed skin is red and distended. "Are you okay, man?"

I crouch next to Slate and put a hand on his shoulder. "He'll be fine. Slate's allergic to pumpkin."

"Shit." Romain reddens. "I mean, *shoot*. Sorry, Gaëlle."

Gaëlle blinks back tears. "This situation definitely deserves a shit. Anyway, off you go. Don't want you to be late."

As he seizes the doorknob, Gaëlle calls out, "I love you!"

Romain's cheeks burn harder, but they also lift with a sheepish grin.

As Slate groans, I look up at Adrien. "Can you help me get him upstairs? And, Gaëlle, can you phone Sylvie?"

Slate presses himself up, teeters. "I'm good, princess."

Adrien catches him right as the man, *who's good*, rams into the shelving unit, tipping two jars which the bedlam had spared.

"Sorry, Gaëlle." Slate's slurring a little, and his eyes are half-lidded.

"You're anything but good." I latch on to his other side, drape his arm over my shoulder, then snare his middle, feeling his back muscles flex beneath my forearm.

God, the man doesn't have an inch of fat on him.

Which may possibly be the strangest thought I've had in a while.

Or rather . . . the most normal one.

With Adrien, we march Slate upstairs to Romain's bedroom, then lay him down on the straightened comforter that smells of adolescent boy and *magie noire* cookies. I figure out the origin of the chocolatey fragrance when I spot a plate covered in brown crumbs on the narrow desk propped under the slanted ceiling.

After a few minutes, Gaëlle trundles up with a jar of neon-yellow slime. "I mixed this up. Aloe vera to soothe, rose and lavender essential oils for pain, and chamomile for inflammation. It should help with the swelling until Sylvie can administer something stronger."

Slate's pasty forehead is misted with sweat. "You may want to revisit your claim that tarantulas aren't venomous, Gaëlle." One of his lids is pinned shut, but his neck bears the brunt of the spider venom. He looks like he's ingested a tennis ball, and it got stuck going down.

"The spiders disappeared. Why didn't the venom?" I push my knotted hair out of my eyes, regretting not having tied it up this morning. Wait, I did. Must've lost my hair tie during the arachnid joust. I perch on the edge of the mattress and lean over, resting my bedazzled hand on the swollen column of Slate's throat.

He peeks out of his working eye.

"Am I hurting you? I was just thinking that maybe the Blood-stone could somehow syphon back its magic."

"You're not hurting me, princess." Slate lifts his hand and places it atop mine. "Just the opposite."

Probably because my fingers are clammy, so they feel like an ice pack.

"Two down. Three to go." His lips barely shift as Gaëlle scoops some goop out with two fingers and plasters it over his inflamed lid. "No chance of this gunk making me blind, right?"

"No. Don't worry." Gaëlle presses my hand away to rub her medicated ointment over his throat.

"Hmm . . . you said the same about the spiders." His deep, skep-tical hum stirs the air between us.

"You're allergic, that's why you're like this. I'll go downstairs and grab some more for you to take home."

If only we'd understood the scroll, understood what completing the Quatrefoil would bring about. I would never have slipped the damn Bloodstone back on. I make a fist, furious with myself for having dragged us all back into this nightmare.

My phone rings just as Gaëlle leaves the room. I stand and pluck it out of my jeans' back pocket. "Hey, Alma." I begin to pace the hardwood floors, anger and guilt warring within me.

Alma is gasping into the phone. "Everyone okay? We felt the ground shake—was that a *kelc'h* turning?"

"Yes. We finished our challenge."

"Wait? Really? Wow. Well, anyway—I just ran into—Sylvie who told me—someone got an allergic reaction—to Tracy. Who was it?"

"Slate."

Adrien, who's leaning against Romain's signed French National Basketball Team poster, tracks my frenzied pacing.

"Where are you?" I ask Alma.

"On our way—down from Fifth—I don't know why we were rushing to get up here—class doesn't start for another hour—but I left in such a hurry, I forgot my bag and coat."

Right. In her version of reality, the spider invasion didn't happen. "Once you get to *Au Bon Sort*, come upstairs. We're in Romain's bedroom."

"'Kay."

After Alma hangs up, I walk up to the window and grip the narrow ledge lined with framed family pictures. My attention lingers on the one of Romain with his father.

Romain, age four according to the number of candles blazing on the *fraisier* in front of him, is sitting on Matthias's lap, gazing up at his father as though the man hung the moon. How would he take the news that he's dead? Would he understand like we did, or would he revile his stepmother? How would Nolwenn and Juda react?

I look across the street at the tavern. Was it infested with spiders too? I find comfort that if it was, Nolwenn and Juda will have no memories of it.

Adrien sidles in next to me, arms crossed. I look away from the silver cobbles and up at him. Twin purple crescents tinge the skin beneath his eyes. I'm imagining he slept as well as I did last night.

"There's something not adding up." His familiar scent wafts off the patch of skin beyond the jutting collar of his button-down shirt and slides into my lungs. "None of us get incapacitated, and yet *he* does? How can you be allergic to magic?" Adrien glances over his shoulder at Slate, whose eyes—eye—is fixed on us.

I glance down at Adrien's hand, the one pricked by a spider. It's not swollen like Slate's skin, but it's definitely pinker than usual. He notices me looking and tucks his hand into his pocket. "It's not the same thing."

I get his hesitation. I really do. But Slate fought right beside us. He helped me find the teacup last night. He told us that we needed to put the things where they belonged. He's proved himself.

Either that, or he's really good at hiding his game.

But, even if I can't wrap my head around Slate's presence, or his odd ear-licking greeting, my gut tells me to trust him. I'm just not sure *why*.

I return my gaze to Adrien's and whisper, "If he were some cursed piece of the Quatrefoil, he wouldn't be on our team. Not to mention, he'd have cursed *us*. It's been more than twenty-four hours since he's appeared in our life."

Adrien's lips thin. "He remembers. *Everything*."

"Because he has *diwaller* blood." A lot about Slate doesn't make sense, I agree. But the *diwaller* blood I completely believe.

Adrien reangles his body to face mine. "Cadence, you know how much I love and respect you, right?"

My heart fires off a beat. *Like a sister.* No more than that. Which is probably best anyway. I glance at Slate, find his poor face crimped in such pain it quiets my inner ramblings.

I really hope Sylvie has a cure against magical venom.

"So, don't take this the wrong way." Adrien murmurs this just as Alma hurtles in with the town doctor and Bastian, hot on her heels. "But you *are* aware he's somehow bewitched you into thinking he's one of us, correct?"

I snap my gaze back to Adrien, my eyebrows slanting a little, then a lot, and then the corners of my lips following suit. "Bewitched me? I may be young, Adrien, but I'm not gullible. The Bloodstone doesn't light up when he's around, and the stone lights up. Every. Damn. Time I'm near Quatrefoil magic." I'm saying it not only to convince Adrien but also to cement it in my own mind, because if I start to doubt my own gut, I'll go crazy.

"Cadence—"

I'm about to return to Slate's bedside, when I wrench my neck back to add, "These trials have disillusioned us all, but I choose not to let them turn me into a cynic. You should, too."

On that, I walk back toward the stranger, who stood on the spider-infested battlefield alongside me, even though it wasn't his war to wage.

32

SLATE

The first thing Sylvie pulls out of her bag is an EpiPen. I throw my legs over the edge of Romain's bed, my only thought: *get the hell out of here*. I've seen demonstrations of those things. They have big-ass needles hiding in their depths that someone jams into your thigh like a sledgehammer.

No. Effing. Way.

I've already been lubed. Gaëlle put so much goop on me, I feel like a used sex toy. The hell I'm getting poked by a needle on top of that.

I hate needles.

But before I can haul ass out of this kid's bedroom, Cadence wraps her fingers around my upper arm. "You need to sit still for this."

The scent of her shampoo hits me at the same time as the pain in my chest. I try to talk, but my words stick like gum in my throat and each of my breaths comes out thinner and thinner.

Sylvie rolls Romain's desk chair toward me. "This will only sting for a second," she coos before gleefully and violently shooting me up with epinephrine.

The needle stabs my thigh, and a deep ache radiates through the muscle. I swear and grit my teeth. Though my heart races, the pressure on my chest decreases, and sweet, *sweet* oxygen trickles down my throat and puffs up my lungs.

"Goodness. What a strong reaction to spider venom." Sylvie touches my cheek. The skin's numb. "If I didn't know any better, I'd think you were rolling around in a tarantula's nest, not simply petting Tracy."

My makeshift hospital room is teeming with people. Alma stands huddled beside Bastian on the shaggy navy rug, ogling me like I'm in a circus sideshow. Her mouth hasn't closed once since she stepped over the threshold. I worry her tongue may dry out.

"I thought the shop downstairs was a mess, but you, Slate . . . wow." Bastian squints like his prescription lenses aren't strong enough.

I snort. "Thanks, little—" I stifle the word *bro* in the nick of time, swapping it out for, "one." It's lame and earns me a raised brow, but at least I don't freak his muddled mind out.

From his spot by the window, Adrien mutters, "Dead ringer for Quasimodo."

"That's rich coming from a guy whose eyebrows were MIA two days ago."

Cadence sucks in a swift breath, flicking her eyes toward Sylvie.

A strand of silver hair falls from Doc's updo as she scrutinizes Adrien's face.

"Adrien was, um . . . trying out looks for my alien-themed birthday party." Cadence smiles at Sylvie. "Which you'll be invited to, of course."

"I have *just* the costume!" Sylvie claps. "Oh and, young man"— she pats my thigh—"don't be alarmed. Your swelling is impressive, but I've seen worse results from human and animal interactions. Much worse."

"Talking about that Pug-German Shepherd nibble? That was nasty." As I say it, Sylvie frowns while Adrien stops breathing. *Yeah, Prof. I was there.* I peer up at him from under my ballooned eyelid. "You ever fix the good doc up with a rare breed of dog?"

His eyes bulge.

Sylvie smiles. "Adrien *did* recommend a fabulous breed for me. A Magyar Agár otherwise known as a Hungarian Greyhound. I got Gaston a week ago. He's the perfect boy." She digs through her purse. "Let me show you some pictures."

Thankfully, we're saved by the sound of Beethoven's Fifth.

Sylvie scoops up her cell phone, and after the initial hello, goes right into doctor mode. "Any allergies? . . . When did the symptoms first start? . . . Any difficulty breathing?"

While Sylvie continues drilling the caller, Cadence turns to me. A minuscule sliver of sunlight penetrates the window, lighting her from behind like she's one of those saints painted on cathedral walls.

"I don't know if it's Gaëlle's unguent or the shot, but the swelling on your face is already going down."

Sylvie hangs up and nods. "You do look much better. You'll still require antibiotics." From her medicine bag, she gives me a blister pack of pills. "I'm glad you responded to the epinephrine because I'm needed elsewhere. Oddly enough, you aren't the only one with a reaction to a bite today. Nothing as serious as yours, but still."

Cadence stiffens. "Wh-what?"

Sylvie slips her arms back into a fluffy down coat that reaches her knees and could double as a comforter. "Five students have shown up at the university clinic in the last fifteen minutes. My student nurse says it looks like wasp or bee stings possibly, but kind of hard to get a bee sting in Brume this time of year. My guess is either a bedbug infestation or some house spiders. Always plenty of those." Her phone chimes, and she checks the screen. "Goodness. Make that *nine* students. So odd. Perhaps the turning *kelc'h* scared all the insects out of their hiding places."

Adrien gives a strangled laugh. "That must be it."

"Rising from the pits of hell," I declare. "I mean . . . Brume. Although, they are quite possibly one and the same."

Bastian grunts, but his eyes spark from my special brand of humor.

Cadence stands as Sylvie packs up and lets herself out. When the slap of Doc's loafers sounds on the narrow, uneven staircase, Cadence tips her chin up and fires a look at Adrien. "Sounds like Slate's not the only one *allergic to magic*." For the last bit, she bends her fingers into air quotes.

Bastian's eyes go super wide. "*Allergic to* . . . You guys had another trial?"

A slight flush turns Prof's neck pink, but otherwise, he ignores Cadence's dig and gets our non-*diwaller* sidekicks up to speed.

"Spiders?" Alma clutches the edge of Romain's desk, her complexion rivaling the last of the milk in the glass Romain left behind.

Brown gaze darting all over the room in search of the hairy, eight-legged beasts he so fears, Bastian jerks backward, knocking into the desk and almost tipping the glass. He seizes it between trembling fingers. It's the same comedy skit as at lunch, but it still makes me smile.

"They're gone. We solved the plague puzzle." Adrien lifts his hands like he's trying to calm a wild animal. "All of them turned to dust."

That doesn't relieve Alma, who grimaces. "Eww."

Slowly, color returns to Bastian's cheeks and luster to his eyes. "So the constellation was the Web of Lies . . ." He licks a finger to gather up cookie crumbs from the plate on the desk.

I'm not even sure he notices he's doing it. Like me, he learned to eat whenever he could, whatever he could. When I made my first big sale, I swore that he and I would never go hungry again, and even though the boy is scrawny, his stomach no longer rumbles like this cursed town each time it tests us.

"In ancient Brumian myth"—he sucks his finger and strikes out at the plate again until it's so shiny it looks like it's been run through the dishwasher—"the spider web represents illusion: meaning that something which seems frail or delicate can actually be surprisingly strong. That's pretty upbeat for the Quatrefoil, isn't it?"

I think of Rainier, how easy it is to dismiss him as frail because of his wheelchair, and sit up straighter, my head swimming with the movement. "Or insightful."

Alma finally peels herself away from the desk. "So, now the Quatrefoil is giving us inspirational memes?"

I rub my throat. The skin is hot and gummy. "No. I think it's trying to tell us something. Something serious. Like on First with the Wrongful Death constellation."

Bastian merely frowns. To think that two days ago, he would've heard what I'm *not* blatantly spelling out and put it together, but he's no longer aware of Rainier's underhandedness.

"What exactly are you saying? That a murderer is on the loose in Brume and that he can somehow create illusions to make others believe he's innocent?" One of Cadence's hands has found purchase on her hip.

"This isn't a whodunnit or some kind of riddle, *Slate*." Adrien spits out my name. "This is a series of challenges we must face to prove whether we deserve magic." His hazel eyes pulse out a glower. "If you're trying to turn us against each other, I strongly suggest you quit while you're ahead."

"Turning you against each other isn't my intent, *Prof*." I make sure to put the same emphasis on his nickname that he used with my name.

One of his eyes twitches. Deep down, I know Adrien's a decent and smart guy, and the only reason he's strapped on some blinders at the moment is because this murder stuff hits too close to home. It must be tough to have a 'stranger' insist a magical clock's pointing out one's mother was murdered.

Cadence inhales too much air and gasps, "My father!"

Yes! Yes, Cadence. That's it—

"I'd better check on him. What if the ground shaking loosened some of the boards keeping Solange inside?" She slides out her phone and dials Rainier.

I sigh. That wasn't my girl piecing the puzzle. That was her being the forever-considerate daughter.

As Cadence speaks into her phone, I find Adrien's eyes leveled on my face, but I don't think he's seeing me. The faint frown lines crinkling his brow, combined with the glaze coating his hazel irises, tells me he's thinking. About his mother? About what I said?

After Cadence disconnects her call, she says, "He's barricaded himself in his office, because a few of the wooden slats blocking off the bathroom splintered when the ground shook." She wrinkles her nose. "You think you could put up some new ones, Slate? I wouldn't want her to get out . . ."

In all honesty, I think it would do Rainier some good to have a monster on the loose in his home. After all, the town has had to endure having *him* on the loose.

"I can do it, Cadence," Adrien offers.

"That's really kind of—"

"I'll go." I all but leap off the bed, cutting Cadence off midsentence. "Wouldn't want you to get rips in your fancy coat and trousers, Adrien."

Adrien crosses his arms over his chest. "I was heading down to the manor to study the scroll some more anyway."

"While you study the scroll, Cadence and I will reinforce the zombie trap."

Cadence puts a hand on my forehead. "Are you sure you're up for that? I mean, the swelling's down, but—"

"I'm good, princess." I'm no longer feeling woozy, and my heart is pulsing regularly.

She reels her hand back slowly, eyes on mine. I keep expecting her to tell me not to call her princess, but her scarlet lips don't part to chastise me. Merely to breathe. In and out. When her pupils dilate, I tilt my face farther down, and her nostrils flare delicately. She doesn't back up.

Someone clears their throat. Bastian. "What's the next challenge?"

Nice cockblocking, little bro.

"I'm not completely sure, but according to what I've pieced together"—Adrien's tone is gruff—"it'll have to do with rocks and order, or something of the sort."

"And the curse, if you guys don't make it in time?" Bastian asks.

Cadence pivots slightly but stays so close her arm brushes against my torso.

"There were drawings of gargoyles on the *Kelouenn*." Adrien buttons up his coat.

"You better call Geoffrey and have him feed the townsfolk another lie to get them off Third," I tell him. "Better yet, out of town."

"Slate's right," Cadence adds. "We were lucky there were no casualties this time around."

Adrien's jaw ticks and ticks. He hates that Cadence is siding with me, but he's rational enough to see the wisdom of my words.

While Adrien places the call, ever-considerate Bastian offers, "Alma and I can help Gaëlle with the clean-up."

"Dad's not answering." Adrien crosses the low-ceilinged space toward the door, eyes fixed straight ahead. "I'll go up to Fifth to make sure he's all right, then meet you back at the manor." Without further ado, he leaves.

"You think something happened to Geoffrey after we left?" Alma murmurs as she and Bastian follow in Adrien's footsteps.

I don't hear his answer, because all my energy is laser-focused on Cadence. Not to mention, I don't much care about the old creeper who stole my spot on the crew.

When Cadence starts to head out, I capture her wrist, my fingers bumping into the glittery emerald charm, before trailing lower, across her palm. "Thank you."

Cadence shivers but doesn't pull away. "For what?" she rasps, the honeyed sound of her voice all but making *me* shiver.

"For trusting me." I run my thumb over her knuckles, and another shiver goes through her body. "For worrying about me." I lift my free hand to her face and cup the delicate frame.

Her fingers finally close around mine, and her breathing quickens.

Maybe our attraction is part magic, fated like Merlin and Viviene's, but I don't give a damn. Magic is real, and so is our connection. When she licks her lips, I lean forward.

She grits her teeth, and her fingers strangle mine.

I freeze and am about to apologize for reading her wrong when she lets out a pained whimper. "The ring."

I drop my gaze to her side, to the hand I'm not holding. "Well, *kaoc'h.*"

The stone glows so brightly it splashes color onto her pallid skin. "Do you think the ground is about to—"

The earth bucks, and we pitch forward. The glass on the desk tips over, hits the plate, then rolls onto the rug, dribbling milk everywhere.

"Do that?" Cadence's question, like her expression, is filled with nerves.

I snare her waist and spin her so that if we fall, she'll land on the bed. And we do fall. I come down hard on top of her, catching my weight on my forearm. She still lets out a little *oomph*. The ground rumbles again, and something glances off my skull—the metal lamp from Romain's nightstand.

Brume really has it in for my skull.

The quaking stops as suddenly as it started. Rubbing my throbbing head, I pry my upper body off Cadence's, allowing her to scoot up.

"Are you all right?"

The worry brimming in her blue eyes makes me want to play up my injury, and I'm about to when Gaëlle yells, "Cadence, we need to get to Third!"

Panic replaces her worry. "I need to go. You should stay here and—"

"And miss out on seeing real-life gargoyles?"

Her pupils flare. "God, I don't want to fight another statue."

I drop my hand away from my throbbing cranium. "Didn't mean to remind you of Ares."

She shakes her head a little as she gets to her feet. "You really do know everything about our first round." It's not a question. Not an accusation either. Merely, an observation.

I reach out and take her hand, the one with the ring, and clasp it in mine.

Her throat dips with a swallow. "We should go. We don't want anyone turning into a gargoyle."

Depends who, really. I wouldn't object to Rainier being immortalized in stone. Or Adrien. He'd make a comely statue.

Cadence tugs on my hand, towing me toward the door. With a sigh, I shuffle after her, down the stairs, and through the disordered shop. Alma, Bastian, and Gaëlle stand outside, all three shaking like leaves. Alma's lips quirk at Cadence's hand clasped in mine, and the tremors stop racking her body.

At least, we're distracting her from her panic. No such luck with the other two.

Suddenly, Adrien's haggard face appears under the swinging sign of Third. "Thirty minutes!" he yells. "Dad just called. We have thirty minutes!"

Gaëlle gasps. "You're kidding?"

"Not to mention, we need to evacuate the *kelc'h*." Adrien's jaw twitches when he catches Cadence's hand nestled in mine.

"The students?" she whisper-yells. "We need to evacuate the dorms!"

"Dad's sending out a town-wide alert," Adrien says.

Cadence bobs her head. "Good. Okay. Good."

I squeeze her hand, trying to ease her nerves. "What's the constellation, Prof?"

"Treacherous Path," he says through barely separated teeth.

"Ah. The celestial embodiment of the domino myth that says that each bad decision generates another, like a long line of falling dominoes." It should really have been rebaptized *Slate's Journey Through Brume.*

Prof's glower is really quite formidable, way more potent than I expected from such a polished blond.

"So what are we up against?" Cadence pulls her hand out of mine and spears it inside her coat pocket. Sadly, I assume it's because of Adrien.

"Street paving," Adrien declares.

Gaëlle's eyebrows streak toward each other. "Street paving?"

"You know that alley between my house and Claire Robinson's? The one composed of uneven and mismatched pebbles from the lake?"

"*La Ruelle Ancienne*?" Bastian asks.

Adrien nods. "Well, we have to repair it, and we have thirty— twenty-six now—minutes to do so."

"That sounds like fun," Alma says enthusiastically.

Adrien scrubs a hand down his face and lets out a heavy sigh. "I guarantee it'll be anything but."

"Let's go!" Gaëlle barrels ahead, breaking into a run.

I start to follow but stop when Bastian and Alma trail after me. "You two stay on Second!"

"But—" Alma says at the same time as Bastian declares, "We want to help."

"Check on my father," says Cadence. "Please, make sure he's okay. But careful of Solange!" She turns, fresh on Gaëlle's heels.

"We'll call you from up there so you can help remotely, but whatever you do, stay the fuck off Third, capeesh?"

With hefty sighs, they both relent. When I turn around to go after the three other *diwallers*, Bastian calls out, "You should stay with us, Slate."

"I've got *diwaller* blood."

He stares steadily at me through his lenses, short locks blowing across his forehead. "So, what? You can't be cursed?"

Oh, I can . . .

Since I don't want him to worry, I slap on a smile and say, "Exactly. I'm immune." And then I run up the hill toward Mercier's ex-wyvern lair, pushing past students rushing out of dorms.

At least, Geoffrey got the campus-wide alert out. As I run, I bang on doors and windows and bellow, "Evacuate Third, people! Evacuate Third!"

That spooks the hordes already streaming down the hill. People move faster, jostling each other like housewives during *Galeries Lafayette*'s summer clearance sale. Made the mistake of going one year.

Never. Again.

"Everything will be okay!" I tack on.

And I honest-to-goodness feel it will. After all, I'm good at manual labor. How hard can paving a puny alleyway be?

My good feeling nosedives when I spy the mound of rubble that reaches Cadence's knees.

I cop a look at my Daytona. Sixteen minutes.

We have sixteen fucking minutes to set down hundreds of stones.

In the right order.

We are utterly and royally screwed. *Note to self: stop underestimating the Quatrefoil.* "What's the curse again, Prof? Gargoyles?"

"We're not sure yet," Cadence whispers, eyes just as wide and troubled as Gaëlle's and Adrien's.

"Guess we'll be finding out soon." Gaëlle's words dangle ominously in the *ruelle*'s deepening shadows.

CADENCE

Cold skitters inside my bones as I stand on Brume's oldest street, a narrow passageway that dates back to the fourteenth century. It's—or rather, it *was*—cobbled with round stones from the lake instead of the square setts inlaid in the rest of Brume.

I know this because I've given many guided tours of the town and taken one myself, mostly to deepen my knowledge of Brumian history. The guide who'd led us through the nooks and crannies of Brume had worn a ridiculous wizard cap and a glued-on beard that had made Alma cackle like a witch. I couldn't count the times I'd elbowed her, even though our tour guide had seemed more amused than hurt by her laughter.

"*La ruelle* was supposedly fashioned with magic," Adrien's telling Slate. Or maybe he's telling all of us, although I imagine Gaëlle's already aware of this lore. "Each rounded stone was set into the sandy mortar, the dark gray ones lined the sides, and the beige ones"—he squats, his coat pooling around him like molten silver, and picks up a pale stone—"filled it in like a carpet."

I frown, because I recall seeing a drawing of *la ruelle* in *Istor Breou*, and it didn't resemble a beige band with a dark trim. But maybe I'm remembering another road. Adrien's the professor after all.

"There are exactly twelve hundred stones. I've counted them."

Adrien spins one of the darker stones repeatedly between his gloved fingers.

Slate snorts. "Exciting pastime you have, Prof."

Adrien stands and faces Slate. "It was for a history lesson."

I clutch my elbows. "Guys, we're down to eight minutes. Should we just push all the stones onto the sand, or dry mortar, or whatever it is, and hope they magnetically pull themselves into their rightful place like the other items did?"

"I think that's a solid plan, princess."

I don't bother sighing at the nickname. For reasons unbeknownst to me, he enjoys calling me princess. I allow him this quirk, because I no longer think he's doing it to rankle me.

Not after we held hands.

I can't believe I held this stranger's hand.

But most of all, I can't believe how natural it felt. My fingers tingle with heat that for once isn't emanating from the Bloodstone.

Gaëlle drops to her knees and starts shoving the pebbles onto the naked stretch of dirt. "I really wish I had some Air power right now. I could just sweep my arm—and voilà."

Soon.

Maybe.

Would it kill me to be positive?

I scrub out the maybe and focus on the soon. *Soon*, we'll have solved the Quatrefoil riddles, proving that we're worthy, because that is the reason it's testing us, right? As I kneel to help the others, I refuse to believe it's all just some Machiavellian game with no end.

Gaëlle always says positive thoughts bring about positive results. So I think positive thoughts until my brain feels like it's bleeding rainbows.

I sense both Adrien and Slate eyeing me as we work in silence, laying out the pebbles as evenly as possible. I'm guessing Slate's looking my way because of what happened earlier between us. What *almost* happened. As for Adrien, he's angry with me for trusting Slate. It rolls off his tight shoulders and saturates the dark air surrounding us. I want to snap at him to cool off, remind him that we're all stressed out, but barking will surely have the opposite effect.

Slate peers at his wristwatch, a bulky, shiny thing. "One

minute." Although I'm no watch expert, or amateur for that matter, it seems expensive, and I briefly wonder how an orphaned college student managed to afford it.

We work faster and harder, pressing the stones down, rolling the ones that sit atop their neighbors, swapping light-colored ones for darker ones to arrange them into the pattern Adrien described. My ring flashes and burns intermittently, and I could swear I feel a magnetic pull each time I drag one of the dark stones toward the far edges of the pale carpet. Except the magnetic pull is tugging my hand away from the sides and toward the middle.

"At least, there's no snow in the alley," I say. *Look at me being so positive.*

Gaëlle glances at the sliver of sky overhead. "Let's not jinx it."

"What are you all doing here?" The familiar feminine voice raises the fine hairs on my arms.

Third was supposed to be evacuated.

I crane my neck to find Mademoiselle Claire blocking out the narrow entrance of *la ruelle*, one gloved hand clutching a mammoth travel mug, the other, the lapel of a long, fitted cape-coat.

"Claire?" Adrien exclaims. "You need to evacuate Third right—"

The ground rumbles.

"Run!" he yells.

But it's too late. If we fail, and a curse befalls Brume, it'll land on whatever poor soul remained on the *kelc'h*. I imagine she's not the only one. Even though students streamed out of dorms earlier, there's no way *everyone* in town read the text alert Geoffrey sent out.

My boot catches on the space between the stones where mortar should be, and I topple backward, coming down so hard on my tailbone my vision crackles. Blinking, I stare at the cobbles.

Please, please, please, stay put.

Brume shakes harder. A pebble pops out of place. Then another. And another. One last shudder and all of them wink out of existence and reappear beside Claire, who stands wide-eyed and wide-mouthed, at the narrow entrance of the alley, her hair fanned out like serpents around her ashen face.

Gaëlle palms her mouth and gasps.

Slate crouches in front of me and offers me a hand. "You think we need mortar, Prof?"

Adrien, who's straightened up already, doesn't answer, his attention on Claire. I knuckle my still-bleary eyes and squint. And then I suck in air because Claire Robinson isn't just ashen, she's gray.

Gray as granite.

"*Kaoc'h.*" Slate's warm breath ruffles a strand of my hair.

Claire's eyes glint as though she's staring out of a mask.

"The curse. It isn't gargoyles. It's *toull-bac'hs*," I whisper.

34

SLATE

At the phrase *toull-bac'h*, I think of Bastian's description of the magical jail cell. I whip out my phone and tap in little bro's number. I only realize after the fact that I'm not supposed to know it by heart, but it doesn't matter because the rest of the crew are all calling their people.

While Bastian's phone rings, I take a few steps closer to Claire Robinson and an eerie sensation crawls over my skin. Even behind the granite, her eyes seem to follow my every move.

The phone keeps ringing.

Fuck. Answer, Bastian.

Finally, he comes on, his voice wary. "Uh . . . *oui*?"

"Took you long enough! You *trying* to give me a heart attack?"

"Who is this?"

Out of habit, I say, "Jesus, it's me," before I even think about it.

"Me who?"

"Slate!" I take a breath to calm myself. I'm supposed to be a stranger, not a psycho-stalker. Bastian rarely picks up for unknown callers, so I should be glad he picked up for me. I clear my throat and say in a soothing voice, "Just checking in. Are you and Alma okay?"

"Uh, yeah. We're sitting with Rainier, who's recovering from a close call. Solange got out of the guest bathroom and followed him into his office. But Rainier went all badass and used a paperweight to defend himself. He got out and locked her in there. I just nailed some slats over the office door, but I'm not sure how long they'll hold."

Hopefully, long enough to keep Bastian and Alma safe, but not long enough to stop Solange from having another go at chomping Rainier's brain.

"Was that the *kelc'h* turning? Are you guys done?"

I run a hand through my hair. "Not even close. Claire Robinson is currently locked in a *toull-bac'h*, so whatever you do, you and Alma stay away from Third, got it?"

A beat of silence, then, "If it's a real *toull-bac'h*, it won't just hold her, it'll eventually turn her to stone."

"Good thing we're bringing back magic then." For all my reassurance, my gut twists at the possibility that this curse will be like Emilie's—irreversible. I shove the thought behind a wall in my brain.

Putting away his phone, Adrien announces, "Dad said he's having trouble calculating how much time we have now. Somewhere between five and forty-five minutes, so we'd better get to work." He drops down onto all fours and starts shoving stones into the dusty mortar.

I snap my attention to Adrien. "Geoffrey can't tell if the clock's ticking faster or slower?"

"Guess not." Adrien's voice is tight, a muscle spasming in his jaw.

"What's happening?" Bastian asks.

I quickly relay our failed masonry job and Geoffrey's total ineptness.

Cadence starts on her own pile of stones, but suddenly she cranes her neck and squints one of her eyes. "You have Bastian's number?"

"Got it during lunch." Hopefully, the impromptu spider show will have muddled her memory a little. To prevent her from digging, I put Bastian on speakerphone.

His voice echoes comfortingly in the alleyway. "Alma can stay with Rainier, and I can go up to Fifth right now."

Gaëlle shakes her head. "No. If we only have five minutes you might be passing through Third when—if—"

"If we fail," Cadence finishes in a bit of a doomsday voice.

But Bastian doesn't give up. "I'll run like the wind."

"No. Stay on—" The call drops, because he's hung up. "*Putain!*" I roar.

"So, are you planning on helping, or will you just be playing phone operator this round?" Adrien doesn't stop adding stones to the line in front of him as he taunts me.

Snickering at Prof's unanticipated sense of humor, I flip him off and crouch next to the others to start on the jigsaw. A few minutes into the job, Bastian comes streaking past us. His pace slows, but one glimpse at Claire, and he's off like a doped-up racehorse again. As Gaëlle and Cadence line up their cobbles like disciplined schoolkids, the silence deepens around us and so do the shadows.

Soon, it'll be night, because the sun doesn't go down in Brume; it fucking plummets. The rising mist isn't helping matters.

A plunk rends the stillness as Adrien drops his rock. He frowns at Cadence, then points to the area of road she's filled up. "What are you doing?"

Instead of a carpet of light stone surrounded by dark, she's set hers out so that, near the middle, the black stones curve into a semi-circle.

She blinks at her design as though just taking notice of it. "Oh, I—"

"The lighter stones go in the middle, Cadence," Prof says, sounding very much like a professor.

Cadence shakes her head, her hair falling over her shoulders. "Are we sure about that? I could swear I saw a different pattern in *Istor*—"

"We're sure. I see it every single day. Multiple times a day!" Adrien's voice is shrill with anger and panic.

"Hey!" I stare daggers at him. "No need to be an asshat, Prof."

"There are lives at stake, *Slate*. Every second counts. And Cadence is wasting time."

"At least she's not wasting space. Unlike some members of your family."

His hazel eyes blacken under his refurbished eyebrows. "Watch what you say."

"*You* watch it. You have no right to take your stress out on Ca—"

Something hard smacks the already sore area on the back of my head, sending shockwaves of pain through my skull. A small, round stone tumbles to the ground.

Gaëlle sucks in a breath.

"Did . . .?" I palm the back of my head. "Did you just throw a rock at me, Gaëlle?"

She scrunches up her nose. "A tiny pebble."

I lift my eyebrows. "A cobble."

"I didn't mean to throw it so hard. Or even at you, necessarily. But we don't have time for this squabble." Her gaze sticks to the ring, which is glowing so bright its reflection resembles a bloodstain on the hastily paved street.

A giggle starts at the end of the street. Surprisingly, it emanates from Adrien. He tries to stifle it, but his lips break apart around a more manly laugh. Gaëlle joins in. While Cadence shakes her head and settles on a grin.

The ground bucks, and whatever mirth was rising in me shoots back down like the sun on the Brumian horizon.

"Stay low!" I shout, uselessly gripping the dirt like it's a lifeline.

My head pounds along with each new tremor. The odor of earth, dust, and iron fills the alleyway as, one by one, the stones pop out of their orderly ranks and explode into chalky fireworks.

A moment later, everything stills, and the rocks appear in a jumble at Claire Robinson's granite boots just as a feminine scream rips through Third. Better not be Bastian who was turned into stone or I will obliterate this entire fucking town. I scramble up to my feet, ready to scale Claire, whose effigy blocks off our access to Third, when Adrien wraps his fingers around my bicep to keep me in place.

"We had fifteen minutes." Adrien's voice cracks. "This time, we'll probably have less." Gone is his earlier glee and anger. Only terror remains.

I shake myself loose from his grip and fish my phone from my pocket. As I redial Bastian, my screen lights up with an incoming call from him, and relief cartwheels into my chest.

I bark, "Bastian? Are you safe?"

"I'm on Fifth," he pants. "Just wanted to let you know—I made it."

"Thank fuck."

"How much time do we have?" Gaëlle asks.

I reiterate the question.

"Give me two secs," my brother says as I crouch and start chucking the cobbles into place. "So . . . it's hard to be precise since I wasn't present during the last round, but from the speed the star hand's moving, and where Geoffrey's indicating it was placed—"

"Spit it out. How much time?" I don't mean to stress him out, but the clock is literally ticking.

Bastian hesitates for half a second before blurting, "Nine minutes."

We speed-lay the stones, and this time, when the ground rumbles, they're all in place. I strain to hear the stone-on-stone screech of the *kelc'h* turning, but instead the rocks levitate off the ground and snap like popcorn, poofing out of existence before once again reappearing at Claire's feet.

A distinctly animal whine soars through Third, only to be choked off midhowl. I'm guessing there's a new canine statue somewhere on this *kelc'h*.

"*Dieu merci*," Gaëlle breathes out, and you know you're in hell— or Brume—when you thank God a puppy's getting cursed.

The clock can't seem to make up its mind. For the next try, we have five minutes, and fail. The following one, we're back to sixteen.

And we fucking fail.

Pretty damn soon, France will be able to rival China for the largest stone army.

When Bastian calls again to say we have twenty-one minutes and four seconds, Cadence rips the phone from my hands. "I need you to go into the archives and look through *Istor Breou*. I remember seeing a drawing of the *ruelle* inside, with a motif, but can't remember it precisely. Send us a picture the second you find it." She shoves the phone back into my hands and wastes no time setting down stones once more, only this time, she works the darker ones into a curved shape at the center of the alley. "I don't know if it's a trick or not, but I'm going to listen to the ring this time. I think it's trying to help us."

Gaëlle, Adrien, and I exchange a look because the Quatrefoil doesn't *help*. It hinders. It frightens. It claws. It barbecues. But it most definitely doesn't help.

Cadence stops sliding her lip between her teeth. "I know you all think I'm crazy, but the Bloodstone *isn't* the Quatrefoil. Besides, I swear I remember another pattern than the one Adrien's describing."

Prickhead's confidence and kempt appearance has taken a serious hit. His dress coat is caked in dust, his cashmere hat askew, and a streak of dirt smudges his left cheekbone and the bridge of his nose.

"Time to try it Cadence's way." Even though I'm still wary, I remind myself that the ring *is* an artefact finder. It really could be showing us the ropes. Just like the celestial dial might be pointing out Rainier's shady character.

I'm ready for some pushback from Prof, but his posture and voice wilt like paper in water. "Fine. Okay. What design do you remember, Cadence?"

All our phones ping with a message. I stare at the screenshot Bastian just forwarded to a group chat labeled *The Crew*. I should be focusing on the actual image, but my insides are too busy transforming to mush at having officially been inducted into the crew.

My phone rings, and I stick it on speaker.

"Did you all—get the image?" Bastian's still out of breath.

"Yeah, we all got it." I study the design. Of course . . .

I set the phone down and start helping Cadence fashion one of the five Quatrefoils out of the darker stones while Gaëlle works on smoothing the pale stones all around and Adrien works the life out of his jaw, clearly miffed he got it wrong. I'm about to make a quip about his historical knowledge shortcomings, but decide the blow to his ego was substantial enough.

"Apparently, when the *diwallers* took magic away from the people," Bastian is saying, "there was an earthquake. The *ruelle* incurred a lot of damage and was entirely reset, but in a different order. The cobbles were laid out as a uniform tableau instead of a Quatrefoil tapestry."

"Thanks for the history lesson. Now go check on that star-hand countdown for us, will ya?" I ask Bastian. "And call us if it goes nuts in its dial."

As I hang up, Adrien brings a hand to the triangle of skin that peeks out from above his coat collar. "This was all preventable." His eyes are wide and haunted. "If I'd listened to you, Cadence—if I hadn't insisted—" He gazes at Claire's stony face. "It's my fault so many were cursed. My fault they're entombed. I'm so sorry." I'm not sure if he's saying it to his work colleague or to us, but the man looks on the verge of tears.

"We all make mistakes, Prof," I reassure him. I start thinking back on all the mistakes I've made. For each stone I lay, a new one comes to mind. Paving the alley becomes cathartic as I bury the wrongdoings I brought about, intentional or not.

In no time, Cadence and I have gotten two quatrefoil shapes down, while Adrien and Gaëlle concentrate on the mass of pale stones.

Sweat crochets down my brow and spine with each minute that ticks away. Twenty. Seventeen. Twelve. Ten. Eight.

Cadence set a timer, and I keep peeking between it and the image Bastian sent us.

We climb to our feet with four minutes and forty seconds to spare.

"Oh my God, we're done. I can't believe we made it." Gaëlle is shivering as hard as the surface of the Nimueh Lake beyond the ramparts.

I squint between my phone screen and the alley. At the heart of the central quatrefoil lies a bare patch shaped like a plus sign. "We're missing a stone!"

I shuffle the stones around to try and fill it in, but when Cadence passes the ring over the shape they zoom back into place as if dragged by a magnet.

Adrien floods the alley with light from his phone while Gaëlle drops to her knees and brushes her hand over the newly paved ground, feeling for any errant cobble.

Cadence zooms in on the photo. "Wait. I don't think that's a pebble in the middle."

Gaëlle, Adrien, and I lean in, our heads touching. The illustration shows something larger, something shaped like a cross, painted red, blue, green, and white.

"The old paving stone in the display case in Town Hall!" Adrien breathes close to my face. Smells like he had garlic at lunch.

"Town Hall's on First. I'll call Alma." The second her friend picks up, Cadence explains what we need her to do.

"On my way." Alma hollers goodbye to Rainier and then pants, as I imagine, she dashes through First. I hear the clacking of her boots, the screeching of a door hinge. After thirty-seven seconds, she yells, "Got it!" making us all jump. "I'm on my way!"

"Don't come to Third. I'll meet you on Second!" I whirl, only to remember we're boxed in by Claire Robinson on one side and the town ramparts on the other. I wrench my neck for a window but none give onto the alley.

Putain de bordel de merde.

The cork that is the astronomy professor is our only way out.

"Whatever you do, don't break her!" Adrien warns. "She doesn't look it, but she's fragile right now."

I suck in my gut and press my back against the stone wall of Adrien's house, sliding centimeter by centimeter past the astronomy teacher. Her hands are out to her sides, fingers splayed and petrified. I shimmy along but her left hand is way too close to the wall for me to get through the thin space. I try the other side. One of my coat buttons snags on the extra-long fingernail of her index finger.

I wrench the button free. At the same time, there's a loud *crack*, then a subtle plink. I stare in horror as the granite stub bleeds thick, scarlet liquid.

I've broken my share of hands and fingers, taken pleasure in the satisfying crack of bone from bullies, but right at this moment, I'm on the verge of puking. Whimpers rise from inside the *toull-bac'h.*

Adrien grabs me and yanks me out of the slender opening. "Cadence, you're thinner! You can get through."

Has he not spotted the blood? Did he not hear the whimper?

He probably has tunnel vision. We're so close this time. We just need the paving stone.

Cadence's face is bloodless, her eyes awash with unshed tears. Unlike Adrien, I have no doubt she saw what I did.

She doesn't take her eyes off Claire's hand as she contorts her lithe body to fit through the black divide of air.

"Forty-seven seconds," Gaëlle announces, her voice already heavy with defeat, because Cadence is still not through.

In less than a minute, another person will turn to stone.

"I can't get through," Cadence growls.

"I'll lift you up!" Adrien barks.

I press my forehead and palms against the cool stone wall and shut my eyes, swallowing down the bile and frustration. Maybe her finger will reset when the *kelc'h* trembles. Maybe—

Just then, Alma's voice comes at us from somewhere on the main road. "I've got it! Don't worry, I've got it!"

I wrench my head off the wall and snarl, "Don't worry? Get off Third, Alma. Get away!"

"Give me the stone, honey." Cadence speaks calmly. "Quick."

From behind Claire, Alma's shadowy form appears. "Where are you—oh—*whoa* . . . Is that—"

"Alma, the stone! Hurry!" Cadence sticks one arm past Claire.

Alma heaves the thing into Cadence's palms.

"Now, run!" Cadence yells just as the *kelc'h* lurches.

I clutch the wall.

Cadence bangs into me. I try to steady her, but the ground heaves and the alley dissolves into a strip of dirt.

We.

Failed.

35

CADENCE

"A LMA!" I wail. "Alma! No! *Nonononono*." I claw at Claire, trying to squeeze around her to reach my friend, who lays supine beyond the professor's *toull-bac'h*.

When the world stops rattling, the cast-iron streetlamps flare to life, and the horror I felt when I saw Alma trip and fall multiplies. A thin shell of granite now encases my friend, blunting her brightness and snuffing out her liveliness.

"No, no, no." Tears salt my cheeks as my fingers finally graze the hem of her stone skirt. "No." *This can't be happening. This just can't be happening.*

A strong arm snares my waist and hauls me back. "Shh, princess. Shh. We'll get her back. She'll be okay. We'll get her back."

I turn in Slate's arms and bury my face in the crook of his neck, finding a measly amount of solace in his solid warmth.

"This is all my fault," I whimper as he holds me to him. "All my fault."

"No. No, not at all. You are *not* to blame."

If only I could stay in his arms for the rest of the night.

But I can't. I've already overstayed his hug. I press away from him, but he doesn't let me go. Not completely.

His palms find purchase on either side of my face, and his thumbs sweep the tears off my cheeks. "Not. Your. Fault."

How generous he is to say this, even though it isn't true.

I press away from him and glare down at the Bloodstone, which flashes like a traffic light. I latch on to the ring and yank and yank and yank, but all I manage is to twist my skin and anger my knuckle.

"Hopefully, this'll hold," Gaëlle is telling someone. I'm guessing Adrien.

I turn to find Adrien beaming his phone's flashlight onto Claire's hand. A yellow minion Band-Aid graces Claire's finger.

"Mom always had plasters on her too." Adrien's bereft tone drags me out of my self-loathing and fills my veins with a renewed spark.

Alma will not end up like Camille.

"Let's finish this!" I clamp my fingers around the cross-shaped paving stone Alma risked her life to bring us and place it where the Bloodstone pulls my hand, at the very center of the alley. And then I return for the dark cobbles and begin building the five quatrefoil outlines.

"You're fucking kidding me? Four minutes and twenty-six seconds?" Slate mutters as he packs one of my shapes with pale pebbles. "Yeah . . . uh-huh. We'll get it done, but, Bastian, stay with Geoffrey, you hear me?"

Blood gushes into my ears as I slap each cobble against the packed dirt.

Adrien crouches beside me, working on the lighter patch of stones. "The Quatrefoil will reverse all of its curses, Cadence."

"Will it?" I snap, my tone so brittle he flinches. "Because Emilie's not back. Papa's still handicapped. Solange is a drooling zombie!" I spear my fingers through my hair, pushing it out of my eyes so hard I tear off a couple strands.

His mouth pinches, and I want to apologize, because he was trying to be nice. To comfort me. But I can't accept his sympathy. Besides, if he'd listened to me when I told him the design was wrong, we wouldn't still be paving the damned alleyway. My best friend wouldn't be encased in a *toull-bac'h*. Claire Robinson's finger wouldn't have cracked off.

He must spot the condemnation in my expression, because his hazel eyes grow as inky as the fragments of sky beyond the mist. He moves away from me. I bet he'd move away from the alley, from Brume and the cursed Quatrefoil, if he could get past Claire.

"Two minutes left, guys," Slate announces.

Keeping my eyes averted from Alma, I dash to the pile of cobbles and grab handfuls, then race back to the side abutting the rampart and line them up on the dirt.

Six trips back and forth later, Gaëlle sputters, "Twenty-three seconds."

My stomach is a knotted rope, and my lungs feel cast from iron. I hurry, the others matching my rhythm.

"Twelve."

"I hate countdowns," I mutter, crouching to press more cobbles into place.

"I have two stones left." Slate's slashing the night with his phone's beam. "Can anyone spot where they go?"

"Here!" Adrien yells at the same as Gaëlle calls out, "Six."

"*Putain*! And this one? Where—" Slate drops to his knees so brusquely I half expect him to mess up our handiwork, but once the stones are in their rightful place, they're magically cemented there.

Until our time runs out, that is.

Then they all fucking airlift and spangle out of existence.

Slate punches the narrow alley just as Gaëlle whispers, "One."

I sit back on my heels, eyes closed, and brace myself for another earthquake, another scream, and another layer of guilt to form over my desolate heart.

The *kelc'h* groans, and I ball my fingers into fists, my nails biting into my palms.

I hate magic.

I hate it with every cell of my being.

It's vicious and cruel and—

"We made it." Gaëlle's awe rushes over the creaking bones of Third.

My lids rise.

My head turns.

I stroke the cobbles, shuddering when my thumb grazes the painted plus at the heart of the smallest quatrefoil, the one in the middle of the alley. I level my gaze on the main road, hoping to see

Mademoiselle Claire and Alma shake themselves free of their granite cocoons, but both remain motionless.

A shadow falls over me, and then knees click as a broad figure impedes my view of the two statues.

"She's still trapped," I croak. "They're both still trapped."

"Only two more trials to go, and we'll break them free."

"What if—" My swallow slips painfully down my contracted throat. "How do we"—my voice shakes with a rising sob—"protect them, Slate?" The sob squirms out, and then another, and another.

"Please don't cry, princess. You're breaking my damn heart."

"I hate this day. I hate this day so much."

More shadows drape over us as Gaëlle and Adrien crowd in around us. Adrien kneels and puts a tentative palm on my shoulder blade.

I turn my head and blink wet eyes at him. "I'm sorry for how I spoke to you earlier. I'm so sorry, Adrien."

He raises the hand not on my back and rests it on my cheek, angling my face farther toward his. "You have nothing to apologize for, Cadence." He leans forward and places his lips on my forehead, and I sigh.

Not out of relief, because I won't feel any until the Bloodstone comes off and this nightmare is over, but out of affection for this friend who's never once been anything but kind and careful with me.

"I love you," I whisper to him, and his breath catches.

Was he not aware that I did? He and Gaëlle are my family. I could never have survived this version of hell without them at my side.

I unlatch my forehead from Adrien's lips and wrench my neck back to look at Gaëlle. She stands behind Slate, who's gone so stiff *he* looks carved from granite. "I'm sorry I dragged you into this, Gaëlle, but I'm lucky to have you in my life."

My heart's not so desolate after all, and my tear ducts not so dry.

I look at Slate last, unsure what to tell this stranger, even though I feel so absurdly much when I look at him.

He stands before I can come up with any words to thank him for his assistance and jams his hands into his pockets, then pulls out gloves, which he wrenches on, his dark gaze tapered on the black leather.

I call to him with my eyes, but he doesn't give me his attention. Instead, he strides toward Claire. "Now, to get past Mademoiselle Claire without chipping her," he grumbles.

Gaëlle's eyebrows lift in time with my own, because he sounds more angry than worried. Is he mad about the broken phalanx or the lack of recognition?

My contemplation wanes as my gaze settles on Alma. If only I could switch places with her.

I swear on my life, I will get you out, Alma.

And then I swear it on each star in the Brumian firmament, hoping that, even though they're cloaked in mist, they can still hear me and will hold me accountable.

36

SLATE

Three days have gone by since our trial on Third, and all's been depressingly quiet. I stare at the ceiling from where I lay on the hard mattress of my elfin hovel, the cheap sheets I bought at Carrefour like steel-wool against my back. A speckled spider tiptoes across its web in the corner of the room, causing an involuntary shiver to snake up my spine.

Fucking Brume. Now, not only do I have mermaid PTSD, but I also have a newfound fear of being bitten by hairy creepers.

I rub a hand over my neck, glad it's no longer puffed like a profiterole, then feel around the floor for my shoe and throw it at the unsuspecting arachnid. The lacy web tears, but the spider drops to the ground unharmed and advances over the hardwood in what I swear is a gloating swagger.

Sighing, I reach out and grab the folded boxer-briefs I bought during my twenty-minute, one-stop shopping trip to the supermarket. Besides underwear and six-and-a-half-count Breton cotton bedsheets, I got comfort food and drinks: three giant bags of lemon-flavored madeleines and a magnum of Cabernet Franc.

I rip the price tag off my new underwear, toss it on the nightstand, then pull on one of the pairs, the spandexy cotton snug against my ass. Plain colors were alas depleted, so thumbs-up emojis decorate my best bits.

The checkout girl had stifled a smile when she'd scanned my

purchases. Usually, I would've cracked some self-deprecating joke, but the post street-paving mosh-fest had put me in a mood. A mood I have yet to kick.

I step into my jeans and yank on a T-shirt. Time to stop moping and take inventory of the good things in my life:

1. Bastian is alive.
2. Cadence is alive.
3. I'm alive.

It's a real short list.

I could pad it. Add positives like oh, the fact that I'm no longer washing my weenie benders in the gritty sink of the *toilettes hommes* in order to wear them two days in a row. Gotta celebrate the small victories and all that crap.

When I compare my *thank-fuck* list to the endless one of baddies, I groan.

1. Emilie is still dead.
2. Solange is a zombie.
3. Claire Robinson turned to stone.
4. So did a junior named Nicolas, and Catherine, a freshman.
5. So did the good doctor's Hungarian Greyhound, Gaston.
6. So did Alma. Fucking full of life, never sit still, laugh-your-ass-off Alma.
7. So did Spike. He's here in front of me, looking mighty pasty.

That's not the full list. There are tons more. But here's the sweet little cherry on top:

100. Cadence loves Adrien.

Not only does she love him, but she also declared it in front of me, ripping out my heart and crushing it against the cobbles right then and there. I almost wish I was cursed to be in a *toull-bac'h*, so my heart could turn to stone.

At least, it would hurt less.

But then I think of the blood that seeped out of Claire Robinson's finger after I broke it off and decide that although my predicament sucks, hers sucks harder. My stomach turns as I remember her pained moan, and I fall back onto the bed, head in my hands, pulse kicking my temples.

Don't think about it. Any of it. Especially not the look of surprise and terror on Alma's face when the granite imprisoned her.

Or the look of joy on Adrien's when Cadence confessed her love.

I've been *not-thinking* a lot these past three days.

Once the *kelc'h* reset, we got to work before anyone dared return to Third. For once in his pathetic life, Geoffrey proved useful, emerging from the temple and hauling a pile of fluffy blankets from his son's home. We wrapped Claire and Alma up and, as carefully as humanly possible, carried them into Adrien's living room. Then we scoured the rest of Third for the other casualties.

We had to break into Nicolas's dorm where he was stone-cold napping. Catherine had been in the middle of a yoga session, stretched out in downward-dog on a foam mat in the common room of her dorm. The others in the class had all run screaming when it happened. Thankfully, they won't remember a thing now that the *kelc'h* has swiveled back. Sylvie's Hungarian Greyhound was petrified peeing. We searched for fucking ever for the last victim but didn't find the unfortunate soul. Until, that is, I got home to a lifelike statue of Spike.

Adrien's living room resembled Medusa's lair when we were finished. An improvement on his old-man style. I almost quipped he should get himself some statues for when his present ones turn back to flesh and fur, but my mood had taken a toll on my vocal cords. Even more so when I saw the exact moment the *toull-bac'h* victims fully turned to stone.

When the thin granite sheen over Claire Robinson's eyes thickened and the kiddie plaster around her finger faded to gray. When there were no more muffled whimpers or cries or whines beneath the surface of any of the stone husks. When the spark of life that even Alma's statue had, just up and died.

Through all of it, Bastian remained clueless and confused. I'm making sure he stays that way to spare him the heartache I'm presently experiencing, because by God does it suck to lose the girl.

While the *diwallers* played art movers, he was tasked with babysitting the clock. Once we were done, I went up to the temple with the rest of the crew. Bastian had searched the group for Alma, which prompted me to lie about her whereabouts. I told him she'd gone off to Paris to meet up with her parents, who'd surprised her with a visit. Cadence and the others corroborated my tall tale.

So, as far as Bastian knows, the paving stone situation went down without a hitch. Problem is, it's been three days, and he's starting to get suspicious because Alma hasn't answered any of his text messages. Bastian may be naïve but he's the opposite of stupid.

I added another deceitful layer to my lie by telling him that in her hurry to get to Paris, Alma had forgotten her cell phone. Then I texted Cadence so we were on the same page.

She sent me a thumbs-up emoji. A fucking thumbs-up, like the ones on my fucking underwear.

Even though I don't want to see Cadence fawning over Adrien, I wish the Quatrefoil would put the next round in motion, just to give me something to do besides wallow and wonder what the everliving-hell will be thrown at us next.

There's a knock on the door.

I glance at my watch. 9:45 a.m. on a Thursday morning. Pretty much anyone I know should be in class right now. So should I, but my whole schedule got wiped out along with my existence, and apart from the astronomy classes, which are not happening at the moment due to Claire Robinson's 'leave of mental health', the study groups are all too small for me to slip in unnoticed.

I duck under the spiteful ceiling beam and unlatch the door. Bastian is in the hall, the light from his phone screen tingeing his skin green. He gives me a half-hearted, "Hey," as he clicks off the device, but not before I spot the list of one-sided text bubbles he's sent Alma over the past few days.

His being here isn't good, because it means he's skipping class, and he only skips if he's hurting. The last time he purposely skipped a class was four years ago when the stray mutt we fed scraps to was hit by a car. Bastian found her dead on the side of the road, and I found him cradling her broken body in his arms. He didn't go to school for two full days he was so shaken.

Skipping is Bastian's equivalent of getting so utterly sloshed he'd steal a cursed ring off a corpse.

I pull open the door wider, and he steps in.

"Don't you have class?" I'm glad to see him but wonder why he came to me. He's still a little skeptical of this Slate Ardoin.

His eyes are bloodshot, the skin under them bruised purple. He gives a shrug. "I've read ahead in the Economics textbook, so no real reason to go."

Alma's in that class with him. So is the uncursed version of me.

He sucks in a breath, and those bloodshot eyes widen.

I follow his gaze, my stomach plummeting as I realize he's spotted Spike. Before he can make any other sightings, I swaddle the Mexican Snowball and Cadence's neon cactus with a black button-down in dire need of a wash. With my toes, I unplug the cord, so it stops glowing.

"What's that?" Bastian's attention thankfully hasn't strayed off stone-cold Spike.

"That's . . . *uh* . . . my sculpture. Made it in *Intro to Sculpting* last month."

Crouching, he takes a closer look. "I thought that was only for art majors."

"Nope. *Non.* For anyone who wants to get their hands dirty." I rub said hands together, trying to get rid of their clamminess. I really hate misleading my brother.

"Huh. It's really good." He studies it again.

"Thanks. Hey, so what brings you by—"

"It's going to sound crazy but"—he's leaning so far forward, his nose almost gets impaled on one of Spike's granite needles—"it looks just like my Steve."

My hands freeze.

"You know, my Eve's Needle that got plant-napped. This sculpture leans the same way he does, even has a patchy area where he got sunburned when the guys left him too close to the window." A deep groove pleats his brow.

I run a hand through my hair while I try to decide which way to play this. "Well, to be honest, I was at that party one of your buddies had a few weeks back." I'm making the assumption that with that many idiots in one house, parties have occurred, and regularly. "I'd been struggling with what I was going to sculpt for my next assignment, but when I saw Sp—Steve—I knew he'd be perfect."

"Wow. That's just . . . wow. Nice." He clears his throat and takes off his glasses, pretending to rub the bridge of his nose when what he's really doing is wiping his eyes.

Bastian's sorrow makes my chest feel like a sumo wrestler's using it as a stool. If the *toull-bac'h* wasn't so fragile, I'd actually give Spike to Bastian, just to see the kid smile. But I can't take any chances, not when my little brother is cohabitating with careless teens.

"So what brings you to my dilapidated domain this early? Just felt like slumming it?"

We're all supposed to meet up in the archives at lunch to pore over *Istor Breou* as well as pictures of the scroll. Pictures, because since Solange is now barricaded in Rainier's office, we no longer have access to the *Kelouenn* the Quatrefoil coughed up during the treasure hunt. I still don't know how Rainier led her up the stairs and got out unscathed, what with being stuck in his wheelchair, but I applaud his craftiness. Anything to keep us from the truth.

Bastian stands and fidgets with his glasses some more, wiping them on his scarf, setting them on his face and then taking them off and wiping them again. I gesture for him to sit on the bed but he stays upright. There's no chair for me to offer. The closest place to sit is on the piss-stained toilet down the hall.

Glasses back on, Bastian heaves a heavy sigh. "Okay. Look, I'm just going to come right out with it. I think the others are hiding something from me. About Alma. About the Third Kelc'h trial."

"Oh?" I force my eyebrows up, affecting a look of surprise.

"I realize we don't know each other well, but that's sort of why I came to you. They care about me, and I think they're trying to protect me. But you, you and I have no history. No emotions clouding our relationship. You have no reason to hide the truth from me, except that maybe they've asked you to. But I'm here to beg you to tell me the truth. Man to man."

The sheer irony hits me with such force, I can't hold back a laugh. It starts off as a chuckle but quickly morphs into an unstoppable wave. I set my hands on my knees to hold myself steady and laugh until I cry. As I do so, Bastian's complexion goes from ashen to beet-red.

Putain. I've got to get myself under control, or I'm gonna lose what little friendship I've regained.

I catch my breath and shake my head. "Sorry. Some situations make me socially awkward. Sometimes, I just laugh without there being a good reason."

"Paradoxical laughter." The ruddiness starts to fade from his cheeks. "I've read about that. Although usually, it's associated with brain damage." He pauses just long enough to make his statement a question. When I don't say anything, he continues, "But sometimes, just being nervous or anxious can cause an onslaught. My guess is the others forced you to keep this stuff a secret and you're uncomfortable now that I'm confronting you."

Right. Or *I* forced *them* to keep it a secret.

Bastian's eyes are pleading, and behind the thick lenses they're magnified to take on the puppy-dog-look that forever gets me. Yet I'm also aware of how ulcerated my heart feels now that Cadence has gone for Prof full-throttle, and I don't want Bastian's organ to become a festering wound like mine.

He clears his throat, but his voice still breaks when he says, "She's cursed, isn't she?"

I don't dare make a sound. I don't even fucking breathe.

"At the very least, Slate, tell me if she's gonna be okay. Just that. I don't have to know more. But I want the *truth.* No bullshitting me. Please."

I give a short nod, realizing I'm basically admitting something happened to Alma. That she isn't in Paris with her missionary parents. My hope is, despite turning into stone, she'll come back to us on the new moon. I sigh and say it out loud, sensing he needs the reassurance. "She's gonna be fine."

Bastian's jaw clenches, but the tension in his shoulders eases. "Thanks." With a hesitant smile, he adds, "Bro."

37

CADENCE

I bluster into the temple, the straps of my bookbag carving up my shoulder even through my five layers of clothing. Today is brutally cold, and considering the thick, white cloud cover, it's about to get a whole lot frostier. When I checked the weather report app this morning, it forecasted a hailstorm would hit Brume by midday. It hasn't hit yet. Maybe it won't. Maybe—

A hard plink resounds through the otherwise quiet temple. Then another, and another, as though someone upturned a bag of marbles.

I spoke too soon.

The hailstorm's here.

The ice pellets pummel the dome with such force I expect the colored glass to fissure but like the rest of the temple—and of Brume, for that matter—it was built with magic, and magic is indestructible . . . when it wants to be.

An icy current travels through the curved bookstacks, lifting the ends of my hair. I turn away from the dome to find Adrien dusting his blond head and dark coat.

"Bloody hell, it's cold out there."

"If we ever get magic, you'll be immune to cold." At his cocked brow, I add, "Your element being Fire and all."

"Huh. How convenient will that be?" He smiles. He's been doing that a lot lately. Probably because he senses we're past the halfway mark.

I cannot find it in me to smile. The mere thought of Alma trapped in granite sends me spiraling into a vortex of anxiety and despair. Not to mention all the others. Hearing Solange's guttural wails and grunts throughout the night is all at once terrifying and heartbreaking.

How Papa stands the noise the entire day is beyond me. I've asked him to leave the manor, leave Brume, take a hotel room in Rennes, or better yet, Paris. The farther away he could get the happier I'd feel—not only that, but away from Brume, his curse would diminish and he could walk—yet my father is stubborn and refuses to abandon me however many times I remind him I'm not alone.

I may not have Alma at the present moment, but I have Adrien, Gaëlle, Bastian, and Slate. Although Slate's been MIA recently. Ever since the last trial, he's been acting a little strange. I think it's the guilt of having broken Claire's finger. Of seeing her bleed. He's probably not accustomed to blood. Most people aren't.

"Slept better?" Adrien asks, unbuttoning his coat.

I sigh. "No. It's surprisingly unnerving to share a home with a zombie."

"I've told you already, but I'll repeat it. Stay at my house until we're done, Cadence."

"I can't leave Papa alone with her. Last time I did, she broke out and chased him into his office. If he hadn't had that paperweight handy . . . *and* amazing aim." I shudder just thinking how close he came to being turned into a zombie, or God only knows what else.

"He can stay with my father."

Our fathers aren't friends, hardly friendly, so that's never going to happen. "I doubt sleeping on your couch surrounded by humans trapped in stone will be more conducive to shut-eye," I end up saying.

"You wouldn't sleep on my couch, Cadence."

My pulse ramps up, driving prickling heat back into my chilled extremities. "You don't have a guestroom."

"I'd take the couch, and you'd take my bed."

Oh. My nerve endings quiet all at once. Of course, he hadn't meant to share a bed. *Mind out of the gutter, Cadence.*

I eye the glass trapdoor that leads down to the archival room, but decide to bring up an earlier, sort of related, incident. "I ran into Charlotte today."

Adrien's posture tenses. "Yeah?"

The unpleasant incident swims back to the forefront of my mind. I was exiting my Comp Lit class when Adrien's ex backed me into a corner of the Bisset Esplanade. I probably could've squeezed past her, but since I didn't fear her—there's little I fear these days besides magic—I reclined against the wall to hear her out.

"She's under the impression we're dating and threatened to expose our illicit affair, starting by telling our fathers."

Adrien's eyes widen before squeezing dangerously, almost viciously. "Is that so?"

It's a look I'd expect on Slate, but not on this even-tempered and mature man. It's absurd how often my mind strays to the stranger with *diwaller* blood. What's even more absurd is how much I miss that stranger. I haven't seen him since we stood in front of Bastian the night of the *toull-bac'h* trial and lied about Alma's whereabouts.

He messaged me once, a clinical-sounding text about having told Bastian that Alma forgot her phone. I'd spent over an hour crafting replies, none of which I ended up sending because they'd either sounded desperate or whiny. Frustrated with myself, I'd sent him an emoji.

Safe.

Emotionless.

Straight-to-the-point.

What emojis aren't though, are conducive to conversation.

I shove my lackluster messaging skills far from my mind. "You really need to set her straight, Adrien, because she clearly didn't believe me when I insisted you and I were strictly friends."

"What we are, is none of her business."

"True, but your career's on the line. You really don't need to get into trouble over a lie."

He clenches his jaw so tight I can hear his teeth scrape together over the steady ticking of the clock and the clacking of the hailstorm.

I sigh. "Get that phone call out of the way and then meet me in the archives. I'll get started on the *Kelouenn* and the nonsensical text."

I circle the recessed clock and pull open the trap door that leads to the temple's underground, already dwelling on the absurd and illogical passage Adrien assumes explains our fourth trial. Just the way it's written—each word is repeated twice but with its letters reversed—is confusing.

Midway down the stairs, Adrien yells, "Cadence, wait!"

Frowning, I pause and crane my neck. Seconds later, he's clambering down, panting like he's run a mile instead of a dozen meters. The rings of brown, gold, and green in his irises eddy and darken as he stares at my eyes, then lower, at my mouth. Lips pressed tight, he flicks his gaze to the rough stone wall behind my head and glowers at it.

"What is it, Adrien?"

Waves of heat course off his body as though his veins had somehow filled with fire.

"Did you forget your phone? I can lend you mine but I'm not sure it'll convince Charlotte we're not together."

His gaze finally returns to me. "I didn't say it back, because you caught me by surprise back in *la ruelle*, but I need you to know that the sentiment is mutual, Cadence."

I tip him a smile. "I know you love me, Adrien."

He blinks, apparently genuinely stunned. "You do?"

"Well, you *have* told me a bunch of times over the years. Your declarations are usually accompanied by how you couldn't have dreamt of having a sweeter little sister."

He grimaces.

After a beat, I put a hand on his arm and squeeze, because he still looks in pain. "We *are* lucky to have each other."

He shuts his eyes. When he reopens them, his gaze falls to my hand. I'm about to pull it away when he raises his palm to my cheek. I freeze.

"Next month, you'll be eighteen." After tracing each one of my fingers with his gaze, he's now tracing each one of my lashes. "But I don't really care. I should though, right?"

I'm perplexed and tense. God, am I tense, because I'm not

entirely certain what's happening, and yet deep down, I'm aware that men don't corner and touch women for no reason.

"I'm not your brother, Cadence."

"I'm aware." My voice sounds funny, thick and wooly.

"Are you?"

I should ease him away, but my jaw feels stuck to his palm, my boots welded to the steps. "Of course, I am."

He dips his face lower until his mouth is a hairsbreadth from mine. "Good."

And then his lips are on mine, and his long fingers in my hair.

Although I spent the last few years harboring improper fantasies about my childhood friend, my body seizes up at the contact, and guilt floods me instead of pleasure. I feel like I'm cheating on someone, and the emotion makes zero sense, since we're both single.

"Adrien," I whisper, but he kisses his name off my lips, then licks away any last attempt at telling him to stop.

I'm not weak, and he's not restraining me. I could end this kiss but I don't. Instead, I see it through.

What a terrible thought . . . I shouldn't be *seeing it through*; I should be reveling in it. For some reason, my mind is whirring instead of my body. I think of my first and only lip-locking partner —Romain—and the kisses we shared at the stroke of midnight each New Year's Eve. Platonic as can be, but sweet nonetheless.

Kissing Adrien oddly feels the same.

It doesn't feel like sunshine and starlight and magic, the way I'd imagined. Both our bodies are stiff, our lips working through the motions, the kiss soft and measured. I wish he were a little rougher, a little more reckless. I want him to steal my breath and I want to steal his in turn. I want his touch to turn more possessive, to press me into him until no space remains between our bodies. But Adrien is a gentleman and hardly pulls me near at all.

Slowly, steadily, my pulse dribbles back down until I all but flat-line, and I ease away from him. I don't feel regret, because at least, now, I know we aren't right for each other.

"I'm sorry." He rubs his mouth. "I shouldn't have crossed that line." I guess he, too, noted the absence of chemistry.

"I crossed right over it, also." I smile, because I don't want this to be awkward.

He peeks at me from beneath his lashes.

"At least, now, we know."

He smiles back, tentatively at first, and then a little more brightly. "Yes, we do." He lifts his hand and curls it around my waist, which has me frowning.

Before I can ask what he knows, because our thoughts are obviously not aligned if his hand has wandered to my body again, the ground rumbles.

Adrien stumbles back, catching himself on the railing, and I hit the wall at my back, my palms taking the brunt of the blow.

As I lock my knees and flatten my spine against the coarse stones, I can't decide if I appreciate the Quatrefoil's timing or despise it. On the one hand, it puts a dent in how awkward it was about to get between Adrien and me. On the other, it's delaying our inevitable 'talk'.

"Cadence!" Slate appears by the trapdoor, Bastian weaving like a reed behind him.

Another hard shake makes Slate's body loom closer. I think he may be falling, but his boots are eating each stair separating us. A heartbeat later, he's on the step over mine, arm extended.

"My hand! Take my hand!"

"She's fine!" Adrien grumbles, reaching out toward me at the very same time.

I look between their hands, between their faces. I end up keeping my hands to myself.

Another deep groan emanates from the bowels of Brume.

Slate lunges down another step, and then . . . And then he just disappears.

And so does Adrien.

And so does the stairwell.

And someone I never thought I would see again appears, an emerald quatrefoil charm shivering from her wrist.

38

SLATE

One second I'm on the stairs, yelling at Cadence to take my hand, and the next, I'm sitting at a table in a restaurant with two complete strangers, yukking it up about Lord only knows what and drinking cider from a frosted tankard.

The shock of this sudden change jolts me, and my cup drops, splattering me with foam before crashing to the floor. I stand, knocking over my chair, and palm my sweater to wipe off the droplets.

Only it's not my sweater.

It's a starched dress shirt topped with a tweed waistcoat.

You've got to be kidding me.

I shriek. Like a little girl. Like twelve little girls. No, like a gaggle of pre-pubescent choir boys.

Hands grab me, squeeze my shoulders, brush my cheek, but I keep screaming. After erasing my identity, the Quatrefoil has now replaced my body with . . . with Adrien's.

"*Chéri*, talk to me. What is it?" I stiffen as an older woman with long black curls frames my jaw with her soft hands, emerald eyes glinting with concern. She has a slight accent, one that adds extra syllables to her words. "Rémy! Rémy, *chéri*, what's going on with you?"

Rémy?

So, I'm not Adrien?

I pat my chest, my neck, my face. Thank all that is unholy, I'm still me. Wearing hideous clothes, but still me.

My legs give out just as a vanilla version of myself rights my chair. My ass hits wood, and I blink up at the man watching me through tortoiseshell glasses. He's got my eyes, my mouth, and my nose—well, the nose I had before it got busted one time too many. His hair is stick-straight, threaded through with just enough silver to look distinguished. His chin's shaved smooth.

The sleeves of his navy corduroy blazer, adorned with actual elbow patches, rumple as he pushes them up. "Nolwenn, could you give us some water, please?"

A round woman carrying a platter of food sets it down and swipes a pitcher from another table. She fills up an empty cup and hands it to me.

I grip the glass but don't drink. Just gawk.

Nolwenn's gained ten kilos around her middle and lost one from her *au naturel* face. Unbelievably, the lack of makeup and the extra padding make her seem softer, younger, and a heck of a lot more blissful. Her hair's still puffed, but all in all, she's a whole other person.

"Would you prefer sparkling, Rémy?" she asks.

I keep gawping as I lift the glass to my mouth and take a sip. The water's cold and tastes of iron, as though it was heaved up from the well in the square. My gaze surfs over the wide-eyed lunch crowd, toward the multi-paned window and the well beyond it. That hasn't changed. Fake flowers sit in the bucket, and its peaked roof is still present. However, everything else is unfamiliar.

I'm sitting in the tavern, but besides its roughcast walls, nothing is the same. Instead of scratched wooden tables, framed old photographs, and clover-stamped floor tiles, this place is all white tablecloths, modern paintings, and polished concrete flooring.

Nolwenn turns to the dozen or so other diners. "Show's over!" And then she bustles back into the kitchen.

A server dressed in a penguin suit cleans up my mess while the concerned, dark-haired couple continues talking to me.

The man puts a hand on my shoulder. "What happened, son?"

Son? I study his features once again, then eye the woman, who's still hovering, a slender groove etched between her drawn eyebrows. I know these faces. They smiled at me from a frame on my mantle before Brume's Broom blustered through my house.

Oscar and Eugenia Roland.

My parents.

My *deceased* parents.

They seem alarmingly alive.

Heartbeat accelerating, I stare around the dining area and recognize several faces from the daily landscape of Brume. Fellow students, one firefighter, the security guard who tased me, and an ex-boyfriend of Alma's. But no one from my crew.

I swallow down the sharp bite of panic.

"Rémy, *chéri*"—my mother's voice is soft, careful—"why did you scream?"

I try to run my hand through my hair, but it's gelled stiff. *Jesus.* I pat the crunchy locks and utter the first excuse that comes to mind. "I saw a spider?"

The minute I say it, I regret it because spiders don't bother Slate Ardoin. Or, well, they didn't until they turned me into Quasimodo's twin.

But Oscar laughs. It's quiet and smooth and soothing, like aged whisky. "I should have known." He shakes his head and grins at Eugenia. "Remember that time he found a teeny-weeny one in the corner of his room? The one we practically needed a microscope to see?"

Eugenia's face brightens, mirth washing away the worry lines on her forehead, and then she kisses my helmet of hair. "You wouldn't sleep in your own bed for a week after that."

Right ... I'm not Slate Ardoin. I'm Rémy Roland.

In this messed-up version of reality, I have a shitty sense of style *and* I'm a wuss.

Also, I'm loved.

My insides suddenly feel compact and sweet like the custard in an éclair.

I shake my head. I don't even know these people.

This must be the fourth trial. Unless tarantula venom has finally breached my brain? To be honest, I'm not sure which would be the better scenario.

While my ... *uh* ... parents take their places at the table once again, Eugenia giggles. "Good thing your brother wasn't here for the spider sighting. I think he's the only one in the world more terrified of those things than you are."

Wait, what? I have a brother?

My mother checks the slim gold watch strapped to her wrist. "Twelve minutes late . . . What are the odds he got lost inside one of his books again?"

"High. Very high." My father smiles, then he raises his arm. "Ah, there's our little bookworm."

An icy wind wraps around our ankles as the heavy curtain over the front door is pushed aside.

Bastian pops through, dressed equally tastelessly, and makes a beeline for our table. He kisses Eugenia's proffered cheek, then drops into the chair beside mine. "Hey, *frangin*."

Whatever weird spin the Quatrefoil has put on my world, I'm glad it made Bastian my brother, even though it gave him an iffy sense of style and old man spectacles—tortoiseshell like our father's.

Our father . . . Insane.

This is all completely insane.

As Bastian shrugs out of his coat, Oscar pours him a glass of water. "You missed quite the excitement. Rémy nearly went into cardiac arrest after seeing a spider."

Bastian shoots right up, gaze darting every which way. "Spider? Is it gone?"

Now it's my turn to laugh. "Thank fuck you haven't changed." I rip off a piece of baguette and toss it into my mouth.

Eugenia frowns. "Rémy, language."

I nearly choke on my bread. No parent figure has ever scolded me for swearing. My mouth was always cleaner than any of my foster families', whose vocabulary was ninety percent four-letter words and ten percent derivatives of those words. My school teachers never thought it was worth the effort to turn trash like me into someone respectable, so they didn't even bother. Swearing became my M.O.

"*Pardon*," I apologize, both annoyed and kind of touched someone cares about what I say and how I say it.

The server takes our orders, then ferries over our meals. The food's fantastic as usual, but the menu's nothing like the one at the old tavern. The *real* tavern. Instead of traditional Breton fare, this is French-Asian fusion. Every dish comes to the table looking like a work of art, and I admire the palette of colorful sauces that accompany my foie gras sautéed with daikon radish.

Conversation over lunch is breezy. It seems that Bastian not only considers himself my little brother but legally is. From what I glean, he was adopted by the Rolands. I wonder what that kind of childhood would've been like. A bout of heartburn seizes me as I contemplate it.

Bastian sits a little straighter, fidgets a little less, speaks a little louder. He exhibits confidence I've never spotted in him before. I decide I like him this way, at total ease with himself. He's glowing. If I weren't mildly freaking out about the Quatrefoil's intent, I might take real pleasure in this alternate reality.

Suddenly, the sunny mood at the table turns somber. Both my parents are staring at the thick curtain and the woman who's stepped past it. Claire Robinson. She's sliding off her gloves and my attention immediately zips to her fingers. They're all there. *Halle-fucking-lujah.* Though I have no clue how she got out her granite prison, just as I have no clue how I got into my tweed jail cell.

My mother seems to be holding her breath as Claire steps up to the bar. When the blonde professor's gaze flits our way, a predatory smile widens her face, and she alters her path.

Oscar sighs audibly while Eugenia crosses her arms over her chest and tilts her chin up.

Bastian looks at me and rolls his eyes.

"Oscar! Eugenia! What a surprise." Claire flutters her over-mascaraed lashes and unwraps a bright-pink scarf from around her neck, revealing the hearty bounce of her cleavage.

"Hello, Claire," my father says on another sigh.

"Sorry to interrupt your family lunch." She doesn't seem sorry in the least. She pulls an empty chair from the table behind her and sets it so close to Oscar's, the armrests clank together. "I was wondering if it'd be all right if I used your lesson on black holes with my freshmen."

While she bats her eyes shamelessly, Bastian turns to me and says, "So? What did Cadence say about"—he makes a little circle with his head—"you know?"

"She exists here too!" I hadn't really stopped to ponder this fact, but wow, am I relieved.

Bastian squints at me from behind his glasses. It's the look he gets when he's questioning someone's sanity.

Merde. He's not aware this is a trial. Or another curse. Or the Quatrefoil only knows what.

Throwing out a fake little chuckle, I shrug. "Gotcha."

He herds breadcrumbs into a little heap on the tablecloth. "What time are she and Alma coming tonight."

"Tonight?"

He lifts an eyebrow. "You know, for the inauguration? Of the cathedral? Geoffrey Keene and the historical society's big renovation project?"

"You mean the *dihuner* temple?"

"I mean the *cathedral*—that big thing on the top of the hill. The medieval monstrosity that's been there for centuries. The building that just got all-new stained glass and saint statues." His voice is sarcastic, but his dark humor's tinged with alarm.

"Right. Yeah. And we're going with Cadence and Alma because . . .?" I look to him to finish the sentence, hoping my cluelessness isn't too obvious.

"Because it's kind of expected for a guy to take his girlfriend to this kind of fancy event."

"Girlfriend? Cadence is my girlfriend?" The unease tearing at my gut abates. That's two good things to come out of this trial—Bastian is my bro and Cadence is my girl.

Bastian leans in closer so that his voice is a whisper. "Are you *on* something? You're acting really strange."

But I don't answer, because right then, the curtain shifts and spits out another customer. A dapperly-dressed one, although that's not a real feat in this town. All one has to do to qualify is avoid tweed, corduroy, and patterns frequently found on tablecloths.

"Berthou! Over here!" Oscar's waving his hand in the air as though we're sitting in a crowded airport instead of a chic restaurant.

Bastian nudges me. "If you don't know when the girls are coming, I guess we can just ask Monsieur Berthou."

Stomping his suede boots on the mat, Monsieur Berthou dusts snow from the shoulders of his cashmere coat before removing it and handing it to the penguin waiter. His ivory cable-knit sweater and stonewashed jeans look expensive and yet don't scream money. The clothes of a fashionable, wealthy man.

As he strides over to us, I get a sense of déjà vu. I *know* him, but can't quite place him. He shakes hands with Oscar and Bastian, then kisses both Eugenia and Claire on the cheeks. He's the kind of guy you instinctively like and trust—his blue gaze is warm and welcoming, and smile lines bracket his mouth.

Claire finally excuses herself, and Monsieur Berthou slides into the freed chair, shooting me a wide smile before turning toward my mother.

"You're not already getting dolled up for the party, Eugenia?"

My mother titters before tipping her wine glass to her lips. "You have me confused with Oscar."

My father shakes his head.

"Well my girls are already at it." Berthou smells like cedarwood and cigar smoke. "Glad to be out of the house."

Cigar—

Holy.

Shit.

Monsieur Berthou is none other than Rainier de Morel.

39

CADENCE

I haven't stopped staring at my mother since the ground shook and transported me to a realm in which she exists.

When I suddenly found myself here, she was standing behind me, wrapping strands of my brown hair around a hot iron while laughing about something or other. I had no idea what, because my mind was wholly focused on making sense of the hallucination that felt eerily real.

I may be wrong about the Quatrefoil's inner workings, but deep down, I've always held out hope that if we defeat the dark magic, we'll manage to reverse all of its curses. Not only Papa's legs, but Maman's untimely death.

My father breezed past us toward his closet—breezed!—announcing he was on his way out to grab a quick drink with friends. He didn't ask if we wanted to come. Then again, we weren't dressed. On his way out, he kissed my cheek. Surprisingly, he didn't kiss Maman's. He barely even talked to her.

I was about to ask if he could see her when Maman said, "Shall we meet on First, Rainier?"

Uh . . . weren't we in the manor on First?

"Or will you come back before then?" Her voice didn't carry much warmth.

"I'll call you." And then he was gone.

My father can walk.

My mother is here.

I knew already then that this wasn't real, but I deeply wanted it to be. I curled my fingers into my waffle-knit bathrobe—my ring-*free* fingers—and absorbed every sound and every movement of this ghost come to life.

That was several hours ago.

Since then, my childlike wonder has abated, the shine already wearing off the apple. In this plane, magic has never existed. The Quatrefoil never existed. And so things are as they would be without it.

Papa kept his last name; Maman never slipped on the Blood-stone; I never fought a vicious hawthorn tree or a terracotta goliath. Even the *kelc'hs* are reversed, with the temple—no, *cathedral*—on First, and our manor on Fifth. Our manor where Solange is not a zombie and my mother's presence fragrances every room.

It should be the perfect world, but it isn't.

In the perfect world, my parents are deeply in love, not strangers existing alongside each other.

"She is *not* cheating on your father, Cadence."

I jump at the sound of Alma's voice, and then I let out a muffled gasp and wrap her in a tight hug. She's alive. And well. Not cocooned in granite.

I press her back, my eyes wet with emotion. "Your hair!"

She frowns and touches a lock of it. "What's wrong with it? And why are you acting like you haven't seen me in years?"

I swipe the skin beneath my eyes, careful not to smudge the makeup Maman applied. Alma doesn't know that this is a parallel world. The same way Geoffrey doesn't seem to. Perhaps he was sent to another plane?

Unless he's pretending . . .

When I greeted him upon arriving at the cathedral, he barely grunted back *hello* as he whisked my mother away to brainstorm birthday presents for Camille. Silver lining: he didn't ogle me. He's got the original object of his obsession back.

"Just feeling emotional today, Alma. As for your hair . . . it's very purple and short."

She smooths a hand down her shoulder-length, chopped curls, tugging on them as though to loosen the tight spirals. "Probably the lighting since I haven't redyed it recently. Anyway"—Alma juts her chin toward where my mother stands, head bent with Geoffrey's— "I think you're wrong about them having an affair."

But there's something between them. I can see it in the furtive glances, the shared smiles, the feather-light touches. Not to mention neither Camille nor Papa are present.

Just as I think of Geoffrey's wife, her voice rings over the cheery din. I spin on my heeled, knee-high boots to locate its source, and my heart vaults into my throat. I can't help but smile, but it's wobbly and tear-filled. How I loved this woman. This tender mother figure. I want to throw myself in her arms, but if I do that, she'll worry something's wrong with me. The same way my mother asked me repeatedly over the course of the afternoon we spent together if I was feeling all right.

Camille walks arm in arm with Adrien, whose eyes grow wide when he sees me. He whispers something in her ear that I don't catch because the temple—I mean, cathedral, which honestly looks more like a Turkish bath with all its midnight-hued stone, glossy columns, and twinkling lights—is cavernous, twice the size of the *dihuner* temple, and rectangular. It's paved in black marble instead of ochre tiles and is littered with statues of saints. The outsized magical clock is gone and so are the curved bookcases. The stained-glass cupola is also nonexistent.

I can't decide if I'm relieved or unnerved by the clock's absence. Even though the *dihuner* was far from a step-by-step manual, it still offered us a semblance of guidance. Just like the *Kelouenn* and the Bloodstone.

I touch my index finger. I don't miss the hot weight of the ring, but what does it mean that it's gone?

Maybe that's our trial . . . we need to find the ring, clock, and *Kelouenn*, and put them back in their rightful spots. No. That sounds too similar to the first trial. Not to mention, how does a giant clock go missing? Unless it's ticking beneath the black stone?

Adrien carves a path toward Alma and me. "Cadence"—his voice is shrill with nerves—"please tell me you remember?"

"Remember what?" Alma's head is so close to mine that her purple curls brush my bare shoulder.

I loose a relieved sigh. "Yes."

Adrien, too, releases a deep breath. "Thank God. I don't know if Dad's pretending but—"

"I was wondering the same thing." My gaze boomerangs toward Geoffrey, who's smiling down at my mother.

"What are you two chattering on about?" Alma clutches my arm a little tighter, her long shellacked nails digging into my skin.

I attempt to come up with a believable answer since Alma's not aware of the Quatrefoil's trickery. "The party we're planning for Camille's birthday. It's a surprise. Actually, Adrien and I need to discuss the final details." I steal my arm from her grip. "I'll catch up with you in a sec, all right?"

Alma frowns but then gets sidetracked by a passing platter of mini quiches. As she skips to grab one, Adrien's hand settles on the small of my back and guides me behind one of the giant marble columns.

"How insane is this trial?" I hiss once we're hidden from the swanning crowd.

"Very. I mean, I'm so happy to see my mother. That's a gift. But everything else . . ." He runs the hand that was on the base of my spine over his gelled blond locks, then over his face. "I'm going to be a father."

"What?"

"In this alternate reality, I'm married, and my wife is about to give birth. She's on bedrest as we speak."

"You're kidding?"

He squeezes the bridge of his nose. "Unfortunately, no."

"Who are you married to?"

He grimaces. "Charlotte."

I snort. I can't help it. "*Wow*."

His hand slips off his face and settles on the wide column next to where I'm leaning my head, his mouth curving into a rueful smile. "Tell me about it. I kept trying to sneak out of my house to come find you, but my *wife* requested *fraises des bois*, because normal strawberries didn't quell her pregnancy cravings, and then she had me massage her swollen feet, complaining the entire time that I was pressing too hard or that I wasn't in the right spot." He shudders as though the mere memory of kneading Charlotte's soles is painful. "I'm so glad my fake wife's on bedrest. Does that make me a terrible man?"

"You married Charlotte, Adrien. That makes you a saint."

He smiles, his gaze dipping over the cobalt dress Maman insisted I wear. "I hope you know I'd never have picked her." He settles his free hand on my waist, and my amusement screeches to a halt.

Crap crap crap. For the briefest of seconds, I debate the merits of pretending like I don't remember what we were doing before the world spun off its axis, but that'll again delay the inevitable. Even though I was hoping to save this conversation for after the trial, we need to have it now.

"Adrien, about what happened in the stairwell . . ." My voice tapers off as a man walks up to the statue nearest us and tilts his head.

His hair's gone fully gray, and prematurely so, but his skin is tanned and unlined, exactly like I remember him.

I duck under Adrien's arm to get a better view. "Is that—is that Matthias?"

"It is."

"We have to find Gaëlle. She must be freaking out." I round the column to scan the crowd for her but find myself looking into another familiar face.

Slate's.

He's here, too. Dressed in a black tux, which he wears over a black dress shirt unbuttoned at the collar, he looks older and more refined. He isn't clean-shaven, but his black curls have been tamed, and his skin is bruise-and-welt-free.

My father stands beside him, looking equally dapper. He waves me over with a smile, while Slate scowls. I'm not entirely certain why he's scowling, but I imagine it's because of something Papa said.

"The kid's here too?" Adrien's gruff voice ruffles the hair beside my ear.

The kid? Slate really rubs him the wrong way.

"Shows he was telling the truth when he claimed to have blood ties to Brume," I say.

Adrien produces a disgruntled sound, as though he disagrees.

"I wonder whose child he is. And do you think he knows this isn't real?" I snag my lip and run it between my teeth as I stride toward him.

I still can't get over how strange it is to see my father upright. He's so much taller and broader. And happier. I assume that last part is because Maman's alive, although . . .

I spot Gaëlle then, pushing a double-stroller through the nave, her favorite yellow scarf wound loosely around her neck and dusting the floor. She *oohs* and *ahhs* at the twinkling spotlights embedded in the vaulted ceiling.

"Gaëlle!" I call out.

Her eyes widen and dart away from me, and then she draws an arc, arrowing straight toward Matthias. When she parks the stroller beside him, his arm comes around her shoulders, and he kisses her temple. So, I guess she's *not* freaked out . . .

"Don't you look stunning tonight, *ma Cadence*."

Still frowning from Gaëlle's brush-off, I look at my father. "*Merci*, Papa."

"When does she not look stunning, though, Monsieur Berthou?" Slate plucks my hand from my side and tugs on it until my body bumps into his.

Heat rises into my cheeks, and I attempt to press myself away. He did not just say that? And why is my father smiling?

"So right, my boy." My father slaps Slate's shoulder. "So right."

The affection between the two is so incongruous that my jaw is surely dragging like Gaëlle's scarf.

"Cadence inherited her looks from Amandine." Papa's blue eyes scrape over the crowd. "Where is your—" His breath catches, and then his lips press tight.

I follow his gaze toward where Maman and Geoffrey still stand close together . . . *too* close together.

My father coughs and then backs up. "I'll see you kids later." There's a hint of sadness inside his voice and on his face. As he fords through the crowd toward a dark-haired couple, his shoulders slump a little.

I grit my molars. How could she do this to him? Act so . . . so . . .

Slate must hear my teeth's enamel grind, because he murmurs, "She's not real, Cadence. Nothing about this realm is real."

I stare up into his dark eyes, grateful for his words, but then I startle. "You're conscious this is all fake?"

"I am." His nose brushes the shell of my ear as he moves in to add, "And by the way, we're dating." He spreads my fingers with his, then gently folds them over mine and lifts my knuckles to his mouth to kiss them. "In every version of this world, you and I . . ." His voice trails off, and I briefly wonder how he planned on ending that sentence, but I get caught up on the first part of what he said.

"We're dating?" My voice sounds as rough as the stone stairs cutting up Brume's flanks—straight again.

Slate nods. "*And* your father adores me."

"I noticed that. It's—"

"Endearing?" Slate supplies.

"Unexpected."

A smile curves his eyes. "Oh, and Bastian's my brother."

I gasp. "No way."

"My parents adopted him from the foster care system."

"How wonderful." Adrien's voice is crisp, his gaze laser-focused on my hand enclosed in Slate's.

I hadn't even noticed he'd trailed me over.

I disengage my hand from Slate's. "Did you find out who your birth parents are?"

Slate nods toward the couple my father is speaking with, and I study them more carefully. Where have I seen them before? My mouth rounds as my brain snares the memory. They were in my parents' wedding album and in the town's obituary.

The Rolands.

Something strikes me then . . . Something truly odd. Odder than this entire situation. Or maybe not odder, because this is all very weird, but definitely equally so.

My spine tingles, and I take a step back. "The first time we met, you said you were their child. How—How is this possible?"

"Yeah, Ardoin, how is this possible?" Adrien's arms are crossed in front of his chest and strain his three-piece suit.

Slate's silent for a beat, then his gaze cuts across the room toward Geoffrey and my mother. "How much help has your father been in the trials, Adrien?"

"I don't see what that has to do—"

"None, right?" Slate slams his eyes back onto Adrien's.

"He fought the mermaid."

Slate barks out a sharp laugh. "Like hell he did. And it was a *groac'h*."

I frown—both at Slate's knowledge of the water fairy and at my own skepticism of Geoffrey's abilities. If I hadn't seen him emerge from that well with my own eyes, I would never have believed it. "What are you trying to say?"

"What I'm trying to say is that Geoffrey has been a placeholder, that's all. He's not a real *diwaller*. Think hard, both of you. Don't you feel like you've forgotten something? Like something has been off this whole time?"

I almost nod. But since when has anything to do with the Quatrefoil felt *right*?

"*You're* what's been off." Adrien glares at Slate.

"Actually, no. I'm the real Water *diwaller*. Always have been. After Cadence's Earth trial against the hawthorn, I was cursed, and my curse was to be forgotten, along with my bloodline. Becoming a nobody was my worst fear." His eyes sweep over every feature on my face, settling briefly on my parted lips before rising back to my eyes. "Well, one of my worst fears." His hand rises and delicately cups my nape, pressing through the hair my mother coaxed into perfect, glossy waves.

I shiver. From his touch. From his confession. From the fact that my mother is alive and that magic has rearranged the world as we know it.

"What you are, is delusional, Ardoin." And then Adrien's fist whispers past my cheek and crashes into Slate's unsuspecting face.

40

SLATE

Adrien's right hook is shit. His knuckles glide off my cheekbone and do more damage to my hairstyle than to my face.

His eyes widen, and he stares at his fist as if he isn't quite sure where the sudden movement came from. Were I back in Marseille, I'd pummel him until he was nothing but a black-and-blue stain on the sidewalk. Slate Ardoin doesn't deal well with unprovoked violence.

But I'm not in Marseille. I'm here, in Brume, or at least a version of it. And I'm not even Slate Ardoin. I'm Rémy Roland. And my guess is that Rémy is a peaceful sort of dude.

Still, my fingers itch like hell to wipe the floor with Adrien's porcelain features.

Instead, I step closer, my voice as close to shouting as I can make it in a whisper. "What the fuck, Prof? You really think it's a good idea to bring attention to ourselves in front of the whole town?"

His gaze cruises over the crowd, who luckily hasn't noticed the near fight, before zeroing in on me. "Fine. But you're not the Water *diwaller* and you're not Cadence's boyfriend."

"Oh? Because you are? Says the married man."

The anger that flares behind his pupils is impressive. Too bad for him, it translates into another lackluster swing.

"That's enough." Cadence shakes her head, her glossy locks glinting like coffee candy in the twinkling spotlights overhead. "We don't have time to debate what is or isn't true. We need to figure out what we're supposed to do."

"You believe me, though, right? That I was cursed?" After hearing her tell Adrien she loved him, now I'm fishing for any little scrap she sends my way.

Jesus, I'm pathetic.

She studies my face and gives me a pitying smile. "I believe *you* believe it."

I don't know why it suddenly feels like I swallowed a butcher knife. Of course, she doesn't believe me. Of course, she won't remember. It'd be a pretty weak curse if I could sweet-talk my way out of it, even though sweet-talking *is* a true talent of mine.

Adrien crosses his arms over his chest. "Cadence is right. We need to focus on the trial, not on you, Ardoin. Dad's pretending—"

"Not pretending," I interject, but Adrien talks right over me.

"—but Gaëlle undoubtedly knows."

"Every trial this time around had to be done as a team," Cadence says. "This should be no different."

I look over to where Gaëlle's laughing with Romain in one wing of the cathedral. "I have a feeling Gaëlle's happy here."

Cadence sighs. "Everyone's alive and well. It's an ideal life."

"For some," Adrien mutters.

"Should've wrapped it before you tapped it."

Adrien glares at me.

"I like you and Charlotte together. You're so . . ." I roll a couple words around on my tongue but decide they'll all earn me a raised eyebrow from Cadence, so I settle on, "compatible."

I think Adrien mutters, "Should've punched you harder," but Cadence has wrapped her hand around my arm, garnering my full attention.

"Boys. Focus. Please."

Oh, I'm focused . . . On *her*.

Even through my suit jacket and button-down shirt, my skin warms where she squeezes.

She releases me. "We need to corner her," she whispers, before taking off toward the curly-haired mother of three and wife of one.

Matthias is way more palatable in technicolor, still a far cry from handsome. Could be his sense of fashion. Seems to be a thing in Brume. One good tailor would do this town wonders.

Adrien and I set off behind Cadence, just as Romain trots toward his father and Nolwenn to help with the twins. Gaëlle leans toward one of the statues Amandine sculpted. Rainier was telling me all about them during our walk up the hill.

His eyes shimmered the entire way. Out of pride for his wife's accomplishment, but also out of grief. Apparently, this Amandine is no saint. He hasn't said much, but I caught him staring at Geoffrey. It reminds me of how I looked at Adrien when Cadence declared her love to him.

I'm really glad he's currently hitched.

As we part ways and circle a still unsuspecting Gaëlle, I wonder if there's any way of leaving Adrien in this dimension.

"Gaëlle, can we talk to you a second?" Cadence asks.

Gaëlle startles and backs up, bumping into Adrien. "No." She spins away from him and smacks into my front. Anger replaces her alarm, and she shakes her head so vigorously her hair comes tumbling out of its pins. "I don't want to go back. I'm not going back."

Cadence runs a hand down the velvet sleeve of Gaëlle's ochre dress. "I know, but this isn't real."

"It could be." She whirls around to face Cadence.

"It's a mirage. It may seem beautiful," Cadence speaks calmly, "but it's engineered by the Quatrefoil, so it's only a matter of time before the beauty fades."

Gaëlle keeps shaking her head. "I'm not going back, Cadence. You all can go, but I'm staying."

"The only way to get back is together," Adrien says.

"*Non.*" Gaëlle's brown eyes fill with tears. "There must be another way. Matthias . . . he's here. He's good and sweet and caring." She wipes her cheek, and her sadness makes my cold, dead heart thump.

Applause thunders under the vaulted ceiling as the orchestra finishes their set.

I wait for it to die out. Once a new classical piece begins, I whisper, "Before we were transported here, did you read anything inside the *Kelouenn* or on the star dial, Prof?"

A nerve in Adrien's jaw ticks. "The only thing I worked out was mirror images. Guess it makes sense." He gestures around him. "A mirror world." His arm settles back against his sapphire velvet tuxedo jacket. "The curse, however, that wasn't so clear. And since we didn't get a chance to see the constellation, or touch the topazes on the *dihuner* before getting thrown in this realm, I have no indication about what must be done to complete the trial."

I give a good, long sigh. "Good thing we're talented at winging it." I'm generous in extending the compliment to Adrien who surely writes lists, and lists about his lists.

"Every trial this far has been to put things in their rightful place," Cadence says.

"But without the visions from the stones, we don't know *what* needs to be put into place." Adrien wilts, his shoulders sloping, his stick-straight spine curving into a question mark. "Mirrors," he murmurs. "Mirror, mirror—"

"On the wall. Get us the fuck out of this ball."

His attention jerks toward me. The ladies, too, look my way. "Sorry," I say. "It was just too tempting."

A faint smile tugs at Cadence's lips but then fades as she bites her bottom lip in thought. "What about pictures of the *Kelouenn*? Have you checked your phone, Adrien?"

He straightens like an arrow and fishes his phone from his inside breast pocket. I doubt there'll be pictures but I don't dare ruin everyone's—Gaëlle excluded—enthusiasm.

Adrien swipes. And swipes. And swipes. He has a lot of pictures of Charlotte. *A lot.* And from the looks of it, either he's shit at taking pics or pregnancy hasn't been all too kind to her.

"They're all gone."

Dun-dun-dunnn. And the Quatrefoil strikes again.

"Maybe they're gone for a reason." Gaëlle looks to where Matthias, Nolwenn, and Romain are playing with the twins. "Maybe that last trial was the definitive last trial, and this is our reward." She fingers her yellow scarf. How she can stomach wearing the thing is beyond me. "Think about it. If there was ever something we wanted out of bringing magic back, this is it, right?

To have the people we lost back? To get the chance to atone for our mistakes?" Her eyes blaze with hope. "The curses are all reversed. Everyone who's died because of magic is alive. My father called me this afternoon. *My father!* I haven't heard his voice in seventeen years. And getting Matthias back . . . not in my wildest dreams did I ever imagine getting him back whole."

"But there's no actual magic in this reality." Cadence's gaze has pinwheeled to her mother.

Amandine's no longer standing beside Geoffrey, but she's also not standing next to Rainier.

"This reality *is* the magic." Gaëlle's words are convincing, and I almost find myself believing we've won all the trials. But the fact that Cadence still doesn't remember who I really am is proof Gaëlle's conviction is false.

Adrien's still swiping through his photos, a hefty crease growing between his eyebrows.

"Look at that ultrasound." More tears tumble down Gaëlle's cheeks. "Look at your baby. You can count all ten of her fingers."

"I'm having a boy," he says, sounding detached. I suppose it isn't a real baby.

"*His* fingers. I tell you. This is our reward." This time, when Gaëlle sidesteps me, I let her pass. I watch her all but sprint back toward Matthias as though fearing he'll be ripped from her life again.

Adrien pockets his phone, all ten of *his* fingers balled into fists.

"You okay?" Cadence squeezes one of his fists, and yeah, it's petty, but I grit my teeth.

"Yeah. Dandy."

I never thought I'd hear someone actually utter that word, but if it's used anywhere in the world, it makes sense it's here.

"I need some air. Come with me?" The look he gives her combined with his pleading timbre almost make me feel bad for him, but when I see his fingers spreading Cadence's until they're holding hands, my pity blinks out of existence.

She tugs her hand from his. "I'll meet you in a little bit, okay?"

I'll be meeting him out there too in a little bit. I don't say it out loud, but I express it with my aggressive posture. She's my fucking girl. In every realm, Cadence is mine.

Reluctantly, Adrien heads toward the cathedral doors.

Once he's gone, Cadence runs a shaky hand through her hair, and that's when I notice she's not wearing the ring. "The Blood-stone's gone."

She nods. "Along with everything else that had anything to do with magic."

A loud laugh booms through the cathedral. It's Alma. She's watching my brother as though he's God's own cousin, and then she kisses him, and he holds her close. The crowd has parted around couples waltzing. My parents are one of them. Camille and Geoffrey another. I catch sight of Gaëlle, thanks to her bright scarf, so incongruous set against her fancy velvet frock. She's got both arms wound tightly around Matthias.

Everyone seems so happy.

Cadence stares at the dancing couples, probably searching for her parents, but they aren't dancing. Her top teeth worry her bottom lip, but then she suddenly gasps.

"What?" I scan the crowd for danger.

She raises a bobbing hand and points.

To a little blonde girl. Emilie's dancing, her toes atop a woman's feet, each step the woman taking becoming her own.

I don't even realize that I've moved until I find myself in front of her and the woman, who must be the mother considering their resemblance. Her mom's eyes widen in surprise. I swallow down my barbed guilt and nod to Emilie. "May I cut in?"

Her mother smiles. "What do you think, *mon amour*? Do you want to dance with Rémy?"

Emilie hops off her feet, a grin puffing up her cherubic cheeks.

I bend so I'm face to face with her. "I have to warn you, I'm not as talented a dancer as your mother."

Emilie smiles up adoringly at the woman. "No one is, but sure." She extends her hands. Once they're snug in mine, she puts her satin-slippered feet on the polished black bridges of my dress shoes. She's not heavy, but I can feel her weight like maybe, just maybe, she's real.

I dance with stiff legs, swaying from foot to foot like a rocking horse.

Looking up at me with big brown eyes, Emilie says, "I dreamed about you."

I miss a step and nearly knock her to the ground. Catching her by her twig-like arms, I say, "What do you mean?"

"It was you. But you were messier. Your hair, your face. What my mom calls 'scruffy'."

I can't help it. I laugh. "Scruffy. Like a stray dog. Just wonderful."

We start rocking again. "So, what was this dream like?"

Her rosebud mouth twists as she thinks. "I'm not sure exactly. But I was scared. Really scared. Then you held my hand and told me it was going to be okay."

The cathedral swims in front of me, the music drowned out by the pounding heartbeat in my ears. My tongue is plastered to the roof of my mouth, my throat dry and raw. But I can't stop myself from asking, "And was it?"

A second of silence, and then she says, "No."

I gently push her off my shoes then crouch down and wrap my arms around her. The smell of her fruity shampoo makes my nostrils tingle. Underneath that is the scent of kid sweat and crayons. I squeeze her tight, but it doesn't stop the yawning ache of regret inside me.

"I'm so sorry," I tell her. "So, so sorry."

She squeezes me back. "Yeah. I know."

41

CADENCE

M y palm crawls to my chest as Slate takes Emilie's hands and swings her around the cathedral to the strum of the quartet. Why did Slate go to Emilie? Does he also remember that she died because of Matthias's ghost?

My mind trades in the six-year-old's rosy cheeks for sallow ones. I blink to clear away the last memory I have of Emilie and superimpose it with the way she looks right now, bright with life.

Maybe Gaëlle is right. Maybe this is our reward.

No.

The ground shook and tossed us here. Instead of living in the moment, we need to figure out a way to escape it.

An arm winds around my waist, and then Maman's perfume—patchouli and clay—drifts into me. "Rémy is looking quite dapper tonight."

I don't admit it out loud, but the boy cleans up really nicely.

"Are you two being safe, *chérie*?"

I frown. "Safe?"

"Are you using protection?"

Oh. A flash flood of heat swarms my body. "Umm. We're not—" I clear my throat. "We didn't—" *Have we?*

"You aren't?" My mother sounds surprised. "You've been together for so long."

"Um. Not that long." I tug at the round collar of my dress as though it's strangling me, but it isn't. This conversation, though . . . "But don't worry, Maman. Camille explained everything to me a few years ago when she took me to the gynecologist—"

"Camille?" Maman sputters, her arm dropping from my waist. "She took you to see a gynecologist? Why? And when?"

Shoot. Of course. In this reality, I surely didn't go to Camille when I had my first period.

"We just, uh—we just happened to discuss period cramps one day, and one topic led to another, and . . ." I'm just about ready to fan myself I'm so uncomfortable having this talk with my mother.

My mother who should be the first person I had this talk with.

Fine wrinkles press into the corners of her mouth and eyes. "Honey, I know I work a lot, but the door to my art studio is *always* open for you."

I wonder who else it's also always open for. Papa? Geoffrey?

I decide I have to know. "Are you having an affair with the mayor?"

"The mayor?" My mother stares at me aghast, and then her lips spread around a resonant laugh which has her head tipping back and tears streaming down her cheeks. "Why in the world"—she gasps for breath—"why in the world would you think I'm"—another sputter of hilarity—"having an affair with"—one more—"Marianne?"

"Marianne? Marianne's"—I'd been about to say alive but swap it out with—"the mayor? Since when?"

"Since forever ago. What's wrong with you today, Cadence? You're acting so very strange."

"Amandine, may I recuperate my girlfriend?" Without waiting for her approval, or mine for that matter, Slate grabs my hand and tugs me toward the center of the cathedral.

He envelops my waist with his arms just as the orchestra launches into a new melody. It's slow and a little sad, the sort of song they play in those war biopics Camille and I would watch on weekends. It was our thing.

"What was that about?" Slate asks as he twirls me. His hands shake as he does so, as if his dance with Emilie was so much more than a few steps on marble.

"Marianne Shafir is alive and she's the mayor."

Slate doesn't say a word. Simply spins us again.

"She didn't die of cancer," I say.

He snorts. "She didn't die of cancer in her past life either."

Even though I'm clutching his neck, I lean away to look at him. He's still spinning us, and I'm momentarily distracted by how skilled Slate is in the ballroom and wonder if it's something from this life or from his real one, but set that enquiry aside for later, because . . . "You really think there was foul play?"

Without missing a beat, he says, "I do. I think she was murdered to cover up another murder."

"Seriously?" My feet stop moving, so his do too, yet the world and everyone in it keep spinning. "That's a huge assumption. You're basing this on the constellation from First, aren't you?"

"Now's not the greatest time for such a discussion, princess."

"Now's *exactly* the time. You can't drop a bomb like that and then skirt my question."

His gaze flicks to a place over my head, a place where my father and mother are fighting quietly but animatedly. My grief at seeing them like this absconds with every last one of my heartbeats. Is this truly what would've happened to them had Maman survived the Quatrefoil? They would've ended up embittered and passive-aggressive?

Slate catches me staring. "It's not really them, Cadence." He shifts me so my back is to my hostile parents.

He's right. It's not.

I have to repeat it several times for it to sink in. "So you were saying? Is this all speculation based on the way the celestial dial lit up, or do you have actual evidence to sustain your theory?"

"Cadence . . ."

"Don't coddle me, Slate, because I'm *really* not in the mood."

He sighs and then leans closer and breathes into my ear, "She was hired to forge Camille's suicide note. I'm pretty sure she was killed because she knew too much."

"What? That's ridiculous." I say, but it's simply reflex.

I've never believed Camille had committed suicide. Never. Still, my dress feels too tight, the air too thin, the noise too loud. I search the sea of made-up faces and crisp attire until I spot Marianne chatting with Nolwenn by one of the black columns.

"Who hired—" I suck in a shredding breath and start again, this time louder. "Who hired her to—"

Slate presses his mouth against mine, swallowing my outcry. I realize he did it only to quiet me, and yet when his mouth begins to move over mine, my mind blanks, and my body warms, and I melt into the kiss.

Slate has just confirmed my suspicions about Camille, and the realization is so earth-shattering that I swear the ground begins to shift and shake. Or maybe it's my heart that's rumbling from the pain of knowing someone stole her from our world.

Slate's velvet tongue lashes at my own as though he's attempting to swipe away my anger with a kiss. He's delaying the inevitable with this kiss, with his arms that band around my back, imprinting my body into his. My polished nails scrape along the hot skin on his neck and thread through his curls, coaxing his face infinitesimally closer to mine.

The man tastes like shadows and sin, and it's intoxicating. My head spins, my body spins, my heart spins. He keeps twirling us as he deepens the kiss, but his footwork becomes clumsy, and then we're listing, and his mouth is brutally ripped from mine.

My fingers spring away from his neck, and his arms from my back. "Slate!" I gasp over echoing screams and rumbling stone, a sound I never wanted to hear again after my battle against Ares.

Suddenly, I'm sitting in front of my mother's vanity mirror, and she's coiling pieces of my hair around a hot iron.

The blood drains from my face as I cry, "Slate! The cathedral!"

"It's made of marble, honey. Not slate." Maman releases the curled lock and starts on another. "Why the sudden interest? Every time Geoffrey and I have tried to tell you about it, you've yawned."

"What?" What the hell is she talking about?

"Amandine!" Papa yells, his footfalls echoing up the stairs.

A groove forms between my mother's eyes. "In here, Rainier!"

He stampedes into the room, his complexion the color of bone. "Oscar just called. Juda had a heart attack!" Tears laminate my father's eyes, making them seem bluer, darker, like the lake that stretches outside my parents' window.

My mother's hands fall away from my hair, and the iron tumbles to the carpeted floor, unhooking from the outlet. Her knuckles rise to her gaping mouth and smother it. "Is he—were they able to—"

"They're trying—" Papa sinks onto the foot of their crisply made bed and hangs his head into his open palms, his entire body shaking with grief. "They're still trying."

Tears roll out of Maman's eyes, but mine stay dry, because this isn't real.

This can't *be* real.

Unless . . . "Was it because of the . . . of the cathedral?"

"Mon Dieu, I can't believe he's gone," my mother says, her voice squeaking around wet gasps.

"Is the cathedral still in one piece?" I ask, because what the hell is going on?

"Why are you so damn focused on the cathedral, Cadence?" Maman snaps.

Her tone hurts, but the realization of what's happened distresses me far more.

Gaëlle was wrong.

This place, this warped version of Brume isn't our reward; it's our trial.

And the cost of failing: people's lives.

42

SLATE

This time when I jolt into the new reality and find myself once again at lunch with my dead parents, spilling cider onto my tweed waistcoat, nobody gives a damn.

This time, Oscar and Eugenia and the whole crowd in the *bougie chic* version of the tavern are focused on something other than my shock.

Nolwenn is standing in the kitchen doorway, screaming, "*Au secours!*" At her feet lay several scattered overturned pots and pans.

Perfectly grilled veal, lightly browned duchess potatoes, and a puddle of gravy, stick to the kitchen tiles. Just beyond that, Juda lies face down in blackberry compote, his skin as purple as the fruit.

One of the guys who'd been eating at a corner table bends over Juda, turns him, and begins CPR. I recognize him as one of the fire-fighters who helped when my *groac'h* made the well overflow. He barks out orders and thumps Juda's chest between bouts of mouth to mouth.

Juda doesn't react. His normally friendly eyes stare up glassily at the ceiling; his grizzled yet muscular arms stay limp at his sides.

"He was fine only a minute ago! How did this happen?" Nolwenn's apple cheeks tremble as she cries. She scans our faces as if one of us might hold the answer. "He was just fine!" When her eyes find mine, guilt hollows my gut. Her stare is so haunted, I turn away. Tasting bile, I push through the small crowd of gawking diners and out the door.

The cold smacks me exactly like my foster father Vincent used to—with such violence it makes my eyes water. Proof that not everything is different in this version of Brume.

I fumble with the slitted pocket of my fugly waistcoat to tug out my cell phone. The wind is wicked, so no one's out on the terrace today huddling over a piping mug of coffee. The only noise in the square comes from the squeaking of the copper sign that now reads FOURTH KELC'H instead of Second.

If I hadn't just seen Juda die, I'd tell myself this is a game like the one Bastian and I used to play when we tried to imagine a different, better life. One where the ceiling was the floor, and yes was no, and good was bad. One where slaps and kicks meant hugs and kisses, and kids like us were the ones to succeed.

Maybe, if we're lucky, and the Quatrefoil gives us a break, Juda won't be dead in the other realm. The *real* realm. Maybe this will all just be some fucked-up dream.

But this is the Quatrefoil. Some of its twisted games aren't games at all.

I tap Cadence's number and get an automated message telling me it doesn't exist. *Fuck*. Of all the things to change.

I scroll through the contacts, knowing she's in there since we're supposedly dating. But she's not under Cadence. Or de Morel. Or even Berthou.

She's under *Sweetums*.

Wow. And here I thought the tweed was my low bar.

Cadence picks up on the first ring. "Slate! Your dad just called mine." Her voice splinters. "It's because we failed." She sniffles. "Juda must've been on his way up to the party—"

"No. He was at the tavern."

"But the tavern's on Second," she croaks.

"In this screwy version of Brume, Fourth is Second, remember?" I glare at the copper sign wishing I could tear it down and melt it. I doubt it would hinder the Quatrefoil, but one can wish. "We've got to evacuate this *kelc'h* until we can figure out how to get back to real Brume. I'll call Geoffrey—"

"He's not the mayor. Marianne is."

I rub the back of my neck. "Forgot about that little detail. Where can I find our favorite accessory to murder?"

Cadence sucks in a shrill breath, which makes me feel minutely bad about the brusque reminder. "In Town Hall," she finally says. "Unless she's at the cathedral, getting things ready for the inauguration."

"They'll probably cancel it." I let the words, *since Juda's dead*, hang in a beat of silence. I doubt anyone will be in a party mood now that a beloved citizen just met his maker. "Actually, I doubt Marianne will listen to me about evacuating the *kelc'h*. We've just got to figure out how to get back before anyone else gets hurt."

Cadence's breath whooshes out. "If *Istor Breou* exists in this realm, it could help us. Come to the library with me?"

Hell, yeah. Never thought I'd get excited about hanging out between bookstacks. Then again, never thought I'd be wearing tweed and be buddy-buddy with Rainier.

"Meet you there in—" I stop, suddenly remembering that the temple slash library is no longer a thing, and I don't recall seeing any books in the cathedral. "Where *is* the library?"

As the question leaves my lips, I catch sight of a handmade sign stapled over a striped green awning across the square. It spans the width of two buildings, replacing what used to be *Merlin's Baguette* and *Au Bon Sort*. I briefly wonder where the hell anyone gets good bread in this town without Merlin. The handmade sign reads: *Bibliothèque Temporaire*. There are also two A-boards baring those same words underlined by large arrows pointing to the glass door.

"So the library's across from the tavern. Where *Au Bon Sort* used to be."

"Really?" Cadence is probably wondering, like I am, what Gaëlle does in this life. "I'm leaving now so I'll see you there in five."

As I slip the phone back into my pocket, Bastian ambles onto the square from First or Fifth or whatever the fuck *kelc'h* is the one below this one, hopping to the side of the road when an electric emergency vehicle speeds by, eating up the snow-capped cobbles and splashing sludge over my brother's pressed trousers. Probably a hand-me-down from my own closet. Wish I could've handed my entire wardrobe down.

Sylvie and another woman slide out of the electric car and

hurry to the tavern ... or as the snazzy silver-and-black sign reads, *Café 4*. The cacophony of shouts and sobbing spills out into the square as Doc opens the door, then gives way to blissful silence when the heavy wood snicks shut.

Bastian's eyes widen behind his lenses. "What happened?"

I give him the grim details and, while he stares in shock at the restaurant windows, I start toward the library.

"Where are you going?" His voice is thin, and his eyes are growing progressively redder and slicker. He lifts his glasses and scrubs the tears that have spilled over.

"To the library. I have a date in the stacks." I'm hoping my humor will alleviate his sadness, but then a pang of anxiety makes me freeze. Even though Juda's death might not be permanent, I don't want it to befall anyone else. Least of all my brother. "I totally forgot! I've got a cactus delivery coming at the house and someone needs to sign for it. Can you please go home and wait for it?"

He nods to the tavern. "I should—in case Nolwenn—"

"The best thing you can do for her is give her some space."

A muffled version of *Never Gonna Give You Up* by Rick Astley cuts off whatever Bastian says next, and I realize with increasing horror that it's someone's ringtone. And that someone is me.

Do I have *no* taste as Rémy?

Sweetums flashes across my screen. "Cadence?"

"Adrien's having his baby! I mean, Charlotte is! She got so upset when she heard the news about Juda that she went into labor." Cadence pants like she's climbing the stairs between *kelc'hs*. "Adrien's on his way to the clinic."

"And Gaëlle?"

"She's not taking my calls."

Because she doesn't want out of this life ... "It's up to you and me to find answers."

"There's Geoffrey—"

"Like I said, Cadence, you and me."

Bastian's eyebrows knit together as I end the call. "What was that about?"

"My cactus package, B! Get the hell off Fourth!"

He blinks his wet eyes at me, and, grumbling, finally gets going. Over his shoulder, he yells, "You'll owe me."

"Happy to." I stay in the square until he passes under the clanking sign and vanishes from view, then carve a wide arc to avoid the flowery well and yank open the library's door.

I expect several hundred square meters of neat bookshelves. What I get instead is a hoarder's paradise. Not only are the bookshelves bursting, every spare centimeter of space is subjugated by books stacked or stuck or crammed every which way. The walls are covered with vintage oil paintings, dusty hunting trophies, and musty-smelling tapestries.

"Oh, good, Rémy, you're here. I just got that book you were asking for." The red-headed dude, Paul, who didn't want to give me Spike when my house turned into a dorm, is standing at a counter piled high with novels, magazines, and old-fashioned video cassettes.

The wall behind him consists of four old mirrors with ornate frames that may be worth something at an auction if they're covered in real gold leaf. The top mirror is cracked—all the way from one side of the frame to the other—but the remaining ones are in decent shape.

"And your usual spot is free."

I lift an eyebrow. I have a usual spot?

More importantly though . . . "There's unused space in here?"

Paul chuckles. "I know. Thank God the big inauguration's tonight so we can finally start putting the books back into the building. Not easy running a library from an antique shop."

So the cathedral is rebecoming a library . . .

Like it's a game of Jenga, Paul gently tugs a book out of an impressive tower of tomes. The thing wobbles but doesn't collapse. He waits until the danger passes, then hands the book to me. *Madame Bovary*.

Did I borrow this one for fun? Who am I?

I set it down. "Actually, I need *Istor Breou*."

"You mean *L'Histoire Perdue*?"

"No. *Istor Breou*."

He bats his bleached eyelashes. "Not ringing any bells."

"Anything about magic in Brume?"

"Just *L'Histoire Perdue*."

This conversation's starting to make me dizzy. "Okay. That

then."

Paul turns, opens a trunk behind him, and removes an old tome. "Here you go. But you can't check it out."

"Yeah, yeah, I know."

The door opens, and the shop fills with the fruity scent of Cadence's shampoo. She's wearing the silver puffer coat and that ridiculous hat with the pompom that she lost in the fire at Adrien's house. Her cheeks are flushed as crimson as her lips. *Damn* . . . the sight of her never gets tiring.

"C-Cadence! *B-Bonjour*." Paul gives her an awkward wave, which sends the tower of books tumbling.

I'm tempted to growl, but I don't think that'd go over too well with Cadence.

I stalk over to her. "Come on. I have the book." I leave Paul to pick up his mess and head to the back of the library where I locate a round table with curled feet and copper insets, the sort that screams doilies and a dainty tea set. I dump *L'Histoire Perdue* onto the lacquered wood. "No *Istor Breou*, but we've got this."

Cadence lifts an eyebrow and starts paging through it. "*The Lost History*? It looks like a children's book."

She's right. Any hopes I had are dashed. The book is old, the paper thin and brittle, the words written in a careful hand. But sweet, colorful illustrations cover the pages.

"I'll go ask Paul for—"

"Wait"—Cadence catches my wrist—"this is actually pretty interesting."

Too quickly, she removes her hand. I drag the second uphol-stered chair over so I'm sitting as close to her as I can get without outright pulling her onto my lap. My shoulder brushes hers, and she stiffens but doesn't pull away.

"We didn't discuss what happened last night," I murmur close to her ear.

Cadence's eyes stay trained on the lines of text. "Technically, it didn't happen."

I stiffen. Is she really going to sit there and pretend we didn't kiss? I pivot in my chair to face her. "Then how come I can still taste your lips?"

Color rises to her cheeks, and her eyelashes flutter. "I meant, chronologically." She darts a glance at me, but it's fleeting. Bashful. "It was a good call to shut me up."

I steal one of her hands from the book and cocoon it between both of mine. "I hope you know that's not the reason I kissed you."

Her throat dips with a swallow. "It wasn't?" Her voice comes out satisfyingly breathy.

"No, it wasn't."

This time, when Cadence looks my way, she holds my stare, and the air crackles. I start to lean in, but she turns her head and nods to the book.

"Slate, we should . . ."

I sigh. "Save the world?"

"Yeah. That."

"Fine, but once we do, I want to revisit what happened."

Still full-on flushed, she smiles and then surprises me by twining her fingers through mine, and damn if that's not the headiest round of foreplay of my life. My pants tighten around me, the stupid fabric scratchy and constricting. How I miss jeans. I even miss my emoji boxers.

As I shift around in the seat, trying to get comfortable, my gaze scans the page Cadence is reading. "What the hell? The title's in French. Why's the text in Breton?"

"Modern Breton, which I can translate." Cadence's voice deepens as she sums up what's on the page, making me feel like a kid at library story time. Not that I ever attended a library story time, but I'm imagining that this is what it would feel like. I watch Cadence's lips as she talks, and I think I finally understand where all the librarian fantasies came from.

"It's the story of a boy who lives in a world of magic. But his magic is so powerful, instead of making friends, he makes only enemies. One day, he sees an altered reflection of himself in a puddle."

"That sounds oddly familiar."

Cadence continues, "So the boy kneels before the puddle and glimpses himself as a normal child with a simple life. There's no magic in the reflected world, and he has friends. Every day, he sits before the puddle and dreams of this other world. But with each day the sun shines, the puddle gets smaller and smaller. One day, when the puddle is nearly dried up completely, he steps into it."

I wait for more, but she stops. "Then what?"

Cadence looks at me. "Then he disappears."

"And?"

"And that's the end."

Talk about a cliffhanger . . . "Well, that's a shitty ending."

She laughs. "You're right, but maybe it's telling us how to get home."

"We need to step through a puddle?"

"Or something reflective like it."

I swipe the book from the table and stalk over to Paul, who's now creating a chest-high skyscraper of books. I hold up *The Lost History*. "Who wrote this crap?"

He startles, and his tower crumbles. "Oh, uh, it's attributed to Merlin."

"Merlin the wizard?" Cadence steps up behind me, so close to my back her sweet heat travels through all the itchy wool and starched cotton.

Being on the spot ignites Paul's freckles. "Um. No? Merlin the author. He was really famous even back in his time, which was like a thousand years ago." He begins to gather up the scattered items. Cadence crouches to help him, so I feel obliged to as well. As I go around the register, I accidentally bump one of the old mirrors, sending the gilded frame swinging.

Paul's still listing facts about Merlin. "Ironically enough, *L'His-toire Perdue* is the only one of his works that survived, yet apparently he wrote . . ."

I don't hear the rest of his words, because all my gray matter is focused on the mirror and the reflection in the glass. I'm not wearing Rémy's tweed monstrosity. I'm wearing my black jeans and my black turtleneck. Cadence, her red coat instead of the silver one. On her finger, the Bloodstone gleams like an alligator eye at twilight. Paul's in the panorama too, but he's standing by another till, handing a ten-euro bill to Romain, while scarfing down a *magie noire* cookie.

Cadence, who's just risen from her crouch armed with a

teetering stack of books, meets my gaze in the mirror, and the blood drains from her cheeks as she realizes, at the same time as I do, that we've found our puddle.

43

CADENCE

My gasp quiets Paul, who swings his gaze around the *bibliothèque* as though expecting an axe murderer to pop out from between the stacks. I guess my paleness is conducive to such theorizing.

I meet Slate's dark eyes again in the mirror, noticing the galaxy of inconsistencies in our reflection—our attire, our surroundings, the ring on my finger, Maman's quatrefoil charm bracelet around my wrist. "We need to call Adrien."

"Why?" Paul asks, still on high alert.

"Um—" I draw a total blank.

"To congratulate him on his baby," Slate supplies.

"No way! I thought his wife wasn't due for another month?"

"She went into early labor," I say.

"Huh. Does that mean you'll be TAing his classes, Cadence?" Paul rubs his palms together but stops at Slate's tapered glower.

The corners of my lips hook up at my provisional boyfriend's show of possession. He's taking his role very seriously. I wonder what'll become of us once we get back. And then I wonder what'll become of Slate once we solve the fifth trial. Will he puff out of existence the same way he puffed into existence? What if he was sent to us just to help?

Stomach flip-flopping, I set down the stack of books I'm still holding. In the mirror, I'm setting down a giant glass jar striated with dried purple blooms, bone-white powder, and green flakes.

"Cadence, look who's out in the square." Slate nods to the window where Gaëlle is shaking so hard her long yellow scarf sways like a cat's tail.

She's standing beside Matthias, whose tearstained face is heartbreaking. They're both watching the fire brigade carry Juda out in a body bag.

Paul drops an armload of books and hurries to the door. "Someone died?"

"Juda," Slate says, a touch of bitterness to his tone.

Even though I'm holding on to the hope that in real Brume, Juda will be alive, I fear the consequences of our failure will carry over. This is why we need to move faster. To solve this quicker. We need to break every curse the Quatrefoil ever cast.

"There are so many people on the *kelc'h*," Slate whispers, and I understand what he's saying.

If the ground shakes before we can get the *diwallers* together in the antique shop-cum-library, the Quatrefoil will have a field day choosing its next victim.

I spot my parents in the thickening crowd. Alma. Other university friends.

My father and Alma are already cursed, so they probably won't be again, although who truly understands the rules outside of the wicked source of magic that drew them up?

My gaze lands on my mother, who's curled around my father, her head burrowed in the crook of his neck. I hate that Juda had to suffer for my parents to suture the distance between them. To think I'm about to split them apart.

Papa won't remember. Only the *diwallers* and Slate will.

My gaze returns to Gaëlle, and a new wave of guilt seizes me. Papa won't remember, but she will. She'll remember Matthias the way he is now: normal, caring, wonderful. Losing him will crush her, but it's not as though we have the option to stay. We must finish this. I can only pray that the next trial will truly be our final one, because I don't think my heart's sturdy enough to go through another round.

I fist my fingers, and even though I can't see the Bloodstone, I swear I can feel the heat and weight of it again, like spider silk, like a phantom limb, like barbed wire.

Nolwenn throws herself over her husband's cloaked body and sobs. The sound of her lament stomps all over my already flattened heart and wrings tears from my burning eyes.

The air churns as a warm hand closes around my balled fist and then another cups my jaw and tilts my face up. The smell of winter —cider, spice, and crackling logs—swells over the musty cold of the antique shop. I inhale deeply because I want to replace every cold place in my body with Slate's heat.

"Cadence, eyes on me. Breathe . . ." He presses his forehead to mine, taking slow, deep breaths I'm probably supposed to mimic. "*Shh.*"

"I'm so angry at myself. Furious. Why did I have to put the ring on? Why couldn't I have just let things be?" My guilt is as hard as the ramparts that ring our town, as deep as the lake, as dense as the forest, as compact as the mist forever clinging to our hill.

"No." His nose bumps mine. "I did this, princess."

I don't know why he wants to take the blame for something that's indisputably *my* fault. Had it been his, the ring would've been on his finger. Before I can contradict him, his lips fasten to mine, gently, sweetly. They don't move, just rest there the same way our foreheads and noses touch. He takes a small step toward me, and the rest of our bodies lines up, each groove fitting against each ridge, each curve fitting against each dip.

The heady intimacy of trading air and heartbeats combined with the gossamer press of Slate's mouth, tips me out of this reality and into another. One where sunshine burns away the fog, where the sky is clear and the forest lush and the lake a shimmering sapphire. A place devoid of grief and guilt and magic. A place where nothing bad can reach me.

How can lips do that?

Blitz away the world and transport you into a new one?

More than ever, I'm convinced Slate is magical.

What other logical explanation is there?

Pulse drumming, breathless, I press him away. "You're not real, are you?"

Slate's eyebrows hang so low over his eyes that they cast them in shadows. He takes my palms and sets them on the stubble coating his jaw. "I'm real."

Impossible. "If the Quatrefoil taught me anything, it's that just because something feels real doesn't mean it is." I murmur this, even though Paul isn't within earshot, since he's slipped outside the shop to get a better view of the weeping crowd.

"Cadence, princess, I'm real. I don't know how to prove it, but I am."

"Then how come—how come . . .?" I lick my lips, taste his.

"How come what?"

"How come you—how come you make me feel so much? I *barely* know you."

"You know me better than you think."

"What's that supposed to mean?"

"The Quatrefoil erased me from your memory. From everyone's memory."

A shard of air slices through my lungs. "You were serious when you said that before?"

"I fought against the hawthorn alongside you, and your piece cursed me."

My gaze rakes across his face, trying to remember, but I don't. I don't remember anything about this man. I certainly don't remember him fighting alongside me. The only thing I remember about that day is feeling so damn alone in that subterranean grotto.

Slate turns his head and places a delicate kiss in the center of my palm. "I understand if you have trouble trusting me, Cadence, but I swear on everything I hold dear—which, until I met you, was a four-eyed boy and a cactus—that everything I'm telling you is true." His gaze settles on the finger where the Bloodstone should be but isn't. "If only I could take you out of Brume to prove it, but since I can't"—his gaze returns to mine—"you'll just have to take my word for it." He wets his lips, then parts them to add, "And store it beside my heart, which you stole the very first time we kissed."

I blink and then snort. I can't help it. The same way I can't help the grin crawling over my lips. I press my palm on his chest, over the organ pumping wildly. "I stole your heart, huh?"

"It's the tweed," Slate grumbles through a crooked smile. "You should hear my ringtone." His obsidian irises take on a slight sparkle. "If sappy were a song, that'd be it."

This time, I laugh.

The wooden floorboards of the shop pop and groan. "Juda is dead, and you're . . . What exactly are you two doing?" Adrien's sharp voice sobers me up.

Slate's heart judders beneath my palm, and his smile disappears. "What we're doing is none of your business, Prof."

I lie a calming hand on Slate's arm, then step in front of him to break the men's glowering contest. "Where's Charlotte? I thought she was in labor."

"False alarm," he says between barely parted teeth. "So what the hell were you doing?"

"We were finding the way back, Adrien."

"Through your tonsils?" he snaps.

I square my shoulders. "Obviously not, since we're both still here. What's gotten into you?"

"What's gotten into me? Really? You kiss me, and a few hours later, you're making out with him?"

Slate stiffens behind me.

"I thought I meant something to you, Cadence. I thought . . ." Adrien shakes his head, his already unkempt blond hair becoming messier. "Obviously, whatever I thought was wrong."

"*You* kissed *me*, Adrien." I knew I couldn't put this conversation off forever, but could he have picked a worse moment for it? Assuredly not.

"Well, you fucking kissed me back," he all but snarls, but beneath the anger there's hurt, and I hate myself for putting it there.

"Which was a mistake. I shouldn't have led you on. Not when I was developing feelings for someone else."

"You made out with Adrien?" Slate evidently has selective hearing because he missed the part about my nascent feelings for another man.

"Yes." I inhale deeply, then pinch the bridge of my nose. "Yes, I did."

"When?"

"Before you, Slate." I throw my hands in the air, exasperated with having to defend myself. "Before we were tossed in this stupid, fake version of Brume, and I became your fake girlfriend."

"You were already my girlfriend," he growls. "My *real* girlfriend."

I flip around, heart walloping my ribs.

"What is he talking about, Cadence?"

Slate grinds his jaw, the bone popping.

"You can't hold me accountable for something I have no memory of." I speak softly because yelling will only add sparks to the fiery tension.

His jaw keeps ticking.

"If you do hold me accountable, though, tell me now."

"So you can go back to Adrien?"

I recoil. "Is that really the sort of girl you think I am?"

I'm not my mother. The thought comes unbidden, and however hard I try to rid myself of it, it clings.

"I had a crush on Adrien my entire life, and then you arrive, Slate, and suddenly, all I can think about is you. You said I stole your heart, but you apparently stole mine too, except, unlike you, I have no recollection of when the theft happened." I turn back around toward my childhood friend. "Adrien, I will *always* love you, even if you stop loving me after today, but I now know that I'll never be able to see you as anything more than a brother. I'm sorry if that's not what you want to hear."

Adrien's chest still pumps harshly, and his hair is still chaotic, but at least, he hasn't stormed out.

"Now that we've cleared the air"—or rather, loaded it—"can we *please* get back to work?"

Neither man replies. They're both way too busy nursing their disgust for me. Or licking their wounded egos, although why Slate's ego would be wounded is beyond me. I didn't cheat on him. You can't cheat on someone you don't remember.

"Look in the mirror, Adrien," I tell him on a sigh.

His fists clench at his sides. "Maybe you should look at yourself in the mirror, Cadence."

Slate's chest knocks into my back. "She meant it literally, asshole. The mirror is our way home."

Adrien goes very still as his gaze climbs to the wall behind the register. He must see himself in the other world because his jaw goes slack. "We need to get Dad and—"

A low rumble resounds, knocking books off their shelves.

"*Putain de bordel de merde,*" Slate mutters before yelling, "Meet back here in—"

Maman twists a lock of my hair, smiling widely. "The cathedral is grandiose, and the lighting Geoffrey managed to create makes the place so dreamy. You're going to *love it*, Cadence."

Have we already buried Juda? Is he dead? Dying? Papa doesn't call up to us or run into the bedroom this time. Maman keeps curling my hair while I take calming breaths, trying to understand what's happening. My phone rings on the vanity table. Adrien's name flashes on the screen.

I pick it up. "I'm coming. Are you all already there?"

"She's dead, Cadence!" Great big sobs roll out of him. "Charlotte just died. Right in front of me. And the baby . . . *my* baby. Oh, God. I don't think he'll make it."

The blood drains from my cheeks.

Maman, who must've heard everything, plucks her phone from her bathrobe pocket. "Sylvie, Adrien needs you. Call him immediately. It's Charlotte." She disconnects whispering a litany of *mon Dieu*s.

Although I'm equally horrified, I'm trying to keep a level head, trying to remember it's not really real. "We haven't even buried Juda yet."

Maman's blue eyes find mine in her vanity mirror. They're the exact same shade, exact same shape as mine. Geoffrey is right. Our resemblance is uncanny. "Why would we bury poor Juda?"

My spine straightens. "He's, um . . . all right?"

"I think so. Why? Has Nolwenn mentioned anything?" Her phone rings, and she picks up. "Oh, Camille . . ." She paces her carpeted floor as she talks with Adrien's mother.

I pick up my phone and scroll toward Slate's name. When I can't find it, I begin to freak out but then remember his name is Rémy here.

I find his contact and hit dial. The second he picks up, I ask, "Is Juda alive?"

44

SLATE

I spill my cider and knock over my chair, my gut clenching with dread at the prospect of seeing Juda's lifeless form once again. But Oscar and Eugenia are smiling at my antics, and a rotund version of Nolwenn laughs while dripping champagne into the fluted glasses of a fancy couple near the window.

There's no screaming or crying or distress calls.

Everyone is happy.

Never Gonna Give You Up starts playing. I pull the phone out of my pocket before anyone can complain about it. Instead, several diners, including my mother, start humming the lyrics, because this here's the perfect crowd for that tune.

"Is Juda alive?" Panic laces Cadence's voice.

I turn to get a better view of the kitchen. Through the porthole window, I catch sight of Juda's ridiculously tall chef's hat bobbing, and my stomach muscles relax. "He is."

In a toneless voice, Cadence says, "Charlotte died."

It takes me a second to process. "Charlotte? Adrien's Charlotte? Pregnant Charlotte?"

"Yes."

"And the baby?"

Her response is so soft I can barely hear it. "Adrien thinks the baby's gone, too."

"*Putain.*" The taste of cider sours on my tongue. "Fuck, fuck, fuck, fuck, FUCK."

My string of expletives gets everyone to stop whistling, humming, singing my ringtone.

My mother's lips pinch around my name. "Rémy." She doesn't add, *language*, but it dangles in the air between us.

"Get Adrien and Geoffrey. I'll call Gaëlle," I growl into the phone. "Meet in the library ASAP." I hang up and stand. "I've got to go."

Dad frowns. "But your brother's coming—"

I cross the room and whip open the velvet curtain keeping out the cold. Before I step outside, I turn back and yell, "Fire!"

"Where?" My parents bounce out of their seats.

Several others also shoot upright.

"Get off Fourth! Run!" Hopefully, third time's the charm.

Chaos ensues. Nolwenn drops the bottle, which shatters, then rushes into the kitchen. Chairs topple, the gilded rungs slapping against the floor. I hold the curtain for the stampede.

"Dad, get off the *kelc'h.*"

His eyebrows pinch, but he takes my mother's hand and tugs her down toward Fifth.

What was Charlotte doing on this circle of Brume anyway? I spot some clothing stores farther up the street. When a sallow-faced Sylvie emerges from one of them, I assume Charlotte *shopped* till she *dropped*.

Oh, you twisted son of a—

Bastian's in the square! I'm about to yell at him to turn back when Mom hooks her arm through my brother's and forces him off Fourth. Letting out a sigh of relief, I finally crunch across the frozen cobbles.

I call Gaëlle. It rings and rings and rings before going to voice-mail. But I'm nothing if not persistent, and I hang up and call again. Hang up and call again. Hang up and call again. Until I've driven her crazy enough to pick up.

"Juda's alive," she hisses.

"Yeah, but did you hear who's—"

"Look, Slate, I'd rather live the same day over and over than go back."

"Gaëlle—"

"Matthias and the kids are here. Happy. Healthy. I want to be here. I *have* to be here, and—"

"Charlotte's dead."

Gaëlle pauses. "But she was on bedrest."

"Guess in this episode, she wasn't."

"But she's very pregnant—"

"And very dead. Both she and the baby." It's harsh, and I feel my stomach roil at the words, but it shuts her up. The sudden silence on the other end of the line is now a deep, black hole. "You still there?"

She mumbles something incoherent.

"We can't stay. If we do, someone else will die, so meet us at your old shop. The one that's now a library. If you're not here in ten minutes, I'll personally come to get you."

The *Bibliothèque Temporaire* sign stapled to the awning flaps in the wind, one corner already coming undone. A cocoon of dust motes and warmth envelops me as I enter the literary dumping ground.

Paul's exactly where he was last time I came in: at the counter, encased in leaning towers of books. "Oh, good, Rémy, you're here. I just got that book you asked me to order."

I shake my head. "I'm not here for *Madame Bovary*." My gaze goes to the mirrors behind him, my breath hitching when I note that this time, not one but two are cracked. "When did the mirrors break?"

He turns around and, although seemingly impossible, pales. "My boss is gonna kill me."

The two remaining mirrors are in perfect condition, apart from the fact that they're reflecting a whole different reality. I blink at my handsomely-dressed self.

As Paul obliviously inspects one of the broken mirrors, I reach around him and press my fingertips against my reflection. Instead of smooth resistance, I'm met with a cold, viscous malleability that engulfs my skin. A shiver travels down my spine, and I yank my hand away before Paul can remark that his mirror is essentially a vat of jelly.

"You'd better get those shards taken care of," I say, hoping to keep him busy. "Someone could get hurt."

Concern pleats his brow. "I'll go grab a broom."

As he heads toward a back room, cold snakes through the shop. Cadence is holding the door open, hat askew, coat unzipped, cheeks flushed from the cold.

Gaëlle slinks in, swiping at her red and puffy eyes. "I didn't—couldn't—say goodbye." She grips the yellow yarn around her neck as though about to whip it off and use it to lasso this realm. "*Mon Dieu,* my heart." Her palm drifts there, settles there.

Cadence winds her arm around Gaëlle's shoulder and pulls her into a hug. "Adrien's on his way. Geoffrey, too."

The toddler in me balls his fingers into fists at the mention of Adrien. *How? How could you kiss him?*

The door swings open then, and Adrien cuts across the cluttered space in three short strides. Geoffrey's not behind him.

I peer into the square, find only the fire brigade's utility vehicle. "Where's your dad?"

Adrien crosses his arms over his chest and glares at me, determination obvious in the set of his chin and the width of his stance. "I didn't bring him because we're not going anywhere. Not until this day starts over again."

"Oh, you're sorely mistaken," I growl. "We're going. Now."

He takes a step closer. "In case you didn't hear, Charlotte's *dead*, Slate."

I close the gap, the toes of my waxed wingtips touching his. "Funny that you care now."

Shock blasts his pupils wide. "Just because we're broken up in the real world doesn't mean I ever wished her dead!"

"Oh, Adrien." Gaëlle slides her palm up and down the sleeve of his coat. "I'm so sorry."

When Cadence, too, starts petting him like he's an abandoned kitten, I have to lock my molars to hold back a snarl.

"She'll probably be alive back home." Cadence tips her head toward the wall of mirrors.

Adrien dries his eyes. "Like I said. We're. Not. Going. Anywhere. I don't want to take the chance that Charlotte being gone here means she's—in the real world. Once the day starts over, and she's alive again, *then* we can go."

Cadence gasps. "But then someone else will be dead, Adrien."

"I realize that." His voice breaks. "But, at least, it won't be Charlotte."

"Wow. So you're ready to play Russian roulette with human lives? Glad you're not teaching Ethics." I point to the four mirrors on the wall—two broken, two intact. "Every time we fail, a mirror shatters, and those mirrors are our only way out. So your little resistance, on top of being soulless, makes you a giant, greedy prick."

The grandfather clock sandwiched between a stack of pastel bodice-rippers and encyclopedic tomes chimes. And chimes. And chimes.

Twelve eardrum-shattering chimes later—how has Paul not gone deaf and crazy?—silence settles again. Until it's interrupted by door hinges, and the freckled boy in question returns armed with a broom and a dustpan, pale face streaked with a sheen of sweat. How vast or deep is this back room?

"Oh, hey. Sorry. I'll be with you in a sec." Paul dashes toward the sharp silvery shards and starts sweeping.

"One more round. All I'm asking is for one more round." A pained look flashes across Adrien's face as he studies the wall. But then he runs a hand through his hair—which I only notice now is no longer growing out from a buzz cut. "I understand that what I'm asking for is selfish, but allow me this. Please."

Cadence drops her voice, "What if next time, it's someone else we care about?"

Gaëlle tightens the loop of her scarf.

"What if it's Romain? Or one of Gaëlle's twins?"

Cadence's impassioned hypotheses make the twitchy mother of three freeze.

"It probably won't be them," Adrien grumbles.

"*Probably*?" Rage tears through me. "How fucking selfish can you be, Prof?" I'll admit that if it had been Bastian who'd succumbed to the Quatrefoil, I may be playing the same game, but the fact is, it's not my brother. And to be completely fucking honest, I'm still bitter about Cadence making out with this asshat.

I sweep a pile of books off the counter and toss them at Adrien hoping they'll knock some sense into the idiot.

"Please call Geoffrey." Cadence's voice is soft but brooks no argument. "Please—"

The ground rumbles, cutting her off midsentence.

Suddenly, instead of books, I'm sweeping dishes off a table. The crystal candleholder, the deluxe china, the chilled bottle of cider—they all shatter against the brushed concrete flooring. Oscar and Eugenia watch me with eyes the size of serving platters. Screams fill *Café 4*.

"*Qu'est-ce qui se passe?*" Juda barrels out of the kitchen. "What's going on out there?"

I don't bother making excuses. I march out the door and head directly for the miserable little makeshift library, calling Cadence as I cross the square.

"Who is it this time?" I snap.

"I don't know. I haven't heard. But I'm on my way."

When I step into the aisles of overstuffed shelves, Paul doesn't call out that he's got a book for me. The only sound is the quiet whoosh of air from the heating ducts. Eyes on the prize, I head for the wall of mirrors, clenching my jaw when I notice three have become a kaleidoscope of splintered pieces.

I roar and kick over a pile of books. One of them thumps against a leg. I freeze as I trail the leg up to a torso and freckled face. A giant shard sticks out from his chest like a cheese knife in a block of Gouda, and blood stains his striped rugby shirt scarlet. I don't bother crouching to feel for a pulse. The kid's chest is motionless.

My gut twists. *Putain de bordel de merde.* I was beginning to like the guy.

Brisk air rushes through the shop as Cadence enters. She's not wearing her hat or even her coat this time, and her hair is curled on the left side but not on the right. Gaëlle hurries in behind her, then holds the door for Geoffrey and Adrien.

"I don't have time for this," Geoffrey is saying. "The inauguration is in four hours and—"

His words wither at the sight of Paul.

I lift an eyebrow at Adrien. "Charlotte doing well?"

He doesn't take his eyes off of Paul as he nods, Adam's apple bobbing as he swallows.

Gaëlle palms her mouth, stifling back a shriek, or her lunch. Cadence sways on her feet. I reach out and snare her waist to keep her upright.

"We're going this time!" I bark, lacing my fingers through Cadence's. "Everyone, hold on to each other!"

"What?" Geoffrey's usually tanned face rivals Paul's bleached one. "Where are we going?"

"You'll see." I grip the wool of his coat in my right hand, and without letting go, shove him head first into the mirror.

45

CADENCE

I trip over my own feet as I tumble out of the mirror and only manage not to faceplant because I'm gripping Slate's hand. After I've steadied myself, or rather, he's steadied me, I slide my hand from his and blink at the very white and spacious room.

The five of us stand—well four of us do, as Geoffrey's sprawled onto his front, groaning—in the hospital room where I recovered after my fight against Maman's goliath.

The real Fourth.

Gaëlle touches her neck, which is bare, her scarf gone, left behind in that deceitful realm filled with ghosts.

Adrien lifts a shaky palm to his hair, sheared again, then pats his coat pocket to locate his cell phone. He starts tapping on the screen almost maniacally. "I need to—Charlotte—I need to check if —" A heavy breath leaves his lungs.

"What is it?" I scrub my clammy fingers over my jeans.

He looks up from his phone, eyes unfocused. "I just—I opened our last chat and—I don't understand how but—"

"If you could finish just *one* of your sentences, Prof, we may be able to help you." Slate is entirely focused on adjusting the cuffs of his sweater so they peek out evenly from his sleeves. "If you want our help, that is."

Adrien's mouth hasn't closed, and since he still seems faraway, I walk up to his side and peer down at his phone. "Is that an ultrasound?"

He manages a nod.

I squint at the tiny white smudge floating in a pool of grainy black. "Did the picture somehow travel back from Fake-Brume?"

"I don't know," he murmurs.

Gaëlle roots around her coat pocket. "I took pictures when I was there. With Ma—" She chokes on her husband's name, and new tears hedge her clumped lashes.

"Oh, Gaëlle," I whisper.

She bats her eyes and sniffs, then stares down at her phone, scrolling through her photos. As she goes through pages and pages of them, Geoffrey presses himself onto all fours with a loud groan.

"My pictures," Gaëlle whispers. "They're all gone!"

Where Slate frowns, Adrien's hazel eyes grow wide.

"What's the date on the ultrasound?" she asks. "There's usually a date."

He blows up the picture and brings the phone to his nose as though he's suddenly nearsighted. "It's dated tomorrow. No, the day after. I don't understand."

I pull my own phone out and look at the date. Three days. We were gone in that other realm for three days. "It's dated yesterday, Adrien. Today's Sunday the twelfth."

"But how? Oh my God, these are real. I'm going to be a father. A real father." The blood drains from his face and then he's falling, and I try to catch him but fail.

Slate shoots out his hands and grabs fistfuls of Adrien's coat.

My friend still ends up on his butt but lands gently. "I'm going to be a father," he repeats slightly robotically.

"Couldn't be happier for you, Prof." Slate *does* sound genuinely thrilled for Adrien, which is strange because, as far as I know, neither man is fond of the other.

"I need to phone Charlotte." Adrien shakes himself out of his trance but stays seated on the floor as he dials her number. It rings and rings, and then her voicemail picks up and drizzles her grating voice over the otherwise quiet room.

Well, almost quiet. Geoffrey's still groaning and grunting as he finally rises, furiously brushing his coat as though to rid it of every last speck of dust from the shiny linoleum.

Adrien tries phoning the future mother of his child six more times before someone finally answers, and from the sound of the voice drifting faintly out of the receiver, it isn't Charlotte.

"Jasmine, hey. Can you put Charlotte on?"

There's a beat of silence.

Adrien jerks. "Excuse me? What's not funny?"

"You asking that!" Jasmine roars loud enough that we all hear.

"She sent me a picture. Please just put her on." His nostrils flare, and he squeezes the bridge of his nose. "What sick joke?" he growls as he pulls the phone further from his ear, probably to give his eardrum a break from all the shrieking.

"I'm at her fucking funeral! The whole town's here, except *you*! The guy she loved! The guy whose baby she was carrying! The guy who can't even be bothered to show up! You didn't deserve her, Professor Mercier," she yells before hanging up on him.

His gaze rockets up the length of my body and settles on my face. I don't think he's looking at me, though. I think he's looking for a point of focus so he doesn't keel over.

"Gaëlle," I whisper, "call Romain."

She's already lifting the phone to her ear.

A moment later, her stepson answers. I can't hear what he's saying until he begins to cry. "Papi, he—oh, Gaëlle . . . he . . ." Romain's voice breaks around a sob that deepens Gaëlle's already heartbroken complexion.

I ease the phone from her lax grip. "What happened, Romain?"

"Hey, Cadence." He sniffs. "Why weren't any of you answering?"

"Because, um . . . we were stuck . . . um, somewhere." I'm not sure where it is we're supposed to have been, so I go for vagueness. "What happened to Juda?"

"He was driving back from the market and about to park in the town lot next to the station when—" His voice breaks like when he was going through puberty. "When he had a stroke. The old Mercedes hit a median, flipped and bowled down Charlotte who was on her way to—on her way to Paris to meet Adrien." His voice is barely above a whisper.

"What about Paul?" I ask, assuming he's dead.

Maybe . . . just maybe though—

"He was trying to get Charlotte out from under the car, when the metal collapsed and crushed him too. A freak accident," he croaks. "Mamie, she's . . . I've never seen her cry this much. Cadence, it's so horrible."

"Where are you?"

"At the cemetery. The funerals are"—another sob squeaks out of him—"right now. Are you—are you all coming? You're with Adrien, right?"

"Yes, he's with me. We're on our way." I power off the phone and hand it back to Gaëlle who drops it into her coat pocket without staring away from the silent EKG machine. "They're all dead."

Slate sighs. "To be expected."

"Expected?" Adrien lurches to his feet and starts pummeling Slate. First his nose, then his cheekbones, then his stomach.

I yell for him to stop, but he doesn't. He just keeps pounding his fists into Slate, who finally cinches one of Adrien's wrists, then the other, and tosses his arms away with such momentum Adrien bangs into the mirror that spit us out.

Slate swipes at his face, smearing blood across his sharp cheekbone.

I hurry to the bathroom and grab handfuls of paper towel, soak them, and sprint back toward Slate. He takes them from me and wipes up the blood dribbling from his split lip.

"What the hell's gotten into you, Adrien?" I yell.

Adrien's jaw clicks and clicks. And then he's rushing out the room, his father tottering behind him, calling out his name.

"We need to go to the cemetery." I stare at the bloodied tissue paper in Slate's hand. "Are you okay?"

Slate grunts. "His swings are improving."

I slant him a contrite smile.

"Slate's here," Gaëlle suddenly murmurs.

I frown and drag my gaze away from Slate.

"The whole town's in the cemetery, but somehow *he's* here," she says this accusingly. "He came through the portal, which means I could've brought Matthias back." She turns toward the mirror facing the hospital bed and claws at her reflection.

I don't really understand her logic. "Slate's of *diwaller* descent,

Gaëlle. Matthias wasn't." Not to mention, Slate wasn't dead to begin with.

"That's not true." She's still trying to climb through the inanimate object on the wall. "Eugenia and Oscar weren't *diwallers*, and they were never parents!" Her anger is a living, breathing thing. It heaves and billows and crushes, pressing in around the three of us.

I look at Slate for help, because *what* am I supposed to say to someone who's obviously losing her mind to grief?

He walks over to her and takes her hands in his. "You're going to hurt yourself."

"I'd just gotten him back," she wails. "I want him back!"

"He wasn't real, Gaëlle. None of what happened back there"— Slate nods to the mirror—"was real."

Wasn't it?

Our kiss had felt real.

Maman's hands too.

I bring neither of these up, because what's the point in disproving a theory that's serving its purpose?

"I want him back," Gaëlle croaks again, softly this time.

"Shh." He rubs soothing circles on her back, then dips his head toward her ear and whispers something that seems to solidify her spine.

She presses away from him and scrubs her face. "You really think so?"

"We'll know soon enough."

She sniffles loudly, breathes in long and deep. "I need to get to the cemetery. For Nolwenn." She backs up and then pivots, still whisking the moisture off her cheeks.

Once she's gone, I turn back toward Slate. "What did you tell her?"

"That we've got to keep trying. That, if we're lucky, Matthias will come back after the final trial. If we're lucky, everyone will. If we're lucky the curses will reverse."

I bite my lip, and although I'd sworn an oath to take Gaëlle's secret to the grave, I whisper, "Except his curse didn't kill him."

"I'm aware."

My mouth parts. "You are?"

"I was there. The day we unburied his bones, then reburied them in my backyard."

My skin pimples as I recall the afternoon we evacuated Bastian's dorm to plow through the frozen earth. I'd take any memory at this point, but none arise.

"*Your* backyard?" I finally ask.

"Yes. The house was Eugenia and Oscar's. They left it to me in a trust." He grinds his jaw. "It's *not* an extension of the campus."

I don't dispute his claim, because he has no reason to lie about this. "It's still so strange that they were actually your parents."

"They died in a fire. A Quatrefoil-caused fire, by the way. Not a freak car accident like everyone thinks. Speaking of car accidents, we should probably head down to First."

He's right. We should.

I start backing away, but stop and lift one arm, reaching for him. His eyebrows pinch together as he stares at my bobbing hand. I start to lower it, but he snatches it in midair and clasps it firmly, as though worried I may come to my senses.

Since when do I hold random people's hands? That's something Alma does; not me. A twinge of sadness flicks my heart at the thought of her. So full of life back in Fake-Brume; stuck in a stone prison here.

We're going to defeat the Quatrefoil. Only one trial left. We can do it.

We have to.

"I'm sorry I kissed Adrien," I say, halfway down the hill.

Slate's fingers slide out of mine, and I shiver, partly from the wisps of icy mist and partly because I already miss the warmth of his skin. But then his arm curls around my waist and tucks me into his side, and his mouth lands on my temple, a spot of heat on my otherwise frigid body.

"I know you forgot me, Cadence, but please never again forget that you're mine."

I crane my neck back and stare into the depths of his dark irises, then twirl in his arm and kiss him, accepting that I am his and making sure he knows that he is mine.

46

SLATE

Brume is a ghost town. Shops shut. Curtains drawn. Even the dogwalkers and perky lunch-hour joggers are missing from the terrain. Our steps echo on the cobbles as Cadence and I make our way down the winding road to First.

"Wait!" Her eyes spark a vivid blue, the color of the sky everywhere else in the world but in Brume. "We can take the stairs. Everything should be lined up except Fifth."

Through the thin mist, the stone steps have indeed lined up, hooking a hard right just before the top circle.

"Four down, one to go," I whisper. "We're almost done."

"Almost. Then I can hopefully stop hating myself for putting on this ring."

My fingers tighten around hers, the oval stone imprinting against the meat of my thumb. "If you want to hate someone, hate me. I'm the one who started this whole mess."

"You mean, Geoffrey—"

"No. Me. Like I told you, Geoffrey's just a placeholder. *I'm* the Water *diwaller. And* the impulsive asshole who stole the Bloodstone off your mother's finger on New Year's Eve."

Cadence stops, and although she doesn't drop my hand, her grip grows slack.

Fixing my eyes on the horizon, which is twenty meters away thanks to the wall of forever billowing fog, I add, "Instead of erasing my element, the droll clover decided to substitute Geoffrey for me. I mean"—I shudder—"Geoffrey. Out of all the souls in Brume."

She stares into the mist for a moment, and I'm terrified my full confession's ruined the fragile bond we've been forming. But then her fingers tighten, and she sighs.

Screw you, Quatrefoil. We're winning. You can't ruin everything.

My good humor collapses as we near the cemetery gates. Sobs curl off the somberly attired crowd and lace around my lungs, thinning my breaths. I suck in a mouthful of frigid air but the cold merely intensifies the pain in my chest.

"Oh, God." Cadence stops short, blinking back tears.

There's three, maybe four hundred mourners spread across the graveyard like black lava. It seems we've arrived at the tail end of the ceremonies, because people are lining up. For what, I'm not entirely sure. Maybe toss dirt into the plots? I squint to make out what they all hold in their hands.

"Sugar." Cadence wraps both her arms around mine and her head lolls onto my bicep as we move closer. "To sweeten the afterlife. It's Brumian tradition."

We stop in front of the caskets, and I startle when I count four. I'm about to ask Cadence who else succumbed to the Quatrefoil when I notice the size of the fourth.

Small.

Child-sized.

My gaze rises to the blown-up photos propped behind the coffins. Although the fourth picture is angled away from me, I know whose face it'll show.

"Emilie," I breathe.

"They found her body," Cadence gasps, gripping my arm harder. Maybe it's to keep herself upright, or maybe it's to keep me that way.

Even though the desire to fall to my knees isn't lacking, my joints are too stiff and my muscles too rigid to fold. I can barely put one foot in front of the other. As Cadence tows me down the frozen path between headstones, the Bloodstone digs into my spasming bicep.

When the kid's picture comes into view, Emilie's gap-toothed grin hits me square in the heart. Her face is larger than life, balanced perfectly on a metal tripod, weak Brumian sunlight creating a slight glare off the glossy paper.

Although I longed—still do—for the little blonde child to return to the world of the living, I'm glad her mother got closure. Or am I? The woman's bowed over her coffin, grief contorting her face into its own death mask. Perhaps I should've weighed down the girl's body like Rainier instructed.

I pull my gaze away from the grieving mother and rub the ache gnawing at my chest. Adrien stands across from us, in a heated discussion with Charlotte's friend. In the half hour since we landed back in Real-Brume, the professor looks like he's aged thirty years.

Beside another dug-up plot of land, this one shaded by a twisted linden tree, Gaëlle's hugging a skeletal woman whose body rattles with sobs. It takes me a second to realize the frail, bony creature with skin like melted wax is Nolwenn. Magic hasn't been good to her.

It hasn't been good to anyone.

I find Bastian next, huddled with a group of his housemates around Paul's casket, shock and horror etched into their youthful faces.

Like steel-toed boots crushing a cockroach, their grief flattens the hope that buoyed me as I traipsed down from Fourth. These trials were supposed to bring us closer to righting the Quatrefoil's wrongs, but this congregation of tear-stained faces bears testament to the fact that we've only gotten farther.

We aren't winning. We may never win. In fact, we started losing the second I slipped on that ring. And after the next trial, who's to say there won't be another ludicrous expedition? We thought the end was in sight last time only to see the finish line disappear. How many people will end up dead because of my drunken hissy fit on New Year's Eve?

The cemetery goes in and out of focus, and my knees liquefy.

"Slate?" Cadence pivots in my arms, one hand gripping the lapel of my coat, the other tapping my cheek. "Stay with me."

I blink and swallow, find my center again, then bury any glum thought. Bury it deeper than any of the coffins in the entire graveyard. Bury it until it no longer exists.

Slate Ardoin doesn't fail, the same way he doesn't faint.

Cadence's breath plumes out of her mouth. "I'd almost gotten used to seeing Papa out of his wheelchair." I catch the grief in her voice. Grief over losing a reality we got to taste even though it was never on the menu.

"Cadence!" Rainier powers his way toward us, the motor buzzing over the quiet laments filling the graveyard. "I cannot believe you left Brume without telling me. Do you know how worried I was?" His gaze connects with mine, teeming with reproach. The ambitious asshole with a deadly determination to come out on top and annihilate me in the process is back.

"Guess we've left Kansas, Toto," I mutter to myself.

I can't help but wonder if Rainier would be Monsieur Berthou had magic not tainted his heart. I wonder if he'd be a decent guy with a modest sense of self. Would a world without magic have given us a Rainier I could actually get along with? Or was everything there just an illusion?

Cadence looks at me. "Talk later?"

I nod.

After Cadence drops my hand, I slip away and into the crowd as though I were no more substantial than mist. A moment later, I find myself in front of Juda's coffin, next to the impossibly thin version of Nolwenn, who's half-heartedly sucking on a cigarette. How I miss the plump, glowy woman from the other realm, her boisterous laughter and all-encompassing smile. Even her hair is flat today, and her skin, which hangs off her bones like an ill-fitting robe, is so translucent, the network of blue veins underneath is bright as ink.

Her husband's the one being put into the ground, yet Nolwenn could pass for the cadaver.

"Nolwenn?" I say.

She turns toward me, her frown deepening as she stares, clearly attempting to place my face. She blows out a weak puff of smoke, then drops her skinny cigarette to the snow. "Ah . . . the boy who made quite the scene in my tavern the other day." She says this with a warm note of nostalgia, as if those were the good old days, when college kids came into her restaurant and got tased.

"Are you okay? You look . . ." I let my words fade out, realizing how wrong that must sound to a widow. What I meant to say was: *When did you lose all this weight?* And: *Are you sleeping?*

"Married forty-six years. How I'll miss my husband. But not for long." She glances down at her hands, the skin on her right one covered in blueish-black script.

What the hell? Nolwenn's not exactly the type to get a tattoo.

She sees me staring. "The words started near my collar bone. They spread over my torso and down my arms. Now they've spilled out onto my hand. Hurts like hell, too. My chest is where most of the poison has pooled. Although, who am I kidding, it's everywhere. Eating away at whatever it is that keeps me alive."

Horror ices my spine. "Poison?"

She unclasps her purse and digs inside, pulling out a rumpled tissue to rub under her eyes. Black streaks transfer to the white wad. She tucks the tissue back into her purse and looks up at me. "Do you believe in magic, boy?"

"I . . . uh—"

"Well, I do. For decades, I've been trying to keep it away, but the funny thing is, each time I destroy it, it comes back stronger than before. Had I been smart, I would've kept my distance. Perhaps, it would've died out on its own. Or perhaps, it would've made things better."

She's not really talking to me, mostly rambling, but I rest a hand on her shoulder, gently so as not to break her. "How have you been destroying it?"

"I sound like a loopy old woman, don't I? I don't even know why I'm confessing this to *you*—a complete stranger."

"Probably because I am a stranger. One who'd never pass judgement." *Come on. Tell me what you did.* When her eyes glaze over, I give her shoulder a light squeeze, praying I don't fracture a bone. "So . . . the poison?"

"I'm not entirely certain how it got into my system. When I try to remember, my head starts to hurt. But I often dream that I pulled a shiny leaf out of the rubble of a demolished building." She gives me a watery smile. "Then again, I also dream I wait tables at the tavern in the nude."

My blood turns to ice in my veins. No, not ice. Burning oil.

Cadence's piece! The one she dropped after fighting Ares!

Adrien and I looked everywhere for the damn leaf. Cadence nearly *died* because we couldn't locate it. And I nearly killed myself because I thought all was lost. Bitterness scorches my throat with bile as I remove my palm from the woman who accidentally sent us for another spin on the cursed, magical carousel.

Something else hits me. Nolwenn fished that golden piece out of the rubble but left Cadence for the rescue team? How could she be so heartless? Did she assume Cadence wouldn't die because she was a *diwaller*?

I step back, glaring at the unnatural tattoo. It's not poison; it's her punishment for messing with the Quatrefoil. Fucking serves her right. Explains why she's been wasting away these past few weeks, becoming this damaged husk of a woman.

"Sorry for your loss," I say in a clipped voice before pushing through the throng of mourners. I want out of this death-fest.

In my haste to get away, I almost miss Bastian, sitting by himself on a stone bench near a row of headstones so old the epitaphs are worn to nothing. He has his head in his hands, and if I had to guess, he's reciting "La Fourmi" by Robert Desnos. It's his go-to poem when stressed. A kid's poem to keep his tears in check.

As I approach, he lifts his head, eyes bulbous and shiny.

"Hey." I set my ass on the icy bench next to his.

"Paul's dead." He says this as if I hadn't heard.

"I'm sorry."

"And Juda. And Charlotte." He takes off his glasses and wipes his crimson eyes. "And they found that little girl—"

"I know, Bastian." I cut him off because I don't want to hear about all that anymore.

"How could you all just up and go to Paris without me? Without telling me? I didn't know what to think." He gestures to the coffins lined up like parked cars. "Now, this."

I sigh. "Look, we weren't in Paris. We had another trial. For the Quatrefoil." Now it's my turn to gesture to the dead. "And we failed. Thrice."

Bastian blinks, then swears under his breath and plops his glasses back. "You mean four times. Or"—he crooks a forced smile—"fourfold?"

I snort but then sober up. "The fourth was from before. Don't you remember?"

He sucks in some air and releases it just as fast. "All these lives interrupted by magic."

I like his way of thinking: *interrupted*. It beats mine: *lost*.

"Are you guys prepared for the next trial?"

I sigh because the four of us—five if you count that imbecile Geoffrey—should be poring over the scroll right now, making battle plans. My gaze skates over the crowd and catches on the diminished forms of my fellow Quatrefoil crew. No one looks ready for battle. In fact, we all look like we've already lost the freaking war.

Bastian taps on his phone, zooming in on a photo.

"You've got a picture of the *Kelouenn*?"

"Yeah. Adrien shared the pictures with all of us when he took them."

When *I* took them. Jesus.

I bite my tongue and squint at the screen. The words are gobbledygook, but the illustrations, for once, are easy to make out. "Triangles."

"Yeah. The elements. Air. Earth. Fire. Water. And look, they aren't only outside the text like the other drawings, these bleed into both areas." Bastian spreads his fingers over the screen to make it zoom further.

Huh. How fucking weird is it that this is starting to make sense to me? "If I had to guess, I'd say our trial has to do with our elements. And, if we fail, the curse will have to do with the elements, too."

"My thoughts exactly." Bastian shoves his phone back into his coat pocket, then sits forward, shuffling his feet back and forth over the snow. "I miss Alma."

I scrub my hands down my face, and it sounds like sandpaper. "You'll get her back soon." I almost add, *I promise*, but bite back the words. I promised Emilie she'd be safe, and she wasn't.

Bastian nods, coffee-colored eyes bright with tears. "The new moon's in two days."

My pulse ramps up.

"What happens then?"

I want to scream *who the hell knows*, but Bastian needs reassurance, so instead I go with, "Magic will make things right."

From the way his mouth purses, I'm not sure I've convinced him.

One of his housemates trudges over. "We're going back to the dorms. Gonna have a beer in Paul's honor. You coming?"

"Yeah." Bastian looks at me. "Want to join us?"

"Nah, you go on, bro. We'll talk in the morning."

I watch him walk away, shoulders slumped, and although it still grates me that he's heading to the Roland estate with four total strangers, I manage to punch back my annoyance.

Once they've faded through the mist, I head up to my dorm room on Third where I have a date with the communal shower to wash away the residue of this interminable nightmare.

47

CADENCE

I lower my knuckles from the door of dorm room number three, which according to Bastian is where Slate currently resides. When I hear no shuffling beyond the wood, I assume the boy I came to see is absent and start to leave. Unlike me, Slate's not trapped in this godforsaken town by a cursed red stone.

"Cadence?" Slate's deep voice stays my swiveling boots. He ambles down the dim corridor toward me with only a towel knotted around his waist, dirty clothes in one hand, shampoo bottle in the other.

"Hey." Could I sound any breathier? "Thought you may have gone out."

"Without you? Unlikely."

As he looms closer, my attention drops to his bare chest. Taut golden skin dusted in dark hair that thickens beneath his navel. Chiseled abs stacked atop one another worthy of being immortalized by a talented artist—if only I had an ounce of my mother's talent.

I live next to a lake, which fills with swimmers in the summer, so I've ogled my share of half-naked men before—and *yes*, summer actually hits Brume . . . a quick visit, but a visit nonetheless—yet the sight of Slate makes my palms sweat and my heart race.

As my gaze treks back up the length of him, I catch details I missed during my first perusal: a small white blemish over one pec;

a thinner, longer scar over his shoulder; a rectangle of melted flesh on his inner forearm.

"What happened to you?" I ask.

"I'd have a shorter time filling you in on what *didn't* happen to me." Slate's eyes go dark as he nods to his pec, the movement making a wet curl flop over his forehead. "Stab wound. The knife-wielding idiot forgot hearts were on the left side of one's body. Unfortunately for him; fortunately for me." He tilts his head to his shoulder. "Stray bullet. Only nicked the skin. I got lucky."

He breezes over the origin of the fainter scars. Some made with broken glass. Another left behind by a pencil whose lead tip's still lodged beneath his skin. Yet another produced by a corkscrew one of his foster mothers used on his thigh. Finally, he lifts his arm to the dim amber glow of the entry hall's spotlights, exposing the waxy patch of skin.

"This one's from the fire that killed my parents. Nolwenn told me Camille saved me. Since it was her element, she didn't get cursed touching it. Whereas my parents . . ." He sighs. "At least, our ancestors figured out how the Quatrefoil worked that day."

A door creaks down the hallway, and out pop two girls, calling out flirty goodbyes to the dorm room owner. Both startle at the back of half-naked Slate. To think they haven't even gotten an eyeful of his front. I suddenly don't want them to.

"We should go inside."

He gestures to his door. "After you, Mademoiselle de Morel."

"It's unlocked?"

"I don't have anything worth stealing in my elf hovel. Not to mention, my key disappeared the same day I did."

"Elf hovel?" I ask as I step past the threshold.

He tosses his dirty clothes on the floor and pats a wooden beam. "See this? I've lost count of the number of times I've walked into it."

Although I *should* be looking at the beam, I find myself staring at his arm and the muscles flexing beneath the skin. I didn't know arms could be so sexy, but pretty much everything about Slate is sexy, and dangerously so. I swallow, my mouth suddenly as dry and brittle as the pages of *Istor Breou*.

A small smile tugs at his mouth. I blush, then shove my curled strands behind my ear. *Damn.* I must look ridiculous. Maman only got to style one side of my head, and I've had no time to rectify the asymmetry. I let a curl run through my fingers, my heart thudding from the memory of her touch.

"You all right?" Slate puts the bottle of shampoo down beside a glowing neon cactus. I know where he bought it because I got Bastian the same one as a dorm-warming gift.

I loose a sigh as weighty as the metronome marking my existence in heartbeats. "My mother put these curls in my hair. I ran out before she could finish, and now she'll never—" I press my knuckles against my teeth to stifle the sadness, which, until now, I've kept bottled up. "I always dreamed I'd get her back. And yeah, she wasn't as perfect as I made her out to be, but she loved me." My voice splinters. "She loved me so much."

Slate takes a step toward me and threads his hand through my hair, smoothing down the half-curled side. When my tears brim and collapse, he drags my trembling body into his. He smells so clean and warm, like laundered sheets and dark spice. Each lungful of him, of his aliveness, beats down my grief until it's again manageable. I reel my bloated lids and slant my head back to look at him. How selfish I am. I may have lost my mother, but he lost *both* his parents.

"I'm so sorry," I whisper.

His eyebrows dip beneath more vagrant curls. "For what, princess?"

"For complaining about my loss when I still have my father and you have neither mother nor father."

"I have Bastian and Spike . . . sort of. And now, I have you." His hand slides down my spine and settles on the small of my back. "Besides, I've made my peace with being an orphan a long time ago."

"It's not fair."

"It's not, but I'm a big believer in working with what life gives you and making the most of it."

My gaze roams over his scars again, and I boldly caress each and every one. "You're a really beautiful man, Slate Ardoin. Are you sure you're real and not one of Maman's sculptures come to life to lead me astray?"

He laughs, and the sound is so bewitching it makes my blood

hum. "Although your mother was incontestably talented, Cadence, I'm as real as it gets." He flattens my hand over his left pec, filling my palm with his strong pulse, then folds each one of his fingers over each one of mine.

"What about that scar?" I dip my chin to a white caterpillar-like patch between his thumb and forefinger.

"Steak knife. Almost severed a tendon. Patched it up as best I could. My needlepoint needs some work."

I lean over and kiss the toughened skin, then roll up onto my tiptoes and kiss this scarred man. It takes Slate a full minute to snap out of his daze, but when he does, he becomes possessed. His hands roam hungrily over my curves, kneading and caressing, pushing and pulling.

We stumble and tumble, knocking into the dresser, then into the statue of a cactus propped on the floor—he really likes his cacti. As my back thumps against the wall, Slate rips his lips from mine and shoots an arm out to steady the spindly effigy. Panting hard, I chase his mouth, return it to mine, and he backs us up toward the tiny bed, which lets out a worrying creak as we land onto it.

Slate breaks the kiss again, bracing his weight on his forearms. "We don't—you know." He nods to the mattress, lips and cheekbones deliciously flushed.

I flick a curl out of his eyes, which have gone inky. "I know." I drink him in. "By the way, who's Spike?"

A crooked grin spreads across his mouth. "My cactus."

"You named your statue?" Forget like; he *loves* those things.

He looks over the hard knob of his bare shoulder toward the gray statue. "Believe it or not, there's a real cactus under the granite." His Adam's apple dips. "Spike's a *toull-bac'h* victim."

"You're kidding?"

"Sadly not." He sighs before returning his attention to me.

A thought takes hold. "Bastian's cactus, the one that went missing . . . it wouldn't be the same one, now would it?"

Slate's half-smile is back and brighter than ever. "Don't know what you're talking about, Mademoiselle de Morel."

I release a small, very unladylike snort. "I've heard of boys fighting over a girl, but never over a cactus."

"Technically, we're not fighting over it. Spike's mine, but somehow, when I got cursed, he became Bastian's, who proceeded to rename him Steve. Of all names." He shudders.

I laugh. "Doesn't surprise me that you two are brothers. You're surprisingly similar underneath your vastly dissimilar attitudes and appearances."

"Besides custody of a cactus, we have *nothing* in common. He's good; I'm ... *not*."

My laugh turns into a headshake and a smile that digs into my cheeks but also into my chest. "So, do you steal *everything*?"

"Define *everything*."

"Cacti ... the real and fake types?" I nod to the lamp, which I now assume he took from Bastian's dorms when he snatched Steve-Spike. "Bloodstone rings? Hearts?"

"You actually gave me that light-up one."

My laughter fades, and frustration sets in.

He smooths the furrow over my nose with his thumb. "As for the other items ... only one ring to date, and only one heart. But yes, Cadence de Morel, I'm a thief. A street urchin. The bad boy daddies warn their daughters away from."

I cup his neck, then spread my fingers over the column of warm skin and drag his face closer to mine. "You left out something in that list."

"Yeah?" His warm breath fans over my parted mouth. "And what's that?"

"You're the boy I choose in every version of Brume."

48

SLATE

I jerk awake to the sensation of spiders crawling over my skin.

No. Not spiders. Just poor blood circulation.

I smile into Cadence's hair, which is fanned out over my arm, and although I'm plenty happy to let her use me as a pillow, I ease my prickling limb from underneath her neck and shake it. She lets out a long sigh but doesn't wake.

Carefully, I stand up and pad over to my dresser, then drop the still-damp towel off my shriveled balls and pruned skin. It's my turn to sigh when I spot my only available pairs of skivvies—heart-eyes or crying-laughing emojis. I choose the heart-eyes but chuck my jeans on the nightstand so I can slip them on before Cadence catches sight of these snuggly uglies and decides she prefers Adrien.

Although Prof probably wears handknit boxers.

Possibly, corduroy.

I lie back down next to Cadence, close enough to hear the gentle pattern of her breaths.

They're so soft. Like everything else about her. So very . . .

THE MATTRESS DIPS AND SHAKES, and hot air streams against my cheek as though Cadence is working through a nightmare.

"Shh," I whisper, eyes still closed.

She snorts and then lets out a deep, wet snore, like a chainsaw cutting through pudding. For a second, I'm shocked she's producing such a noise, because it's so un-Cadence-like, so low-pitched and aggressive. Not that girls can't snore heartily—my first foster mother's snores used to drown out the screeching subway that ran beside her house.

I smile and whisper, "You're a noisy one," before nuzzling the side of her neck and dragging my lips over her cheek.

Instead of soft, sweet skin, I'm met with bristly hairs and the odor of earwax.

My lids jounce open.

It takes my eyes a moment to adjust to the moonlit darkness, but when they do, my body lurches away from the man dozing beside me, head of graying hair denting *my* pillow.

"What the fuck?" On instinct, I shove him, managing to roll him off the bed.

He lands with a thud and a, "*Kaoc'h!*"

Trimmed and buffed nails push back a black satin sleep mask, revealing Geoffrey Keene's weasel eyes.

"What the fuck?" I repeat.

He blinks, still getting used to the dim light. That's when I notice he's in his pajamas. In some Versace monstrosity that looks like someone swallowed a set of watercolors along with Louis the Fourteenth's entire living room and puked them up on Adrien's old man. The turquoise, forest-green, and black silk is decorated with an overabundance of illustrated golden baroque leaves and Greek vases. GK is monogrammed in shiny thread over his non-existent left pec.

"What the fuck are you doing here and what the fuck are you wearing?" It seems my expletive vocabulary is rather limited when in a state of shock. I'm usually a man of more than one four-letter word.

Geoffrey dusts his pajama bottoms and glares at me. "I could ask you the same thing, kid!"

I look down at my heart-eye emoji ball huggers and reach for the jeans I left on the nightstand. Only, they're not there. Neither is the nightstand nor the cobweb in the corner or the crafty beam.

"This your place?" I ask Geoffrey, though I know the second the words tumble out that the answer is no. We're most definitely *not* in Town Hall.

He stuffs the sleep mask into his monogrammed breast pocket and taps the skin under his eyes as though to get rid of the puffiness. "Where the hell have I sleepwalked to now?"

"Wait, you don't know where we are either?"

"No, but it looks vaguely familiar."

The room is long and rectangular, the ceiling vaulted, the tall beams holding up the gabled roof painted over with strands of shimmery quatrefoils. The sole window is clover-shaped and set in the highest part of the peaked wall opposite us, with a ledge wide enough to double as a window seat, had it been closer to the floor.

Covering the lower part of that wall is a giant tapestry depicting two wizards watching water tumble down a three-tiered fountain. On the neighboring walls hang more embroidered panoramas showcasing seascapes with freaky aquatic creatures—puffer fish with fangs, razor-backed eels, cephalopods with tooth-lined beaks, claws protruding from the tips of their eight appendages. The details are so vivid I can make out each tapered spine fanning up from the eels' bodies, each glassy bubble streaming from the fanged fish. Even the fury lighting the black eyes of the ugly *pieuvre*-slash-freaky-beaked-mollusk-with-giant-tentacles is woven to such perfection, the hairs on my neck stand on end.

Carved into a cubby on the fourth wall, beneath a rusted plaque with two interlocked Rs, sits a replica of the fountain from the first tapestry, only this one's dry and covered in a geometric frieze of inverted triangles that flare to life, casting the room in an eerie blue light.

Geoffrey steps over to the fountain and stares at the plaque. "The Keene family crest."

"Uh . . . don't you mean Roland?"

"*Quel idiot.*" He points to a big-ass R. "See the K?"

"That's an R."

"That's a *K*. For *Keene*." He huffs.

I drop it because he's obviously seeing what the Quatrefoil wants him to see.

"You asked where we were earlier. Well, this is my ancestors' manor, the one that perished the day the Quatrefoil was broken into four pieces. Camille showed me graphite drawings of it in *Istor Breou*." He looks over at where I sit on the bed and cocks an eyebrow. "You'll know it today as the university amphitheater. If you actually attend our school, like you insist you do . . ."

As I slide off the sheets to get a closer look, the whole bed vanishes from underneath me. Startled, I murmur, "*Putain*." I think about Cadence, how I wish I could call her to make sure she's all right wherever it is she ended up. I assume that, since I'm in my ancestral home, she's in hers. My breathing comes in quicker at the thought that she's on her own. "Don't happen to have a phone in that monogrammed breast pocket of yours, Geoff?"

A glower reshapes his face. "No, *kid*, I don't." After a beat, he adds, "This must be my last trial."

No, it's mine. Why the Quatrefoil's keeping up this charade is beyond me. I mash my lips to keep from making a fuss and go back to scanning the room for clues as to what I'm contending with.

"I just wonder why you're here instead of the others."

I crack my knuckles. "Because the others are in their respective homes."

"Huh . . . so I suppose the Quatrefoil sent you to assist me with my final round."

He believes I'm his lackey? Here I thought age was supposed to bring wisdom, but I guess the older you get in Brume, the more your mind deteriorates. Must be the blood-congealing mist.

"Odd, isn't it, that the Quatrefoil thinks you need assistance considering how valiantly you fought and how assiduously you worked on every trial?" The sarcasm's stronger than I am.

Geoffrey notches up his chin and sniffs, offended.

I squint around me, on the lookout for a door. There's got to be one somewhere, maybe behind one of the monstrous tapestries. I stride around the room, peeling the heavy woven things from the wall, unearthing plenty of dust motes but zero door.

A cool breeze whispers across the room. Rubbing my bare arms, I approach the fountain. White lines of calcium deposit stretch across the stone. I shove past Geoffrey to inspect the giant copper box nailed to the wall beside the lowest basin, finding a collection of harpoons and a Poseidon-sized trident.

I slide my gaze over all three tiers. "I can't believe there's a fountain inside a house."

"This was the Keene training room." Geoffrey, who's crossed the room, probably to get away from me, is presently nosing one of the tapestries like a truffle hog.

"Training?"

"I know why you're here!" He spins toward me. "You're my sacrificial lamb. Or rather, minnow since we Keenes are Water *diwallers*." He smiles as though it's hilarious.

"*Bajaneg*," I mutter under my breath.

"What was that?"

I almost repeat it but decide to take the high road. Soon enough, the town will remember. Cadence, Adrien, and Gaëlle will remember, and Geoffrey will return to his state of honorific larva mayor with a penchant for tweed and a revolting obsession with the doppelganger of his lost love.

"When you say training room, you mean the gym?" I scan the beams, the gable window, the space.

Stroking the sewn form of the younger wizard, whose dark curls obscure most of his face, Geoffrey releases a dramatic sigh. "The use of magic required training. How to wield spells. How to harness one's element and use it in a fight. Sometimes, near the end of their training, wizards tested their students, setting a challenge for them —a monster to attack, an element to beat down, a situation to survive. That was done indoors, where the magic could be contained."

The fountain emits a slow gurgle and a thin line of liquid trickles out of the spout. It zigzags over the basin, then drips down the side of it and splashes the flagstone floor.

Two heartbeats later, the trickle becomes a stream, and then it becomes a river.

49

CADENCE

A damp chill skitters across my skin. I reach for my comforter to pull it up, but my fingers close around air. Did I kick it off the bed again?

Wait... I didn't fall asleep in my bed; I fell asleep in—

My lids open, and I wrench my upper body at such an awkward angle that a few of my vertebrae crack. When I notice the bed's empty and no longer in Slate's dorm room, I sit up, heartbeats scattering through my blood along with a heavy dose of adrenaline.

Did the ground shake?

Is this my last trial?

Am I dreaming?

The bed winks out of existence, and I land hard on something damp and dark. My tailbone stings from the impact, confirming I'm wide awake, and this is real. Or as real as magic gets. Not to mention the Bloodstone is swirling like molten lava and burning up my flesh.

I flatten my palms against the ground to heave myself up, but damp grains of sand suction my hands and feet. Pushing into my heels, I manage to hoist myself into bridge before flipping around. The second my knees hit the ground, they begin to vanish beneath the granular surface.

Apparently, this isn't normal sand. Why would it be? After all, it's Quatrefoil-made.

I'm still not sure where I've landed, but if this is the last trial, my guess is somewhere on Fifth.

My wrists vanish. I yank back my hands, managing to unearth them, then push myself up to standing. The second I'm vertical, I sink faster. I'm tempted to drop back onto all fours and crawl over to one of the dark wainscoted walls. Scientifically, the sand should be firmer the farther I move away from the center.

I snort at my stupidity.

There's no science in magic.

Just as I think of magic, bright-green light flares from one of the walls in the shape of an enormous slashed triangle.

Not that I had many doubts left, but the enchanted Earth element confirms trial number five has well and truly begun. How long do I have? And more importantly, *what* must I do?

Still uncertain of my sand-density theory, I trudge toward the edge of the room like an infantry soldier, lifting my legs high and stretching them far to lessen the number of limb-uproots. By the time I reach the wall, sweat beads along my hairline, and my thighs tremble, but my muscles don't burn, and I'm not out of breath.

Although the sand still suctions my bare feet, the grains aren't as loosely knit, so I sink slower. Squinting around me for an exit, I tread along the wall, palming the carved paneling for hidden seams. By wall number three, claustrophobia worms itself behind my breastbone.

With Slate last night, we'd talked about the triangles on the scroll; we imagined we'd need to battle our elements again, but we assumed we'd be doing so together. Instead, we've all been cast into separate arenas.

Or at least, that's what I assume.

What if the rest of them are together, and I'm all alone?

By the time I've scoured the last wall, and I'm standing beneath the luminous Earth sign, my fledgling panic makes my lungs feel like two wadded-up wet tissues. I gulp in breath after breath, and yet no oxygen seems to trickle down. I go dizzy from hyperventilation.

Come on, Cadence. You've faced so much worse.

I think . . .

Maybe this will be the worst.

Balling my fingers, I work hard on evening out my breaths as I wait for the Quatrefoil to launch something at me. Although I'm not certain of much when it comes to magic, I'm certain my trial isn't a demented gym session in a litterbox.

I jump as something slithers against my ankle.

And so it begins . . .

50

SLATE

A current rushes over the fountain and into the room. Within a minute, the frigid water is as high as my ankles, crawling its way up my hairy calves. Silt floats to the top, and the room begins to reek of musty damp.

Geoffrey's frantically rolling up his pajama legs. "These cost over a thousand euros!"

"Oh, will you fucking forget your pajamas and help me find the exit?"

I wade back over to the tapestries and heave up a heavy corner, then squeeze behind it and spider-walk laterally, sweeping my palms over the wall on the off chance that I missed a hidden panel during my last go-around. I sneeze nonstop as I slosh through the rising liquid, finding no doorknob, no hinges, no seam of any kind. The water now reaches my knees, and my feet have gone numb.

I squeeze out from behind the first tapestry just as Geoffrey does the same on the opposite wall. "Anything?" I holler, my voice skipping across our kiddie pool.

He shakes his head while pulling his silken trousers up so high the waistline now cinches his chest.

I crane my neck to glance at the quatrefoil-shaped gable window and the slice of sky it affords us. For a second, it feels like I'm back inside the *puits fleuri* anticipating a mermaid attack.

I squash my mounting PTSD. "Maybe the water will rise high enough to carry us to the window."

Geoffrey pales, then wheels around and claws the edge of the tapestry like he's trying to climb the thing. "I can't swim!"

"You're kidding me?" Cold squeezes my nuts as the water rises farther. Jesus, is this coming directly from the North Pole?

He shakes his head so hard his gray hair falls out of place.

The cold hits my waistline. "How the hell did you defeat the *groac'h,* then?"

"I ... um ... the others hooked me onto, um ... ropes." His brow furrows as though he's trying to recall the trial, but my guess is he doesn't have a fucking clue, because he never actually got his feet wet. "Ropes and a breathing tube."

However entertaining the image of Geoffrey as a puppet is, the fact remains he's going to make this trial twice as hard on me if I have to succor his Versace-clad ass.

I mutter with a hefty dose of sarcasm, "And you say the Keenes are Water *diwallers.*"

"Our power is to manipulate water, not swim in it!"

My nipples harden against the rising pool. "Look. Hang on to the edge of the tapestry. The whole goal is just to tread water and keep your head above it until we're close to the window. It's a waiting game. Compared to everything else we've faced, this'll be easy." I say it to him but pound it into my own head, because I need to convince myself that it'll be a piece of cake and that the best eight inches on my body—presently reduced to one—won't crack off like an icicle before this is over.

As I pump myself up, a ripping noise whooshes over the rushing water.

"What was that?" Geoffrey's eyes widen so much there's a lot more white than hazel.

My soles are no longer touching the floor, and I have to paddle to keep my head above water. Like the underwater lights in fancy swimming pools, the inverted triangles glow through the cloudy liquid, creating the illusion that the embroidered creatures are moving through the churning current.

The ripping sounds again. This time, I find the source.

Stitch by stitch, the clawed tentacles of the octopus start to pop off the tapestry and fill out like that novelty grow toy I scored Bastian once from a broken vending machine. The thing took a week to go from flat and flea-sized to a slimy, tennis-ball-sized mess.

But this is instant.

And the creature is a fucklot larger than a tennis ball. Each one of its tentacles spans the length of the room.

I swallow as a massive head tears itself from the tapestry, each purple thread ripping like strips of Velcro. A translucent film stretches over the thin line of the *pieuvre*'s pupils, but then it blinks, and clears the fog. Shiny black eyes focus directly on me.

While I swear under my breath, Geoffrey screams.

51

CADENCE

Agreen stalk topped with a bulb pierces the dark sand. Treading in place, I watch it grow and overtake my knee. The bud swells then bursts open in a firework of long, slender white petals.

I have very little knowledge of plants and flowers—I wasn't exactly raised an Earth witch—but I've seen flowers like these in books. Chrysanthemums. The token of the living to the dead.

I gape around my adult-sized sandbox as more white chrysanthemums sprout and blossom. My head spins faster, my vision swims, and my tortuous breaths shorten.

The Quatrefoil's planning on burying me alive!

For all I know, the dark sand is actually sugar, the same we Brumians use to sweeten the afterlife. I lift my palms to my face and inhale. Sure enough, a treacly scent leaps over the potent floral one.

Dread lances through me, and I sag against the wall. "Very funny!"

When I'm calf-deep in brown sugar, I realize I've stopped stepping.

Shit, shit, shit.

Clutching the slender frame of wood on the panel at my back, I wrench my legs, desperately trying to unearth them. My kneecaps crack from how hard I'm pulling. I'm going to end up dislocating them.

As my knuckles go white from the strain of holding on, I start twisting my bare feet to create space. I manage to get one leg up a couple centimeters but at the cost of my other leg lapsing.

Growling, I wriggle my deeper-buried foot, hoisting it so hard my abs scream. Whatever leverage I'd achieved with my other leg vanishes along with both my kneecaps. My fingers slip off the barrette of wood, and I hinge at the waist, tumbling headfirst into the carpet of chrysanthemums. I squeeze my eyes shut as the petaled balls sweep across my forehead, cheeks, and arms, leaving traces of their funerary scent behind.

When I hit the ground, I shove up immediately, driving the flowers into the sugar. Because they're magical, they don't tear or bruise, just jounce right back up the second they slip free. Sweat plasters my hair to my nape, and glues sugar to my jaw and arms. I lick my lips. When the cloying sweetness hits my tongue, I gag, then spit until I've cleared my palate.

I want to cry.

Cry and rage.

Instead, I latch on to the indestructible stems and pull. I don't magically rise from the quick-sugar, but at least I stop sinking. One hand fastened around a bunch of stalks, I release the other and swing my arm out to snare stalks farther away, my quatrefoil charm glittering wildly, darkly.

I pull and pull, attempting to bend my elbows, but the opposing forces drive my arms into a rigid line. The sugar sucks harder at my body, so hard my fingers slip up the stems toward the round clusters of petals.

Please don't break off. Please.

Although the bulbous heads stand strong, my body slides down another inch. Cool air glances across my soles. *What the—*

My toes pop out of the glutinous sugar, and then my ankles.

There must be a chamber underneath me.

Is it my funerary chamber or another exit-less room that'll suck me deeper into the bowels of the earth?

I guess I'm about to find out, because my knuckles fail me and spring my fingers open. I just have time to rake in a breath and shut my eyes before the sugar reaches my neck and propels me under.

52

SLATE

"**K**ill it! Kill the thing!" Geoffrey shrieks.

I will. After it eats you.

I wait a second. Then a second second. Finally, I decide not to sacrifice him and begin thinking logistics.

There was a weapon box beside the fountain. To reach it, I'll need to swim across the room and around the giant *pieuvre*, which is using the place as its personal paddling pool.

I take my eyes off the colossal cephalopod long enough to see that Geoffrey has suddenly turned tree monkey and is scaling up the tapestry. Despite how entertaining he is, it's the tapestry that steals the show. Where moments ago there were two wizards in robes eyeing a fountain, now, there are two dudes bobbing in a pool, an older one in ugly PJs and a younger one in heart-eye emoji briefs.

I lift my middle finger, and the guy on the curtain does the same. Well, I'll be damned. The Quatrefoil really does have a sense of humor.

Steel-gray stitches appear in the upper corner of the hanging. The woven shape fills out at warp speed, its form a lengthening shadow. A shadow that's slithering downward, toward the stitched version of Geoffrey's head.

Fuck.

Skimming the wall to avoid colliding with the outsized octopus,

I windmill my arms and flutter-kick, reaching Real-Geoffrey just as he releases the tapestry. Both he and a massive tentacle hurtle down. Geoffrey lands on me, and pain lances through my forehead as his skull bashes mine. We go under, and I inadvertently take a breath, the water a sharp knife to my lungs.

Before I can even swim to the surface, we're catapulted into the air by the *pieuvre*'s tentacle which has ripped completely free from the tapestry. I fly like a circus acrobat before piercing the water like a bullet, Geoffrey hot on my tail. The silence underwater engulfs me, but the second I reach the surface, it's all yelling and sobs. Geoffrey's thrashing around and grabs my shoulders from behind.

"Let go!" I splutter as he starts to pull me down. I rip his hands from my shoulders but not before I inhale another mouthful of water.

Geoffrey's legs circle my waist, and he tries to climb me to keep his head above the surface. His arms tighten around my neck, and we both sink. My lungs burn as I suck in more water.

Putain. Panic jolts through my spine. He's going to drown us both.

I reach over my shoulder and punch him. The shock of my knuckle sandwich slackens his grip. Gasping and coughing, I whip around and punch him a second time, hard enough to knock him out. No way am I dying because Geoffrey can't calm the fuck down.

I wrap my arm around his shrunken biceps and hold him in a vise, making sure his head stays above water.

Another tentacle soars upward and comes crashing down. I dart to the side just in time to avoid being smashed, but the impact whips us into the air and flips up as though we were pancakes on a griddle.

A third tentacle comes at us in this twisted game of Whac-a-Mole.

We splash-land near the fountain, almost colliding into the copper weapon box, which apparently wasn't nailed to the wall and isn't made of metal since it's bobbing on the surface. Hopefully, the weapons are floating too, but a quick glance around the glowing aquarium proves they aren't.

I shove a groaning Geoffrey toward the box. "Hang on to that!"

Blinking, he scrabbles atop his makeshift life raft and hugs it for dear life.

Keeping my eyes open, I stick my head underwater, spot a nifty harpoon gun directly under me. I inhale a breath and dive, reaching the gun just as a tentacle grazes my calves. I shove off the floor as though there were burning coals and shoot to the surface, harpoon in hand.

The *pieuvre* narrows its already slitted pupils on me.

Fuck. Fuckity, fuck, fuck.

The barbed weapon looks like a splintered toothpick compared to the sea creature.

I shoulder the weapon and shoot, but the trigger mechanism is broken—or fake—because no metal barb flies out.

53

CADENCE

I land on solid ground, in a room made of packed, pale dirt with walls cobbled in stones shaped like small *n*s. One of the walls bares a marble plaque with the carving of an Earth element that glows lime-green, single-handedly vanquishing the subterranean dark.

As I push myself to standing and dust my palms on my jeans, I peer up at the ceiling, then reach up and stroke it. The pale dirt is smooth and solid and smells of damp and cold instead of floral-infused crème brûlée.

I am *never* eating sweet custard again. Never. And not because I'll be dying down here. I add this footnote for my morale, which is in dire need of a boost.

The floor begins to rumble.

We must've run out of time.

My pulse, which had quieted from my lowered amount of effort, spikes right back up, driving the taste of metal up my throat. I scramble backward, pressing my back against the wall for support, and brace myself. Will the Quatrefoil send me back to the quick-sugar or will I remain down here?

The vibrations in the packed dirt rattle the cobbles in the wall that clank like my chattering teeth and tickle my flattened palms. The quaking intensifies as two door-shaped segments of wall lower, disappearing straight into the ground.

I wanted an exit.

I now have two.

But where do they lead? Deeper into the earth or upward? Am I supposed to pick one? What if I pick the wrong—

I fling my attention to the Bloodstone, then hold out my hand like a metal detector and move toward one of the entrances. The stone doesn't glow harder. Heart hammering, I cross the small cellar toward the other opening, willing the stone to flare.

When it doesn't, chills rain down over my skin.

I really have to stop expecting magic to help me. The malefic thing only ever tests and hinders.

I peer through both holes, but whatever tunnel or room they lead into is pitch-black. I close my eyes and tap into my gut. Right or left?

My gut is balled so tight it fails to answer me.

I flip open my lids and sigh. I'm going to have to go in blind.

Wait . . .

I move back toward the wall and claw at a cobble to toss into the black rooms.

It takes my nails precious minutes to scrape away the dirt from around the rounded stone and then more precious time for my fingers to get enough of a grip to pry it from the wall.

And when I do, bile shoots up my throat, because what I hold isn't small and flat.

It's long and curved.

And it isn't a piece of stone.

It's a human bone.

54

SLATE

As the octopus closes in on me, I do the next best thing to shooting it . . . I poke it. Straight in the head. The sharp tip of my weapon skids against the creature's rubbery skin, but the *pieuvre* jerks back, so I'm guessing it felt the jab.

A sharp pain saws across my calves, and blood ribbons around them in a dark swirl.

I spin around to see one of the monster's tentacles lift, my blood staining its curved claw.

I yank the spearhead back, then thrust the barbed point directly into one of the suckers peppering the fleshy arm, impaling the snake-like thing. I feel a satisfying squelch as the weapon penetrates.

"Watch out!" Geoffrey yells.

Sure enough, a second massive tentacle is soaring right toward me.

I try to pull the harpoon out of the first one, but the barb's lodged too deep. "Fuck!"

I dart to the side, avoiding the weight of the tree-sized arm, but not fast enough to come out unscathed. One of its claws slices my waist, coaxing more blood from my body. My head spins, and my grip falters around the harpoon still tucked into the *pieuvre's* limp appendage. The room goes bright at the white-hot pain drilling my side like a firebrand.

The water has risen so high that we're almost level with the gable window and the animal's eerie eyeballs.

"We're going to die!" Still atop his floatie, Geoffrey paddles frantically toward the window, his splashing catching the attention of the crazed cephalopod.

I take advantage of the distraction to shake myself out of my daze. Even though I feel lightheaded, I concentrate on ripping the stuck spearhead out of the monster's limb. At the same time as I manage to wrangle it out, the creature smashes a tentacle right into the old man. The box pops out from underneath Geoffrey and bobs alone on the surface of the water.

"Take that you oversized octopus!" I poke its slitted eye, praying it blinds the damn thing.

The creature screeches.

Now, to locate Geoffrey.

55

CADENCE

Dropping the femur or whatever bone it is I'm holding, I suck back the bile clogging my throat. It goes down sideways and burns a fiery path into my already raw lungs. I wheeze and hack, refusing to choke on my own vomit inside a . . . a . . .

Blanching, I stare around me at the stacks and stacks of bones packed in as tightly as the dirt around them.

Why does this place have a cellar full of bones? And whose bones are they?

I look at the one at my feet. It seems human but hopefully isn't. Not that I'm into sacrificing animals, but if these are all remnants of people . . .

Oh, God . . .

Vomit spews from my mouth as the mass grave's dank reek envelops me. I picture Maman's skeleton in its silken dress and heave again, staining the pale dirt around my feet. At least these bones have been picked clean of flesh.

After I rub my mouth on the back of my hand, I roar, "*Espèce de Quartefeuille de merde!*"

I don't even care if insulting the source of magic renders it crueler. How much more cruel can it get?

Actually . . .

My gaze vaults over the wall of bones and scours it for flesh-eating maggots. When nothing squirms, I shut down my train of thought so the magical clover doesn't siphon it from my mind and make it real.

Revulsion fueling my desire to beat the Quatrefoil once and for all, I crouch and seize the bone, and then I walk to one of the openings and toss it inside. It clanks against something solid. I unearth a second bone and lob it into the other opening. A more muted thud resonates from the chamber, but still a thud.

Heart beating out of alignment, I murmur, "Eeny, meeny, miny, mo," to pick where to go next. I end up heading into the first chamber.

As I pass the threshold, I hold my breath, waiting for something to happen. The ground to rumble. The doorway to vanish. Minotaur hooves to clop. Bats to shriek and flap. Rodents to scurry. None of this happens. I don't know whether to feel relieved or worried.

Maybe I picked the wrong chamber. I start backpedaling when the entire ceiling lights up with the neon-green glow of my element. Like the previous chamber, the walls are tiled in bones and the ceiling is made of packed dirt. However, this space is rectangular, with doorway-like openings running the length of it. I count five— three on one wall, two on the other. If anything emerges from them, be it fabled animal or monstrous humanoid, my heart will jump ship.

One hand pressed against my drumming chest, I lean over and scoop up my bone, then tiptoe along the corridor of possibilities. I peek inside each room—two are square chambers with no exits, or at least, no visible ones; two are hallways dotted with more doorways; and one is a foyer of sorts with only one opening.

Except for the rush of my pulse and the muted thud of my footsteps, all is silent inside the catacombs. Hauling in a deep breath, I step into the chamber with the most openings and peer into each one. The rooms beyond mirror the ones I've just seen.

This is a labyrinth.

My trial is a *freaking* labyrinth!

I imagine that to win, I must find my way out.

I lift my forearm and mop my brow, giving my forehead a good sugar scrub in the process. I look down at myself then—my white tank top and skinny jeans are speckled in damp, brown stains, my toes are pale white from the bitter cold and stained brown like the rest of me. *Lovely*.

How I wish I'd had the foresight to wear shoes, but who wears shoes to bed? If only I'd kept the sweater and socks I shed before curling in next to Slate. At least, I kept my clothes on. An itty-bitty smile curves my lips as I think of Slate who fell asleep with only a towel knotted around his waist. Is he still in his dorm room or is he on Fifth, fighting his own element? Or is Geoffrey the one fighting? Although I trust Slate, my mind cannot dissociate the well trial from the image of a neoprene-clad, ashen-faced Geoffrey.

I refocus on the here and now: me and my labyrinth. What happens if I choose wrong? How far do these underground tunnels lead? Could I get lost down here forever or will my time eventually run out? And what happens if I do run out of time? Does Brume reset? Does the ring fall off my finger? Since we locked nothing into the clock for the celestial dial, will the Bloodstone spill crippling poison inside my veins like it did to Maman? Will my bones find their way into these walls of fragmented skeletons?

What I wouldn't give for a baguette. And not because I'm hungry. I don't think I could stomach food after wading in viscid sugar and traipsing through fusty catacombs. I want bread so I can sow crumbs in my wake like *Little Thumbling*.

Papa would tell me that story before bedtime.

Oh, Papa . . .

I stare up at the ceiling, wishing I could plow through it with the Bloodstone, but if I could somehow tunnel through, I'd probably emerge in the pit of brown sugar and chrysanthemums.

I stop pining for an easy way out, and since nothing good comes to those who wait, I pick a door and go through it but stop before I turn another corner and eye the bone I'm gripping. It slipped out of the wall rather easily. Even though the idea of extricating more bones turns my stomach, I scratch at the wall until another eases out, and then another, and another.

Hugging my bouquet of human remains, I start down one of the tunnels and drop a bone.

Bread crumbs and balls of yarn have nothing on my tomb mapping.

56

SLATE

A tentacle and an eye have been maimed, but the *pieuvre's* toothy beak is intact and producing an alarming hiss-shriek combo that rattles the walls.

I dive under, scanning the depths for Geoffrey. I find his body floating beside the behemoth trident. I swim toward them, my calves and waist on fire, and latch on to the back of Geoffrey's collar with one hand and the trident, which is easily my own height and twice as wide as my shoulders, with the other. Thankfully, the water makes both weigh practically nothing. Still, they slow my ascent.

As soon as I break the surface, I shake Geoffrey until he splutters and hacks, then spear the tapestry with the tines of the trident to create handholds.

"Hold on to the wall rug!" I yell into his ear to make sure he's conscious.

"This is *not* a rug," he huffs.

Yeah. He's good.

When his fingers loop through the piercings, I turn and hoist the trident, sinking a little from its weight. A pop, followed by a dull ache, sounds in my shoulder. *Bordel de merde*. I think I dislocated the joint.

The octopus's hooked beak opens around hundreds of needle-sharp teeth and another screech, which drives a foul-smelling current into my heaving chest and propels me into Geoffrey. I lock my jaw from the galaxy of mind-shredding pains that erupt every-where in my body as we collide.

I shove off the wall again, heft the trident over my other shoulder, more determined than ever to murder the octopus. As my elbow bends, and I take aim, a memory flashes across my brain: Cadence, right before my trial with the *groac'h*, frowning over a glossy book, saying, *"The giant Pacific octopus has three hearts, nine brains, and blue blood."*

I can picture the illustrated anatomy under her tapping finger. Three hearts. All of them cocooned at the back of its bloated balloon of a head. Even though I have no idea if a magical *pieuvre* shares its anatomy with the Pacific octopus, it's worth a try.

"Hey, Geoff, keep it distracted, all right?"

"Dis-distracted?"

"Wiggle around. Shriek some more. That sort of thing."

"Have you lost your damn mind? I'm not going to . . ."

I dive under as he does exactly what I want without even realizing it. Skimming the wall, I circle the beast until I'm positioned behind its head. When I pop back up for a breath, I catch a couple of Geoffrey's shrill whimpers.

Good.

Perfect.

I dip back down, bend my legs, and flatten my soles against the wall.

Here goes something.

57

CADENCE

Hours. It feels like I've been walking these catacombs for hours.

I've reached so many dead ends and gone around in so many circles that I'm beginning to lose hope. When I reach the initial chamber, the one with my vomit and elemental insignia, I want to lob my armload of bones at the wall and roar.

I do just that. "Can't you give me a break? A hint? Anything before I lose it?"

Come to think of it, raging against a magical clover is probably the first sign of dementia.

The pale room splashed in neon green blurs as tears slicken my eyes. I don't want to perish in fucking catacombs lit up like a drug den. Not that I've ever gone to a drug den, but I bet it's done up the same, complete with skeletons and lurid lighting.

Wiping my eyes, I stare at my triangle until it splits into a string of triangles. I blink, and it's back to being alone. I retrieve one of my bones, stride toward the luminescent element on feet gone numb from cold, and bash the freaking plaque until my makeshift bat splinters and the bones in my arms begin to rattle.

Nothing happens to the symbol, of course.

Not a damn thing.

I choose another bone and go at the plaque again. When my weapon cracks, I march over the only threshold I've yet to step past.

There's no light in this room. Not that lighting would be necessary since it's the size of a one-car garage. One very small car. The ceiling grazes the top of my head, cool and damp, and my lungs cramp from the soggy consistency of the air. I turn back toward the 'foyer' when something wriggles atop my head.

I freeze.

The wriggling continues.

Heart walloping my ribs, I dive into the glowing green, acrid-smelling chamber, drop the femurs, and scrape both my palms over my hair in rapid succession. Something plops on the puddle of vomit in front of me.

Something small, glossy, and tubular.

A worm.

I palm my hair again in case there are others, but no more fall. Just the one. I crouch and study it, then pick up a bone and prod the creature. It doesn't magically inflate, just squirms away, heading back toward the shoebox-like room of damp dirt.

Pulse quickening, I stare at the black chamber. If there are worms, then the ground is soft. If the ground is soft, then I can tunnel through it.

This is how I get out.

This is my exit.

The treacly scent of brown sugar streaking my body tamps down my hope. The sugar was soft, and look where that got me.

A tremor goes through the ground.

Oh, no. What if I've run out of time? I'll to have to start all over.

Mon Dieu, I don't want to start over.

The grinding gets louder, and the floor shakes. Still crouched, I fan out my fingers against the packed dirt floor for balance. I'm tempted to close my eyes, but I'm not sure I could get my lids to come down if I tried. They're stretched as taut as the rest of me.

Suddenly, I grasp the source of the grinding. The stone thresholds are rising and slowly filling in the doorways.

It's not the *kelc'h* turning, so I haven't run out of time. But I am still essentially starting over.

"*Why*?" I yell. "Why are you doing this to me?"

I'm not claustrophobic. Not usually. But the air is growing thinner, and my muscles firmer. If I don't spring out of my crouch, I'll be locked in this position for all of eternity.

I'll be *buried* in this position.

I jolt to my feet, my knees screeching from the abruptness.

As the ground rattles, I stare toward the chamber with all the openings and hallways. The one that led me nowhere. Then I stare around me, at the room that led me here. And then . . . then I stare at the chamber of soil flecked with worms.

By deduction—or by sheer idiocy—I assume it'll lead me *somewhere*.

But where?

I trade relative safety for the unknown, grab the edge of the rising stone wall, toss one leg over, then the other, duck, and stumble into complete and utter darkness.

58

SLATE

I spring off the wall like a three-headed dart. Pain ripples through my arms as I plunge the weapon in the back of the octopus's head.

The tines go right through.

I'm so stunned I almost drop the trident, but instead I wrap both hands around it, give it another hard shove, then wiggle my giant fork around to make extra sure I skewered something vital. Or, hopefully, three somethings vital.

Thick, blue blood gushes like a cloud of dye.

Tentacles lifting as if in surrender, the *pieuvre* screeches one last time, almost as stridently as the mayor, and drops, sinking with my weapon of aquatic destruction.

Its head lolls back, and its black eyes grow milky as I swim over it toward Geoffrey.

"Get on your back."

He doesn't question me. He must sense I'll kill him next if he doesn't comply.

I grab a handful of his collar and float him over toward the gable window that's even larger than it looked from down below.

Outside, the sky is still dark and misted with smog or . . . Is that smoke?

Is that a flaming tower?

Since it's coming from the direction of the Mercier building, I'm guessing it's exactly what it looks like. Even though the buildings around the temple aren't the familiar modern ones, we're most definitely on Fifth.

I lug Geoffrey onto the stone windowsill, then lift myself. Now to figure out how to break the glass without cutting ourselves to ribbons and get down without breaking our bones.

Geoffrey groans.

Or is that me?

Every bit of me reverberates with pain.

There's a gurgling noise, like a drain being opened. The water, which comes right up to the sill, starts to recede. One of the *pieuvre*'s tentacles slips slowly down with it. I reach out, grabbing onto a claw. The giant keratin spike is hard as rock, and the appendage slippery and long as a water slide.

I laugh.

"What's so funny?" Geoffrey's eyes are open but don't seem to focus.

"We're about to head down in style, Geoff."

It only takes one forceful tap with the claw to smash the window. Glass rains down onto the snow below, and frigid air bites my wet skin, glazing me in an icy sheen.

"*Putain.* I hate winter in the North."

Geoffrey shivers and hugs himself, his ugly silk pajamas sticking to his slouched frame.

Fire shoots through my shoulder as I grip one of the steering-wheel-sized suckers on the underside of the tentacle. "A little help here?"

The old man blinks at me and grimaces, but must sense it wasn't a yes or no question, because he snatches the edge of the rubbery sucker.

"Heave!" I yell.

The pain is enough to make bile rise into my throat. I choke it down as we manage to pull and then push the tentacle through the window frame.

"Again!"

We grab and heave, grab and heave. My digits redden from the cold yet sweat darts along my brow.

Just when we've threaded enough of the beast through the window to get us to the ground, Geoffrey sobs, "I can't anymore."

"Help me roll the tentacle so we can slide down."

"Slide?" Geoffrey squeaks.

"Would you rather scale the suckers?"

He stares down at the giant suction pad. "No."

Once we've rolled the rubbery limb over, I push Geoffrey down the makeshift octo-slide, then dive after him, landing against a pillow of snow. Geoffrey's shrill shrieking catches the attention of two people on the quad. In perfect synchronicity, they wheel around and carve through the quad to reach us.

I lift my head, groaning from the pain lancing through my shoulder and waist, and squint into the darkness, praying one of them will be Cadence, but Gaëlle's bouncy hair and Adrien's ironing-board body are unmistakable.

If my girl's not with them, it can only mean one thing.

She's still fighting.

59

CADENCE

Once the wall settles into place, sealing me into a chamber so small it could very well be my final resting place, it dawns on me that I forgot all my bones in the other room, and I'm not talking about the ones in my body.

Those are packed in tight.

I take swing after swing at the wall. It's not mushy enough that my fists go through, but the soil does cushion my knuckles.

I yell until I'm out of breath, and my lungs burn just as terribly as the rest of me. Suddenly, I snap my mouth shut. The room is small. How fast will I deplete it of oxygen?

Bastian would know. He'd relate the answer while pushing up his glasses. How I wish he were down here.

And Alma. She'd deem this an epic adventure—as long as no spiders attacked—and fill the silence with nonstop chatter. How I miss the sound of her chirpy voice.

I sag to my knees and hang my head, wanting nothing more than to curl in on myself and wait for this to be over. I rue the day I dug the Bloodstone ring out of the safe and put it on.

If only Papa hadn't brought it home.

If only he'd changed the code to the safe.

If only he'd dumped it into the trash, or buried it in our backyard, or thrown it in the lake.

Tears lining my eyes, I shove every last *if only* from my mind and focus on *what now*. That's what Slate would do if he were here. He'd focus on where to go instead of where he's been, and drop plenty of jokes along the way.

"Oh, Slate," I whisper, blinking back the pooling moisture.

If I could choose one person, just one, with whom to solve this challenge, it would be him. Not Adrien. Not Papa. Not Gaëlle. Certainly not Geoffrey.

I'd choose Slate.

Just thinking about him injects a little vigor into my backbone, and I crane my neck to look up. Not that I can see anything. Not even the Bloodstone is glowing.

Drinking in a breath that doesn't seem to inflate my lungs fully, I press my palms into the ground to stand. My fingers hit something hard. My mind lights up with the image of a shovel, but it's merely the bone I tossed in earlier, before I wandered through the maze of quartered skeletons.

Better than nothing, I suppose.

I grip it, and its solid weight tops up my dwindling levels of courage. I stand and press the knob against the roof of earth, denting the worm-haven. The wiggly things rain down on my bare arms. Instead of being disgusted, I'm heartened, because the more there are, the looser the soil.

And boy, is it loose. It's plopping down like sloshy snowballs. I drop the bone and begin digging with my bare hands.

The air seems to grow denser and colder, as though more oxygen is trickling in. Am I getting closer to the surface? Is that why? Or is it merely an illusion?

Please, let it be real.

When I have to push up on tiptoe to keep clawing, worry clambers down my spine and flattens my bubbling hope. I still haven't reached the surface! How much farther do I need to dig?

I crouch and feel the writhing earth for my bone. The second I seize it, I spring up and hit the ceiling, sweat dribbling down my neck in rivulets.

I won't stop.

I'll never stop.

I'm getting out of here.

Something cold drifts over me, colder than the worm-riddled earth.

Something that melts.

Snow.

My heart holds still, and then it thrashes anew as I work my bone quicker against the widening gap.

Snow means I'm out.

Snow means I'm free.

More flakes pepper my cheeks, and then a huge clump of white falls on my upturned head, stunning me. I brush it off with my forearm just as a trickle of voices carries toward me. Adrien's. Gaëlle's. Geoffrey's. Slate's. They're all out on the quad, all done with their trials, all alive. And from how clearly I hear them, they're all nearby.

I start yelling, because if I can hear them, they can hear me. I clamor each one of their names until suddenly, they start yelling mine back.

Footfalls pound overhead along with a couple gritted Breton swear words, and then the hole grows wider. My fingers are so stiff, they're still bent around the bone that thuds against my thigh.

An arm appears. Bruised, and bloodied, and ropy with muscle. Then a shoulder and a face, chiseled and topped with wet black curls.

"Hey, princess. About time you joined the pajama party on the quad." He spots the femur in my hand, and his Adam's apple dips. Then his dark eyes lift back to mine. "Guys, she's here! Adrien! Gaëlle, Cadence is here!" His skin is a mottled mess of bruises and bleeding cuts, yet no man has ever looked handsomer. "It's over, baby. It's over. Just grab my arm, and I'll lift you out."

Lips trembling from exhaustion and relief, I finally let go of the bone, which bumps dully against the mound of earth at my feet, and reach up to grasp Slate's proffered hand. I try to take it, to close my fingers around his, but my knuckles are swollen and unbending, my fingertips caked in mud and blood.

"Cadence!" Adrien pops into my line of sight, and although the sky is still dark and the moon thin as a fingernail clipping, I notice he's lost one of his eyebrows.

Gaëlle appears behind Slate's other shoulder, her curls teased into a dark halo around her haggard face.

Their elements did a number on them.

Slate wraps one hand around my bicep and closes the other one around my aching fingers. "Grab her other arm, Prof."

Adrien crouches and positions his hands like Slate's, and together they haul me out of the earth.

60

SLATE

The mix of terror and exhaustion on Cadence's face makes a raw ache build in my throat and chest. I hold her to me and tell her it's over, but the whole time I'm also telling myself, *She's okay. She's okay.*

She's here. She made it. She's alive and in my arms.

And fuck me, does she smell good. Like crème brûlée or sugar-laced crêpes.

Stiffly, Cadence squeezes me back. My shoulder reverberates with pain, but it's no longer coma-inducing thanks to Adrien resetting the bone. Who knew history buffs doubled as chiropractors?

When she loosens her grip, my gaze falls to her top which used to be white but has become a mixture of brown from her trial and red from my blood.

I'm about to apologize when one corner of her mouth tips upward. "Cute underwear."

I glance down at the heart-eye emojis and raise a cocky smile. "Remember . . . it's what's inside that counts." *Alas, it's not counting for all that much in this cold.*

The ground suddenly buckles, the screech of stone on stone echoing through Fifth. As the *kelc'h* clicks back into its rightful spot, I hold Cadence, and she holds me.

A full minute after the last vibrations, Gaëlle whispers, "We did it." She looks at us, one by one, her knotted crown of hair shaking, her voice growing louder. "We did it. We fucking did it!"

Adrien lifts the skin of his newly re-scorched eyebrow. "Never heard you swear."

"We'll have to check the clock to be sure." Cadence steps out of my arms and turns toward the temple.

It's only a hundred meters away but feels like it's on the other end of the planet. A collective sigh of fatigue escapes us.

Geoffrey squints away from the library and at the teased nest atop Gaëlle's head. "What was your trial? A wind tunnel?"

"More like a tornado." Her hand goes to her hair, then drops to her curves, which have become misshapen lumps under at least three layers of clothing.

Her nightclothes take me back to Foster Home Two where, to save on the heating bill, Hector would turn the radiators off at night, forcing us all to sleep wadded-up in the entirety of our wardrobe.

Until now, adrenaline has kept me numb, but the rush is crashing, and the numbness starts to feel like a thousand needles under my skin. My toes are purple. Cadence's, too. Don't know about Gaëlle's and Adrien's, as apparently, they both sleep in socks. Gaëlle in two pairs, actually. The top pair hand-knit in the same yellow yarn as her old scarf.

I blow in my hands. "Why don't we pick up this nice little chat after we're dressed?"

But Geoffrey speaks over me, nose crinkling. "What was your trial, Adrien?"

"Fire salamanders. I never want to see anything lizard-like again."

"And yours, Cadence?" His slimy gaze roves over Cadence as he leans in to sniff her. "How come you smell like a bakery?"

She rubs her skin, and something that looks like coarse brown sand flakes off. "I was dunked into a vat of sugar before—"

"Sugar?" Geoffrey spears his hand through his wet hair, removing newly-formed icicles. "That sounds nice."

"Well, it wasn't. Especially after it swallowed me whole and delivered me into a catacomb labyrinth."

I wrap my arm around her waist and drag her toward me, partly to share body warmth and partly to hinder Geoffrey's leering.

"Were the catacombs anything like the ones in Paris?" Geoffrey wrings the water from the hem of his silken top. "Such an exquisite landmark."

Cadence glares at him, teeth chattering so hard she doesn't answer him. Or maybe she doesn't answer because he's a condescending idiot. Gaëlle pulls off her chunky duster sweater and drapes it over Cadence's shaking shoulders.

"Th-thank y-you, Gaëlle."

She gives the top of Cadence's head a motherly kiss.

"You know what wasn't exquisite?" Geoffrey continues. "My *pieuvre*."

I lift my fist. It takes every ounce of my willpower not to smash it into the old man's nose. After disparaging Cadence's exploit, the larva has the audacity to complain about his trial's hardship? He fucking bobbed like a toy duck in there.

He takes a step back from me, his bare feet crunching over the snow. "You really need to stop using your fists to send messages."

I bare my teeth, in no mood to discuss my manner of dealing with assholes.

"Hey, Dad?" Adrien runs a hand through his hair, which is gray with ash. "Could you go check on the *dihuner*? See if the celestial dial's changed?"

Probably fearing I may go through with the punch, Geoffrey scuttles toward the temple.

Adrien sighs. If Cadence smells like sugar buns, he smells like burnt toast. And looks like he was roast on a spit. His T-shirt and pajama bottoms are charred through in places, and peeking out from underneath is . . .

Wait. "Is that"—I grin—"Charlotte's face?"

He startles and tugs at a flap of plaid, trying to hide the mosaic of Charlottes blowing kisses from his banana hammock. And here I was concerned about my underwear.

"It was a birthday present, all right? After what happened on Fourth, I—" Adrien's face starts to crumple.

"Hey." I gesture to my own outfit, or lack thereof. "I'm not judging. These weren't even a gift."

Gaëlle snorts; Cadence laughs.

Adrien scrubs his flushed jaw, offering me a smile as tight as his briefs, before turning his attention to the Roland Amphitheater, magically back from the Quatrefoil's storage facility. "I don't mean to sound like a broken record, but how did you find yourself mixed up in Dad's trial?"

"Because I'm. A. *Diwaller.*" Exhaustion's making me testy. "Which you should be fucking glad about, 'cause without me, Daddy Dearest would be paddling around in the belly of a giant octopus right about now."

He purses his lips like he's sucking on something sour, just as a heavy bang makes us all spin toward the temple.

"The *dihuner* looks like it did at the beginning!" Geoffrey pants, yanking on his wet pants. "The star dial's reset, and the stones are shiny but blank."

Cadence touches the giant ring on her finger, then tries to tug it off. *Stuck.*

I wrap my fingers around hers, dragging down her hand before she chafes her delicate skin attempting to twist it off like I did last time. "It'll come off at the new moon."

Adrien stares at our linked hands. "Let's hope so."

"There's no hoping, Adrien. We won, so it will." Gaëlle touches Cadence's shoulder. "It will," she says again. "Now, I've got to get back to the twins, and you all need to get changed and warmed, but let's meet up later to properly celebrate. Because we deserve to celebrate."

That we do.

We all head down the stairs, breaking off at our respective *kelc'hs.* Cadence heads to the dorms with me under Geoffrey's frowny gaze.

"Aren't you heading back to First?" he asks her.

She nibbles on her lip as I whisk her away, because she doesn't owe Geoffrey any explanations. "I still think we should head to the clinic. You need stitches." She stares at the caked blood on my stomach.

"I'm not facing Sylvie. Not after we petrified her pooch."

"But it's got to hurt."

"Pfft. This is nothing compared to the pain of you not remembering you're my girlfriend."

She smiles and rolls her eyes, and it chases away some of the horror of the night from her beautiful face.

AFTER I'VE REVIVED my extremities with a hot shower and I've dressed in more than just a pair of boxers, we head out of my dorm room and through the square toward Cadence's house.

Although I suggested she shower at my dorms—with zero ulterior motives—she gestured to her grimy clothes, telling me there was no way she'd want to put them back on. She did end up scrubbing up her arms and face before pulling on last night's sweater.

"Nolwenn's up." Cadence motions to the tavern with her chin.

Through the lacy curtains, I catch sight of Nolwenn sitting at one of the tables, head cradled in her hands. Any anger I'd had for the woman earlier dissipates at the sad sight.

Our steps slow.

"She seems lonely." Cadence raises her blue eyes to me. "I wish I could tell her Juda's coming back, but . . . but I'd rather not give her false hope."

I understand what Cadence means. What if the Quatrefoil sends us on another hunt? What if reversing human curses is all a myth? Oh, God . . . what if it *is* a myth? What if no one *ever* remembers me?

"Coffee?" she asks me.

I nod, deciding it wouldn't matter, since Cadence and I have made new memories.

The tavern door's unlocked. Instead of being greeted by the usual scents of ground beans and baking bread, we're met with the stale odor of depression. Nolwenn lifts her head as we enter. Her face is gaunt, her usually puffy coif is a flattened mess. Instead of a crisp button-down and simple slacks, she wears a shapeless lavender chenille bathrobe.

She frowns at us, then at the lightening sky outside, as though confused as to what time it is. "I don't have any food ready." She pours herself a glass of *chouchen* from a sweating half-empty bottle. "I—Juda—"

"We're not here for food, Nolwenn." Cadence tucks herself into the seat beside her.

I drop into the seat opposite the ladies. "We're here for you."

Her face softens. "Aren't you two sweethearts. Let me get you some coffee. You look like you need coffee. Unless you want *chouchen*?" She nods to the bottle.

Cadence wrinkles her nose. "Coffee sounds great." When Juda's wife wobbles to her feet, Cadence catches one of Nolwenn's bruised, veined hands and coaxes her back down. "Allow me."

As Cadence ventures to the bar and turns on the machine, cold air sweeps across the room.

A hand draws open the curtain, and then Adrien enters, hat pulled low over his brow. "Morning. I thought we were meeting at *Au Bon Sort*, but I saw you all through the window." He gives Nolwenn an empathetic smile and nods at me and Cadence. "Dad's not coming. He's soaking in a bubble bath."

"Hope he doesn't drown," I mutter as Cadence carries back two espressos. She sets one down in front of Nolwenn before asking Adrien, "Coffee?"

"God, yes." He takes it from her and swallows it like it's a shot of vodka before even sitting.

A moment later, Cadence returns with more black gold. The bitter, hot liquid is like heaven after my twilit water aerobics session.

"How are you holding up?" Adrien fiddles with his empty cup, twirling it around and around.

Nolwenn reaches across the table and captures his twitchy hands, holding them tight. "I should be asking you that question, Adrien. Charlotte was so young."

Adrien's mouth opens, when his attention narrows to a point— the back of Nolwenn's hand. Lines of indigo chicken script cover the lax skin. I squint and recognize a few words—*eventide, beating heart, Brume.*

"What's this?" Adrien grips Nolwenn's hands tightly.

"Oh, that." She coughs. "Nothing really—" She tries to pull them back, but Adrien doesn't slacken his hold.

"She's cursed." I shrug a shoulder over the rungs of my chair, the stretch feels heavenly for my spine but painful for my abs. "I didn't get a chance to tell you, because I found out right before we were whisked off to Fifth, but she stole Cadence's leaf from the wreckage of the Beaux-Arts building. Which is why we never found it."

Both Adrien's and Cadence's mouths part. Their shock would be comical if the result of Nolwenn's meddling didn't suck so hard. I know she believed she was doing the right thing by whisking that piece away, but so much pain and so many curses could've been avoided.

I tug on the fabric of my black button-down, which has fused to my skin. I must be bleeding again. "Wouldn't happen to have a first-aid kit on hand, would you, Nolwenn?"

Nolwenn frowns at me. "The Beaux-Arts building was in ruins?"

That's what's sticking? Here I'd imagined it would be the part about her wrecking our hard work.

"First-aid kit? Duct tape?" I wad one of the checkered napkins and press it against my wound. From how heavy the fabric gets, I fathom I'm bleeding quite a lot.

Cadence stands. "I know where it is. I'll go get it."

Adrien finally comes to. "Her curse is a tattoo?"

Nolwenn stares at her skin, then into her glass of *chouchen*. "If it makes you feel any better, every new word that appears on my skin makes me sick, and not just mentally but physically. It's like each letter is filled with poison."

"Your pain doesn't make us feel better," I say.

Her eyes flick to mine, and her colorless lips sketch out a smile that vanishes around a deep sigh. "I've tried everything I could to get rid of them. Scrubbing them off. Scraping them off. I've even cut my skin in places . . ." She trails off and shakes her head. "Nothing works. They just keep returning. More and more words every day." She links her knobby fingers around her glass.

Cadence returns with the first-aid kit. She shoos Adrien out of his seat so she can tend to me.

He springs up mechanically and comes around the table toward Nolwenn. "May I look at them more closely?"

Nolwenn hands him one of her arms. As he pushes her chenille sleeve up, he gasps.

"What is it, Prof?"

Cadence splashes antiseptic against the long cut, and I hiss, while she grimaces, probably because the alcohol is stinging her ragged fingertips.

"I'd swear these words come from the *Kelouenn*." Adrien's nose is practically touching Nolwenn's skin.

Cadence looks up from the gauze she's unrolling. "You're kidding?"

"No. Look." He points out a sentence.

Cadence and I both read it. "They're in French."

"Not only are they in French, but they're in Maman's handwriting." If I thought Adrien was pale before, he's downright pasty now, with a slight tinge of gray—Brumian white.

Cadence's eyes trail over the lines on Nolwenn's arms. "They're Camille's lost translations..."

"Stolen," I correct. "Not lost."

Both Adrien and Cadence stare at me.

I sigh. "You guys don't remember, but I was in the archival room when Cadence opened the box."

Adrien shakes his head. "Why would her curse be Mom's translations?"

Nolwenn pulls her arm from his, pours herself some more *chouchen*, then, hand shaking, lifts her cup to her mouth and drains it. Guilt pooling into her wrinkles, she says, "Because these translations... someone gave them to me four years ago."

"*You* have them?" Adrien sputters.

She swallows. Pours herself another glass, but Adrien steals it from her hand.

"Who gave them to you?" he grits out.

"Marianne. Marianne gave them to me."

"Marianne Shafir?" The surprise in my voice is evident.

She nods.

Adrien's forehead pleats. "Why did she have them?"

"She was asked to steal them. She never told me by whom, although I always had my suspicions. Marianne told me to keep them safe so that person didn't retrieve them." Nolwenn stares past my shoulder at the dawn-lit square. "She told me to hide them." She closes her eyes.

"Where are they?" Adrien slings his gaze around the room.

"I stashed them in Juda's wood-burning stove. I thought—I thought the world would be better off without them."

Adrien blanches some more. "You—You burned them?"

Cadence and I stare at each other in shock.

"Marianne was so upset when she came here. Near hysterics." Nolwenn's eyes are still shut. "She kept saying she was on her way to confront the evil plague of Brume. That she would no longer be part of the illness."

Cadence whispers. "Did you read them?"

"I did."

My heart, which has been slowly ramping up throughout Nolwenn's story, now pounds vigorously.

"Those translations would have made it easy for someone to bring magic back. Too easy. Magic is so terribly evil. It killed my Matthias. It killed your Maman, Cadence. Camille. Marianne. It killed so many people. That's why I guess I took your leaf away. I didn't want you to bring it back. That's why I burned those translations. That's why I destroyed Viviene's statue. I hungered to destroy magic's very roots."

My blood churns as pieces of the puzzle begin to fit together. "Nolwenn, I don't think the evil Marianne was referring to was magic. I think it was human."

Nolwenn's lids reel up. "But magic is evil."

"Agreed," I say, everything clear now, "but Marianne, like Camille, was killed by a person. I'd bet my life on it."

"What?" Adrien wheezes. "By whom?"

The moment I utter my theory, which at this point, is more than a theory, I'll destroy Cadence's relationship with the only parent she has left. Or with me, if she thinks I'm lying.

"By whom?" Adrien repeats, enunciating each syllable.

I run a hand through my hair and forge on with what I know, even if it makes me sound like a creeper. "I had a detective look into some things—"

"A *detective*?" Adrien splutters.

"He found out that Marianne Shafir was paid to forge a letter. Your mother's suicide note—"

Adrien's eyes glaze with shock. "Dad had Marianne check it because he thought it had been forged!"

"And Marianne confirmed it was written in Camille's hand." I lower my shirt now that Cadence has finished taping the wound.

"Oh *mon Dieu* . . . Marianne." Nolwenn's palm crawls up to her mouth.

Cadence has already heard this part of the story, but tears fill her eyes nonetheless.

"Who? Who paid her?" Adrien's voice is as sharp as Juda's cleaver and icier than Brume's cobbles.

My lungs feel packed with steel wool. I can't look at Cadence as I say it. I just can't. As much as I hate Rainier, I love his daughter. And this will hurt her. "According to my detective, she was paid by a man in a wheelchair."

No one gasps or sobs or swears. They don't even breathe. The only noise is the humming of the refrigerator behind the bar.

I finally dare look through my lowered lashes at Cadence.

Her brows are knit tight, her hands balled into fists. "Papa's not the only man in a wheelchair," she whispers. "Not even in Brume. There's Monsieur Dubois. Yves Babin. Jean Lambert."

I prop my elbows onto my thighs and reach out to take Cadence's hand, but she keeps both out of my reach, rolling the gauze up and shoving it back into the first-aid kit.

Sighing, I look toward Nolwenn, who's staring at Cadence with such pity, because *she* knows it's Rainier. She's always known he was capable of something like this.

"Nolwenn, do you happen to have an ink spill on your body?" I ask, because I'm sure Rainier stained the *Kelouenn* to hide something. Something Camille found out when she was translating the scroll, and which cost her and Marianne their lives.

Nolwenn frowns. "Actually, I . . . I do." She unties her bathrobe, revealing a pink flannel nightgown that skims her ankles, then tugs down her V-neck collar. The skin there is a sea of bluish-black ink. "I imagine this is what you're referring to?"

Illegible. I swear under my breath. There goes my dot-connecting. I still have proof of Rainier's involvement in Marianne's forgery —the two hefty money transactions he made from my trust account. Although, since I've been forgotten, the trust my parents established in my name sadly doesn't exist.

"But look what happens when I touch it." Nolwenn presses her

356 | OLIVIA WILDENSTEIN

index finger against the stain, and the excess ink recedes into her hand, leaving a red oval surrounded by two lines of curved text.

Stone and blood with moon will bind. Dark night will blood and stone untwine.

I read it aloud. Twice. It takes that long for the meaning to hit me.

Holy.

Fucking.

Shit.

"What does it mean?" Nolwenn asks.

Adrien murmurs, "It means the Bloodstone binds to our body—to our *blood*—when the moon shines and slides off when it doesn't."

"But Papa ... He ..."

"It means the ring was never going to poison me," I breathe.

"And it didn't poison Amandine," Adrien finishes.

Cadence stands so abruptly her chair skids back and tips over. A choked sob flits from her trembling lips. She stares at the door, and then she's rushing toward it and out of the tavern.

"Fucking A," I breathe, before shooting out of my chair to go after Cadence.

61

CADENCE

"Cadence, wait!" Slate's voice skips over the glassy ice crust, which has formed over Brume during the frigid night. "Wait!"

I *can't* wait.

I need answers.

I need to understand what—*who* killed Maman, if it wasn't the Bloodstone.

Slate circles me and blocks my path. I stare down at his boots, reluctant to look up into his face, because I've heard his theories, and I dislike them completely.

If he's right about my father being involved in Camille's murder, in Marianne's . . .

If the trial on First about the secrets of murderers holds any truth . . .

Oh, God.

All of it hits too close to home.

All of it *hits* home.

"Maybe those words on her skin aren't really the ones beneath the ink spill." I try optimism on for size one last time.

Slate grips my upper arms gently. "Maybe." His voice is low and crackles like charred logs. "But everything points to your father paying Marianne to steal the translations. To forge Camille's suicide note. And then Marianne conveniently dies after all this?"

I close my eyes as fatigue and dread well up behind my lids, threatening to course down my cheeks. "I left Fake-Brume convinced I'd see Maman again." My voice catches. "But if those words are true . . ." An icy draft tunnels between our bodies, kicking up my hair and carrying away the rest of my sentence.

Slate's hands unfasten from my arms to slip around my back. I don't hug him back. I can't. My fingers are too stiffly balled against my hip bones.

"I'll never get her back," I murmur against Slate's thumping heart, against the black material of his shirt that smells of brine, blood, and warmth. "Even if the curses got reversed, I'll never get her back."

I suddenly wish he'd tell me I might. That I shouldn't give up hope, but Slate, unlike Papa, isn't a liar.

A sigh lifts his chest as he smooths back my hair. "Walk me through your plan, princess."

"Right now, going home and confronting him." The Bloodstone feels like a noose around more than my finger.

Slate's lingering silence tells me he's not pleased with my strategy. Was he expecting a more elaborate one? Was he hoping I'd slip a knife from the tavern and torture the truth out of my father? Kill him like he killed—

I cannot even think the names of the women he *may* have killed.

"Well, I don't want you doing that alone."

I pull out of Slate's embrace and gaze up into his somber eyes. "I *need* to do this alone."

"He murd—"

I press my fingertips against his lips because Brume has awakened, and I'm not ready for the town to hear my father's sin before I hear it from him.

Stone and blood with moon will bind. Dark night will blood and stone untwine. The translated line swirls through my mind like an epitaph.

Slate drags my hand off his mouth. "Here. Take this." He digs his key chain out of his pocket and removes something slender and silver, like a penlight. "If you press here, a pick slides out."

I balk at the weapon. "Slate, I know I've done some questionable things during the trials but I could never stab my father. Not even if I find out . . ." Again, I stifle the words. "Besides, he'd never hurt me."

Slate's jaw ticks. He probably believes I'm delusional, but I'm not. My father may have faked his regret at Maman's passing and his grief at Camille's, but his love for me is real. And although I hope it's because I'm his daughter, I'm not naïve enough to forget I'm also his last chance at getting magic.

When Slate tries to tuck the weapon into my hand, I back up.

Again, he grinds his jaw. "Then I'm coming."

"No."

"I'll stand outside."

"Slate . . ."

"I swear I'll stay outside. Your father won't know I'm there. Only you will."

I sigh. "You're going to come even if I tell you to stay back, aren't you?"

"Yes."

I raise a half-smile that's not very bright. I'm not sure there's much brightness left in me. As I turn, Slate steals one of my fists and winds his fingers through mine. Even though we could take the stairs now that all the kelc'hs line up, we choose the long road home.

As we pass the black gates of Town Hall, it dawns on me that I can't live in the manor. Not if any of my suspicions are true. "I'm going to have to visit the Housing Department."

Slate frowns.

"If Alma wasn't . . . wasn't—" I study the striations in the hedge of snow that sits on either side of the road like a raised sidewalk. "I'd go live with her, but until the new moon—"

"No need to visit the Housing Department." Slate raises my fingers to his mouth. After kissing my knuckles, he says, "You owe me another sleepover. A proper one this time. No going coyote ugly on me in the middle of the night to visit morbid historical sites."

I snort but sag against his side. "Do you really think the catacombs existed?" I'm trying to distract myself from my forthcoming confrontation.

As he glances toward the hill, he releases my hand and winds his arm around my waist instead. "Wouldn't surprise me if this town was built atop a few bones."

And blood.

So much blood.

"I really hate magic," I croak.

"And I really hate that you won't let me assist you with your cross-examination."

"You'd kill him, Slate."

He doesn't deny it. After a beat of silence, he says, "Before you confront him, I want you to pack a bag of clothes and anything of sentimental value, and bring it out to me."

My quatrefoil charm bracelet has the greatest value. I tug my wrist toward my chest and hold it there as though to feel closer to my mother.

Too soon, we're standing in front of my family home, and although there's no blood splatter on the windows and no dead bodies spiked to our fence, an air of foreboding lingers on the property.

"In Fake-Brume, you two were so close," I whisper.

"In Fake-Brume, your father was a nice man."

My heart squeezes like a fist at the memory of Papa's warm smiles that lost their luster when my mother stepped into the picture. I suck in a breath.

"What?"

"Nothing . . ."

Slate whirls me so that I'm facing him. "You gasped. I want to know why." When I still don't share my sordid speculation, he drops a threat: "Or I won't stay outside."

"Fine. I was wondering . . . What if it was an accident? An argument gone terribly wrong? What if it had nothing to do with the Quatrefoil and everything to do with Geoffrey?"

Slate's body goes eerily still. "Whatever your father's reasons, he's still a murderer."

"Presumed murderer. Maybe my mother—"

"Took her own life like Camille?"

His sarcasm makes me bristle, not because he's wrong, but because hearing it said aloud makes me realize how ridiculous my accident theory sounds.

I was raised by a man whose hands are soaked in blood, a man who used those hands to stroke away my nightmares and clap at my achievements, to hold me up and hold others down. I swallow hard and steel my spine as I turn back around to stare at the manor and the giant quatrefoil studding the blue door.

I thought the world as I knew it had ended on New Year's Eve, but I was wrong. It ends now, under the patchy peach sky of dawn.

I breathe in long and hard as I step down the path to our house, my boots bruising the fresh snow. Inside the manor, no oven-warmed pastries or freshly-squeezed orange juice fragrance the air. The foyer is dark and quiet. Only the rhythmic thudding of Solange's head against Papa's office door livens up our otherwise deathly still house.

My father isn't a late sleeper, so I assume he's awake. He's probably still in bed, reading a book. Or maybe he's getting himself ready for another day as everyone's favorite dean.

I steal up the two flights of stairs to my bedroom, gently click my door shut, then toss off my clothes and shoes. Twenty minutes later, showered and packed, I carry my bag downstairs. I'm about to go outside and hand it to Slate when rubber squeaks against marble.

"You didn't come home last night."

My shoulders square as I carefully set my bag down by the front door and turn.

Papa sits in the double-wide entrance of the living room, an espresso cup tucked in his hand. His gaze travels from my bag to my bejeweled finger. "Where are you going?"

I may still be shackled to Brume, but I'm not shackled to him. "I'm going to go stay with a friend."

"The same friend you stayed with last night?"

"Yes."

"I assume that friend isn't Alma."

"Alma's locked in a *toull-bac'h*, so you assume correctly."

His mouth parts. "She's . . .? How—"

"She was in the wrong place at the wrong time."

"*Mon Dieu, la pauvre chérie.* She must be terrified."

"Yeah. She must be, but hey, we completed our last trial a little over an hour ago, so as soon as the new moon rises, we're expecting the Quatrefoil to release everyone it ever hurt from their respective curses. How exciting is that, Papa?"

His shock wears off fast at my harsh tone, and then his eyebrows lower, smoothing out his creased forehead.

"You're about to get your legs back." I look at the landing. "Solange will finally recover her mind and humanity. Juda will rise from the dead, and so will Emilie. Adrien will get his pregnant girl-friend back; Gaëlle, her father; Slate, his parents. It'll be one hell of a reunion." I pause. "But you know who I'm the most excited to see? Maman! She'll finally come home."

Although no light has been flicked on, and there are no windows in the foyer, I don't miss the blood draining from my father's face, making him look as pale as Matthias, who unfortu-nately, won't make it to the reunion, since the rolling pin which ended his life wasn't very magical.

I step toward my father, forcing his neck to bend. "You don't seem very excited to see her."

His mouth flattens. "I'm merely having trouble wrapping my mind around the fact that she'll be coming home after seventeen years. That is, if the Quatrefoil can truly reverse the curse of someone so long gone. It's unlikely."

I stare down at him, willing him to stop perpetuating this charade of his own free will, instead of deepening his pit of lies. "You know what I had to do during my last trial, Papa? I had to find my way out of a catacomb. A catacomb, Papa. A place filled with so many skeletons. So many more than the ones we found in your closet."

He flinches. "What skeletons?"

"Oh, right. You don't remember our first trial. The Quatrefoil sent us on a little treasure hunt through First. We had to carry Mari-anne's bones from your closet back to the graveyard, Camille's suicide note and teacup from the van's glovebox back to Town Hall, and—" I stare past him at the statue on our coffee table. The shreds of doubt I still harbored that my mother's death may have been accidental evaporate, and as they do, my heart dries out and hardens like clay. "And Maman's bonsai from underneath your pillow." I blink away the image the words conjure and stare down at my father. "Is that how you killed her? You smothered her?"

"What has gotten into you, Cadence?"

"The truth. The truth has gotten into me."

Silence. Such terrible silence rings between us.

Here I was expecting more deflection, a couple gasped non-guilty pleas. I get *nothing*. Nothing but labored breaths.

"Did you kill her?"

One of his eyes twitches.

"Did you kill *them*?" I raise three fingers. "Maman." I fold the middle one. "Camille." My index finger comes down next. "Marianne." My thumb, which is still bleeding where I filed it down to the quick, bends.

"Camille committed suicide, and Marianne died of—"

"Cancer?" I let out a humorless laugh. "Nope. Not cancer."

Loaded silence echoes anew.

His grip around the coffee cup is so tight I'm surprised the fine porcelain hasn't yet shattered. "Who filled your mind with such poison?"

"Ha." My lips quirk into another roll of humorless laughter. "Why, the Quatrefoil, Papa. The same one that supposedly leaked poison inside Maman's veins." I wiggle my aching fingers in front of his face, the red beam of the stone cutting across his colorless features.

He catches my hand, squeezes my fingers a little too hard. "You're acting like a lunatic, *ma chérie*."

"In my defense, it's not every day you learn your father's a murderer." I try pulling my hand free. For a moment, I don't think he'll let go, but he does. "*Stone and blood with moon will bind. Dark night will blood and stone untwine.* Ring any bells?"

Papa grows as still and stiff as Maman's statues.

"Do you remember how, when I was small, you'd sit me on your lap and point to the creepy drawings on the *Kelouenn* and tell me not to fear them?" The memory of my father the protector, the vanquisher of nightmares, is a dagger to the heart, but I forge on. "How often would we study that scroll together? I learned my very first Old Breton word from it." I swallow as I twist the blade deeper through my ribs. "You know what else I remember from all those years ago? I remember the *Kelouenn* not having a stain, even though you swear it was always there. Too bad the only people who could confirm my recollection are all dead." The pain in my chest is so raw I expect blood to bloom over my university hoodie at any second. "*Stone and blood with moon will bind. Dark night will blood and stone untwine.*" I repeat the words that have lain dormant beneath the stain, and as I do, every piece of this horrid puzzle falls into place. "Camille realized you murdered Maman, since the ring didn't, and threatened to disclose it to the town. You had her silenced with arsenic. That's what you paid Marianne to do: steal the translations, since you couldn't access the archival room"—I glance down at his legs—"and forge a suicide note. Just tell me one thing, did you pour the poison yourself, or did you send Marianne to do your bidding?"

A vein throbs in Papa's temple.

"I guess it doesn't matter. Her death is still on you."

"Stop it, Cadence," he snaps.

"Or what, Papa? You'll poison me too?"

His whole torso jerks, and his fingers spring open around the cup, which collapses and peppers the marble in shards of porcelain as delicate as egg shells.

The front door flies open, and Papa narrows his eyes. I know it's Slate without looking over my shoulder, and I raise my hand to keep him back.

"Just tell me *why* you killed my mother? That's the least you can do before I walk out of here."

"I did not—"

"Don't. Lie." My clipped roar shuts him up. "I deserve the truth! Is it because she was having an affair with Geoffrey?"

From his string of rapid blinks, I fathom Maman's death wasn't a crime of passion. Maybe in this version of Brume, she was faithful to my father. She was the good guy, and he was the bad one.

"Why, Papa? Why did you take her away from us?"

He throws his arms in the air in exasperation. "Because she refused to try again! She refused to save all those who were cursed! She refused to help me! And she sent . . ." His eyebrows collapse over his eyes as though he's trying to locate a memory. "*Geoffrey* away. She . . . she hid him." Confusion contorts his face.

I'm certainly confused, because this is the first I'm hearing about Maman hiding Geoffrey. I don't remember him ever being gone from Brume.

"Not Geoffrey," Slate says. "Amandine sent *me* away, because I was a toddler. A toddler who wouldn't have survived a battle against the Quatrefoil. Nolwenn told me before my curse set in, and you all forgot about me. She helped Amandine get me away from Brume because she was worried Rainier would force me to fight since my parents were dead, and I was the only remaining Water *diwaller*, so no one else could recover my piece."

"What is this boy going on about?" Papa sputters. "Who the hell do you think you are?"

Slate's hand spirals down my arm and links through my trembling fingers. "You'll remember me soon enough, Rainier. According to Bastian, in thirty-six hours." He tugs on my hand, shouldering my bag. "You got your confession, Cadence. Now, let's go."

But I dig my heels in, because I want an apology, remorse, something to show me that my father isn't entirely cruel. Neither apology nor remorse warps his expression. Only anger. Terrible, frightening anger.

"The second your legs work, use them to run. And run far, Papa, or your crimes will catch up with you and end your miserable life."

Every bone in his face seems to press into his skin as though he were about to scream, but no sound seeps from his unbolted mouth. Only hasty, muted breaths.

I blink back indignant tears as Slate leads me away from the monster in the chair I used to love above everything in this cold, misty world.

62

SLATE

Right outside the manor's gates, we bowl into Adrien. His face is scarlet, his breathing hitched, his eyes like loose marbles in his head. I know the look. Hell, I've worn the same one Lord only knows how many times. He's doped up on anger and adrenaline, riding so high he's capable of snuffing out a human life with his bare hands.

He pushes at me with those hands right now, keeping his murderous gaze on the manor. "Out of my way, kid."

I plant my feet firmly in the snow. He tries to skirt me, but I mirror his stomping.

"I said, get out of my way!" Spittle flies out of his mouth and onto my cheeks.

I don't—not to save Rainier, because I don't give a rat's ass about the old man—but to make sure Adrien doesn't commit a crime he'd regret for the rest of his life.

"Adrien, please," Cadence starts.

"Don't *please* me. Your father had my mother murdered!"

I guess he put three and three together.

He shoves me again, this time with enough force to unsettle my balance. One of my soles skids on the frozen ground, and he lunges to the side, nearly getting past me, but I thrust out my arm and grab his coat, yanking him back so hard the move nearly dislocates my shoulder. *Again.* I grit my teeth and hang on.

"Oh, God, Adrien, stop, just stop." Cadence starts to cry.

"Yeah, cool the fuck off." We're chest to chest now. He's using all his strength to keep going forward while I'm using all of mine to keep him in place.

Cadence strains to keep his left hand in a vise, which helps me recover lost momentum.

"*Cool off*?" He screams, more banshee than future Fire mage. "I'm going to kill him." The fevered glint in his eyes is exacerbated by his right eyebrow's absence.

I cinch his biceps harder because I know he'll go through with it if he gets past me.

"It's not worth it," I say. "*He's* not worth it. You'll go to jail—"

"*He fucking murdered my mother!*" Pain reverberates along my spine as he slams me against the gate and turns to Cadence, a snarl in his voice. "He murdered my mother, Cadence. He murdered her!"

"He murdered mine, too!" Cadence drops her head into her hands as her knees buckle and she lands into the snow. She's wailing now, huge sobs that break my fucking heart. I want to go to her but don't dare let go of Adrien. "He murdered my mother, too."

Adrien's muscles tauten, then slacken like a pair of sweaty socks. "What are we going to do?"

I toss his arm away. He falls to the ground next to Cadence and reaches out. She leans into his chest, her shower-damp hair spilling over his gray coat. Adrien wraps his arms around her, crying into the top of her head. They cling to each other in their grief, right beneath the golden *Manoir de Morel* plaque.

For once, I don't throw out a sarcastic barb, or growl like a papa bear at Adrien's proximity to my girlfriend. For once, I ignore my own jealousy at seeing them together and instead give them the moment they both need. They share something I have no part in. Something awful.

I swallow down a bitter ache and turn back toward the manor. I'm glad the picture window is on the other side, overlooking the lake, because I don't think I could handle another glimpse of the man's hateful face.

I've done some bad shit in my life, really bad shit, but nothing like Rainier de Morel. This whole time, we've complained about the viciousness of the Quatrefoil, but the Quatrefoil was the one telling us to look beyond people's appearances. It showed us truths we didn't want to see. It also led me to Cadence and held me hostage in this town, forced me to become a better man.

Like the ancients wrote in *Istor Breou*, it's not the magic that's destructive; it's the extent people will go to in order to get it. Or in Nolwenn's case, to stop it.

Adrien and Cadence have now melded together like forged pieces of iron.

Putain. I'm not jealous. *Really.* I'm happy to give them time.

But maybe not *so much* time.

I crouch behind Cadence and lay my palms on her shoulders. Even though I don't pull her, she pares herself away from Adrien and tilts her head up to look at me. With a sigh, she touches my hands, and I help her stand.

And then I reach down and offer Adrien my hand. He swipes at his cheek, then slaps his palm into mine, and I hoist him up.

"So, we just let him live?" Adrien asks between labored breaths.

"Killing him would be a mercy." I stare at the front door, which is the same blue as Rainier's eyes, a darker shade than Cadence's. "His past finally caught up to him. Let him exist with that for a little while."

WE DECIDE to blow off steam among the *toull-bac'hs* that litter Adrien's living room like the fast-food wrappers in Vincent's Peugeot.

Although still pale, Cadence's shoulders are straighter, and she's stopped shivering. At the sight of Alma's statue, though, my girl almost loses it again. I squeeze her to me, promising her that tomorrow evening, her best friend will be free. I have no right to promise it, because I have no clue if that's what will happen, but I'm willing to say or do anything to lessen Cadence's pain.

I circle Adrien's guests, studying their stone faces. They're cold and lifeless. Officially, I suppose, no longer *toull-bac'hs* but proper statues. I shudder, accidentally nudging Gaston. The dog frozen mid-wee wobbles. I steady him, then back away before I can inflict any more damage.

There's a knock at the door, and then Gaëlle blusters in, smelling like freshly baked bread and chocolate cookies. She removes a tray from a paper bag and slides it atop Adrien's messy coffee table. "I brought sustenance: a platter of *jambon-beurre* and *magie noire* cookies. I can't stay long, though. Romain opened the shop but he needs to—" She stops as she takes in our faces. "Something happened."

Adrien sits unmoving and unblinking on the suede couch, moaning sporadically while staring at the oil portrait of his mother, which had vanished in the *guivre* fire but reappeared after the hawthorn trial.

Gaëlle slips off her coat. "What happened?"

"It's . . ." Eyes reddening, Cadence sinks into the bulky armchair. "It's . . ." She tries again but doesn't get any farther.

I give Adrien and Cadence a chance to tell their story by heading into the kitchen to stack plates, glasses, and napkins, and fill a pitcher with water.

"Okay, you're scaring me . . . which is saying a lot considering what we just lived through. What the hell happened?" Gaëlle has taken a seat beside Adrien.

I shove books aside to make room for my loot, then slide a sandwich onto a plate and hand it to Cadence, who shakes her head.

"I'm not hungry."

"Doesn't matter." I push the buttered baguette filled with ham her way. "You need food."

"No, I—"

"Just one bite. For me."

With a little huff, she takes a bite and chews. I kiss her temple, grateful she swallowed the damn thing. She needs energy and sustenance, and although I'm aware food can't fix a broken heart, it'll fuel her mind and body, which in turn will help her think more clearly.

Since neither Cadence nor Adrien have answered Gaëlle, I impart a piece of the story. "We found the translations. They're tattooed across your mother-in-law's body."

Water flies out of Gaëlle's mouth as she chokes on her sip. It's enough to bring Adrien out of his stupor. He pounds her back until she stops coughing.

"Th-those were the translations?" She starts tugging on one of her long curls. "She told me she was forgetting things. That it was a list to remember. I made an appointment to speak with Sylvie next week because I was worried it might be the onset of Alzheimer's."

I sigh. "Her memory's intact. The only things she's forgotten are the ones the Quatrefoil made her forget."

"Oh, thank God. But . . . but I still don't understand." She points between Cadence and Adrien, silently asking me why they look like someone just died.

So I lay it out for her. Starting with Rainier's obsession to possess magic. How he killed his own wife because she refused to try again. How he lied about her death being caused by the Blood-stone, and how everyone believed him until Camille uncovered his secret when translating the scroll. We tell Gaëlle how Nolwenn ended up having the translations, and how she misinter-preted the meaning of what Marianne said when she warned her about evil.

Unlike Cadence, grief sparks Adrien's hunger. He's devouring the *jambon-beurre* like a lion ripping through its prey. "If instead of burning those papers, she'd shared them with me, or with *you*," he's yelling, "we could've dealt with Rainier *four* years ago! We could've had fucking closure!"

Gaëlle blinks at him, at us. "I can't believe it," she murmurs. "I can't believe he'd do—" She bites her lip, probably remembering Rainier's calm, take-charge attitude when she accidentally killed Matthias.

Maybe that should've been a clue.

Gaëlle frowns at me. "How did you find out about the payments?"

"I hired a . . . lawyer—" I start.

Adrien stands, knocking into the coffee table. Water sloshes over the rim of his glass onto the brown area rug, but he doesn't seem to care. He starts pacing the room. "Call your lawyer! I want to know what he's got. I want to nail Rainier's ass to the wall."

Cadence stiffens.

"Punishing Rainier isn't going to bring anyone back, Adrien."

Normally, I'm all about revenge, but that's because *normally*, I'm not worrying about collateral damage.

"I won't kill your dad, Cadence. I swear I won't." Adrien's voice is so loud Rainier can probably hear him two *kelc'hs* over. "But I also won't stand to let him run free in Brume, or anywhere else in the world. He took *our mothers* from us."

A tear trickles down Cadence's cheek. She sniffs and brushes it away, then crooks her head to look up at me. "Does your lawyer have enough evidence for an arrest?" Her tone is deceptively flat, a storm brewing beneath the surface.

I sit on the arm of her chair and knead the base of her neck. "He does." Not everything we've gathered is admissible in a court of law, but I know a judge or two who could be incentivized to make our gatherings legal.

"Call him," she says.

"Right now?"

"Right now."

I sort of wish I could brief Philippe, but Adrien and Cadence are so broken, and Gaëlle in such a state of shock, that I doubt any of them will be enquiring how he goes about his information-collecting.

Philippe picks up on the first ring. "Hey. Sorry for my radio silence, but I got a little, uh . . . sidetracked by business down here." He's the lawyer for some seriously bad people in the South of France. I'm assuming he was either being tortured by an employer, or he was doing the torturing. The fact that he's on the other end of the line, breathing, points to option two.

"I've got you on speaker. I'm sitting here with three friends who'd like to know if you found out anything more about Marianne Shafir."

"There's some weird shit happening, Slate. That trust you had me trace the payments from? I did some re-checking. It was there one night and by morning, it up and fucking disappeared, just like my ex-wife. I've got screenshots, printouts, the whole shebang is documented, but even the usual footprints are gone. I swear—"

"Yeah, don't waste time on tracking my trust. It'll probably show back up tomorrow." *Damn curse.* Hopefully, the glitch is temporary. I'd really hate to part with that much money.

"I wasn't able to place the forged letter with any illicit sale or underground auction, but there was a funeral in that town you're staying at, two days after Marianne met with the man in the wheelchair. So I called the bistro in Rennes again. To make a long story short, the neighboring business has a security camera out front, and they don't record over the old footage. Their files go back five years, so we got lucky. They have a few seconds of the guy in the wheelchair who met Marianne as he passed in front of their door. I'll send you a visual."

Cadence's fingers squeeze mine as my cell dings. I tap the screen. The photo's slightly grainy, as if there wasn't much light, but despite the poor quality, there's no mistaking the identity of the man.

Gaëlle leans across the table to look, her hands covering her mouth. Adrien stops his pacing long enough to study the picture in depth. Rage builds in him anew.

"As for Marianne's death, I've talked to every fucking coroner, every registrar in Brittany. Her death was never reported. The funeral director in Brume is way past his prime, by the way. Seems his eyesight is so poor he didn't notice the certificate he got to bury Marianne was a fake." Philippe pauses, and I hear the sound of flint striking, then him inhaling what's most likely a Marlboro Red. "I can dig deeper, but that'll require—"

"More money. Yeah. Let me see if we really want to pursue that lead. I'll call you back." I hang up. "So we have Rainier with Marianne on the day the second wire transfer left my account."

"Your account that's MIA," Adrien duly notes.

"I'm cursed, remember? By tomorrow night, that should be fixed."

"What if it isn't?" he asks.

"If it isn't"—Gaëlle slides her palms up and down her thighs— "I'll go in front of a judge and testify. Accessories to murder—"

"Absolutely not, Gaëlle!" The force of Cadence's refusal rattles the widow. "You're not ruining your life, your children's lives, just to put a ... a ... to put him behind bars."

What word had she been about to use to describe her father? A criminal? A monster?

"Rainier needs to pay for what he's done, Cadence," Adrien says calmly.

"I know, Adrien! I know and I agree that he needs to be held accountable, but not at the cost of any more lives." Cadence shuts her eyes. "Gaëlle will *not* go down alongside him."

"Agreed." I lower my mouth to her crown of brown hair and hold it there as she turns her head and presses her cheek into my chest.

After inhaling deeply, she looks down at her lap, then at Alma's statue. "I think I need to . . . take a walk. Clear my head."

She stands, and so do I. She doesn't tell me not to come. She must sense it's a waste of breath. There's no way in hell I'm letting her out of my sight. Not with a smashed heart and a wrecked spirit. Sure, a magical Bloodstone keeps her in Brume so she wouldn't get far, but I don't want her stumbling into Rainier, who's bound to seek her out for a 'talk'. I bet he's going to try and convince her there was a perfectly good explanation for everything he did.

Cadence shrugs back into her coat, her skin looking extra pale against the red nylon. She hugs Adrien, who stays so rigid you'd think he was embracing Rainier, then Gaëlle, who's crushing a cookie into a thousand pieces on her plate.

I hold out my hand, and Cadence takes it, her fingers gliding through mine and settling in their rightful place. The sun's no more than a dim ball behind a thick haze as I lead her to that lookout point Adrien once took me to. She perches on my lap, both of us quiet, until the day fades into night.

When the cast-iron streetlamps flare, she turns in my arms and pushes an errant curl from my brow. Her fingers are ice.

I capture her wrist and stream hot air against her skin before stamping a kiss to each one of her ragged fingertips. "Home?"

Her breath catches. "I'm currently out of one." Fresh tears crystallize on her lash line.

"No, you're not." I flatten her palm against my thudding chest. "You'll always have a home. Right. Here." I descend from Merlin, but there must be a little Victor Hugo in the mix, otherwise, I got no explanation for the sappy crap that just came out of my mouth.

She smiles and kisses me.

Right there and then, ass cheeks frozen to a bench in the middle of bumblefuck Brittany, with a throbbing cut weeping blood into a band of gauze, I decide that if such declarations are the way to this girl's smiles, I'm trading the thug life for the bard one.

I stand, taking Cadence with me, and don't set her down until I've stumbled into my dorm room and slammed the door so hard it rattles the murderous beam that, as always, clubs my forehead.

63

CADENCE

S late curses. I'd say for a change, but he curses quite often. All the time, really.

I crane my neck to see what's interrupted our kiss. Find him rubbing his forehead. "The beam again?"

"The beam," he growls, setting me down. "Thank fuck I'm a soon-to-be Water warlock or I'd incinerate the damn thing."

"Mage."

"What?"

"Warlocks are evil. Mages are good."

He shoots me a wicked smile that makes his eyes squeeze and curve just as wickedly as his lips. "Adrien can be the mage. I'm calling warlock."

"Mages are genderless."

"The more the merrier then. I'm still calling warlock."

I roll my eyes, and it hurts because my lids are so bloated. God, how much have I cried today? The second I start wondering, I think of Papa, and a mix of anger and grief constricts my chest. I don't want to think about him, so I unbutton Slate's shirt, which has him growing statue-still.

His smile fades, replaced by a look of utter concentration. Or is it consternation? He wraps a gentle hand around my wrist. "You don't need to change my bandage, Cadence."

"That wasn't my intent, Slate." However, after a glance at the wet, crimson gauze, I press pause on my intent. He's in no state for what I was planning.

"What *was* your intent?" His voice is so husky that goosebumps scamper across my arms.

"Something you're clearly unfit for."

He grunts. "If it aligns with what I'm thinking, then I can guarantee you that I'm entirely fit for it."

I smile. "Your abdomen was sectioned by octopus claws hours ago, and you're bleeding half to death."

"Were you planning on making me do some crunches?"

"No." My smile grows. How can this boy find ways to make me smile even on the darkest day of my life?

Slate steps into me, probably to prove how *fit* he is. But then he gently tucks a lock of my hair behind my ear, glides his fingers to my jaw, and tilts my head up. I heft my mind out of the gutter. All he's proving at the moment is how sweet he is.

"You've been through so much in one day. More than anyone should ever have to." He drags his fingers back up to my ear and through my hair to cradle the back of my head. "You don't want your first time to be associated with this day."

Blood rushes into my cheeks. "How—how do you know? Alma!"

"No. Not Alma. You told me."

I frown. "When? I'd remember . . . *Oh.* Before?"

"Yes. Before."

I lick my lips. "I can't believe I told you."

"Cadence, you were my girlfriend." He sighs, then strokes his thumb along my hairline. "Tomorrow, it'll all come back to you. Hopefully," he adds under his breath.

How I hate the Quatrefoil and its stupid curses!

Maman would be alive had it not been for the Quatrefoil cursing my father. I shut this train of thought down, because it makes my anger well, and I don't want the emotion to pollute this moment.

"I want you to make me remember this day for another reason." My gaze falls to Slate's chest. "Unless it'll hurt you." I roll up onto my toes and kiss the knife-edge of his jaw. "I'll be just as happy to make out some more and fall asleep against you."

His breathing quickens, jostling a nerve along his jaw that tickles my parted lips. "You're sure?"

"About being satisfied with kisses and a sleepover? Yes."

He grunts. "Yeah. You're getting those either way. I was asking about the first part."

I detach my mouth from the stubble I'm peppering with kisses to stare into his eyes. "Yes. A thousand percent sure."

"That's some terrible math skills, Mademoiselle de Morel." He backs me into his bed until my knees buckle. "And math isn't even my forte."

Heart beating a mile a minute, I push his shirt off his shoulder and roll it down his arms. "And what *is* your forte, Monsieur Ardoin?"

He flings off the button-down without taking his attention off me. Even bruised and bleeding, the man is magnificent. "I used to think it was conning people."

I shrug out of my coat and hoodie. "And now?" I'm expecting something lewd that'll make me roll my eyes and grin.

"Now . . ." He leans forward, forcing my spine to unspool against his messy bedsheets, and plants one palm on either side of my body. "Now, I believe, it's making you smile, because you do that a lot around me."

The smile collapses from my lips. Out of all the possible answers, never did I expect the one he just gave me.

Slate's eyebrows furrow, almost connecting. "Guess I was over-reaching."

I cup the sides of his face. "I love you, you selfless boy."

"Man."

"Man." I shoot him a watery smile. "And you weren't overreaching. No one has ever made me smile as much as you. *No one.*" I'd lay my palm over the Quatrefoil that I loved him before I forgot him.

"Yeah?"

He sounds so uncertain that I tow his mouth down to mine and whisper the confirmation across his lips.

"I've never been loved. That is, by anyone other than Bastian and Spike, but only Bastian's ever professed it, because cacti are the strong, silent, prickly type."

I laugh.

"Ah, there's that beautiful smile." Slate kisses the raised corner of my mouth before trailing his lips down the column of my throat. "I fucking love you, too, Cadence, and it scares the hell out of me, because I'm not sure how to do it."

"Do *it*?"

"Love you."

I dance my fingers across his back, drinking in the play of tendon and muscle. "Just keep showing up and making me smile, and I'll love you forever."

"Forever, huh?"

Goosebumps crop up on the skin I caress. "Does that scare you?"

"I'll have you know that the Almighty Vanquisher of Fanged and Clawed Aquatic Creatures is scared of nothing."

I shake my head, my cheeks hurting from how far my smile extends. "That's an awfully long title."

"How about we make up acronyms later? Right now, I'd like to give your magnificent body my full attention." He drags the hem of my tank top up, pulsing warm breaths across the bare skin around my navel, then he lowers his mouth to my stomach and kisses it gently, before proceeding to kiss the rest of me.

The *whole* of me.

64

SLATE

I hold Cadence's hand in a near vise-grip as we climb the hill toward Fifth. I'm aware the moonset's not a death warrant for the wearer of the Bloodstone—the *Kelouenn*, or rather Nolwenn's collar bone, assured us of that—but I'm still worried about what the Quatrefoil has in store for us.

As we cross the edge of the quad between the stairs from Fourth to Fifth, the glint of metal under the clinic lamplight garners my attention. Staring off into the mist that's billowing over the Nimueh, Rainier de Morel sits on his silent, souped-up snowmobile, almost in the exact spot he'd parked the night the Bloodstone fell off my finger a month ago.

I can still hear the engine rev, still see the spark of malice in his eyes.

Bile rises in my throat as I recall the night. Because of him and of his lies, I came so very close to throwing myself off the roof of the clinic and onto the jagged rocks below. And when I didn't jump, he was there, lying in wait like a predator, ready to ram into me with his snowmobile. Had Cadence and the others not rushed out the door at that moment, I'd most likely have become one with the snow and stars.

To think he was able to keep up his ruse thanks to *our* hard work and momentous discovery about cradles and locking the leaves into the clock. To think we all fell for this convenient twist of fate. To think Rainier's dirty little secret was that I would have survived the Bloodstone regardless.

Cadence stills as she spots her father. He must sense her looking, because he turns, his blond hair glinting silver, his face pale as the snow below. Even from across the quad, I perceive the desperation in his gaze.

He wants his daughter to come back to him.

Fury sears my lungs as I twine my fingers harder around Cadence's and plant my boots firmly in the snow. If I let go, I'm going to jet over to him and shove him off the edge of the earth.

Cadence's chest heaves with ragged breaths and her eyes wreathe with tears as she watches him watching her. Gulping, she tugs at my hand and leads me toward the narrow stairs to Fifth.

"I can't believe he came out tonight."

"He's probably made the pilgrimage up here to reminisce on the moment he urged me to jump off the clinic's roof in order to avoid the Bloodstone's poison."

Cadence stops midstair, shock lighting the whites of her eyes. "What? He told you to commit suicide?"

Right . . . I hadn't shared that little plot twist. "It's in the past—"

"Talk."

Sighing, I give her all the pieces of that night that she missed out on. Her gaze tumbles back down the hill toward the clinic, though it's barely visible now between the darkness and the fog. The shock of my story dries her tears and thins her lips. By the time I'm done, tendrils of white stream out of her nostrils.

I release my grip on her fingers to cup her face and angle it away from her past and toward her present, her future—me and the temple and her fellow *diwallers* who are both waiting for us on the hill. I brush my lips over her forehead, cheeks, nose, mouth to remind her that I'm here, and that she's cherished, even if it isn't by the man she assumed would be the one to treasure her forever.

"Hey, guys! Only seven minutes and twelve seconds before moonset." Bastian grins down at us a tad ruefully, his hand going to the back of his head and mussing his hair. "Sorry to interrupt."

I tuck Cadence's hand into mine and finish the climb. "No worries. Cadence and I like picking up where we left off."

When I reach the temple door, I'm out of breath and twitchy. I don't like unpredictable things, and nothing has proven more fickle than magic. Well, except Rainier.

Cadence fits her quatrefoil skeleton key into the iron lock. The latches pop with a solid thunk. Before removing the key from the lock plate, she glances at the Bloodstone that sits quietly, almost innocently, on her finger, as if it weren't the cause of so much malevolence and heartache.

"This is it." Geoffrey rubs his palms together.

I'd momentarily forgotten about the little loophole. Hopefully, the Quatrefoil will *fix* things without an intervention on my part. If he becomes the Water *diwaller*, then—

"Is it, though?" Cadence's voice cuts through my musings.

I shoulder the door open to allow the others through.

Geoffrey glances at his watch. "Where's Rainier?"

"He's decided to sit this one out," I deadpan.

The mayor blinks like he's not sure what to think. But then a smug grin buds on his lips. "About time he stays where he belongs. He doesn't even have magic in his blood."

"Right." It's all I can do not to flick his forehead and call him a *bajaneg*.

Bastian lingers on the cleared flagstones, shifting from one boot to the other, eyes jumping between the hill and the temple.

I nod to the door. "Hey, honorary *diwaller*, get your ass in there!"

He freezes and blinks at me, his lenses amplifying the movement. But then he returns his gaze to the hill, and I realize he's waiting for Alma.

"She's coming home tonight."

"That the truth?"

I fucking hope so.

He blanches. "Oh, God."

I wrap an arm around his scrawny frame that feels even scrawnier since Alma and Paul were cursed, and draw him into me. "She'll be back in your arms in no time. Just focus on that. She and Paul are coming home *tonight*."

My conviction and hug don't do much for his complexion, but hopefully they've worked on his spirit.

"Go on."

He trundles in ahead of me.

A duvet of snow covers the cupola, rendering the space even darker than usual. In the obscurity, the curved bookshelves look like an army of soldiers waiting to strike. The hair on my nape tingles, and I brace myself for something to lurch out of the blackness.

Cadence flips on the switch, and relief washes over me in time with the light bathing the room. No soldiers, no monsters, no ghosts. Just a bunch of books and a goddamn ticking clock.

Cadence waits for me beside the railing. A fierce determination sharpens her features, making her look far older than her age.

Gaëlle, who must have realized she'd go bald yanking at her hair, is wearing a new scarf. This one's orange with green tassels. She's back to squeezing the yarn like it's a venomous snake she's hoping to suffocate.

Adrien's jaw is set in a hard line as he helps his father over the plexiglass guardrail. He obviously hasn't told his old man about Rainier's hand in Camille's death, but I'm sure he will after the ceremony tonight.

"No knife this time, Geoff?" I quip, grabbing Cadence around the waist and depositing her safely on the other side.

He frowns at me.

"You know, to make sure you get a spot on the Council?" I help Gaëlle up and over next.

He scoffs. "My spot's already secured. Has been for centuries."

As he settles in front of my symbol, I mutter, "Yeah, keep telling yourself that."

I hop over the protective barrier and advance toward the Water element.

Geoffrey shoots out a hand to stop me. "Whoa, kid. Just because the Quatrefoil let you swim with me during that last trial doesn't mean you have any right to be here with us *diwallers*. Get behind the rail. When it's time for us to share the magic, we may decide to give you some. We'll see."

"With all due respect, Geoffrey, don't be a dick." Cadence's calmly delivered rebuke makes everyone but me balk.

Yeah, I'm smiling. How could I not, when my girl just put a giant jerk in his place with such carefully curated words?

She forges on, "Slate's fought right alongside us—alongside *you* —so he deserves to stand here just as much as you do."

Geoffrey works his jaw as though he were masticating a piece of gum. "Fine. But he stays back."

I half-lean, half-sit on the clear barrier and cross my arms.

Bastian stands on the other side of the rail, right smack behind me. "Two minutes and eighteen seconds." He pushes his glasses farther up the bridge of his nose as he checks the timer on his phone.

Gaëlle's toes abut the glowing white slashed triangle. She looks down, tugging at her pumpkin-colored scarf. "Do we need to touch our symbol?"

Adrien crouches. The red light spilling out of his icon gives him a slight demonic air. "The *Kelouenn* didn't offer guidelines, but why not?" He loosens the tie around his neck—because, of course, Adrien would wear a tie to a magical ceremony—and something in my chest twinges. Brotherly affection? Ever since he lost Charlotte and discovered his mother was murdered, I've developed a soft spot for the fashion-stunted professor. He's no Bastian, but he's wormed his tweedy way into my heart, just like the rest of the crew.

Minus Geoffrey.

"One minute and twenty seconds." Bastian's voice is more air than sound.

As she sinks to her knees in front of her glowing green symbol, Cadence releases a protracted breath, reels one in, lets it out. She sets a trembling hand down on Earth. The urge to go to her is strong, but I don't trust the Quatrefoil for shit and want to be ready for Geoffrey if push comes to corporeal shove.

"One minute."

In one minute, everyone will remember me again.

In one minute, I won't be a nobody.

Except, as I look around, I realize I'm not a nobody.

I came to Brume a scarred and angry orphan with little self-worth and with, for only family, another orphan and a cactus.

I thought I was set for life. That I would never need more. Yet, here I am. Part of something more. Something larger. Part of a crew. Of a family.

And I like it.

"Thirty seconds," Bastian announces.

The pounding of my heart drowns out the relentless ticking *dihuner*.

Geoffrey counts down under his breath.

"Bastian?" I say.

"Yeah?"

"I've got a confession to make." *Eighteen. Seventeen. Sixteen.* "I was the one who stole Steve from your dorm."

The shock and confusion in his eyes both breaks my heart and makes me laugh. He starts to yell at me, but the alarm on his phone brays.

I brace myself for the ground to rumble and the temple to come crashing down around us. Instead, there's a heartbeat of silence. Then Cadence gasps.

The Bloodstone slides off her finger, lifts into the air, and soars toward the center dial.

Cogs grind, and a small recess appears right where the star and moon hands connect. The Bloodstone hovers, then plunges, and the indent seals over. The crunch of glass as the magical stone shatters echoes through the silent library, and then . . .

And then the clock bleeds.

Four scarlet rivulets surge out of its heart and snake over the star and moon dials, tapering toward the four elements, snuffing out their glow.

"What now?" Gaëlle's voice is rife with nerves.

When each golden element is seamlessly outlined in red, the blood shimmers and then sinks into the metal, and four beams flare, illuminating the entire temple like a concert light show. It becomes so bright and shiny, I can hardly see anything past the scorching blue glow of my element.

I blink to rid my vision of the glare and cut my eyes toward Cadence, who's cloaked in an emerald aura. She looks back my way, and her hand crawls up to her mouth.

Shit. Am I bleeding out? Did I vanish? I pat myself—still in one piece—then drop my gaze to cop a look at my body.

A smug grin flips up the corners of my mouth and grows ever smugger when I glance at Geoffrey.

Guess the Quatrefoil's more trustworthy than I gave it credit for, 'cause the person glowing like a radioactive smurf . . . that person is *moi*.

65

CADENCE

I remember.

I remember Slate.

I remember the first time we met, how he slipped and fell at my feet and my family heirloom tumbled from his pocket.

How he told me to make my own luck when the clock struck midnight.

I remember how deeply I loathed him the night he revealed he'd slipped on the Bloodstone ring.

I remember my relief when he surfaced from the well.

My first glimpse of his scarred and battered body in my bathroom.

His awed and pained expression when we visited his childhood home and he caught sight of the painted block letters of his name —REMY.

I remember our first kiss at the tavern.

Our second kiss.

Our third.

All of them.

I remember when I woke up to his face at the clinic after my coma.

How my heart shattered into a trillion pieces when he kissed me goodbye, and then how those pieces fused together when the new moon set and the ring fell off his finger.

I remember his anger fueled by worry when he returned from Marseille and found the ring on my finger.

How he'd stayed awake for days, waiting for my piece to manifest, and then jumped into the earth after me.

I.

Remember.

Every look.

Every kiss.

Every touch.

Everything.

66

SLATE

G eoffrey's meaty fist collides with my jaw. "You thief! You stole my magic!" His right hook's stronger than his son's. "We struck a deal! That Council seat was mine!"

While Gaëlle, Adrien, Cadence, and I shine like glowsticks, Geoffrey glistens from sweat alone.

I rub my jaw and chuckle, my blue halo making me feel saintly enough not to punch him back. "You should never make deals with a con man."

Geoffrey lifts his fist again, but Bastian hops over the railing and steps between us, a fierce mama-bear look screwing up his placid face. "Leave my brother alone!"

It's a complete turnaround of our formative years where I was the one banging heads and telling bullies to leave him be.

His protective stance gives me heartburn. It's alarming how sensitive this town's made my esophagus.

Swearing in Breton, Geoffrey fumbles with his coat pocket.

When I see his wallet make an appearance, I say, "You don't have enough money to pay me for my seat *or* my magic, Geoff."

Glowering at me, the man takes out a red credit card and presses his thumb over it, sliding out a blade. "This doesn't end here," he growls, poking his thumb with the blade before getting down on all fours and slathering blood over the Water element. "Come on. Come on."

But it's too late. The magic is sloshing through my veins like blueberry granita.

Now that the danger's averted, Bastian spins and wraps his arms around me. "I'm so sorry I forgot you," he sobs against my shoulder. "I can't believe—I can't—"

I squeeze him back hard. "That you renamed Spike *Steve*? Me neither. I mean . . . What sort of pussy name is that?"

A laugh bubbles out through his snot and tears. He pulls back and shakes his head so hard his glasses slide down his nose.

"Slate?" Cadence's voice warbles as though she, too, is crying.

I pat Bastian's back, check on Geoffrey, who's still trying to sacrifice bits of himself to the Quatrefoil, then give my girl my full attention. "You look like you've seen a ghost."

She stares and stares at me, her lips trembling around quiet breaths. And then she cups my jaw and pulls my forehead down to hers. "I loved you."

"Ouch. Past tense?"

I feel her smile even though my attention is on her eyes. "I still love you. More than ever." She kisses me gently. "More than ever."

There goes my heartburn again. As I rub my chest, and she deepens the kiss, my hand falls to her waist and tugs her indecently close.

I'm about to suggest getting out of here when Bastian yells, "Hey, you guys stopped glowing!" so close to my ear that my drum shudders.

Cadence and I pry our lips apart but not our bodies. Yeah, I'm not letting her go again.

Like Bastian announced, our skin has stopped glowing. I crane my neck to see Adrien and Gaëlle, who no longer resemble party favors at a rave. Our palms still shimmer, but that's it.

"Dad!" Adrien shouts.

Geoffrey's made his way to the center of the clock and is now hacking at the gold, trying to excavate the spot that absorbed the ring, dripping blood everywhere.

"Dad, stop it! Stop it and *look*!"

Grumbling, Geoffrey stands and squints at his son whose hands are bathed in gloves of fire.

"Oh my God." Cadence laughs. "Adrien!"

He slowly flips his hands over and around. "It doesn't even burn."

"Hey, Prof, you got your eyebrow back!"

Cadence hisses as he lifts his flaming hand to his face and prods the new growth.

Realizing what he's just done, he pops his blazing fingertips off his brow. "Shit. Did I just singe it off again?"

Slightly awed, I say, "Nope. It's still there."

"That's amazing!" Gaëlle claps, then shrieks as a gust of wind leaps off her palms and blows her hair horizontally. She sputters, then barks out a laugh worthy of Alma.

As Cadence stares at her palms, probably trying to coax out her magic, the tremor I was expecting at moonset hits the temple. I cage her body with one arm and fling out the other to grip the guardrail. Dust falls from the ceiling, books tumble off shelves, one of the ceiling bulbs pops, breaking like the Bloodstone earlier. My muscles seize, and I grit my molars.

It's not over.

It's. Not. Fucking. Over.

We should have known.

One by one, the topazes on the celestial dial ignite, sending up rays of glittering light so bright they sear my retinas. Still hugging Cadence to me, I squeeze my eyes shut and keep them sealed until the ground stops shaking. When it does, I cautiously open one eye, then the other, before my mouth joins the fray and parts ridiculously wide.

Before me, standing taller than his usual meter and festooned with additional spines and claw-like leaves, sits Spike. His branches reach toward me like arms, each one topped with a cup-shaped, coral bloom.

Someone's had a makeover.

I almost hug him, but, well . . . I'm not that crazy.

"Hello, Spike." Cadence runs a fingertip along one of his brand-new petals after Bastian fetches him.

The happy yips of a dog echo off the temple walls as Gaston bounds out of a beam of light. He stops at Geoffrey's feet, lifts his hind leg, and finishes the peeing job the Quatrefoil so rudely interrupted.

Geoffrey grumbles out the dog's moniker, making the poor thing cower.

More movement disturbs the celestial light.

Juda, Paul, Charlotte . . .

Adrien stares and stares at her, and then he strides forward and engulfs the petite, pixie-haired woman carrying his child in a tight hug, which she returns with just as much vigor. They'll go the distance, those two.

Claire arrives next and shoves aside the hugging couple with—thank fuck—her finger fully intact.

Yoga-girl materializes, and then napping boy, and then—

"Alma!" Both Bastian and Cadence scream, ridding me of several decibels of hearing.

Cadence gets to her friend first, seizing her in a giant, tear-filled hug. The second she loosens her grip, Bastian whirls his copper-curled crush into his arms and plants a kiss worthy of a sappy romantic movie.

I chuckle, but my laughter peters out as more people materialize from the magical topaz glow. I'm waiting for one in particular, but the people the clock spits out are all adults. After the *toull-bac'h* victims, a startled Solange comes out.

And then nothing.

The topazes keep glowing.

The clock keeps ticking.

Come on.

Come—

A tiny, blonde wisp of a girl materializes, and I let out the mother of all exhales.

Emilie wears her fuzzy unicorn pajamas. As her little head swings around the temple, I stride over and scoop her up, then spin her around and around. She's warm and solid under my grip, and even though her brows shoot up, a giggle escapes her lips at my exuberant welcome. Goosebumps—the good kind, the *great* kind—rise on my skin.

She's real. She's back. She's alive.

When I stop spinning her, she wraps her arms around my neck and her legs around my waist. She smells like strawberry shampoo and toothpaste and playdough. I hold her so tight my arms ache.

"Monsieur?" Her brow's furrowed. "Are you okay?"

"I am now," I croak.

She touches my cheek. "Then why are you crying?"

Laughing, I hug her to me again. "They're happy tears, kiddo. I'm just happy to see you."

"I'm happy to be back, even though the other side was kind of fun."

"The—the other side?"

"Yeah. I got to do all sorts of things! I flew. Like a bird. And it was sunny. And Papi Merlin told the *best* bedtime stories."

I stare at her in shock.

"He's not my *real* papi. He just told me to call him that." She suddenly purses her button lips. "He sort of looks like you actually, except he's *super* old, like at least forty, and has this really long beard. Anyway, he and his lady friend, Viviene, taught me all sorts of stuff."

Her forehead ruffles anew as Cadence steps over to us, smiling and wiping the moisture from her cheeks.

"Hi, Emilie."

Emilie tilts her head, her blonde curls draping over my arm. "You said you couldn't come back with me."

Cadence's palm freezes on her cheek. "Uh . . . what?"

"Wait a minute . . . you're not Viviene."

"You met Viviene?" Cadence breathes.

Emilie nods. "Uh-huh. She and Merlin told me I'd be going home soon. That you just had to prove you were *poor of art.*"

Cadence's lips quirk. "I've always been pretty poor at art. I can't even manage stick-people."

I laugh softly. "Are you sure she didn't say *pure of heart*, Emilie?"

"Oh, yeah. That's it. Can I see my mom now?"

"Of course, kiddo. Let's—"

But Juda's already tugging Emilie from my arms, kissing the girl's forehead. "I've got her. I'll bring her back to her mom."

"Juda, it's good to see you." I shake the old man's hand.

"It's good to be back. How's my Nolwenn?"

"Lost without you."

He glances over his shoulder at Gaëlle who's now hugging a tall man with a bunch of tattoos and white hair cropped close to his scalp. "Matthias wasn't with us there."

Cadence's hand finds mine and crushes my fingers.

I shake my head. "You have to understand—"

"I just need some time." He sighs a deep, soul-smooshing sigh before shooting us a smile. I help him step over the guardrail, then wave to Emilie as they exit the temple and enter the dark streets of Brume.

"Slate, Cadence." Gaëlle's eyes are so red her irises look like two tiger's-eye cabochons. "I'd like you to meet—*remeet*—my papa. Pierre." Her voice shakes with so much emotion that it rattles her entire body. Even her scarf shakes.

"By God, how you look like Amandine." He smiles gently at Cadence. "And you . . ." He frowns at me. "You look familiar but—"

"You'll remember me as Rémy. Rémy Roland."

Pierre's eyes widen. "Oscar and Eugenia's son. Of course." His smile grows. "What a pleasure it is to see you both again. And thank you—all of you—for bringing us home." He squeezes his daughter to him. "Although I'd love to stay and chat, I'm dying to meet my grandbabies. Besides, you've got people waiting . . ." He nods to the bright beams before taking off with a chattering Gaëlle.

I turn around, find Oscar and Eugenia gaping at me as if *I'm* the one who just rose from the grave.

"Rémy!" Eugenia steps closer, her green eyes roving over every part of my face. "Oh, *mon amour*, look at you. Look how grown up you are. Taller than your father." Tears spring out of her eyes and course down her cheeks.

"Not by much." Oscar lifts his glasses to swipe at his eyes, a smile clinging to his lips.

All my life, I've created scenarios in my head where I met my parents. Early on, they were fantasies of courageous rescues, my mom barging into my foster home and yelling, "Unhand my boy!" while my dad fought off the system with ninja stars and round-house kicks. Later, they turned into something else, something that resembled a reckoning, with me spitting in their faces and telling them to fuck off.

"Rémy . . ." my mother whispers again, her accent adding a breathy vowel before the 'r'.

I give her the usual *bise*, a greeting of kisses on the cheeks. "I go by *Slate* now, Eugenia."

She envelops me in a hug. "Well, I still go by *Maman*, Slate."

My fucking heartburn acts up again. Big time.

This is better than any dramatic rescuing or vindictive insult. I squeeze my mother back, a ridiculous smile perched on my face.

After she releases me, Maman turns toward Cadence. "You must be Amandine's daughter."

Cadence smiles. "I hear I look like her. Like Viviene, too, apparently."

"You really do." My mother engulfs a startled Cadence into a hug. "You really do."

My father grips my shoulder, squeezes. Unlike my effusive mother, he's quiet . . . contemplative. "How did you end up choosing the name Slate? I mean, I like it. I guess, I'm just—curious. It's not very French. Or Spanish." He ticks his head toward my mother as though to remind me of my ancestry.

I grin. "It's a long story, pops."

He smiles back at me, and it's strange, because it's like looking at my own face with two extra decades of life on it. "Good thing I like long stories, son."

I rub my chest as I start from zero.

Well, from age three.

67

CADENCE

After a long hug and short chat with Eugenia, a silky, feminine voice drowns out any further possible communication. "Professor Roland! Yoo-hoo."

Eugenia sighs, an indulgent smile hovering on her lips. "*Ay Dios mío*. I was hoping that one would be staying with Merlin and Viviene."

Claire Robinson bustles up to our small group, eyes bright with excitement, smile as large as her bosom. "I thought I spotted you in that sunny place, but it all passed so quickly that I didn't get a chance to say hello. Guess what? I'm a teacher now, too! I teach astronomy, just like you did!"

Oscar scratches his head and nods, a fixed smile on his face. "That's—that's wonderful, Mademoiselle Robinson."

"Will you be going back to work at U of B? Because we could share lesson plans. I've been introducing the freshmen to the ancient Brumian constellations—"

"Mademoiselle Claire! Thank goodness you're back! Astronomy emergency here." Alma strides over and snatches Claire away from Oscar. "Bastian has soooooooooo many questions about constellations." As she leads Claire across the clock where Bastian waits, she looks over her shoulder at us and winks.

"Now *that* girl, I like," says Eugenia.

"Alma's the best."

"Are you ladies done talking yet? Or will I need to wait another seventeen years before officially greeting Cadence?" Oscar's eyes curve into dark rainbows, just like his son's.

I hold out a hand. "Nice to finally meet you, Monsieur Roland."

"Oscar." He steps close and then gives me a one-armed hug that's as solid as Slate's, as solid as my father's.

My father . . .

Is he walking?

And if he is, where is it he's walking to? Toward the temple or toward the train station?

When Oscar releases me, I glance toward the heavy door of the library, half-expecting to find Papa standing there, chin tipped high, shoulders back, proud man that he is.

Is he still proud?

He didn't look all that proud sitting atop his snowmobile.

He looked broken and haunted.

Why was he sitting there anyway? Did he have an appointment with Sylvie? She usually comes over to—

The blood drains from my face, and I back up from Oscar and Eugenia. I bump into the guardrail, then whirl and place my palms on the thick edge to hoist myself over. My legs tremble so hard I worry they'll give out before I reach the rooftop of the clinic.

Because that's where my father is.

I feel it in my bones.

In my marrow.

I run.

I don't think my heart beats once as I skid down the *kelc'h* to Fourth, bruising my tailbone on the icy cobbles. Although my hands glimmer green, as though to remind me I have magic, magic I may be able to use to reach the clinic faster, I don't call upon it.

I wouldn't know how.

Soon, I'll know. But now. *Now*, I run.

Sure enough, when I reach the snowmobile, it's riderless.

I climb the stairs two at a time and emerge on the roof with all my vital organs wedged inside my throat. "PAPA!"

He turns from where he stands at the edge of the roof that could very well be the edge of the world, what with all that mist billowing between lake and sky.

I step toward him, slowly, carefully, afraid that if I go any faster, my momentum will disturb the air and tip him over. I stop close enough to pick out each one of his eyelashes but far enough that he can't reach out and touch me.

"What are—you doing?" My breaths are labored, and my heart rate a wild thing behind my ribs.

His gaze slides over my face, then down to my hands, which are balled at my sides. A smile presses into his haggard face and brightens his reddened eyes. "How strong you are, *ma chérie*. How brave. I didn't do many things right in my life, yet somehow"—his Adam's apple joggles—"somehow I made you." He starts to raise his arm but must realize I'm unwilling to be touched because his fingers plummet back to his side. "Somehow I made and raised this marvelous, pure-hearted girl."

I suck down the sharp jab of pain each one of those words provoke in me. "Why are you—standing on the roof—of the clinic?"

Papa looks back toward the tendrils of mist that ebb and flow like the waves of the lake crashing against the jagged rocks below. "I was contemplating my life."

"And you couldn't—do that—from the manor?"

In spite of the moonless sky and the dull pinpricks of stars, Papa's eyes are luminous. His cheeks too. He's crying.

My father is crying.

The sight wrings a gasp from my lungs. "*You* killed *her*. You have no right to cry!"

"I'm human, Cadence. Just human. Unlike you." He smiles, and it's gentle.

I don't want it to be gentle. I want it to be cruel and devious, because I don't know what to do with gentle.

"Cadence!" My name rings through the darkness. Over and over it rings. Like the tolling of bells.

"That boy truly loves you. *Rémy* . . ." He speaks Slate's birth name almost reverently. "I used to love Amandine like that boy loves you."

"*Don't* compare yourself to Slate. That *boy* . . . he'd sacrifice himself to save me. You . . . you sacrificed Maman to save yourself!"

My father winces as though I've slapped him.

"How could you wake up each and every morning in your

marital bed and stare at yourself in the mirror? How could you go on? And—" I rake in a breath. Another. "And then do it again? Do people's lives not matter to you?"

He stares at his legs as though to show me he was punished. Or maybe he's still marveling that they work. "I went on because I had you. Otherwise . . ." He stares back out into the gauzy vastness, lips pressed firmly together. After a long minute during which my name is called out so many times it sounds like a chant, he says, "Camille was going to tell you what I did. She was going to take you away from me. I couldn't lose you."

"Of course, you couldn't," I say flatly. "I was your last connection to magic."

"No. You were my last connection to my humanity."

Boots thud, and then Slate appears at the top of the stairs, chest pumping so fast he seems to be vibrating. Alma skids to a stop beside him. Adrien. Charlotte. Bastian. Oscar. Eugenia. They're all there, slowly spreading out to form a line.

Papa gasps, and I follow his gaze toward Slate's parents—ghosts from his past.

Slate's mother breaks rank by taking a step forward. "Rainier." She rolls every r in his name.

"You brought them home." Papa sounds awed. "You managed to bring them home. If only Amandine—if only she'd tried when I asked, we could have . . ."

"Slate was *three*, Papa. I bet she'd have tried once he was a teenager."

"Non, *ma chérie*. She wouldn't. After our failures, she changed her mind about magic. She believed it was the source of evil. She tried to cast the ring into the lake the night of the new moon. I found her on the shore. I . . . I managed to stop her from making a terrible mistake." His eyes are locked on his feet.

The plank! "You hit her with the plank from our dock!" The blood on the wood was my mother's blood.

"Only to stop her from making a grave mistake. It just knocked her out." He raises his gaze back to mine, and although I hate all I see, I cannot look away. "I managed to pull her onto my lap and bring her back to the house. I put her to bed, hoping she'd change her mind when she came to. Hoping she'd see reason. But she didn't. And when she tried to strangle me . . ." He sighs. "Well, I'm here, and she's not, so I guess you know how that story ends. Don't think for a second it didn't pain me to part with her."

Bile sloshes around my stomach. "You're a monster."

A scuffle followed by a growled, "Unhand me!" makes me spin around.

"Dad, no!" Adrien races after his father, skidding on the slick rooftop. He goes down hard. Charlotte rushes to his side. With her help, he picks himself back up. "Dad!"

Geoffrey is barreling toward us like a bull, puffs of white streaming out of his nostrils. "Murderer! You fucking *murderer!*"

Papa doesn't even flinch. Probably because he knows he deserves every ounce of Geoffrey's fury.

Adrien's father shoves mine, pushing him precariously close to the edge.

"Geoffrey, stop," I cry out. "Stop!"

But he doesn't.

When Papa stumbles, I shriek and grab onto the back of Geoffrey's coat. "STOP! Stop it!"

But he keeps assaulting my father.

An arm hooks around my middle and yanks me back. Although I kick and scream at Slate to let me go, he doesn't listen. He just keeps dragging me farther and farther away from the scuffle.

Papa rubs at his mouth, smearing blood over his cheeks. "Oh, and Geoff, in case you still wonder if my wife ever harbored feelings for you, the answer is yes."

Geoffrey freezes.

"Amandine thought you were a repulsive man and pitied Camille to have been saddled with—"

Geoffrey grabs the lapels of Papa's coat and shakes him as though hoping different words might fall from his mouth.

Even though Adrien's father has never been my favorite person, my heart hurts for him. For all his faults, lusting after someone else's wife doesn't compare to murder.

Papa smiles. "Come on, Geoff. Be a man and avenge your wife."

"Geoffrey, no!" I wail.

Slate's arm stiffens, squeezing so hard my stomach hurts.

"He's taunting you, Dad!" Adrien yells, Charlotte holding on to his arm to keep him from getting any nearer. "If Rainier wants to take his life, let him take his life."

Geoffrey lifts my father and dangles him over the void with a force I never thought him capable of.

"I love you, *ma Cadence*. And I'm so prou—"

Geoffrey lets go.

My father vanishes.

And the momentum . . .

It makes Geoffrey slip.

Slip and fall.

Right over the edge.

Right after my father.

68

SLATE

The funerals were meant to be private, but they become a town affair. It starts with a couple people dressed in black, slipping in through the graveyard's gates and hanging back in the shadows to mourn without encroaching on Adrien and Cadence's privacy.

But then a few more people trickle in, then more. And more. By ten o'clock, all of Brume is packed between the cemetery gates, sugar packets in hand, condolences on their lips, and grief in their hearts.

Yes, we're burying a villain and an idiot, but the townspeople only see their gracious dean and their stately mayor. They see two men who were, for so long, the face of Brume. Two men they admired and adored, whose sudden and accidental passing have left them all horror-stricken.

The story we told: Geoffrey and Rainier were evaluating the technical possibility of adding an extra floor to the clinic when a freak tremor shook Brume and made them both plummet to their death. The new mayor of Brume—none other than my mother—and the new dean—Adrien—are currently designing a tall guardrail for that treacherous rooftop.

Nolwenn and Juda move toward the de Morel mausoleum, their weary but dry gazes riveted to the blossoming sunshine-yellow chrysanthemums Cadence planted around the crypt using her Earth magic.

My girl said she could never forgive Rainier, but I assume she has. Not completely, but a little. After all, in spite of all he did, she still buried him inside her family's crypt.

The funerary flowers' treacly scent is thicker than the fog blanketing Brume. Fog I have yet to understand how to dispel. Gaëlle and I are working hard at it, using the pocket-sized grimoire Dad handed over after the rooftop faceoff, the one Viviene and Merlin entrusted him with.

"*Ma petite chérie.*" Nolwenn laces arms, no longer stained with ink, around the girl she's always considered like a grandchild.

Juda and I look on as they talk quietly. I imagine about Rainier and Amandine because I hear the words *papa* and *maman* mentioned a few times.

"I miss your galettes," I say to Nolwenn's husband, arms folded in front of my chest.

A small smile bends his pale lips. "I miss making them." The wind teases his white mane and bushy eyebrows, and although he isn't his usual ruddy self, he no longer resembles a cadaver.

After Nolwenn releases Cadence, she turns to me. "Eugenia keeps asking me why I call you Marseille. Mind explaining it to her? I don't yet have the energy or the heart to revisit how"—she swallows—"how I lost track of you."

Her guilt for having given her cursed son her full attention instead of me still ravages her. She shifts her grief-filled eyes to Juda, who picks up her hand and cradles it in his. Although they don't know the gory details of Matthias's demise, they're aware he died while trying to harm Gaëlle.

They're also aware magic is real, along with everyone who stepped out of the *dihuner*, because this time, Viviene and Merlin didn't tamper with people's memories.

To think that soon, the entire town will know, and then the whole world.

I get a rush and a slew of goosebumps just thinking about it.

After Nolwenn and Juda leave, when enough sugar has been poured atop the earth to give every Brumian ant diabetes, when Adrien and Charlotte exit the graveyard arm-in-arm and head-to-head, Cadence closes the crypt door and cries. I wipe the tears from her cheeks, and with a flick of my wrist the salty droplets hover in the air, turning to ice crystals. They float like shimmering confetti onto her flowers before settling on the petals like dew.

My hat trick brings the smallest of smiles to Cadence's mouth.

"I know he did some horrible things, but I'll miss him. God, how I'll miss him."

I pull her to me.

"How is it I can miss a monster?" she croaks.

"Because that monster loved you."

EPILOGUE
CADENCE - 5 YEARS LATER

"You do understand that if you don't accomplish the Quatrefoil's test by the next new moon, you don't pass go and collect a magical power, correct?" Slate refills my empty glass of water with a flick of his fingers.

The thirty-six-year-old Italian carpenter who stands before us nods, his green gaze cutting across our heads for a glimpse of the astronomical wonder.

After it finally gave the four of us magic, the tightly-guarded secrets of our town spread like wildfire across the globe. Today, the *dihuner* has become more famous than the Eiffel Tower or McDonald's golden arches even though so few have seen it since it started ticking. Neither tourist nor prospective student can enter at will. Especially not now that U of B has become a school of magic, fenced in by the same wards that used to confine the Bloodstone wearer.

On the cold February night that will forever remain stained with awe and heartache, inhabitants impure of heart were transported out of our town. The worthy were permitted to stay, but only those who completed the Quatrefoil's tailor-made trial were given magic.

"You do understand that if you don't succeed in the allotted timeframe, you will be removed from Brume and forbidden from applying again, right?" Gaëlle's knitting needles clack as she clarifies the *dihuner's* vetting process. She's almost done with the second lavender baby bootie, and just in time.

"*Si,*" the man says, as I shift on my seat, trying to get comfortable, a feat in my ninth month of pregnancy.

I lay my palm over my stomach just as my little girl makes her presence known with a sharp elbow jab. "You may proceed to the clock and touch the elements, Massimo. And remember, your element will choose you; you don't get to choose *it.*"

"I'd say good luck"—Slate drapes his arm over the back of my chair—"but no amount of luck will save you."

Massimo blanches. "S-save me?"

"Slate," Adrien hisses, before turning to our prospective student of magic. "You won't die, Massimo."

"But you will be cursed if you fail." Gaëlle looks up from her knitting. "Nothing *too* awful."

The curses the *dihuner* inflicts nowadays are watered-down versions of the curses from the past. From the accounts we hear over the news from disgruntled candidates, they range from selective memory loss, cyclical hives, uncontrollable flatulence, poor financial returns, bad luck in love, a black thumb . . .

Although I've learned to appreciate magic and admire what it can do when wielded for good, I've never forgotten how wicked it can be and how profoundly it can taint hearts and minds. I have no illusion that someday, our descendants may have to remove it once again from the world.

Slate calls me pessimistic, but I consider myself a realist.

Hopefully, our lengthy and assiduous method of educating our new mages will result in a safe and constructive use of magic for generations to come.

My daughter kicks again, and I stroke her little limb through the blue silk of my ample dress.

Slate, eager as always to get in on the action, presses my hand away and rests his in its place. "Ouch. She's strong." He shakes out his hand dramatically, at which I roll my eyes.

Massimo clears his throat.

"Yes?" Slate drawls.

Massimo frowns, probably because he, like every human who steps into the temple and stands before the Council, expects us to be these grand, formidable sorcerers. They forget we're merely humans with an unusual skill set.

"May I, um . . . " He gestures to the clock.

"You may!" Slate thunders, making Massimo jump.

I shake my head at his antics, while he kisses my cheek and whispers, "Did you see how he shook, wife?"

"I saw."

Massimo crouches in front of the Water element. He touches it, but nothing happens. He moves to the next element, Gaëlle's, and a beam of white light shoots out.

"*Bon voyage!*" Slate booms, but the man's already gone, vanished into that parallel world where Merlin and Viviene orchestrate the trials. I hear they keep things exciting. Even though I'm in no hurry to meet them, I hope to someday.

Just as Gaëlle raises her hand to open the temple's door and let the next candidate through, a fifteen-year-old girl, who traveled all the way from Nairobi for a chance at getting magic, appears on my portion of the clock.

Her dreadlocks are tangled with brambles, her dark skin glossy with sweat, and her clothes reduced to tatters but she's smiling, and that smile grows when she turns to face us. "I did it! Oh, Great Quatrefoil, I did it!"

I get up to congratulate and welcome my newest Earth mage. "You did, Elektra. *Félicitations et bienvenue.*"

"That. Was. Wild." Her chest rises and falls fast.

Slate cocks a brow that gets lost beneath a corkscrew of black hair. "You actually sound like you had fun."

"I wouldn't call it fun, but it was *definitely* a memorable experience."

"The beginning of a lifetime of memorable experiences," I tell her. "Now, proceed to House de Morel. You'll be given all you need for your time at our school."

She starts jogging toward the grand doors, apparently bursting with energy. "Can I phone my parents?"

Adrien nods. "You can, and you should. Who knows how long it'll be until Brume releases you back into the world."

We've discovered that some mages reach their full potential in a matter of months while it takes others years.

Gaëlle flaps her hand, and the door grinds open, letting Elektra out and allowing the next hopeful in.

"How many more candidates do we have to see today?" Adrien checks his wristwatch, probably in a hurry to get back to his four-year-old son. Or maybe he's excited to get back to Charlotte. However *difficult* I still find her, she thinks Adrien walks on water—or rather, on fire—so I make an effort to be friendly.

Alma's stilettos click against the tiles as she ushers in a woman in a skirt suit and heels, who looks like she's interviewing for an office job, except for her windblown hair. "Eleven. Bastian just blew the last one up here. Literally." Alma rolls her eyes but smiles at Bastian's little show of Air power. She tilts her head for the woman to stand before our long vine desk. "Brume's officially sealed for the lunar month." Before exiting, she calls out, "Hey, Adrien, it's getting chilly in the waiting area. Can you make the air temp a couple degrees warmer?"

"You don't want me to make it rain?" Slate winks at her. "Or snow?"

She laughs. "You do that, and I put Spike Steve on our balcony."

Despite getting his memory of Spike and Slate back, Bastian couldn't seem to shake the love for the cactus he was calling Steve. So much so, that Slate allowed Bastian and Alma to share custody of the Eve's Needle and give him a middle name. They get him every other week.

Slate's eyes narrow. "You wouldn't dare."

"If anything happened, I could always replace him." She takes a handful of dirt from her Chanel fanny pack and flips her palm up. Threads of green magic weave together to form a miniature version of Slate's favorite cactus. Like me, Alma is an Earth witch. She tosses the little plant at Slate, who catches it in spite of its thorns, then spits out curses like a sailor as he pries the tiny thing from his skin and holds it gingerly in his palm.

"Are you two done?" Adrien glowers between Slate and Alma.

Alma steps out, her contagious laughter ribboning in her wake.

"What should we name her?" Slate asks me as Adrien begins to explain the clock's vetting process to the prospective sorceress.

I stroke my stomach. "Why . . . Viviene. Viviene Amandine Roland."

"You want to name Spike's new gal like our daughter?" He shrugs. "I mean, it's a good name."

"I thought you *meant* our daughter." I shake my head but can't help the smile enveloping my mouth. "Are we really bringing this one home, too? I'm thinking we'll need to build a new wing for all the stray succulents."

Slate stares at me in shock. "You know the rule, princess: no cactus left behind. Not a tiny Eve's Needle, not a giant Saguaro."

As Adrien sends another pointed glower our way, I murmur, "Fine. She can come home with us, but find her another name."

"That's my girl. Always making room for another prickly heart."

ACKNOWLEDGMENTS

KATIE:

Writing a book is a huge undertaking that requires time, a certain level of insanity, and lots of support. I want to thank my critique groups (who are the BEST in the world), my family, and my friends. Without you, I would be a gelatinous pool of doubt and unfinished projects. I also want to give a huge thanks to those of you who read and enjoyed *Of Wicked Blood*. Your enthusiasm for the continuation of the story kept me going during a really tough year. Thank you, too, to the wonderful people in The O.K. Crew on Facebook. You have been a source of humor, inspiration, energy, and love. I'm so glad to have virtually met you all! I do hope that even though this duology is done, there will still be enough bookish banter in the group to keep us all connected. To our beta readers—a HUGE thank you for your feedback and willingness to read the book when it was still rough around the edges.

Thank YOU, dear reader, for picking up this book and reading it until the end. I hope you sincerely enjoyed every minute.

And last but not least . . . thank you, thank you, thank you, Olivia Wildenstein. Words are insufficient to express my gratitude for your willingness to work with me on this duology. Writing two books with you has been crazy nuts and—when I wasn't freaking out—soooooo much fun. You're such a gracious and generous person both in your life and in your writing and I'm happy to have gotten to know you better. I am so glad we met on that literary boat ride going from Geneva to Morges. Who knew that we had the same strange sense of humor, the same appreciation for dark twists, and the same reckless way to go in 'pantsing' while writing a book! Thanks for putting up with me throughout my writer's blocks, my doubtful periods, and my obsession for made-up legends. Thanks for sharing this journey with me. It was well worth the ride.

OLIVIA:

It's funny to be thanked by your co-writer for something that you did as a team and that you had so much fun doing every grueling step of the way. Katie, it was a blast, and maybe someday, we'll cook up a fresh plot with a new batch of characters—animate and inanimate ones—and stir everything together to make another zany concoction.

However sad I am to leave Brume and our endearing crew behind, I'm so happy with where we've left them. Anyone who's read my books knows that happy endings aren't a guarantee. I hope that you've enjoyed the magic, that you laughed, cried, and gasped along with Cadence and Slate.

A heartfelt thank you to our first readers and cheerleaders—Erika, Astrid, and Theresea—to our brilliant editor, Anna, and to our hawk-eyed proofreader, Laetitia.

And as always, to YOU.

Here's to filling up the world with magic, one book at a time.

LOVE,

THE O IN OK

OTHER WORKS BY THESE AUTHORS

KATIE HAYOZ

The Clockwork Siren series

IMMERSED

SUBMERGED

SURFACED

ENSNARED (spinoff novella)

The Devil of Roanoke series

THE CURSE THAT BINDS US

The Quatrefoil Chronicles series

OF WICKED BLOOD

OF TAINTED HEART

Standalone

UNTETHERED

OLIVIA WILDENSTEIN

The Lost Clan series

ROSE PETAL GRAVES

ROWAN WOOD LEGENDS

RISING SILVER MIST

RAGING RIVAL HEARTS

RECKLESS CRUEL HEIRS

The Boulder Wolves series
A PACK OF BLOOD AND LIES
A PACK OF VOWS AND TEARS
A PACK OF LOVE AND HATE
A PACK OF STORMS AND STARS

Angels of Elysium series
FEATHER
CELESTIAL
STARLIGHT

The Quatrefoil Chronicles series
OF WICKED BLOOD
OF TAINTED HEART

Standalones
GHOSTBOY, CHAMELEON & THE DUKE OF GRAFFITI
NOT ANOTHER LOVE SONG

Cold Little Games series
COLD LITTLE LIES
COLD LITTLE GAMES
COLD LITTLE HEARTS

CPSIA information can be obtained
at www.ICGtesting.com
Printed in the USA
BVHW081928220721
612369BV00001B/84

9 781948 463447